the
QUEEN

MORTON COOPER

the

QUEEN

PRENTICE-HALL, INC., Englewood Cliffs, N.J.

Design by Linda Huber

The Queen by Morton Cooper
Copyright © 1974 by Morton Cooper
Copyright under International and Pan American
Copyright Conventions
Printed in the United States of America
Prentice-Hall International, Inc., London
Prentice-Hall of Australia, Pty. Ltd., Sydney
Prentice-Hall of Canada, Ltd., Toronto
Prentice-Hall of India Private Ltd., New Delhi
Prentice-Hall of Japan, Inc., Tokyo

10 9 8 7 6 5 4 3 2 1

Library of Congress Cataloging in Publication Data
Cooper, Morton.
  The queen.
  I. Title.
PZ4.C7786Qu [PS3553.062]   813'.5'4   74–3341
ISBN 0–13–748202–7

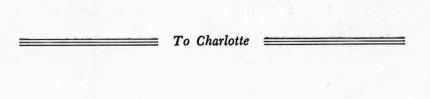

To Charlotte

the
QUEEN

She stood in the late Saturday night rain on a lighted corner of East Eighty-sixth Street, hailing taxis that whizzed past her. Two young men suddenly appeared beside her, and one circled her in grinning appraisal and told the other that the three of them could have some fun tonight. She wasn't frightened, because they didn't seem sinister, but she crossed the wide street to the downtown subway, glancing back over her shoulder. They were following her, shouting schoolkid obscenities, but she didn't see them when her train pulled into the station.

She purposely avoided an empty car and vowed never to be out again after midnight, alone, in this city. She had worked through the afternoon and evening in Judith's office-apartment to clean up long overdue correspondence, and could of course have stayed there the night. Her boss, Judith Harrison, was out of town, too, and surely wouldn't have minded her sleeping in the flat. Her husband of three months and three days was in Rochester, explaining to his boss why he and his bride should not be moved to the Zurich office, so there was no pressing reason to go home. But she had wanted to be there in case he called.

Scarcely a minute after the train started, she looked up and saw them. They sat down on either side of her, still grinning, and before she could get up one of them breezily draped his arm around her shoulders and the other patted her head and asked his friend how long he figured it would take for her to get friendly. She struggled, angered more than frightened, and demanded that they go away, and that made them laugh. There were perhaps a dozen other riders in the car. A few dozed, some had their faces carefully hidden behind newspapers, some passively watched her struggle. An elderly man waddled to them from the opposite end of the car as it began to slow for its first stop and ordered them, in a heavy Jewish accent, to leave her alone, scolded that they ought to be ashamed of themselves. They laughed at that as well, and one of them said they weren't hurting nobody, Pop, and the other asked the elderly man if he wanted them to save a piece for him.

The door opened. She saw a policeman on the station platform, and broke free, and bolted out of the train, hearing them happily yelp as they hurried after her. The policeman wasn't a policeman, she realized, but a subway worker in a blue uniform, and she told him what was wrong, and he blandly told them to get lost or he'd call the cops. Yes, sir, they chortled, and whisked her up the stairs and out of the station.

Some apartment lights were on across the way, and there were street lights, but the rainy night was dark and the area was empty of people. A hand covered her mouth as she screamed for help and hit her when she bit it. She fought as the taller man held her and the shorter one hastily worked at the buttons of her slacks. They talked constantly, cheerfully, never to her except to warn her that if she kept hollering they wouldn't be responsible for what happened to her face. She tried in vain to kick a groin as she had been taught, and she was pinned to the sidewalk as the slacks were yanked off, and she knew it was possible that she could be killed but she screamed all the more.

A siren sounded and they fled. The patrol car did not find them, and she sat in the back seat and shivered with hurt and humiliation. She could file a formal complaint at the precinct now, one of the patrolmen advised her, or they could take her to a hospital emergency ward if she thought she was injured, or they could see her home where she could rest up and decide if she really wanted to go through the rigamarole of a complaint and mug shots that would take a long time and most likely come up with nothing. In a flat, lifeless voice unfamiliar to her, she asked to be taken home. As she shivered, the more talkative patrolman called her lucky. Some chicks out alone in this jungle of a city at night wound up with their throats cut, he said, and just because they were looking for a little harmless action. Not that there wasn't such a thing as forcible rape, but by and large the girls who kept out of jams were the ones who gave certain men absolutely no cause to get ideas. There'd been this cute college kid only last week over on . . .

2

She was flooded with anger, and then with self-loathing. Judith wouldn't only have answered him back but would have insisted on that trip to the precinct. She wasn't Judith. She was who she was, a just-talk feminist who would never bring herself to tell even her husband what had happened this night. Her father, she knew, would be outraged. He would roar about the atrocity done to his baby, and at some point, ever so indirectly, he would suggest, ever so delicately, that she must have somehow invited it. By wearing short skirts, or tight pants, or maybe just a pretty face.

The policeman talked and she thought of the only person who had been concerned enough to try to help her. The elderly man with the Jewish accent. Judith, who rarely spoke about her personal life, had once mentioned in passing that her father was a rabbi, somewhere in Pennsylvania. She imagined the night's horror happening to Judith, imagined Judith dealing with it in strength, strength given her in childhood by a kind and wise and loving and wholly accepting father, and was envious.

The police car stopped in front of her apartment house. She thanked them, mechanically, and went into the building, wanting only to bolt the door and take a long, very hot bath. Riding up in the elevator she thought of Zurich, which she knew only from pictures and books. She imagined it gleaming with clean white snow, with streets that were bright and safe. Before her bath, she would call her husband in Rochester, and they would talk some more about that position in Zurich.

The rabbi was brought awake in the darkness by an insistent thirst and an ache in his belly. He shifted his slight body to lie on his stomach, and thought of indigestion and then thought of death. Yankel Blum, the cigar seller, a year younger than he, had cracked jokes two weeks before, full of plans for a vacation, and the next day the rabbi had buried Yankel Blum.

Indigestion, the rabbi decided, hoped. Soon I am sixty-seven years old, please God, he thought. A man soon sixty-seven years old does not eat stuffed cabbage at ten o'clock at night. I did. *Meshugeh.* I'm *meshugeh,* and my stomach hurts and my tongue is like the desert.

Sleep would not come. He shifted his weight again, and considered nudging his wife to get up and bring him a drop of water. Frieda was snoring lightly. He reached over to touch her, for a formless fear had begun to well in him, and touching her eased him a little. Frieda continued to snore.

The hurt in his stomach receded, but the thirst and the restlessness did not. Silently he spoke the *Mayde Ani,* thanked God for having gracefully and generously restored his soul to him after sleep, and then sat up and slowly swung his legs over the side of the bed. He leaned forward and washed his hands in the basin of water he kept beside the bed. His temples throbbed as he sat up again and he felt pressure, not pain but pressure, in his upper arms. He dressed in his flannel robe although the month was June, and shambled, barefoot, to the bathroom, pausing on the way to switch on his daughter Esther's bedroom light—Esther was in her own home, of course, with her own family—to read the electric clock. Nearly six o'clock; time to be up, anyway.

At the bathroom sink he drank water—only a little because his law proscribed drink as well as food until after morning prayers—and felt small, rolling waves of dizziness and nausea. He poked about in the cabinet for Alka-Seltzer—he would be forgiven if he really needed Alka-Seltzer—and a collection of bottles and vials fell from the cabinet shelf and clattered into the sink.

"Yasif?" his wife called.

"All right, nothing wrong," he called back in Yiddish.

Frieda came to him and he said it was just a little indigestion and complained that he had ordered her a thousand times to clean out this cabinet; what were these green pills for, for instance, why was she keeping pills with a 1959 prescription date, where was the Alka-Seltzer? Frieda, who always spoke Yiddish to him although she had been born in Plainfield, New Jersey, told him he looked like a ghost and felt his forehead and gave him an Alka-Seltzer and said she maybe should call the doctor.

The rabbi shook his head. "Indigestion. Go to sleep," he said, and gathered his clothes from the bedroom and walked downstairs to the parlor of this old house that he hated. His wife followed him and argued that he belonged back in bed. Joseph Hershkowitz, whose life as a rabbi and man of God had been spent meekly and obediently jumping through the hoops of congregations that could always count on his meekness and obedience, frowned at his wife and raised his arm stiffly, firmly, a gesture she understood well, a gesture that commanded that nothing more was to be said, for he was the head of this house, this family.

In the parlor, reading the Pittsburgh *Post-Gazette,* he considered the wisdom of telephoning his daughter Esther's husband, Myron, to drive him to the synagogue. Myron Glantz, more like a son than a son-in-law, never missed *Shahris,* the morning service, and would have been only too happy to drive him there and back home; he had said so often. The rabbi had always refused, except in very bad weather, stubbornly arguing that the exercise of walking was necessary to him. The prospect this day of walking the nine streets, most of them hilly, was not at all pleasant, but he decided against the telephone call. There would be questions and concern. It was easier not to impose.

At half-past six, dressed and ready to leave, he realized that he felt much better. The Alka-Seltzer had helped his stomach and his head. There were brief, sly twinges now and then, mostly in his arms, but the nausea and the dizziness were gone, thank God. At the front door, Frieda warned him that if he ever ate heavy food again late at night she would call the police.

Time and hard work, like heavy winds, had bent Joseph Hershkowitz a little, but he stood erect now, and grinned at his good wife, and kissed her cheek. "Make tea for when I come home," he said. "You want to go dancing? Tonight I'll take you to a contest in a dance hall and everybody will vote for you."

Frieda laughed and playfully slapped his nose and called him a crazy comedian.

Regal City's Orthodox synagogue was set in a neighborhood of poor black people, foundry worker families who were Poles and Czechs and Italians, and a handful of old Jews who were too poor to move or who had come there when it was still a respectable part of the town and refused to leave the security of the familiar. The neighborhood was not respectable now. People didn't paint their houses or sweep their sidewalks. There were beer gardens, and loafers, and there was the rumor for many years of a regular whorehouse on Lincoln Avenue, only one street away from the synagogue. The shame, the *shunda* . . .

In the eighteen years that Joseph Hershkowitz had been rabbi there, the *shul*'s windows had been broken by rocks more times than he could remember. Roughneck *goyim* didn't know how to paint their houses, but they knew how to teach their children to paint swastikas on the synagogue door. The despair, the sense of personal defeat and hopelessness, was often great in Joseph Hershkowitz; not despair for his timeless religion, but for his failures as a teacher, a molder. There was rarely a *minyan* any more, the gathering of ten men at one time to form a community of worshippers, except on the High Holidays. The devout old men were dead or dying, and their sons, if they went to services at all, took their families to the Conservative synagogue at the other end of Regal City, the fancy end. He had a Hebrew School student body of exactly two children. In October, please God, the Eisenberg boy would be Bar Mitzvah, and was almost certain not to attend Hebrew School afterwards. That would leave the rabbi with a *cheder* of one student, the Katz girl. Not even a boy; a *girl*.

Daily and painfully, the rabbi was aware of why he had been

retained at the *shul* for eighteen years and would probably never be discharged. He allowed himself to be pushed around by the congregation; he let himself be treated, even by Feldman the janitor, as hired help rather than a scholar and teacher. His salary was small because he should have demanded increases and was always afraid to, afraid that he would be let go, to go—where? Nowhere; possibly nowhere. His few loyal friends and defenders were dead or had moved away. As a boy in his Kiev village, he had boasted to his friends that he would grow up to be a great rabbi. As an old man in the United States of America, he was afraid to talk back to people who had been trained—by him, he knew—to look down on him, to regard him as a convenient punching bag, as less essential to the *shul* than Feldman the *shammes*.

How did I fail my faith, my people? the rabbi asked this day, perspiring and breathing heavily, as he approached the street leading to the synagogue.

How can a man, soon to be sixty-seven years old, look back at his life and remember so little fulfillment? How can he look ahead and see—nothing?

Quickly he begged God's forgiveness, for to whine was to sin. Much had been good, much was still good. Health; for the most part, there has been health. A wife who gave me no sons, but a fine wife, a selfless woman. A daughter, Esther, never a minute's worry, she married a splendid boy and gave me grandsons, gave her mother and me no heartache, only peace and pride.

He would not think about his other daughter.

Yet he did, as he always did when he determined he would not, every day of his life. He cursed her and he ached to hold her and kiss her eyes and tell her he would cherish her always.

At the synagogue's doorpost, he kissed his fingers and touched the *mezuzah*, the small, slanted case that contained instructions of prayer and Israel's affirmation of faith, and entered the sanctuary that was dank despite the bright day outside. Two men had arrived before him, and two more came within minutes after him. Myron, his son-in-law. Feldman the *shammes*. Yankel Blum's brother Hyman, whose son had married a Gentile girl, a modern daisy. Morris Marcus, who was eighty-one years old and stone deaf and a fine gentleman. The rabbi looked up to the balcony and was not

7

disappointed. Mrs. Marcus was there, already praying; she could barely see and she knew the morning service by heart, but she held her prayer book an inch from her eyes and her lips moved like lightning. Once that balcony had been filled with women, pious and dutiful grandmothers and mothers and wives and daughters and granddaughters, women without these fancy modern notions about how it was supposed to be somehow wrong for men and their women to be separated during worship services. But there was Mrs. Marcus, devout and constant. Old and sickly—climbing those stairs to the balcony surely had to be harder with every passing week—yet nothing could keep her from *Shahris*.

Waiting for the *minyan* they knew would not be, the rabbi and Morris Marcus laid *tefillin*, Hyman Blum and Myron Glantz chatted, and Feldman read a newspaper. Presently the rabbi sighed loudly, the signal of hurt and sadness at no *minyan*, and the partial community of individual prayers began, all the men mumbling the same words, each man at his own pace. Perhaps tomorrow will be different, the rabbi thought. Tomorrow, perhaps, God will choose to bring ten men together under this roof to greet and worship Him.

Why am I dizzy again? Not pain, just a dizziness . . .

Softly reciting *Shemona Esrei*, the eighteen benedictions, he felt a gentle tap at his shoulder, and he turned. Behind him, Myron, seated on one of the ancient pocked benches that squeaked, looked worried and asked if something was the matter. The rabbi shook his head fiercely and returned to the benedictions, his vision blurred now but his mind and memory of the benedictions clear.

The prayer book dropped from his hands. He bent down to retrieve it, and lost his balance, and cried out ". . . *Mechayei hameisim, atah chonen*—" thanking God who resurrected the dead, and sank to the bare floor and was silent. He heard his son-in-law's voice, and tried to remember what came after *atah chonen*.

1

On the day that Joseph Hershkowitz fell ill in Regal City, Pennsylvania, the United States Supreme Court in Washington knocked down a whole slew of state laws passed in an effort to circumvent the Court's previous ruling on abortion. That ruling, the culmination of a long fight that had often been nicknamed "Judith's Crusade," had severely restricted the rights of state or local governments to interfere with decisions properly belonging to individual women and their physicians. Since that ruling there had been many skirmishes on both sides of the issue, and Judith Harrison had been in the middle of most of them, campaigning tirelessly for every woman's right to control her own life and her own body. She had battled to free all imprisoned abortionists and to have medical licenses reinstated, she had traveled widely to publicize pockets of resistance to the Court decision, and she was still working ceaselessly to clean up the residual injustices from the period before the historic Court decision.

And now, as a result of constant public pressure by Judith and others, one of the distinguished names under consideration for a vacant Supreme Court seat was that of Paula Demling. The betting among Court reporters and buffs was that Judge Demling would indeed become the first woman to sit on the nation's highest bench.

Martha Hanaday, reached in New York by the wire services, said she naturally was gratified by the Court's newest decisions, and that yes, she did believe that Paula Demling would be appointed to the Court, and that this might well be the greatest triumph of all for the cause of women's liberation. Asked about Judith Harrison's contributions, she replied, "The battle has been going on for a long time, and some of us were in it before it was fashionable. But one of the chief strengths of the women's movement is, or should be, the absence of a personality cult—especially one based on glamour. As for me, my credentials ought to speak for themselves." After that brief telephone interview, the man from UPI pondered her statement and wondered if it was as confusing as it read in his shorthand notes. She seemed to want it both ways: to reject all individual personalities and at the same time to play up her own. He filed the quote.

And on that day, in Chicago, Judith Harrison changed her mind and agreed to tape a television appearance on *The Mel Kruger Show*. She had first promised to do the taping, then had canceled out later when she rechecked her itinerary and discovered that she was to catch a mid-afternoon flight to Hartley. Then a telegram came from Andrea Lane, of the Hartley Women's Club, asking her to take a later flight, the 5:50, instead; there were complications, minor ones, the telegram apologized, but someone would be at the airport to meet her at 7:05. Judith Harrison therefore phoned Mel's producer and rebooked herself. There were legitimate excuses for her to have postponed the appearance till her next time in Chicago—she had been traveling at a suicidal pace for many weeks, had averaged three hours sleep a night and would look like the Sea Hag on camera—but Mel Kruger was a good friend from the days when she had needed good friends.

The taping began at four o'clock and Judith Harrison did not look at all like the Sea Hag. She was, as she had been on countless television shows and magazine covers, a distinctly beautiful woman. Her deep, even tan and huge, candid green eyes were a striking contrast to her rich jet-black hair, and her faultless figure was still much too young to be thirty years old. One of Mel's other guests, seated next to her, was Randy Grant, the actor, in Chicago to plug a picture he knew was a bummer. He and Judith hadn't seen each other in many years—since the Coast, soon after she had been Judith Hershkowitz and soon after he had been Vincente Bugliosi—and he hadn't known she was in Chicago till now. Jesus, she was a knockout. His famous loins were hurting, and she was smiling at him, friendly as hell, and maybe with just a little Randy Grant persuasion . . .

By four o'clock, the word about the Supreme Court was known, and the Martha Hanaday quote had come in over the network's news wire. Mel Kruger read the quote to Judith Harrison, on camera. She barely blinked. "If that's an accurate quote, I'm sorry," she said and crossed long legs that did nothing to ease Randy Grant's loins. "The women's movement owes a great deal to Martha. While we professional pom-pom girls were jumping around chanting, 'Rah rah, we're man's vessels and vassals,' she was out on the battleground calling for equal pay for equal work, for broad social reform, for basic attitudinal changes. When the history books about mid-twentieth-century women are written, Martha Hanaday will be on most of the pages."

Kruger (gently): "That's awfully generous of you, considering that she seems to have gone out of her way over the past year or so to say some pretty unkind things about you. When she was on this panel six or seven months ago—"

Harrison (sweetly): "Mel, I really don't think your audience wants to hear about a war that doesn't exist. The real news is that this country may soon have new laws that will finally give women, half the population, the right to make fundamental choices and decisions on their own. That's far more fascinating, don't you think? Women *are* changing. The more self-sufficient we become, the more genuinely useful we become."

She talked about going from here today to Hartley, the heart of the Midwest, to participate in a three-day seminar on unfreezing long-frozen assigned roles between the sexes. Randy Grant heard *sexes*, liked it, became more determined to persuade her to stay in town for the night at least. She'd been in Hartley not quite a year ago, she was saying. The climate then had been entirely different. "The auditorium where I spoke was less than a quarter filled," she said. "That may well have been because we weren't much of a drawing card, to begin with. Or because the baby had a temperature, or it was bridge night, or maybe because the men didn't care for their women—I say *their* women advisedly—to start asking questions. Incidentally, there was exactly one man in that audience that night. One.

"Here we are, less than a year later. I'm told that every chair at the seminar that begins tomorrow morning was reserved within two days after the announcement. And that something like fifteen percent of the participants will be men."

Kruger (gently): "Could be that a lot of them want to see the famous Judith Harrison."

Harrison (sweetly, shaking her head): "No. Thank you, but no. I'm convinced that both sexes are slowly waking up to the fact that they needn't stay any longer in prescribed sexist traps, that—"

Pretending to listen, the thought suddenly and gloomily occurred to Randy Grant that maybe she *believed* that cow crap. How do you hump snatch that yammers about sexism and changing roles? Sweet Christ, maybe she's turned dyke since the Coast! Please, Sweet Christ, don't make her a dyke, he prayed. You wouldn't play a dirty trick like that on me, would You?

His hopes sprang again during the short break, when she threw that five-thousand-watt smile at him. They'd talked only for a second or two before the show and she asked now, "What're you into these days, Bugliosi, besides being a beg moom pitchur star? The last time I saw you, you were on your way to visit your parents in Parma."

"Wow, that's a *memory*, Hershkowitz!" he marveled.

"Mm. They call me the Total Recall Kid."

Turn her on fast, he thought. "What'm I into? Your pants, if you stick around town a while."

The smile's voltage wasn't as high, but she didn't switch it off. "Two things never change: the hills of Parma and the romantic nature of Vince Bugliosi."

"Positively. Stay, okay? There's always a later flight. Okay? For old times' sake."

She laughed. "I do love you, Vince. You're the most uncomplicated, direct lecher I've ever slept with."

Pleased: "Yeah. So?"

"So no."

Not pleased: "We made it great on the Coast, remember?" She nodded. "So give me a good reason why no."

Kruger was getting ready to roll again. "I'll give you two," she said, and sat back and the smile was just about gone. "One, I'm expected in Hartley. And two, I've become a virgin."

"Again?"

"Most of the time, yes."

"Man, that woman's lib shit must've really got to you, you know?"

"It must've. The lower half of Hershkowitz still functions, you can tell the boys down at the gym, but now the upper half functions, too. Shhh," she said and pointed to Mel Kruger, who was relighting his cigar, set to go.

12

Sullenly, though on his mark to sprint into a grin or an expression of thoughtfulness in case a camera aimed an eye at him, Randy Grant examined Bobbi Westerfield, who sat at Kruger's left. Bobbi Westerfield was a singer, headlining Mister Kelly's, and Randy Grant had learned to steer clear of singers; they couldn't ball worth a damn. She was blonde and button-cute, breathless with the announcement that it was all just like a *dream,* and she was saying that she certainly respected and admired Miss Harrison, but as far as she was concerned a girl's best bet for happiness was to love and be loved by some great big lug of a wonderful guy.

Randy Grant half expected her to burst into Rodgers and Hammerstein. When he was sure the cameras were off him, he furtively glanced at his watch. How soon was Kruger going to let him sell *Tomahawk Canyon?* Maybe he'd wind up with the Westerfield snatch if nothing better materialized. He hoped, with the philosophy of the temporary loser, that Hershkowitz wasn't a dyke. Bumpers like those were much too fine a feast for butches in army shoes.

2

And in New York on that June day, I, Sam Gallagher, boarded a flight to Hartley, a town I ardently wished never to see again, in search of Judith Harrison.

The Martha Hanadays were old potatoes. Judith Harrison was today, very much today, incontestably the queen of the women's movement. (I was about to call her the movement's Moses, but I've been warned to cool the male chauvinism.)

One reason I didn't want to go to Hartley was that it was Hartley, a nasty little distillation of all that was narrow and ultraconservative in middle America. Another reason was my suspicion, justified by now, that Judith would go on refusing to see me or anyone connected with *Rowland's Weekly*. She had made that clear, through various lieutenants, from the time she learned we were preparing a cover story on her.

I couldn't really blame her. *Rowland's* had printed a bitchy little piece about her when she was a princess but before she became a queen, and what guarantee did she have that this piece wouldn't leave her bleeding, too?

The fact that I was doing the story obviously cut not a sliver of ice. Early in the game, she'd sent *Rowland's* a letter that read, "I do remember Sam Gallagher with fondness, but I am unwilling to cooperate in any interview that touches on my past life or present personal life. As a journalist myself, I well understand that an article is incomplete without juicy tidbits and occasionally even a fact or two about the subject, but I simply do not choose to assist in my own crucifixion. With some exceptions, usually trivial, I have found *Rowland's* characterizations of women to be condescending and demeaning. I naturally wish that your publication would write nothing about me. I also realize that I am helpless to stop you. Please be advised, however, that my friends and associates are being asked, if called upon for interviews, to give you absolutely no cooperation whatever."

Good for you, kid.

Congratulations and sympathies. Truth is, a subject as newsworthy and controversial as Judith Harrison who refuses to sit for an interview generally *is* helpless as hell. The more she and her cronies clam, which is their right, the more reporters must rely on the memories and opinions of unfriendly sources, which is not at all right.

I'd been working at *Rowland's* for seven years, been writing cover stories for three, and this was one assignment I wanted out of. The arguments I gave Howard Bracken, the store's executive editor, were sound ones. I'd recently returned to the States after corresponding from Europe for a year, and I sincerely believed I was a foreigner to the mood and pace of the States. All I knew about recent feminism or women's lib or whatever the hell its name was, if it did have a name, was the skimpy stuff I'd read in the International *Herald-Tribune* and the overseas editions of *Rowland's* in Rome, I argued. I was out of touch, I argued; in restaurants, I was still automatically translating menus into Italian. I argued that I couldn't even remember how American women screw.

Howard Bracken, snowhaired, Sackville Street-tailored, the consummate Wasp listening and talking softly to this shanty Irisher, assured me that they screwed the same way they had before I'd left—depressing news, incidentally, after twelve months of Italian girls. Anyway, softspoken Bracken, who was always eight feet shorter when he stood away from his desk—which had once been Moby Dick's backbone—stayed behind his desk and softspoke me into taking home Xeroxes of the magazine's file on Judith Harrison, in the transparent hope that I'd get hooked. He wanted me to do the job, but of course he wouldn't force me; a writer seldom came through with strong copy while under the whip.

Why didn't I want the assignment, the real reason or some of it? Because ten years before, when Judith was twenty and I was twenty-four, we had been in love. I'd been, at any rate. The active part of it, not the memory part, had lasted three weeks, three intense, round-the-clock weeks, barely pausing for lunch. Ten years later, I was still in love. No perpetual unbanked fire, nothing like that, but in different ways at different times. If I was responsible for the cover story, I would be sure to find some warts, and I would be obliged to print them.

Why, finally, did I say yes? Because the Xeroxes gave me a bewildering gallery of young women, all of them named Judith Harrison, challenging puzzles upon puzzles to be solved. Because I could control, to some degree, what the final copy would be. Because although someone else's research and typewriter might describe her rightly—that her social activism was changing this country around—it was more than probable that the central focus of the story would be to tell us everything we always wanted to know, tee-hee, slurp-slurp, about her activism in a whole lot of famous bedrooms.

Yeah, okay, enough of the noble, protective Sam Gallagher, over-age boy knight. I'll tell you why I said yes. I read the clips and studied the photographs of her, and the fantasy went, *I'll see her again and a light will flash on above her perfect head. The two of us, Jeannette Mac-Donald and Nelson Eddy, will ride to the mountaintop and sing "Sweetheart" together, and magically off will come my Royal Mountie uniform and her rustling petticoats and for the rest of our lives we will love each other, bliss uninterrupted.*

I'm a thirty-four-year-old man, frequently bright, often sober, and I actually had that fantasy. My apologies.

I flew to Hartley because *Rowland's* secret police had learned that she was going to lead a three-day seminar there, and in effect to spit in the rheumy eye of Oliver Starn, who lived in and operated his newspaper publishing empire out of Hartley. Three days in one place was most unusual for Judith; her pattern seemed to be to appear somewhere just long enough to deliver her lecture, stir up the female natives, and disappear before the local reactionaries and their barefoot, pregnant wives could club her to death.

The secret police had also learned that she would be staying at the Airport Inn, which was situated roughly halfway between Hartley and the state's largest city. The office had reserved a room for me there. We'd been researching Judith for nearly a month, chasing down too many hot-flash avenues that turned into dead ends, but we were going to have to go to press within a week or be scooped by the other news weeklies; if Judith's friend Paula Demling was named to the Court, as now appeared likely, we couldn't hold off much longer. I had a good share of the cover piece organized and written. What I didn't have—nor did the other weeklies, we'd heard and were praying—was Judith. With a break, something I needed, I would track her down at the Airport Inn.

Basic facts about Judith Harrison, some of them cloudy in detail, had been nailed. She'd left her rabbi father's home at seventeen and never gone back, because she'd displeased his strict sense of morality and wasn't invited back. I'd spent several days in her hometown, a Western Pennsylvania foundry town that, by comparison, gave drowsy Hartley the ambience of Capri. Her family wouldn't talk to me. The old schoolmates and the one retired high school history teacher who did talk, talked about a grab bag of Judiths:

Pro: She was beautiful, even as a child; we just knew she was destined to marry rich or be a big movie star. Con: Agree.

Pro: She was well liked and popular, even though this town didn't like Jews then and still doesn't. Con: She always elbowed her way in where she wasn't wanted and tried to take over, the way they all do. Pro and Con: Don't use my name, fella, because my missus'll kill me even after all these years, but ol' Judy was just about the best tail I ever had in my life and I must've had a couple of hundred till the ball and chain and I tied the ol' knot. Naturally, Judy and I couldn't date in public in those days, not in this neck of the woods, what with her the Chosen People, *you* know. But she certainly was terrific in the hay.

Pro: Some of this women's lib stuff makes sense, most of it is a bunch of baloney. Looking back, though, we should have figured that she'd be in it, in *some*thing big. She was a natural-born leader. She just never had the chance to do very much in Regal City. Con: She was a natural-born troublemaker. She made fun of everything we decent folks hold to be right and proper. She mistook the Holy Father's gift of physical beauty for license to transgress moral laws, and we're satisfied that she left our community none too soon.

Regal City, Pennsylvania, led me back to New York, where it had led her. Her formal education stopped before high school graduation. She used her wondrous good looks and charm as entrée into the magic circles of the wealthy and powerful; she lived on their

17

private yachts, flew in their private planes, dined with them at Fouquet's, slept with Croesus—and many of his friends. She was a jet-setter while the term still connoted glitter and all attendant goodies.

And turned gradually from Gorgeous Jekyll into Gorgeous Hyde. The opportunism didn't slacken, but the frivolity was peeled away, bit by bit, and dropped overboard. In her mid-twenties she was a celebrity—not a superstar, as she was to become, but still a celebrity—courtesy of her romances with Croesus, courtesy of her flirtation with Hollywood and her fluffy but enormously successful TV show, courtesy primarily of her singular genius for wooing and achieving personal publicity, for surrounding herself with Important People.

The television show—*Judith's World*—grappled with such burning questions as whether actresses should marry actors or how it feels to be the wife of an ambitious young politician. The guests she interviewed—with antic wit and increasingly sharp perceptions— were the Gabor-Gingold-Copa comics syndrome at first. But then she began to bag guests who otherwise seldom or never appeared on fluff shows. Senators. Human rights leaders. Presidential candidates. She was damned good at her job. She knew how to pose direct and thoughtful questions, questions you and I would like to ask these estimable folk, if they happened by our living rooms and if we had the nerve to tackle them. She got the guests because she had the right addresses, the right phone numbers, the right friends of friends, and the nerve to tackle them, anytime and on any subject.

Then, it seemed, Judith was everywhere. Everywhere. And all at once. Organizing or helping to organize peace protests and marches. Electioneering for and occasionally helping to elect progressive candidates to public office. (Which surely had to be one of the scores of reasons Oliver Starn knew her to be the anti-Christ: the Senatorial election of his handpicked hack was a guaranteed cinch till Judith uncinched it by bombarding his state with sales pitches for the hack's goodguy opponent. The good guy won; not by many votes, but he won.)

When she discovered women's liberation, there was the charge—mostly by Martha Hanaday's circle, who fancied that formidable lady as owning the movement in something of the same way that Oliver Starn fancied himself as owning the Midwest—that Judith had signed aboard late, after the Hanadays had worked like mules to get the movement rolling in the 1960s. Judith agreed that the charge was accurate. But once she signed, she signed for the entire voyage. And in doing that she automatically, willfully or not, stole the mantle from earth-mother Hanaday.

Martha Hanaday *had* been a legitimate shaker and mover in her day, but her day as a force was over, either because she'd let her finger slip off the pulse of the present or because—as some were whispering—there were severe emotional demons riding her. In any case, her 1970s contributions to lib were mainly Barnum and Baileyish, counter-productive affairs, and sometimes embarrassing ones—leading a ragtag army of Wednesday afternoon feminists and television cameras to invade a men-only saloon on Third Avenue, screeching that housewives were as persecuted as Mississippi share-croppers, denouncing marriage in the same breath that demanded state-sponsored day-care centers for *all* children.

Judith Harrison never screeched. There were speculations that the Hanadays could open beer bottles with their bare vaginas. Judith, never. The strident libbers called her a shuffling Aunt Tom for wearing sexy clothes and consorting with the enemy, while the Starn types—and there were many of them in varying degrees of enthusiasm—called her a menace to the American Way of Life. The truth, at least from what my digging turned up, lay somewhere between the two charges. She identified herself with none of the 137,598 lib groups, except to lend her name to this or that letterhead or to lend a hand in this or that isolated scrap. She was essentially a loner. And cucumber-cool, and obviously happy at being female, and probably ridden by some private demons of her own. And loaded with finished homework and a reasonableness in argument that were clearly paying dividends: by changing fixed sexist at-titudes, the sexy playgirl turned sexy proselytizer was turning some of the country around. And as her presence grew, so did the number of guns aimed at her.

Which brings me back to Oliver Starn and Hartley.

I'd interviewed Starn and several of his key henchmen a few years back for a *Rowland's* cover story. That story reportedly inflamed his duodenum, and he took initial steps to sue the magazine *and* me for character assassination, but the truth was that I didn't uncover much. The harder I worked at prying open closets containing Starn skeletons, the cleverer he and his henchmen were at keeping them stuck shut; I would get *this* close to proving that Hartley was his personal fiefdom, that he owned its judges and cops, that he was above the law and therefore not above wrecking whatever and whoever threatened or even annoyed him, and then—blanko. His influence indirectly owned holding companies which indirectly owned banks which directly controlled zoning boards; if he didn't want a building to be built it wasn't built, despite abundant reasons why it ought to have been. I re-raked his one great public embarrassment, the Government's charge that he had personally attempted to bribe the head of the F.B.I., no less, into dropping its case against Chet A. Bourne, labor leader and convicted jury tamperer, whose pension fund a few years earlier had bailed Starn out of a financial jam with a three-million-dollar loan.

The Government had a beautiful case. And Starn beat the rap. Midway through the trial, the U.S. attorney shifted gears from killer to wrist slapper. Near its conclusion, the attorney was almost kissing Starn on the lips.

Why? Everyone and no one had an answer, to that question and a peck of others. I kept getting blankos because those few people in Hartley who fed me Starn goodies balked at being quoted or furnishing firm sources, fearful of retaliation if those goodies were traced back to them. I was repeatedly given the name of Noah Walters as the one Hartleyite entirely unafraid of Starn, an old-line civil liberties lawyer who had jousted with Starn and Starnism often over the years. The Gallagher luck that winter was that Noah Walters was seriously ill and his wife wouldn't let anyone near him. The story, such as it was, ran. Starn certainly didn't get the puff piece he'd expected was his due, but he certainly didn't get his ass kicked very forcefully, either, simply because most of my proof that morally and legally he was an outlaw couldn't at the eleventh hour, press time, be proved.

What did this have to do with Judith? The nine Starn newspapers in Hartley's state and the states surrounding had been directly instrumental in defeating such local scourges as fluoridation, mental health programs, school sex education, the election of a Mexican to the school board. They couldn't repeal the right of women to vote, however, nor could they totally crush its ultimate consequence, the women's liberation movement. Oliver Starn knew that the central headquarters of that movement was Main Street, Moscow, and starting roughly a dozen years before, he had successfully put up the proper roadblocks that had kept Martha Hanaday from speaking at any important lectern anywhere in or near his semi-dynasty. But Judith Harrison was something else; she was infinitely more effective at disturbing his peace than Hanaday had or ever could have been. She was fresh air and light, more people were listening to her, and Starn, the powerful caveman, was powerless this June to keep her back where she belonged, with the Atheist Eastern Jew Commie Plotters.

Excuse one more male chauvinism, but Judith had, among other attributes, balls. She was heading into enemy territory. My information was that the last time she'd gone to Hartley to speak, the trip had been a dud because Starn had still enough muscle to scare enough townspeople away. Not this year, though, evidently; a revolution had taken place. I didn't know yet whether it was full or partial, nor could I know what if anything Ollie Starn had up his strongarm sleeve to fight the descending locust named Judith Harrison.

Well, I found out. What happened affected Judith, and Hartley, and Hanaday and all the Hanadays, and me, and damn near everyone in that year's fast-changing country and world.

3

Judith Harrison's plane from Chicago landed at 7:05 in a drizzle and she was met by a slender black man who touched his chauffeur's cap and said, "Excuse me, ma'am, you be Miz Harrison?"

"Yes," she said and smiled. "And you are . . . ?"

He smiled, too. "Luther, ma'am. Miz Lane ast me to fetch you to the Polo." He was dressed well and appeared to be in his thirties, and she wished he would take that scraping and shuffling out of his smile, an otherwise nice smile.

"The Polo? What's that?" A motel, he answered. "I thought I was to stay at the Airport Motor Inn."

"Yes, ma'am, that's what the fussin' was about, why Miz Lane ast you to take a later airplane," he said, guiding her to the luggage carousel. "Least that's how Miz Lane explained it to me. She figgered she wouldn't have to make you no reservations at the Motor Inn 'cause they hardly ever full up. Then she foun' out today they *was* full up and she went racin' 'round tryin' to find you a decent place. Way she figgered. if you came later, you wouldn' have to set aroun' while she was lookin'. Don't rightly know why, but all the hotels and motels 'round here's busy this week. Anyways, the Polo's not's nice as the Motor Inn, but Miz Lane says you'll be comf'table there. It's only a four, five minute drive from here."

Waiting for her bag to be unloaded, he explained his instructions and himself. He was a cabinetmaker by trade, and he did other odd jobs on the side, such as private taxi servicing. He didn't know Mrs. Lane, but he had done some work for a neighbor who had recommended him to the Lanes. Mrs. Lane had hired him to take Miss Harrison to the Polo to freshen up, wait for her and deliver her to Mrs. Lane's house on Three Oaks Drive.

When she spotted her bag and he went to retrieve it, Judith considered telephoning Andrea Lane—they had never met but they had corresponded, and the woman's home number would probably be in the directory—if only to verify that everything was kosher.

Why, for instance, wouldn't Andrea Lane have come herself to the airport? Paranoia, she cautioned herself, and pushed the thoughts aside.

On the drive, she asked his last name. "It's Cobb, ma'am. Luther Cobb," he answered. "But nobody ever call me nothin' but Luther."

"Well, Mr. Cobb, I wish you'd do something for me."

"Ma'am?"

"Quit calling me 'Ma'am.' That's what I wish you'd do. Makes me feel like a school teacher."

He nodded. "Yes, ma'am."

Judith sighed. "Where are you from?"

"Oh, here, ma'am. Hartley, goin' on twelve year."

"Originally, I mean."

"Oh. Jus' outsides Waycross, Georgia."

"Are you married?"

"Oh, yes, *ma'am!*"

"And children?"

"Naah, never did have no kids. We wanted 'em—I got thirteen brothahs an' sistahs, nine livin' las' time I heard—but me and Rosetta, we didn' have none, things din' wuk out that way."

"Do you like Hartley?"

He shrugged. "It's like ever'place else, I guess. Live right, do a job proper, an' nobody bothahs nobody."

"What's your opinion of Oliver Starn?"

He frowned. "My *'pinion?*"

"Starn pretty well owns this town, doesn't he? You must have some feeling about him."

After a moment: "Beggin' your pardon, ma'am, but you bein' from outsides Hartley an' all, maybe you don't know how people live here. Natchully, ever'body here knows Mr. Starn—least knows who he is. It's like I say: nobody bothahs nobody, 'less'n somebody's looking for some kinda trouble."

"I apologize. I'm prying, and I don't have that right."

"No nevah mind, ma'am."

The Polo was neither first class nor a dump, but every second-class motel in the world, clean and functional and totally innocent of personality. The desk clerk, a lemony-sallow young man, acknowledged that someone had made a reservation, and Judith registered, and the clerk gave Luther Cobb the key. Luther Cobb preceded her

to 5, a low-ceilinged room with the obligatory faint scent of disinfec-
tant and framed reproductions of kittens and wheat fields, and set
her bag on the luggage rack. "You like me to go get you a sangwich
or somep'm while you fixin' up, ma'am?" he offered.

"Thanks, no, I was fed on the plane," she said. "Let's see now: I
can be showered and changed and ready to go in twenty minutes.
How far is Mrs. Lane's home from here?"

"Um, Three Oaks Drive . . . shouldn' be no more'n fifteen minutes, there'bouts. I'll set out in the car an' wait on you, ma'am."

Hesitating, never comfortable with people who were obsequious,
Judith said, "That rain's making everything so gloomy outside.
You're more than welcome to wait in here. I'll change in the bath-
room and you can watch television."

"Naaah, ma'am, thank you, I be fine, thank you," he answered,
and the telephone rang, and he left the room.

The caller was another lady from the Women's Club, bubbling
apologies for the confusion and inconvenience, compounding the
confusion and inconvenience with absurdly complicated explanations. Judith interrupted the babble to reassure her. "I'm not sure
I'd know how to function without just a little chaos now and then,"
she said. "No problem. I'll be there soon." They said good-bye and
Judith replaced the receiver, not at all in favor of chaos. Sharon
Fuller, her secretary and friend, normally traveled with her and
kept chaos at bay. But a week ago irreplaceable Sharon, who
preached complete freedom and independence for women, had
moved to Zurich, where her husband had been transferred.

Judith did not bolt the motel door, but she did draw the feces-
colored drapes, blotting out the view of the parking lot and lowering
the volume of speeding cars. She kicked off her shoes and pulled the
tightfitting green print dress up over her head. She switched on the
TV set, as she always did in a new hotel or motel room, never
interested in the screen but to hear someone's voice or someone's
music, to have a connection, and inspected the dresses in her bag to
find the least wrinkled one for tonight's meeting. Naked, she
stretched and yawned, wished she weren't alone, wished she could
plunk herself on that inviting bed and sleep for a week, and headed
for the shower that would get her going again.

Nearing the john, she heard her voice. She saw herself on the
screen, remembered the show but couldn't remember whose show it

24

was, where she had taped it, even when she had taped it, remembered only that Nature had not intended for people to live out of
suitcases. She put on her shower cap and turned on the shower
faucets, but was compelled to peek back in on herself. And softly
groaned. There she was, Hot Sheets Harrison, crossing and uncros-
sing legs, making certain there was frequently a piquant expanse of
thigh to be seen. She saw herself sit upright at one point, her chest
thrust at the camera as if to remove any possibility of doubt that she
owned breasts.

Shaking her head, she hurried into the shower, soaped herself
vigorously, and thought, What in the name of all that's unholy was
wrong with me that day? Am I always that transparent? Do I always
throw it around like a Ninth Avenue hooker? Why didn't Sharon or
someone order me to cool it? Watch it next time, Harrison. You're
recruiting true believers, not studs.

She emerged from the shower and the john, drying herself, and
her breath stopped; Luther Cobb stood at the side of the double bed,
completely naked, his face blank, his clothes on a chair. The bed's
blankets and top sheet had been pulled down, action-ready, and
Judith instinctively clutched the towel to her, covered herself from
her neck to her thighs. *Run,* she thought. *Run back to the bathroom and
lock the door.*

And stayed, because this was insane, in a well-populated motel in
broad daylight. Surely she could reason him back into his clothes.
"I—can't seem to think of any bright comments to make now," she
said, her voice strained and therefore perhaps a framed announcement of her fright. Then, speaking as flatly as possible: "This would
be a bad mistake, Mr. Cobb."

He didn't move. He had neither expression nor erection, and the
awful silence and the awful uncertainty were endless. "I am going
into the bathroom, Mr. Cobb," she said, striving for evenness, with
absolutely no glimmer of whether she was in danger or if he was
merely some poor dumb yuk of a thirtyish adolescent who imagined
this was the way to get laid. "Nothing is going to happen between us.
I'm going into the bathroom, and you're going to get dressed and go
outside. It's as very, very simple as that."

She backed into the john, neither hastily nor slowly, and shut the
door after her and locked it. And found her breath again, and still
clutched her towel, her shaking body still wet from the shower, and

thought, Did he terrify me, am I still terrified, because he's black? Judith the color-blind flaming liberal—am I hooked on the locker room songs and stories about black men? Something like this happened once before. When? A few years ago, in Colorado . . . the Room Service waiter brought me a tray of food and jabbered about the weather, and suddenly he was exposed and grinning at me. I got rid of him after I made clear that he was barking up the wrong girl and after I promised I wouldn't report him. I was uneasy, of course, and sorry for him, but I don't remember being frightened . . .

Why not? Because he was white? How disgraceful of me if that's what it was, how rotten-redneck-antiquated-no-character disgraceful!

All right, what do I do now, now that I'm safely barricaded with no clothes, no telephone, not even a Gideon Bible? Call out to him and ask if it's okay to unlock the door? Judith removed her shower cap, annoyed and still shaken but now vaguely amused by the situation that was straight out of *Perils of Pauline* and *Sally the Sleuth*. I'll wait, she thought. But how long? She almost laughed at the absurd image of herself growing old here, bathing a lot and growing wrinkled. Room Service would slide pancakes and newspapers under the door and say, "Yep, he's still there. Ninety years old, but he's still there."

Hardly a minute after she had locked the door, she heard noises, a shrill and angry human voice. An agitated female voice, Southern and high, was screeching, and Judith could hear Luther Cobb say he wasn't doin' nawthin', and soon she supposed she understood what was going on and thought, *O no* . . .

Then the shrill female voice was at the other side of the bathroom door, and a fist pummeled at the door, and the voice was bleating, "You come on out theah, you heah, hussy white woman, you open up! Vurry *idea,* I seen ya, I folla'ed ya, I seen ya! Come on out! You comin' on out, you white hussy, or I call up the *police?*"

Luther Cobb: "But it ain't like you think, Rosetta."

Shrill female voice: "Ain't like I think! You bluejay naked and it ain't like I think?"

Dazzled, Judith opened the door. A tiny woman, black, looked at her, glared, seemed ready to strike her. "Ain't like I think!" she squealed. *"You!* What kind woman you be, white hussy ho-ah? Cain't leave him alone a single secon', he lookin' roun' for il-*licit,* but this heah's the first time I knows of where it's *white* hussy, not even his own kin'. I seen him! And *you!* Both of you dancin' roun' mothah-naked, an' it ain't like I *think!*"

The woman kept yelling, obviously near hysteria, and Judith stood there clutching her ridiculous towel and waiting for a pause in the torrent. Then, out of the corner of her eye, she saw a movement in the open door, and it hit her suddenly that there could be a crowd forming out there, drawn by this commotion. She took two quick steps to the door, and in the instant when she took one hand away from the towel to push the door shut—just as a corner of the towel slipped away from her still-damp breast—she saw the sallow face and wide eyes of the desk clerk in the doorway, and thought *O, wonderful . . .*

She shoved the door shut and turned back to the babbling woman. "Mrs. Cobb!" she said sharply. *"Please."*

It worked. The tiny woman's fingers rushed to her mouth. Judith saw the marriage band, and the frail body, and the bewildered eyes, and the pain, and said with as much compassion as she could muster within her own bewilderment, "You must believe me. I did nothing to seduce your husband. I'm not simply defending myself . . . well, yes I am, but . . ." She began to re-create what had taken place from the moment she had been met at the airport, sorry for Mrs. Cobb but determined to make her see the truth, preposterous as it was . . .

The ripping sound of a zipper stopped her, and both women turned to see Luther Cobb stuffing his shirt into his pants. He saw them looking at him and began again to protest to his wife, and then the tiny woman was bleating once more, tangled phrases of veiled threat and of being deceived the last time and of God smiting all hussies, and then Luther Cobb was fleeing and his wife was running after him, her shrill voice fading away in the sound of slamming car doors and coughing motors.

Alone, shakier than ever and simultaneously detached, as if she had been a walk-on in some grandly campy stag movie, Judith regarded the mirror over the desk and said aloud, "Welcome to Hartley. After the fireworks display, there will be cigars for the gents and flowers for the ladies."

Disturbed, empathetic, suspicious, tolerant, rattled, now removed and now incensed, certain that the ballet had been orchestrated by Captain Kangaroo and Kafka, she sought out the Hartley telephone directory when she was able to loosen herself from the madness of the past quarter hour or so. There were three listings of Lane in the book, one on Three Oaks Drive.

The Andrea Lane who was called to the phone was totally mystified. She had met the earlier plane, had of course not met Judith, and had been making worried long distance calls to Chicago. She asked when Judith had arrived at the Airport Inn.

"I'm not at the Airport Inn. I'm at the Polo Motel."

"The Po—That flophouse? What're you doing *there?*"

Judith explained, and recounted the incredible scene with the Cobbs.

"My Gawd!" Andrea Lane said hoarsely. "That's *fantastic!* I didn't send you any wire, and I'm sure no one else in the club did. I can't imagine who could have called you. This is *fantastic!* I'll be there in ten minutes."

Judith was dressed and fairly composed when the knock came. Andrea Lane, feather bobbed and perhaps forty, a casually dressed and comfortably built woman with the aura of fashionable suburbia about her, bustled in and they greeted each other and exchanged nervous smiles. "I promise I'm *the* Andrea Lane," the woman declared. "Would you like to see my driver's license?"

"No, only a drink if you happened to bring one," Judith teased. "I've left communities one jump ahead of tar and feathers, but this is the first time I've come to one and broken up a happy home within a matter of minutes."

"*Fantastic!*" Andrea Lane repeated. "There must be an answer to this, and I assure you we'll find it. I just came a minute ago from the lobby, and the clerk told me someone reserved a room for you this afternoon by phone. Well, not *this* someone; I wouldn't reserve space for Oliver Starn in this hole! Oh, incidentally, I'll bail you out of here and move you to the Airport Inn. Okay to do it after the meeting? My house is full of people waiting for you."

"Later's fine." In a gleaming new station wagon, its rear seats a blizzard of dolls and toys and books and pamphlets, they sped into the country. After more questions about the weird business at the Polo, Judith said, "You mentioned Oliver Starn before. Pardon my paranoia, but what are the chances that Starn was behind—well, whatever that was?"

Andrea's lips pursed. "No, I think I'd discount that," she said finally. "My family and I live here, right under Starn's all-knowing, fascist nose, and I wouldn't put anything treacherous past him, except stupidity. He's a postgraduate schmuck, but he's not a fool. Anyway, he's not even around; he and his wife, Ilse Koch, have been in Europe for the past couple of weeks."

"Where? Their summer home in Auschwitz?"

Andrea laughed. "Probably. Not that he doesn't have his own S.S. Elite Guard here to follow his orders, but no, this doesn't feel like him. I'm sure he'd love to cause you trouble, but you're not some anonymous nuisance; you're who you are, and he's too smart to risk getting caught in some conspiracy that ultimately could only help the movement and make him look like a jerk. Schmuck, yes; jerk, no."

"Mmm. And you've never heard of Luther Cobb?"

"Never. Obviously *someone*'s been playing games, and we'll track it all down. Look, I'm *terribly* sorry you were put through that obscene grinder. I'll bring it up tonight; somebody may know something, or may have overheard something, I don't know what but—"

"Oh, let's not bother," Judith said. "The purpose of the meeting tonight is to rap out an agenda. I'm up to here with important meetings that became one side issue after another and ended four hours late with nothing solved."

"What about the drink?"

Judith grinned. "I can do without that, too. I may wake up in the middle of the night and remember what happened and go crackers, but for now let's meet the people."

The Lane estate was good-naturedly pretentious and appeared to have everything but a moat, and the people—Judith made a rough house count of between fifty and seventy, perhaps ten percent of them men—rose, most of them, and some of them applauded, damn it, and Andrea betrayed her, not by alluding to the Polo Motel but with an introduction that was almost indecently flowery. If I don't clear my throat and stop her soon, thought Judith, she's going to give me full credit for the smallpox vaccine and the conquest of Atlantis.

Shortly after nine o'clock Judith began to speak, informally describing how seminars had been conducted fruitfully in other communities, offering views of how she believed the Hartley one might go, inviting comments and disagreements.

At about nine-thirty she noticed that the beaming Andrea had stopped beaming. She seemed to be motioning to someone in another room to go away, and finally got up and tiptoed, all too conspicuously, out of the stadium-sized living room.

Scant minutes passed and an anguished Andrea returned for all to see, and whispered to Judith, "There are two policemen outside, and you'd better come out or they say they're going to come in." Judith stared at her for a moment, hearing and not comprehending. Then there was nothing to do but to excuse herself and follow Andrea to the house's broad foyer.

Two uniformed policemen were waiting. One, holding up a forbidding looking paper, asked, so loudly and with such careful elocution-class diction that it had to be somebody's Halloween joke, "Is your true name Judith Harrison?"

Judith frowned.

"Is your true name Judith Harrison?"

"Yes."

"This is a warrant for your arrest."

"For my *what*?"

The charge was fornication, the policeman announced as though he were reciting an antacid commercial. The complainant was Mrs. Rosetta Cobb. The witness to the act was Lyman Bester, the night desk clerk of the Polo Motel. The arrest warrant was signed by his honor, Judge Harvey H. Curry, and she was to gather her belongings if she had any and come along.

Judith turned to Andrea Lane, scared but angry. "What the hell's all this about?"

Andrea faced the cops. "You have no right to barge in here and—"

"This paper says we do, ma'am," declared the cop, who then turned to Judith and again directed, "If you have a coat or a pocketbook, you have the right to go get them."

Andrea insisted they wait until she telephoned a lawyer; she was told she could telephone anyone she pleased but their instruction was to take the lady in at once. Andrea insisted that she go along, was told that was against regulations. "This is *unbelievable*!"

When her purse and jacket were brought, the policemen led Judith to a squad car in the Lane driveway. One of the men slid behind the steering wheel, the other opened the back door, saw that it was locked from the outside after she was seated, and walked around the front of the car and sat beside the driver. The car moved, and one man asked the other, "You try the new Chink place yet?"

The other shook his head. "Grace took the kids. She said it looks okay but it's still the same old chow mein-chop suey crap."

Anger and indignation intensified as the car rocked through the center of Hartley and beyond, as the cretins chatted, ignoring Judith, as though they were delivering not a person but a parcel. When they reached the front of a solemn building and one cop unlocked her door, her contained fear was suddenly sharp and chilling; her legs became water as she got out, and she lost her footing and stumbled. The cop instinctively reached out to catch her, and for an instant he was human, and then just as quickly he took care to rest his beefy hand on her buttock. Judith slapped it away and slapped the side of his face. He glowered, rubbing his jaw, and said, "You watch yourself there, sweetheart. Assaulting an officer don't go around here."

They guided her up a series of concrete stairs, flanking her, and she thought she might suggest handcuffs to be sure she wouldn't make a run for the border, and decided to hell with sarcasm, to hell with any talk until she found someone in authority. At the top of the stairs, a grinning man with a camera called, "Hi! Let's have a big smile, okay?" and snapped the flashbulb. The policemen took her into a large and cluttered room, where she saw men milling, some in uniform and some not, and where a sergeant lounged behind a desk, talking with a cop, talking and talking and talking; he knew Judith was there, had to because she was barely a dozen feet away, and he didn't even glance at her but kept talking and talking and talking.

One of her escorts disappeared. The other one, the one who had helped her out of the car, pointed her to a wooden bench. She took a deep breath and advanced to the sergeant and said clearly, satisfied with the firmness and absence of trembling in her voice, "I assume you're in charge here."

The sergeant stopped talking, but still refused to glance at her. Then he let a long moment pass, then slowly turned to her and answered, "You assume right. And you're gonna set down over there and assume I'm gonna get to you when I'm ready to."

"I believe I have the right to make a phone call."

His brows came together. He sat motionless, then with a subtle flick of his hand he dismissed the cop to whom he had been talking, and he brought his swivel chair around to face her, his small eyes dark and steady and cold. "Umm. You do now, do you?"

"Will you have someone show me to a telephone, please," she said.

She was baiting him, she knew, and she was successful. The sergeant manufactured a tentative, phony grin. "That's an order, is it?" he drawled, and addressed the cop he had just dismissed. "Chuck, how long you been on the force?"

"Soon be nine years."

The sergeant nodded. "Nine years. In nine years, how many ritzy ladies from out of town can you recall throwing orders at me like I was their butler?"

Judith felt a new wave of fright, but then came a stronger sense of revulsion at being played with by these tin-horn Torquemadas. "Listen, you, what's your name?" she demanded.

The busy room hushed. The sergeant's eyes grew darker. Too quietly he said, "Whoahh now . . ."

See it through, she thought; don't let him play any more. "I asked you your name. The reason is that when this farce is brought into the open, I plan to tell the world your name and that you questioned my constitutional right to place a telephone call."

He rubbed his tightened jaw, surely humiliated in front of his audience of lackeys, surely unused to backtalk. Lighting a cigarette, he nodded to a crewcut officer at the switchboard and said, "Get the number from the duchess, Harry." He surveyed Judith and drawled, flatly, "The name is Sparks. Sergeant Earl Sparks. Now I'm gonna tell *you* something before you get tucked away for a good night's sleep. We know who you are, been reading about you and seeing you on the TV, but that don't make you special. You're being arrested and booked in this state and this county on the crime of unlawful fornication. You bring in all your big-city big shots you like, and I'll tell them what I'm gonna tell you: Earl Sparks is a duly appointed police sergeant of Granum County. Earl Sparks isn't some hick-town rube you big-shot Easterners go around making fun out of. Earl Sparks expects folks, especially unlawful fornicators, to keep a civil tongue in their head. Everything clear now?"

His curtain speech concluded, Earl Sparks then directed himself to a waiting call. The officer named Harry motioned Judith to a telephone on his switchboard table and asked her the number.

Suddenly, preposterously, she went blank. She wanted to call her attorney, Raymond Pallino, in Rye, New York, but hadn't the number, she said, and asked him to call Information. Only local calls were allowed he said. Mr. Pallino would accept the charge, she said. The officer eventually got the number, tried it, and told her, "Nobody answers." Panic building, wishing she had had the presence to instruct Andrea Lane to phone and keep phoning Ray if necessary, she asked now that Mrs. Lane be called. Earl Sparks heard that and rumbled, "The apprehended made her one Constitutional call. Constitution don't allow two. Let's get to work. I don't have all night."

She was booked. A matron, squat and piano-legged, with the face that modeled for iodine bottles, wearing a wooden badge that read *N. Tompkins* above her left Breughel breast, accompanied her and the policeman named Chuck to a small, square, empty room. The policeman fingerprinted her and said to the matron, "Looks like you got yourself a real high-class guest tonight, Nell."

The matron nodded happily. "Nothing but the best."

Then the matron led her to another empty room and directed, "Okey dokey, strip down to the beaver, honey. You're not concealing anything but let's just make for sure." The fury and the hemmed panic gradually gave way to near numbness, and Judith obeyed, and the matron clucked, "Yummy yum, I had a shape like that once, believe it or not Ripley." She gave Judith a faded, wrinkled cotton robe, watched her dress in it, and took her through a door that led to a cell. She unlocked the cell door and purred, "You'll love these accommodations honey. They say it puts the Waldorf Astoria in the shade. Pleasant dreams. You want tea and crumpits, you just ring for room service," and Judith entered and the heavy door clanked shut.

Two other women were in the cell, one young, one comparatively old, both wearing copies of her robe. The comparatively old one, her robe unsashed, face and legs mottled, front teeth prominently missing, drunk or demented or perhaps both, squinted at Judith and cackled. The young one, obviously no more than fifteen or sixteen, was blonde and lovely, with enormous blue eyes filled with horror. The cell contained five cots, a sink, and a toilet with no seat. The older woman cackled again. Judith went to the child, whose body jolted away as if certain she was about to be struck.

Pausing, cautioning herself not to swoop, Judith gently said "Hello." Another pause, and she sat beside the child and said, "My name is Judith." The child's eyes brimmed with tears and she wept, her sobs racking and terrible, and the older woman cackled all the louder, and Judith extended her arms and the child rushed into them.

The child was from Norfolk. She and her boyfriend Craig had asked her father's permission to spend the summer on a supervised organic farm in New Mexico, to learn farming and to share what they knew and had studied about natural foods with Indian families there. Her father had listened to the idea, had said maybe, and the day before she and Craig were to leave had said no. She and Craig had left at dawn the next day, riding buses part of the way, hitchhiking part of the way, guilty yet certain that they belonged in New Mexico. An all-points bulletin had caught up with them in a Hartley diner, where they were arrested at seven o'clock tonight. She had watched Craig being pushed and shoved in the policemen's room outside. She—her name was Cheryl—had been told that her father would have her claimed when he was good and ready, had had her fingerprints taken by a policeman who seemed nice at first but who grabbed her breasts while she was washing the ink off her fingers. She wrenched herself free, and he just laughed and said he was from West Virginia and neighbors ought to stick together.

She wanted her mother, who was in Paris. She felt sorry for Craig, but she had realized, minutes after they had left her home, that she didn't really want him. She wanted her father, who had been reached and sent word that a little taste of jail would be the best thing for her, would teach her a lesson she would never forget.

Judith could only hold her; there was no honest way to comfort her and offer hope. For a time she considered an appeal to the matron, was tempted to plead with her to call *someone* so that this child could be removed at least from behind these obscene bars. And knew that would be pointless; even if N. Tompkins had the authority, she clearly savored the pleasures of her job. The Hartley police enjoyed theirs, certainly.

The older woman cackled at a cockroach. The child saw the roach and held on tighter. The night would be very long, but morning would come. And I'll be ready, thought Judith.

4

Martha Hanaday returned to the Columbia Heights apartment at half-past nine, depleted yet exhilarated by the long day, looking forward to a hot tub and to tomorrow's flight to Boston.

Lights were on, but Norman wasn't in the apartment, and the emptiness mildly disappointed her and made her vaguely uneasy, for she disliked coming home to an empty flat. Being alone in hotel rooms in strange cities never bothered her much, oddly enough, but home was different. She hung her raincoat in the hall closet and started to dial the answering service to check if Norman had called in, but then she remembered that they had agreed to cut expenses by stopping the answering service at six o'clock in the evenings rather than midnight. Penny wise and pound foolish, she thought.

She ran the bath and turned on WNYC for company. The Pierre cocktail party for Norman was expected to finish no later than seven or seven-thirty, he'd said, so he certainly should have been home by now. Well, maybe not. Cocktail parties, which Martha detested, rarely finished when they were supposed to, and Norman—private, limelight-shy Norman—was probably eating up the back slaps and cheek kisses. She hoped he wouldn't make a fool of himself, hoped he wouldn't drink—not that he was a drinker of any consequence, but almost overnight the publishing of his little book had transformed him from a quiet history teacher into something of a minor celebrity, praised and fawned over, and any human being would have to be affected by such unaccustomed attention. In the morning he would begin a two-week (or was it three-week?) publicity tour. He wasn't used to hopping from city to city and hotel to hotel and interview to interview, as she was, and if he *had* to go on that tour, which she had rightly advised him against, he owed it to his health to pace himself properly in advance.

The radio played Sibelius, and the hot, soapy bath felt wonderful.

With a pleasure that was only incidentally sexual, Martha Hanaday cupped her small, firm breasts in her hands, lazily rubbed them, tenderly squeezed them, watched the nipples come alert. Her hands roved her body slowly, exploring angles and planes, summoning agreeable rather than profound sensations, and presently her thighs pressed together, in teasing good humor, clitoris hiding, finger fooled for only a while. The touch comforted her as it warmed her, and she paused and pondered why she was doing this infantile thing, supposed she ought to work to trace what had prompted it.

The pondering lessened as the pleasure grew, lessened, grew, lessened. *The strangest thing,* she imagined herself telling her analyst, Stephanie Wall, at tomorrow's session. *In my bathtub last night I masturbated!*

What was your fantasy?

None. Absolutely none. I don't mean I actually masturbated—not to any climax, certainly. But I did stimulate my genitals and I manipulated them. I haven't done anything like that in years!

Was it gratifying?

. . . Yes. Until I reminded myself that I'm a mature and responsible adult. Yes, it was nice—and upsetting. Fantasy? I've talked about this before. I fantasize that if I lose control over myself just once, if I let go sexually, I'll do every sick sexual thing conceivable. I'll be a dam bursting, I'll go mad . . .

What sick sexual things?

I can't say them. Not now. Not yet.

Velvety pleasures mounted, thrill and guilt racing toward a non-existent finish line, and Martha Hanaday, face flushed and pulse pounding, barely managed to pull her hand away in time when she did indeed remember that she was a mature and responsible adult.

Lying back, taking consciously measured breaths, she forced herself into the present, into reality. She thought about Norman.

She was satisfied that Norman would be well over his temper tantrum by the time he got home.

He had been uncharacteristically peevish at breakfast this morning.

"We don't have to stay too long at the Pierre," he'd said. "I want you with me."

"Really, Norman, it's out of the question. You don't need me for support anyway. You'll handle yourself beautifully."

"What's *support* got to do with anything? The publisher is giving me a party and I simply want my wife to share it with me."

"Oh, Norman really . . . This is *your* party, Norman. You don't want to be there as Martha Hanaday's husband—and you know how the discussions all turn to the women's movement when I'm around. Honestly, you'll handle yourself very well, all on your own. This is going to be a ferociously busy day for me. I have far too many important things to do to stand around and listen to chitchat and watch people get drunk. *Please* don't *glare* at me, Norman. I've promised to read your book, haven't I, and I will, the moment I have time. I'm taking a copy with me to Boston tomorrow; I've told you that. You might at least appreciate that, just a little, instead of badgering me."

"I don't think I'm badg—"

"No, I know; I'm sorry. But let's not quarrel, all right? I have to dash now, or I'll be late for my session. Norman dear, don't look so *dour!* You won't need me, honestly."

Stephanie Wall, who seldom had ventured an opinion in eight years of treatment, had remarked at this morning's session that finding an hour or so to join Norman at the party might have been an act of simple kindness.

"Do you think I was insensitive?" Martha had asked.

"It's more important what you think," Dr. Wall had answered.

Martha shook her head and said, "Norman will be fine," and presently repeated her concern that Dr. Wall looked awfully tired and drawn. Stephanie Wall, aging and overweight and sedentary, had suffered a slight heart attack not quite two years before, when Martha had most needed her, and had spent months recuperating. She was supposedly fully recovered now, but she didn't look at all well during the morning session, seemed somehow less sharp, less vital than usual, and she thanked Martha for her concern, calmly assured her that nothing was wrong, and reminded her that this was the patient's hour, not the doctor's.

From the doctor's office Martha walked to the Russian Tea Room to keep an appointment for lunch—her one real meal of the day, every day—with Nicole Rooney, the New York Chapter president of Sisters of Sappho, to discuss tomorrow's work in Boston. Then, because she would be away from her typewriter for as many days as Boston would need her, she took a subway home to Columbia

Heights to write some advance syndicate columns, to put finishing touches to the September article for *Feminists Forever* and to catch up on her mail.

At mid-afternoon the reporters' calls began to come in about the newest Supreme Court decisions and the probable nomination of Paula Demling, and of course they insisted on baiting her with Judith Harrison's name. She answered the questions guardedly at first, then forthrightly, wishing the Harrison name didn't invariably jolt her temper, however carefully she concealed it. After the third or fourth call she swallowed her third Valium of the day and told her secretary, Nancy, that she would take no more telephone calls. At eight o'clock, in a Lenox Avenue meeting hall, she addressed the BFA—Black Feminists of America—urging the nineteen of her black sisters who were in attendance to free themselves of the sexist and denigrating role in life as bolsterers and wetnurses to their black men, to see themselves as individuals, as *persons*. At nine-thirty, in her apartment, she called to Norman and heard nothing.

At ten o'clock she stepped out of the bathtub and dried her body, a healthy, compact body that had weighed a constant 103 pounds since she had been sixteen years old. Martha Frerichs Hanaday was forty-five now, had borne two children and innumerable spiritual calamities since those horrid beginnings in Vermont, but no horror, no pain showed on her face. It was a good face, attractive, perhaps a trace more than attractive, features small and clean. She regarded her reflection in the mirror as she brushed her teeth and thought, You're no Judith Harrison, with the cheap-thrill good looks and the acre of breasts and the mile of legs. And that's fine. She got to wherever it is she got to by thoroughly vulgarizing the movement. I'm where I am and I'm who I am because the movement is a serious commitment to me, not some sexed-up circus act.

At half-past ten, in bed, the image crossed Martha's mind of Norman leaving the Pierre with one of those professionally sensuous swinger types that hung around the corridors of the publishing world. She rejected the image as ludicrous—Norman wasn't an adulterer; she knew she could not possibly survive it if she ever discovered that he was—but she was worried about him now because Norman was always steady, always reliable, never stayed away late without contacting her. She picked up the telephone from her night table, dialed Information for the number of the Hotel Pierre, then dialèd the hotel's number. Someone at the Pierre kept her waiting for an interminable length of time and finally came back on the line to tell her that the R. A. Storm cocktail party had concluded at approximately eight o'clock.

At a few minutes before eleven she heard the front door unlock, open and close, and she was relieved, largely because she was having trouble keeping her eyes open. She heard something fall—a chair turned over, maybe—and then Norman was framed in the bedroom's doorway, obviously tipsy and possibly downright drunk, his eyes unfocused, the corners of his mouth down, his graying hair rumpled. Martha had seen him like this only once before—she couldn't recall when or why, it had been so long ago—and she smiled at him and was nearly as amused as she pretended to be.

"Good evening, m'lord," she greeted.

"Late," he said.

"Yes. But you're home and safe."

"Broke up 'bout eight o'clock. Went with Prostin and Andy Masters to a bar. That's why I'm late. We started talking."

"And making enthusiastic trips to the well, too, I see. I'm happy you had a nice night out with the boys and I'm glad you're home." She switched off her light. "In the morning, I want to hear all that happened."

"I'll tell you now."

"In the morning, dear. I've been on the go all day and I can't keep awake. Drink two or three glasses of water before you go to sleep. That's supposed to reduce the size of a hangover."

She had a dim awareness of his saying something, but she fell asleep. Minutes later, maybe hours later, she was brought out of that sleep, partially, by the feel of his hand under her nightgown, traveling up her thigh. "No," she said and turned away from him. Seconds later, maybe minutes later, she felt his head close to hers as though he was about to kiss her, felt his penis touching her thigh, smelled the revolting smell of whiskey, and wriggled farther away from him. "No," she said again.

"Sweethear . . ."

"I'm not having relations with you while you're full of alcohol. I'm not an object and I won't be treated like one. Now go to sleep, Norman."

He persisted, and as he fondled her she became sharply conscious

39

of his closeness—*how could he maintain an erection? didn't heavy drinking make that impossible?*—and for a time, though it was important not to give any signal of response, she found that she liked what he was doing, liked being touched there, wondered if she dared guide his head there.

No. He would expect the favor returned. The very thought was barbaric, humiliating.

Firmly, without harshness, she said, "I'm surprised at you, Norman. If you're so terribly desperate to have an orgasm, I'll get up and find my diaphragm. But I'm surprised if all you see me as is a receptacle. *Is* that the way you see me?"

It worked. He slowly left her twin bed to go to his own.

"You understand I did offer myself, don't you?" she asked.

Silence. Of course he understood.

Minutes later, maybe hours later, something wakened Martha yet again, and she saw that Norman wasn't in his bed. The bedroom door was open and the light in his study, directly across the hall, was on. Childish of him to sleep alone, she thought drowsily, glad he was safe.

Norman wasn't in his study when Martha wakened, shortly before eight. She showered quickly, regretting that she hadn't let him talk about himself last night, for she had little time this morning and she was in no mood to listen for long; her session with Stephanie Wall was at ten o'clock—the last session till after Boston—and there were last minute things to attend to before the flight. It would have been convenient, even pleasant, if they could ride out to the airport together, but her flight was fairly early in the afternoon, his somewhat later. Yesterday she had remembered to instruct Bernice, her gem of a cleaning woman who came in four days a week, to pack Professor Hanaday's suitcase for him; Bernice was a genius at packing, and Martha had neither the talent nor patience for it.

She swallowed the day's first Valium, dressed in her housecoat, brushed her short, honey-colored hair, and found Norman in his kitchen chair, drinking coffee he had perked and smoking the one cigarette of the day he allowed himself. He hadn't shaved yet, but he didn't look nearly so awful as she had expected, considering the ocean of liquor he must have put away.

"Well! How's the guilty alcoholic this morning?" she said cheerfully, pouring the one cup of coffee that comprised her daily breakfast.

Norman Hanaday, professor of modern history at Columbia, was six feet tall—a foot taller than Martha—fifty years old, reed-thin, and handsomer than she was attractive. Like Martha, he had learned to allow few emotions to show in his eyes, but there was anger in his eyes this morning, and Martha sighed inwardly, for the last thing she had the patience to endure this day was one of Norman's sulking performances.

"Sit down," he said firmly.

She cocked an eyebrow at the tone. "Hangover grouchiness is the first warning of incipient alcoholism, I read once," she teased, her own tone still light.

"You read too much. Sit down. There."

"I do your bidding, O master," she said, playing along, and sat.

"You read too much and that lets you off the hook: you don't have to feel."

"Oh my, Karen Horney at breakfast," she said, and smiled, wishing he would get on with it and let her get dressed. Norman was an extremely intelligent man, frequently surprising her with his sensitivity, but he had his silly season, too, when he became tiresome.

"I want a divorce," he said.

Martha's coffee cup was halfway to her lips. She looked fully at this man she had known for half of her life, observed the hammy frown of disapproval that he never brought off with success, and she laughed.

He was furious. "What did I say that's so funny?"

"Norman, dear Norman. 'I want a divorce,' " she mimicked, her voice stentorian. "Not only psychiatric analysis at breakfast, but melodrama, too! What old movie did you hear that line in? And the *reading* of the line, my—"

His hand shot out and slammed his cup on the table so forcefully that coffee gushed out of it, and he shouted, *"Damn* you, shut your overeducated mouth and pay *attention* to me!"

The violence and the shouting were new, very new. They had had disagreements and ugly discussions and days of simply not talking to each other in their twenty-two years together, but this behavior was totally unlike Norman. Martha nodded patiently, looking at the wall clock behind him. She hadn't yet dressed, and she needed to allow herself three-quarters of an hour to get to her session, but there was a little spare time. She paid attention.

" 'Want a divorce' is wrong," he said quietly. "There are bad marriages and sleepwalking marriages. We've had no marriage; we've been roommates when we've been even that. What we have to show for twenty-two years together are two children, both of them messes. I did my share to help mess them up, yes—I should've destroyed those psychoanalytic textbooks you were raising them by, and I didn't. I should've done seventeen hundred things differently, and I didn't."

Martha nodded to indicate that she was hearing him. Evenly she began, "If I understand the nature of your complaints correctly—"

"Drop that unemotional doctor-to-patient tone, Martha," he said, rising and pacing. "Jesus, can't you lower yourself to even show any feeling? Must you always sit on that throne and think you can intellectualize *all* problems away? You can't even have sex without thinking it through to a climax."

Stay calm and stay rational, she warned herself. *If you blow up or break down, he'll have won whatever nasty little game it is that he imagines he wants to win. That wouldn't help either of us.* "I'm sorry if my voice bothers you, Norman. I respect the fact that you're upset, and why. You wanted me with you at your party yesterday and I was too busy to go. Then I frustrated you further when you came home and wanted sexual release, and I refused you because your whole affect was loveless. Obviously there was a part of you that *wanted* to be rejected, otherwise you—"

"Horseshit, Martha."

That kind of language was new, too.

She watched Norman stand beside her. The anger seemed to drain out of him, and it was replaced by weary resignation.

"Horseshit," he repeated, and the ultimate indignity was that he stretched his arms, as though he were about to yawn. "I was hoping that for once in our lives you'd listen to me."

"I'm lis—"

"I think you're not. I think that while I'm talking, you're preparing neat little epigrams to impress me with, and that's not good enough anymore, Martha. One of the things I learned about myself last night was what you've been saying all along: I don't need you. I was content—fairly content—to stay in your shadow year after year and be mother as well as father to the kids, because I admired most of what you were doing outside. Well I'm just plain fed up now. I do care about you, even though love hasn't been an especially relevant word for a while. But I'm going to be fifty-one in November, Martha, and—"

The kitchen telephone rang.

"—this is the day you and I have to—" He interrupted himself as Martha went to the phone. "Just a minute!" he said sharply. "Phone calls can wait!"

"It could be important," she said, and answered the call, and it *was* important. Stephanie Wall's service reported that Dr. Wall would be unable to see Mrs. Hanaday this morning, and would Mrs. Hanaday telephone for another appointment on her return from Boston?

A rush of fear stabbed at her. "Is the doctor ill?"

"We don't know anything about that, Mrs. Hanaday. We're just delivering the message."

She slowly replaced the receiver, shaken and worried—the last time an appointment had been so abruptly canceled had been the time of Stephanie Wall's heart attack—and she wondered if she had the right to ring up Stephanie's private number. No, that probably wouldn't be proper.

Staring blankly at the phone, she told Norman who had called, and the message. He didn't answer.

He wasn't there. She walked through the living room and down the hall to find him. His study door was shut. For a moment she considered tapping at the door, and decided against it; there would be more abuse, more inconsideration, and she had enough things to deal with. In her own study, she used the time that would have gone to her session in cleaning up more loose ends at her desk. The work helped keep her mind off Stephanie, for minutes at a stretch.

Norman's study door was still shut when she was dressed and packed and ready to leave. She heard his voice, couldn't hear words, and assumed he was telephoning someone at his publisher's. Despite those disjointed and atrocious charges he had hurled at her, she wanted to wish him good luck, wish him well, let him see that she

43

meant it sincerely, let him know he needn't be afraid. That was why he'd behaved as he'd behaved, of course: he was basically a cloistered man, comfortable with privacy and small classrooms, and now he was about to begin the frightening adventure of exposing his face and verbalized thoughts to the press and on radio and television, perhaps before thousands upon thousands of people at once. She remembered her own early public appearances. They had been terrifying, and why should they be any less terrifying to Norman?

She decided not to disturb him now, not while he was surely still sulking. She went to the living room and asked Bernice, who had arrived at nine, to call down to the building's doorman to hail a taxi. In her case was a copy of Norman's itinerary, along with a copy of *How Fascism Won,* his book which she was *determined* to dip into, in the airport limo on the way to JFK. Tonight, she would surprise him. She, in her Boston hotel, would phone him at his hotel in Cleveland—or was it Detroit?—and she would be sweet and warm, and the distance of miles between them would dissolve, would serve to enhance all that was genuinely good and worthwhile between them. She would be supportive in ways she could not seem to be when they were face to face, and everything would be good again. She would forgive Norman because to punish someone dear who didn't understand himself was to be equally immature and masochistic.

"You watch yourself up in that sky," Bernice directed. "I still wish you'd take the train. I never met an airplane I was settled to trust."

Grinning, Martha said, "You'll see that Professor Hanaday gets off all right won't you, Bernice? He won't admit that he's scared of his trip, but he is. He's been snapping at me, which isn't at all like him."

"Him? Snapping? Don't you go expecting me believe that."

"He's a very little boy in some ways, but he's a fine, fine man. Pamper him a little before he goes, will you? You're marvelous at that kind of thing, and I know he appreciates it. Tell him he's going to be magnificent."

And with that problem solved, she started down in the elevator, worrying about the much more vexing problem of Stephanie Wall. Perhaps she could try the answering service again from the airport; maybe they would have more information by then.

5

Me again. Sam Gallagher.

Judith hadn't checked into the Airport Motor Inn when I got there at six last night, but there had been a message for me to phone Burt Oehlrichs. Burt managed *Rowland's* news bureau in the major city a dozen miles east of Hartley and I remembered him from the other time I'd been here, on the trail of Oliver Starn. I had registered, bought that day's issue of the *Statesman-Patriot,* and up in my room I had slipped the bellhop a five to ring me the moment Judith Harrison appeared.

I dug a bottle of Dewar's out of my overnight bag, poured a restorative shot—first things first—and rang Burt, hoping he'd still be at his desk. He was, but some Midwestern voice twanged that he was on another line and would call me back, and so I waited for the return call by applying myself to the Scotch and the *Statesman-Patriot.* I knew the paper and considered it a first-rate job technically—it was simplistic and essentially evil, but it distorted the news with such conviction and unfaltering nineteenth-century consistency that I never failed to be impressed. The presence of Oliver Starn—who would have released his slaves after the Civil War, anyway—was on every page and in every item in much the way one used to see the Hearsts and McCormicks on every page of their papers, right down to the comics and the cake recipes. All of the Starn papers were successful, partly because of weak or nonexistent competition but mostly because they were immensely readable. The credos were simple and unswerving. Honor comes above all else. Faith moves mountains. Poverty is the result of indolence. The nation began to gallop to the grave on the day Grover Cleveland left the White House. The Lord is a Caucasian Baptist. If women can't be pretty, it is incumbent on them to at least smell pretty. God loves and looks after America; all others pay cash.

It went down easily. The most frightening thing about Starn, maybe, was that he was such a beautiful pro.

There was a front-page editorial signed by Oliver Starn, dateline Corinth, rhapsodizing over the magnificent Greek Government. There wasn't a word, anywhere in the paper, about Judith, but she was present and accounted for, indirectly. The lead piece on the regular editorial page savagely attacked the Supreme Court for having agreed with the arguments against state bans on abortion. It was scarcely a secret that nonlawyer Judith had choreographed that test case, and that the selfsame evil destroyer of American values was due to appear right here in Hartley. The connection, then, however indirect, was unavoidable.

Burt Oehlrichs phoned me, welcomed me to fun-filled Hartley, and I asked him if he knew or thought the glaring omission of Judith Harrison's name was on purpose.

"Our information here is that there's no information, Sammy," Burt said. "One of our contacts, works night rewrite on the *Statesman*, tells me Starn's sent down orders that there's to be a complete and total blackout on Harrison, but that could change any minute."

"Starn's in Greece."

"Ollie Starn is ubiquitous," Burt corrected. "You should know that, Sammy—you investigated the bejesus out of the gent last year or so, remember? My hunch is that he's getting smart in his old age and figured the best thing is to just ignore her and that way she'll go away." I told Burt that Judith hadn't shown yet, and asked if he knew where to find her if for some slipup reason I missed her here. "She's scheduled to start freeing women from bondage at ten tomorrow morning at Addams Hall—that's within walking distance of where you are," he said.

"Come on over and have a drink," I invited.

"Um. Wish I could Sammy, but no way. I didn't learn you were coming till this morning—we can always set our watch by the New York office for meticulous efficiency, can't we?—and I have to take the present Mrs. Oehlrichs to an unbustable dinner party. Look, I really am sorry, pal—I haven't seen you in it must be two and a half, three years. How about lunch tomorrow, if you're not too busy *shtupping* Harrison?"

"Maybe. We'll see what happens."

"I'll leave lunch free. Hey, by the way, did I hear right, about you and Alma being divorced?"

"Yeah."

"Reason I ask: Hartley closes at sundown except for the pinball machine at the bus station. If you somehow don't connect tonight with Harrison, you'll be a lonely type, won't you? I'm suddenly a very guilty sonofabitch, Sammy; I *should* break that dinner party, but I can't. You want to hold on a minute, I'll round up a phone number. She's from Norway and she has a water bed full of gin and to show you what a friend I am I'll put her on *my* expense account."

"You're a prince among men, Burt, but I'll be fine. We'll talk in the morning."

At eight o'clock, Judith was still expected and still hadn't arrived. I realized I was hungry and, yeah, a little lonely; I've been alone in an Excelsior suite and in Holiday Inn boxes, and after a point in time they become equally depressing. I phoned the restaurant downstairs. It was closed. At eight-thirty, Judith still expected, I walked into the heart of Hartley in search of food, found three restaurants, all of them dark and locked. A man wearing a floral-banded straw hat and an American flag tattoo and a polo shirt with a picture of Snoopy on it advised me to try Walgreen's up the block. "There's a couple places outside town if you got a car, but they shut down around ten," he said. At the Walgreen food counter I ordered the Number Three, sirloin and salad, and settled for the Number Zilch, a Swiss cheese on cracked wheat, because the kitchen was closed for the night. I shared the counter with a middle-aged couple who sat beside each other, the lady reading one section of the *Statesman-Patriot,* the man reading the other. I know their names were Marge and Lloyd because that's what the counterman called them. The three of them chatted about niggers, good niggers and bad niggers. From there it was a skip and jump to this here women's lib. The counterman explained that he would beat up on his missus—"proudly"—if she went in for any of that stuff. Lloyd explained that what most of those kind of women needed to set them right was a good roll on the lawn. Marge told Lloyd to hush such language in a public place, but she grinned the most lascivious grin I've ever seen on Norman Rockwell's mom.

Back at the Motor Inn, Judith was still expected. I left word for her to ring my room, stripped to my shorts, drank some Dewar's, saw my Judith Harrison cover story running without Judith Harrison, grew glumly resigned to the likelihood that our love would remain under separate cover, watched *The Prisoner of Shark Island* on television and identified with him, finished the Dewar's. Eventually I fell asleep, but not before I drunkenly cursed myself for having turned down Burt's offer of the Norwegian water bed.

This morning, more than slightly hung, I was paged in the coffee shop. Burt Oehlrichs was on the line to tell me that Judith had come to Hartley, all right. She was in the slam.

Burt didn't meet me at the court house. He sent Johnnie Snedden, a reporter I'd never met but had heard good things about. Snedden filled me in on the little he knew about the bust, and I remember that all I could do for a moment was simply gawk at him, as if there had to be more to the story. "She was busted and locked up here for the night for *balling* some guy?" I asked. Snedden nodded. "Not shoplifting or homicide or smoking on the bus, but *balling* some guy?" Snedden nodded.

Juicy news evidently traveled as fast in Hartley as it does in every other part of the world, because the courtroom was getting crowded. I recognized a few wire service men; Al Chase spotted me and winked. Johnnie Snedden pointed out a small thirtyish man with thinning pink hair and a vest and granny glasses. "There's Clarence Darrow," he said. "Here he goes under the name of Lester Farr. He'll represent Harrison at the arraignment."

"*Is* he Clarence Darrow?"

"He's Darrow like I'm Richard Harding Davis, but I understand Harrison's big-gun lawyer in New York's been contacted," said Snedden. "Over there is the county prosecutor, Cliff Albright. Farr clears his throat a lot and says thank you to self-service elevators. Albright's tough and shrewd as they come."

A side door was opened and Judith was brought in.

She looked as beautiful and composed as anyone so obviously

exhausted could look. Composed and seething, both at the same time, an aristocratic eyebrow cocked as she walked regally to her chair, her expression haughty and authoritative and clearly announcing, *I'm going to murder some bastards before this day is out.* I couldn't be certain if she recognized me or even saw me. She sat down, her back to us. The Judith I'd known in Hollywood had been royally insecure—not emptyheaded, certainly, but rather without defined goal or purpose other than to be directed and taken care of, often by shlubs who knew nothing much but who knew all they needed to know about her vulnerability.

That was in Hollywood. This Judith sat tall, very tall.

The judge's name was Jamison, and he managed to combine the look of Lewis Stone with the bearing of some local politician's fifteenth choice for the bench. A formal charge was droned at Judith and these, I swear, were the incredible words droned:

"You are charged with violating Section 1285 of the State Penal Law in that you on the seventh day of June at approximately 8 P.M. at the Polo Motel did engage in sexual congress with one other than your spouse who was at the time married to another, how do you plead?"

Lester Farr said, amid throat clearings, "On behalf of my client, your honor, a plea of not guilty is entered."

And then Judith spoke. "Just a moment. I'd like to add something," she said.

"Add what?" asked the judge.

"I want it made clear that my plea of not guilty is based on my belief that the violation I'm charged with is ludicrous and unconstitutional."

The room's stirrings and rumblings were low but very audible. The judge squinted at her. "Do you happen to be a constitutional lawyer?"

"No."

"Do you have a layman's expertise in constitutional law, or law in general?"

"No, but—"

"Then it's strongly recommended that you leave the interpretation of law to the bench. Is *that* made clear?"

"Almost nothing has been clear to me since I arrived in this town,"

49

Judith said, "except that this charge is idiotic and thoroughly reprehensible."

"Uh-oh," said Johnnie Snedden.

More rumblings. Jamison snapped, "That will do." He summoned Farr and Albright to the bench, and after a while he said to Judith, "You have the right to a preliminary hearing to determine whether the complaint actually charges you with a violation of the criminal statute—a determination predicated on professional law, not on layman opinion. Do you understand?"

"Yes."

"Or you may waive the preliminary hearing and set the matter down for trial."

"I believe I have the choice of either a speedy trial or a trial delayed at my request," she said.

"That is correct."

"Then I request a delay."

Next came the matter of bail. Albright thundered that the felony (*felony?* had I heard right?) warranted a high bail inasmuch as the defendant, a stranger to the community, had done severe damage to the community's sense of morality and propriety, and a light bail would only serve to encourage immoral behavior. He asked a bail of fifty thousand dollars. Farr cleared his throat and respectfully called the request excessive (not a preposterous joke; excessive), reminded the court that Miss Harrison was a well-known public figure, unlikely to flee, and asked, much too timidly, that she be released in her own recognizance.

Bail was set at five thousand.

Wait, there's more. Judith didn't have any five grand, and it became evident that she was going to be returned to the cooler, presumably to stay there alongside her fellow cutthroats, until someone sprang for the tab.

Guess who stood up with the offer. Yeah. Judith turned to look at me, and her face lighted up in recognition, and she smiled, and turned front again and said she appreciated Mr. Gallagher's offer but she preferred to decline it.

The judge rumbled that no trial date could be set without posted bail. Then he solemnly lectured, "You might ponder something, young lady, for your own good. The bench is exercising considerable leniency in view of your disrespectful conduct in this court-room. You were wise to control your outbursts when you did, because a few more words would have earned you a contempt citation. Ponder that. Ponder that seriously. Next case."

They led her away.

There were five of us newsmen in the corridor when Lester Farr trotted out of the courtroom. I collared him first but he was too fast for me or the others; he didn't walk away, he scurried.

Presently Albright came out. The reason I tell you now that I'm just a shade under six feet tall and still in fairly solid athletic shape is that Clifford Albright immediately made me look like the ninety-seven pound weakling those beach bullies kick sand at. He was mammoth, up and across, a spike-haired, ruddy-faced behemoth with the aura about him of powerhouse authority.

Albright saw the press and instantaneously went onstage; I haven't bumped against all that many public prosecutors, but they do seem to share a common passion to be regarded as superstars. His grin was expansive, and he answered the questions he wanted to answer, and this was the essence of the quickie conference: Conviction allowed for imprisonment of from five to twenty years, and he was going to go full blast for that. Obviously there was a tryable case; he had little patience with cases he wasn't darn sure he could win. The fact that the defendant was Judith Harrison and not universally admired around these parts was completely irrelevant; fornication was on the books as a crime and his responsibility was to prosecute crime. The fact that the man she was accused of banging was colored was also completely irrelevant.

Al Chase of Associated Press attempted to prick the pomposity behind that absurdly inappropriate grin. "Come on and level," said Al. "Do you honestly believe screwing is a crime?"

"Look, boys, don't make me out to be a Sunday school teacher," Albright said. "I did more than my share of cutting up before I was married. But I'm an officer of the community as well as the court, and no, I *don't* see carnality outside marriage as something the community I live in and raise my children in and go to church in should be asked or expected to tolerate. Illegal cohabiting may be perfectly acceptable in the big cities across this country, but I'll tell you one thing: random fucking wasn't what made this country great—better change that to 'promiscuity.' I'm raising three daughters, twelve, fourteen and sixteen years old. I'm certainly not going to let any of them be left with the impression that we condone hopping in and out of beds like animals."

I was purposely staying a bit in the background because I wanted this baby for myself at some point later, but I couldn't resist one small jab: "You say the penalty on conviction could be five to twenty years. What's the penalty in this state for second degree murder?"

Surprise, surprise, he didn't much like that. "I don't think I know your name," he said.

"Sam Gallagher. *Rowland's*," I said.

He knew the name, all right, and the dark glare I got clearly meant that in a better ordered society he would have the authority to remove at least one of my testicles. Sam Gallagher, after all, had once written an unadoring story about Oliver Starn, which meant that Sam Gallagher's name was known in these parts.

"That's all for now, boys," said Albright, his grin quickly back in place. "Time to head back to the salt mines." And off he padded, down the corridor.

Johnnie Snedden chuckled. "Talk about Sunday school teachers. Cliff Albright the Christer leaves town twice every year, once to take his wife and kiddies fishing, and once by himself to the annual lawyers' convention where he gets bombed out of his skull on booze and works at being the world's most energetic cocksman."

We swapped speculations with the other reporters for a while, and they went off to file their stories. "What now?" Johnnie asked.

A good question. When a news story as hot as this one spreads its seductive arms and pants to be investigated, the absolutely worst thing that can happen to a reporter is what appeared to be threatening me: forced immobility. Judith could conceivably stay in the pokey all day. But there was also the chance that she would be sprung while I was away for half an hour, and that she would cannonball herself out of town, a most depressing prospect.

But what the hell, we were reporters, right? "Now we hope she stays put for a little while, and we go and do some digging," I said. "Let's find out what in the name of Starn is going on here."

6

Airborne to Boston, the day's second Valium taking tranquilizing effect, Martha Hanaday opened her briefcase and studied the Sisters of Sappho material that Nicole Rooney had given her. She saw Norman's book and vowed she definitely would get to it, before or after working hours in Boston.

Martha had never had a homosexual experience in her life, nor could she recall ever having thought much about having one, other than in occasional odd dreams that she was always able later to interpret as something more significant than simple sexuality. She was not even wholly convinced that lesbians mattered very much except to other lesbians. But the Massachusetts Sisters of Sappho had asked for her help, and she could hardly refuse. She had been annoyed that they had first asked help from Judith Harrison, who "wasn't available," but then she had seen it as a challenge. She would show them all that she didn't flee at the first sign of real controversy.

She re-examined the facts of that controversy. The contract of a young Boston public school teacher named Elizabeth Kyle had not been renewed for the coming autumn because Elizabeth Kyle was an admitted and quite vocal lesbian. The American Civil Liberties Union was preparing to handle the case, solely in civil liberties terms. Martha Hanaday's role was to represent it as a feminist case.

There were, she knew, critics of Sisters of Sappho, critics who claimed it was not a responsible organization intent on gaining public understanding and support so much as a raucous group of mindless hysterics perversely committed to losing battles, the better to dramatize their oppression. Perhaps, she thought, although she had found Nicole Rooney, her one contact with the group, to be reasonable enough in conversation. What mattered was that publicity was guaranteed. She had come to realize, particularly with more and more newspapers dropping her column in the last year, that she would benefit from all the publicity she could get.

At Logan Airport she bought a local afternoon paper to see if there was anything about her arrival in town. On the front page was a photograph of Judith Harrison, and the caption below said she had been arrested in a town called Hartley on an adultery charge. Martha's initial reaction was a feeling of satisfaction, that the empty, self-serving, headline-hunting plastic doll deserved any punishment she received. But she re-read the caption in the cab and thought, The charge is preposterous. How humiliating it must have been for her to be behind bars, for even a minute!

The brief story on page three was from the AP wire, and it was sketchy and implicitly lurid behind its sketchiness. She read the skimpy details with a mixture of distaste for Judith Harrison's playgirl cavorting and disgust with the men's locker-room guffaws that were there between the lines. The woman would probably even be brought to trial on this insulting charge, she thought—and the papers would be full of nothing but Judith Harrison for weeks, no doubt. She read on in the final paragraphs of the story, which went into a description of Judith Harrison's career and recent activities in connection with a series of Supreme Court decisions. They referred to her as "Ms. Women's Lib," the "acknowledged leader of the feminist movement." As if Judith Harrison had invented the movement. As if Martha Hanaday had never existed. She threw down the paper and sat back in the taxi, brooding.

The Ritz-Carlton desk clerk welcomed her and said, "I believe there's a message for you, Mrs. Hanaday. Would you wait just a moment please? Front!" He returned with a message and a brightly ribboned package. "Yes, here we are."

"Thank you very much," said Martha. "It looks like a Christmas present, doesn't it?"

In the elevator she took the message from the envelope, frightened—unrealistically, foolishly, she knew—that it was bad news from or about Stephanie Wall. Stop it, she thought, that's being hysterical, positively infantile. The message read SISTER MARTHA: WELCOME TO BOSTON & THE STRUGGLE WE SHALL OVERCOME. WILL CALL ABT. 4. SISTERLY, JAN.

The room reserved for her was perfectly adequate and cheerful. From her window she could see the Charles River, and she watched a swan boat glide along the lagoon and loved the sight, loved Boston, one of the cities she flew to reasonably often but still never really had the time to visit. She gave a quarter to the bellhop, who blinked at the tip without enthusiasm and let himself out, and she performed the same orderly rituals she always performed on entering a new hotel room: She unpacked, hung dresses and skirts in the closet, carefully placed blouses and underclothes in bureau drawers. And, passing the bureau, saw the newspaper photo of Judith Harrison there where she had dropped it. She stopped, looking at the cover-girl face, and thought. When did we meet?

December, three years ago, the Thursday evening before the Christmas holidays. She'd written me a flattering, perfectly nice letter, asking if she might attend one of the Thursday evening meetings. Ruth Ingram warned me the letter was a trap: "It's like Eichmann asking to attend a B'nai B'rith meeting. You know who and what she is. She has all the social and moral commitment of a mink. Tear the letter up."

I knew who and what she was. And I invited her to the apartment. Why? Maybe the prospect of recruiting such a caricature of women into awareness and usefulness was an appealing challenge. Or maybe it was simply that so much was going so well that busy, productive December. My newspaper column had forty-one outlets. The envious backbiters hadn't yet congregated to make those systematically destructive jokes about my book and me and all I was accomplishing. I couldn't keep up with all the lecture offers. That same week, after a long tug-of-war, the Union National Bank had finally capitulated and agreed to hire women in key executive positions—a thumping victory, my victory. I was feeling on top of the world, not giddy but rightfully pleased with myself and my unquestioned place in this valuable movement.

She arrived early that evening, by herself, charming, poised, ingratiating. She'd read my book, she said, was moved by much of it, had hopefully honest quibbles about several points that Private Parts *raised, and was eager to listen in on the give and take of women gathered together in a basic cause.*

It was an ambush, deceptive and skillful, and I leapt right into it. I welcomed her, I personally introduced her to each of the dozen or so women who came, including Ruth Ingram, who refused to shake her hand and who said, "I think it's only fair to tell you that I strongly advised Martha to ignore your request to come here tonight. We've seen you and we've read about you. All you've done for the image of modern woman has been to denigrate it and set it back. Why don't you—"

I broke in, said something about courtesy and trust, got everyone seated, with Judith Harrison near the picture window, at the opposite end of the living room from Ruth. The meeting began, and the first matter at hand that evening was the Union National success, its delights and its ramifications. Then on to an open-floor discussion of the next battles to be won. Child care centers. Free abortions on demand. The civil rights of lesbians. Full rights for all women in all areas.

She was silent through most of the meeting. Till someone asked if she had a comment to make.

She had a comment, yes. A number of comments; they were in the form of questions, asked quietly and respectfully, but they clearly had been calculated to cause damage, and they succeeded.

"I don't argue with any issues, but I can't help wondering sometimes about emphases," she said. "I keep wondering whether anyone's right to make decisions can be based on the fact that she's a woman, or perhaps oughtn't it to be based on being a human being?"

She went on to ask about the proposed free day-care centers, "Certainly the facilities should be available to mothers who need them," she said. "But shouldn't we be more concerned about economic need than about the suburban mothers who feel unfulfilled with stuffing dirty diapers into the washing machine? When a woman makes a conscious choice to have a child, doesn't she automatically take on a responsibility for that child's well-being?"

We argued that one for a while, and Ruth said, "Why is it always the mother who takes on the responsibility? It takes two to make a baby, as I'm sure you know. What is the man's responsibility?"

"To earn the money, if that's the way the couple agreed to conduct their lives. Or to stay home and stuff those diapers while she earns the living, if that's their life style. But my point is that it's for them to decide, isn't it, when they have that baby?"

She raised a question about abortion, agreeing that it should be legalized but wondering if we shouldn't place more emphasis on preventing unwanted pregnancies rather than selling the risky and unpleasant aborting of the fetus as a panacea. Interesting in view of her recent activities.

The meeting, which had begun on a note of triumph and solidarity, disintegrated into bickering and bad temper. Ruth got angrier by the minute, and finally, during an argument about whether we were placing too much emphasis on the career-oriented woman to the detriment of the homebody, she exploded that Judith Harrison was simply trying to stir up argument for the sake of argument, and what the hell did a bed-hopping playgirl know about serious careers or the problems of the housewife?

Judith Harrison, who had been arguing with a kind of relish, stood up at that. After several tense seconds of stony silence, she said, "I'm sorry. It seems I have intruded on a private club. Excuse me." And as we all sat there, she began fumbling around looking for her coat.

I hadn't realized that Norman was even in the apartment, but he must have heard part of the argument. It was he who found her coat, helped her on with it, and then, with a cold look around the room, took her down to find a cab.

We tried to regain the mood we'd had when the evening began, but after a while it seemed hopeless. The women drifted out one by one, and Ruth, the last to leave, started to say something about her, that next month she'd be back on somebody's yacht while we went on with the real work. But she saw I was tired and depressed, so she left.

By the time Norman returned, an hour later, I was furious. "I don't know what you thought you were proving with that little display," I said quietly as he hung up his coat. "But I think you owe several people an apology, beginning with your wife."

He looked angry for a moment, then sighed and shook his head. "Differences of opinion are one thing, Martha," he said softly. "But she was a guest in our home."

He went on into his study, and we never spoke of the incident again.

And I never saw Judith Harrison again, at least not in person. But in magazines, in the press, on television, and now on this newspaper's front page, she had done her bit for the dignity of women. Oh yes . . .

Martha turned from the newspaper photo, and saw the package and went to it. Her name was printed in block letters on the festive, red-and-green striped paper, and she felt some of the eagerness of childhood Christmases as she opened the oblong package.

Inside the package was a box, and in the box was a phallus, long and pink and grotesque.

Martha Hanaday gasped and dropped the thing as she would have dropped a live coal, dropped it to the carpet where it rolled out of the box. She heard her heart thump, felt sick, gazed at it grimly, turned away as if to seek escape, looked at it again, was convinced she was going to be sick, would have to be sick.

Who on earth, what warped sense of humor would do such a . . .

She sat, and stood, raised and lowered her eyebrows repeatedly, a purposeful exercise to separate herself emotionally from the sickness of the joke, to detach and free herself. The box contained a card. She retrieved it, still irresistibly drawn to the object. The obscene thing must have been rubber—she had no intention of touching it—and it had prominent veins, and the opening at its head was a large black oval. She began to carry the card to the bathroom, and on the way she buckled ever so slightly and sat in the chair nearest her, and raised and lowered her eyebrows again and took deep breaths, and could not see the object from this chair, and looked at the card and swiftly looked away from it, and finally read it.

Hi Martha.

Read you were coming (ha ha ! !) to town and so am enclosing what you need most. Do not be afraid. It will not bite you unless you tell it to. Have seen you and bet you have not had one in you in years, so thank me for thinking of you.

Love and you know what.
A Friend.

She sat, simply sat. The thumpings began again in her heart, and the viciousness of it, the violation, built and encompassed her so that her face and her armpits were wet, and crying would be idiotic and she tried to understand it all, even a bit of it, and could not. She remembered the field mouse. Soon after her daughter Audrey was born, she and Audrey and Norman had lived for a year near Fort Tryon in Manhattan in a rent-controlled apartment house next to an

58

empty lot that was full of field mice. The field mice came into the apartment continually, and they would dash fearfully from corner to corner, while dinner was being cooked and eaten, more than once while she and Norman were entertaining guests in the living room. Field mice were completely harmless, they had been told; a nuisance, to be sure, but harmless. Their landlord offered to send them his pest exterminator, but they had declined, partly because she and Norman did not believe in cooperating in the killing of anything alive, partly because they feared that their cat, Sassy, would get to and eat whatever the exterminator put down. Finally, when the field mice seemed to be overtaking their apartment and threatening their sanity, Norman brought home a supply of mouse traps, set them where Sassy could not reach them, and late at night or in the morning would dispose of the field mice in the traps.

When Audrey was nine or ten months old, Norman had to go out of the city for a week. Martha wakened one morning to a nasty odor, traced it to under the bedroom radiator, saw that a field mouse had been long dead, phoned down to Mr. Wijomlik the super and was told that Mr. Wijomlik wouldn't be back till late in the night. By afternoon, the smell pervaded the whole apartment. That evening, she knelt at the radiator with an A & P bag, saw exactly where the trap was and, with eyes shut, quickly shoved it into the bag. The trip through the apartment and to the incinerator, surely no more than a twenty-second walk, felt like a lifetime, and washing her hands with soap when she came back was not nearly enough, so she had showered.

Now, in this bright hotel room, she worked up courage (she could hardly phone down for a bellhop) and returned to the object, her eyes slits, and scooped it into the package's paper wrappings and dropped all the contents into the bathroom waste basket. She would dispose of it, somehow, before a chambermaid found it.

Martha stripped, and opened the shower faucets, and felt an anxiety attack about to hurtle toward her. She had promised Stephanie Wall—who hadn't asked for a promise—that she would pace herself to three Valiums a day, but she had taken two today and it was only the middle of the afternoon. She found her purse, could not find the vial of yellow tablets, turned the purse over and let everything in it fall onto the bed. I must be going mad, she thought, her eyes filmed, her body taut, her head swirling; what am I looking for? I can't remember what I'm looking for . . .

The anxiety attacks, once weekly assaults, had diminished in intensity and pain and had been gradually, finally banished three or four years before, had never come back, would never come back. An attack came now, in full and frenzied force, one of the worst ones, old and fresh, splintering every nerve and muscle, chortling at her, suffocating her, and she strode the width and length of the sunlighted room, desperate to dock herself to something concrete, anything concrete, her body and her mind a clutter, unable to concentrate. *Stephanie,* she thought, *Stephanie* . . .

Stephanie's number . . . Plaza something, Plaza Plaza Plaza what? Yes, now I know, I'm sure I know. What's the area code for New York? Two-oh . . . no wait; yes, two-one-two. She dialed it direct. There was a busy signal that wouldn't stop, and she placed the receiver on its cradle and walked again, fast, heard the shower, saw the billows of steam, and hurried to the shower to turn it off. She could not reach the faucet because the water was too hot, and it scalded her and she screamed. She ran from the bathroom, screaming once more, and called for help to no one, to everyone.

"Stop it!" she said aloud. "Stop it, stop it, stop it, you're acting like a psychotic!" At the telephone she dialed the New York number again, and again it was busy. She walked, saw herself in the bureau mirror, saw herself dressed, couldn't remember dressing, dimly remembered that she had seen herself naked. The telephone rang. She jumped and scooped up the receiver. "Yes. Yes."

"Sister Martha? Sister Jan here. You sound out of breath."

"What?"

"Jan Atwell—Sisters of Sappho. You got in safely, I see. Sisters Mac and Helen and Marilyn and I are ready to come by when you are to—"

"What?"

"—something the matter? Is the connection bad?"

Pull yourself together; no one must see you this way, she thought. "I . . . Would you leave this line free, please? I'm expecting a very important call. Call me back later, would you, please?"

"Of course. Like . . . ah . . . when?"

"Later," she said, and replaced the receiver, shook her head to clear it (*Did I take a Valium? Yes. I think so*) and lifted the receiver and dialed Stephanie and got a busy signal. I'll go out, she thought. It's this room, the transience, the impermanence of it, these walls, I'll go out and walk along the lagoon and I'll be fine again. Yes.

She snapped up her key, left her purse, left the shower on, and fled to the corridor. By the time the elevator brought her to the stately, bustling lobby, the attack was gone as magically as it had come, and once outside the hotel, walking fast and with a secure pretense of direction, all of the comic-opera conniptions in the room were grim imaginings of conniptions that could not have happened. Bostonians, like San Franciscans and unlike people in most other cities, smiled at her when her eyes met theirs, and she smiled back and the contagion warmed her. She came upon a Good Humor truck, bought a Fudgicle, bit into it, and wondered what the white-jacketed man was waiting for, why he wasn't going about his business. "That'll be twenty-five cents, lady," he said.

Twent—Oh, for heavens'sake . . . "I'm *terribly* sorry! I must've left my money back in my room. And I've already bitten into this, haven't I?"

"Yes, lady, you have."

"How long will you be here? Ten minutes? I'll run back to my hotel and bring you the money."

"I'm not sure how long I stay here, lady. If yes, then you pay me. If no, then good luck with the Fudgicle I have to pay for."

Martha retraced her steps back toward the hotel, forgot its name, forgot where it was, to the right or the left, walked and walked and found it and tried to remember why she was returning so soon. She remembered: to telephone Stephanie. Waiting for the elevator, anxiety came back, anxiety and the realization that there was no reason for Stephanie's line to be busy, certainly not more than once; when Stephanie didn't pick up her phone, her answering service did.

In the room, steam now pouring into it from the shower, Martha dialed the number. This time it rang, rang many times but rang. She was relieved; and startled, as she waited, to find herself wearing her slip and shoes and nothing else, startled and revolted to see the grotesque pink object not in the waste basket but on the other twin bed. Then at last she heard Stephanie's housekeeper's voice, and she identified herself, and Mrs. Crosby told her that Dr. Wall had taken sick late last night, had gone to Mount Sinai Hospital where she died, at around noon today, that the telephone hadn't quit ringing for as much as a second—

Martha burned her fingers and wrist, but she turned the faucets off. Composed, gracefully composed, she opened her briefcase to look up Norman's hotel in Cleveland or Detroit. He would board the very first flight and comfort her.

Norman's itinerary wasn't in the case, and Martha supposed she must have left it on the apartment's foyer table. Bernice never left the apartment till six-thirty or seven, so she phoned there, rather surprised to notice as she dialed that the hotel room's ceiling light was on, on this gloriously bright afternoon. She let the phone ring a dozen times or more before she hung up. Then she phoned down to the desk and said, "This is Martha Hanaday. What time is it, please?"

"It's three minutes past twelve, Miss Hanaday."

"Twelve o'clock midnight?"

"That's right. Would you like to leave a wakeup call?"

"No. Thank you very much. Good night."

"Good night. Have a good sleep."

"I'll do my best. Thank you," she said and sat again.

7

Gallagher again, hotshot reporter.

As it turned out, Judith did stay in the pokey all day, because the Hartley bondsman didn't receive the okay from her New York attorney's bondsman to put up the five thousand until early evening. Or so we were told. By the time word came that she was finally to be released, Johnnie Snedden and I *had* done some digging, together and separately, and we learned a few things. We learned who Andrea Lane was. We learned from the Lanes' maid that Mr. and Mrs. Lane were out of town and couldn't be reached. The doors at Addams Hall, where the seminar was to have been held, were locked. Lyman Bester, the Polo Motel desk clerk, had heard shouting in the motel's Room 5, had looked through the window and seen black Luther Cobb, naked, white Judith Harrison, naked, black Luther Cobb's wife yelling at white Judith Harrison, and he'd called the cops. Room 5 was empty when the cops arrived. Rosetta Cobb, on her own, had filed a complaint at police headquarters. Lyman Bester had told the police that Rosetta Cobb's story was correct. Lester Farr refused to be interviewed, on or off the record. Luther and Rosetta Cobb were nowhere to be found. Lyman Bester had been advised to say nothing until the proper time. The police had no comment to make. No one had a comment to make. Andrea Lane, Judith's staunchest supporter, had retained a lawyer for Judith, a lawyer who couldn't fix a parking ticket for the Virgin Mary in Vatican City. The odor of a frame was enough to stop up nostrils.

At 8:20, the area outside the jail was filled with reporters, photographers, and television cameras. Judith emerged, dress wrinkled but hair impeccably brushed. There were gushes of questions. She held up her hand.

"I'd rather not answer any questions, mostly because I'm terribly tired and need a little time to sort things out," she said, regarding everyone and spotting me. "But I will say this: The fact that I was arrested and subjected to a series of personal humiliations isn't important, except to me. What *is* important is that whoever engineered my arrest possibly did it with the quaint idea that I and everything I believe in could be demolished in one fell swoop of cheap scandal. Whoever that party is or parties are made a grave mistake in judgment."

She looked at me again, briefly.

And went on: "That's really all I'm prepared to say to you now. I have lawyers to consult and perspective to get before I say anything more, but I can assure you this is just the beginning."

The questions kept gushing. She walked toward me. Johnnie Snedden, whom I'd subtly invited to split if it seemed I was going to make actual contact with Judith, conveniently split.

She smiled at me. "Hello, Pulitzer. Am I a friend or a story?"

"I'll tell you after I rescue you from those jackals."

"Fine."

I'd rented a Plymouth at the airport, and we drove off. "Where do we go?" I asked.

To the Polo Motel and her suitcase, she said, and explained the little she knew of how she had been checked into the Polo and not the Airport Motor Inn. "You see what happens?" I teased. "I leave you alone for one minute and you go getting into all kinds of trouble."

She nodded. "Um. One minute and how many years, Pulitzer?"

"Ten. And lay off the Pulitzer." (And herewith a short autobiographical note. Four years before, until I'd had a stomach full of agony-watching, I'd filed stories for about seven months from Vietnam. *Rowland's* had run the pieces. I'd stitched them into book form, and the book, *Saigon Diary,* had gone and won a Pulitzer. That's enough autobiography for now, mainly because that first book had been my last.)

A kid at the Sunoco station directed me to the Polo Motel, and I started to drive there. But then I looked at Judith, who seemed tense and weary. She smiled. "What I need more than air is a bath, a long, sudsy bath," she said. 'And I also have a long, sudsy inclination not to go anywhere near the Polo Motel."

That made abounding sense. "I'll drop you at my place and go and get your things."

"Would you? Sam, you're too good, you have far too much charac-ter to be associating with a common jailbird."

"Why didn't you let me stake you to the bail? Did you enjoy those extra hours in the clink?"

"Not wildly, no," she answered. "But I would've enjoyed less having *Rowland's* subsidizing my—you should excuse the expression—martyrdom."

"There are worse outfits than *Rowland's*."

"Of course. And there are worse infections than gonorrhea. Let's drop *that* moral argument, okay? I'm walking enough high wires as it is."

"Okay, martyr."

"You *know* I was kidding when I said that, don't you?"

"Do I? I'm the world's nicest man, but I don't have a sense of humor."

She laughed. "You still haven't answered my question. Am I friend or a story?"

"Hopefully both. A friend first. I'll keep my secret wristwatch tape recorder turned off if that's what you want."

"I think so," she said. We rode in silence for a couple of blocks and then she said, "Golly, it's nice to see you again, Sam!"

At the Airport Motor Inn we passed a gaping desk clerk and I showed Judith to my room. "I just had a Mack Sennett fantasy," I said. "The desk clerk phones the cops and you're hauled off again."

Judith grinned wanly, now obviously exhausted. "That's not likely, even in Hartley. Or if it is, then to hell with it. *Let* them squint and goggle. Maybe it's perverse and self-destructive, but I'd like to hand this town a few shocks." I shrugged at her logic, took the key she fished out of her purse and she stepped away from me, lithely and with a wide smile, when I made a move to give her a light kiss. "No, you don't!" she cried. "I haven't been near soap and water in years, and no one touches me till I'm all pink and fresh."

"Ungrateful tramp," I said and drove to the Polo, acutely con-scious of wanting her and not happy about it. I was suddenly walking high wires, too, and I couldn't see a net; except for the harmless and safely shapeless daydreams, what I hadn't seriously counted on when I'd agreed to do the cover story was that I was going to fall in love with her again. Falling in love with your subject is one hell of an intrusion on a job of work.

All right, all right, I know that's straight Andy Hardy out of Faith Baldwin. After ten years, a man doesn't fall in love again in ten minutes with the same woman. Right? Wrong. Remarkable.

The Polo had all the charm and homeyness of an iron lung. I found Room 5 and began to collect Judith's stuff into her suitcase. Among her things was a black brassiere. I held it up, turned it this way and that, examined it, cupped it to my ear and heard the ocean, and for a little while, a deliberate, conscientious while, I was your everyday smirking 42nd Street fetishist, full of steamy images of waves breaking against mammoth boulders, of eternal serenity discerned and contained in the valley of Judith Harrison's faultless, yielding breasts.

Enough already, I thought. I packed the suitcase, fast, and closed it.

I considered trotting off without paying the bill, to stiff them and let *them* collect the rent from the Andrea Lane who'd made the reservation. Instead, I took the key over to the office and said to the sallow-looking man behind the desk, "Checking out of 5, Lyman." Maybe he wasn't Lyman Bester. Maybe Albright's office had parked Lyman Bester in a closet. But this was one way to find out.

His jumpy eyes said Lyman Bester, all right. "How do you know me?" he asked.

He was under strict orders to talk to no one from the press, Johnnie Snedden had told me. I was not only from the press, I was Starn-knocker Gallagher from the press, and it was awfully unlikely that he'd favor me with any choice confidences, but I tried, anyway. I identified myself and took a wild swing: "What are they giving you to be a witness at the Harrison trial, Lyman?"

His eyebrows met. "I don't know what you're talking about."

"Sure you do," I said and took another wild swing. "Tell me exactly what you saw or didn't see in Room 5 the other evening, and it's worth a thousand dollars."

"A thou—"

"One and three big zeroes."

"Just to say I seen that lady and the nigger screwin'?"

"If that's what you saw, yes."

"What's the hitch?"

"No hitch. You simply tell the exact truth and I type up the statement and you sign your name to it."

His jaw moved from east to west. "I don't sign any paper."

"It's worth a thousand today. Tomorrow it's worth five hundred. The day after tomorrow it's worth nothing. Nothing is little zeroes, Lyman. How many days a week are you offered a thousand dollars to tell the truth?"

I watched the wheels revolve. Then he walked away from me and came back with a bill. "Thirty-six eighty, including tax," he said, plunking it in front of me.

I paid it and folded the receipt. "Talk a thousand dollars quick cash over with your wife after I leave," I said. "I'm at the Airport Motor Inn."

"You go and stay there," he said. "You pester me again and I'll have the law on you."

Nothing ventured, nothing gained, as we phrase-makers often put it.

There was a message at my motel to call Howard Bracken at *Rowland's*. There was also an unstamped, hand-delivered letter. The letter read,

> Galger—Get out of Hartley fast if you know what is good for
> you. Go back to your jew magazin in N. York City & leave
> decent christans alone. Hartley was nice to you last time you
> were here, we "Learned our lesson". No body want you here.
> Go home this is a warning.

"When did this letter come?" I asked the desk clerk. He didn't know. "Do you remember what the person looked like who delivered it?" He didn't.

I phoned Bracken from the lobby. It was nearly ten o'clock now, nearly eleven back East, and I was put through to Bracken's home in Weston, Connecticut. His information about the arrest was scattered and incomplete, he said. I filled him in on what Johnnie Snedden and I had been able to piece together (he was Snedden's boss but had never heard of him), and I said that much was a maze of mirrors so far but I was thoroughly convinced that some nasty conspiracy was beyond question.

"Have you got to Judith Harrison yet?" he asked.

"Odd you should ask that," I said. "She happens to be up in my room, right this minute."

"Oh? How lucky for her," said unflappable Howard.

I explained how she came to be there. He took that to signify her change of mind, her willingness now to cooperate on the cover story. "All it signifies, for the time being at any rate," I cautioned, "is that she sees me as a friend, not necessarily a friend who's a reporter."

"That romantic subtlety escapes me, but then most subtleties do," he said. "In any case, I was hoping to run the cover the issue after next, but what started out as a Harrison cover is now Harrison plus Hartley. As long as you don't make a leisurely career out of the story, it's good in a way if the competition scoops us. While they're racing one another to press, you'll be assembling an in-depth profile of a sexist conspiracy—*if* that's what it is—with your legendary skills and wit, and with the help of Judith Harrison."

"Wait a moment, Howard. I never knew you smoked pot. You're wafting along on some rosy dream. The lady may be looking for all the forums she can find, especially now, but she plain hates *Rowland's*. We burned her once, and you're asking her to help on a story she has no reason to believe will be anything but another putdown. You're asking—"

Bracken calmly interrupted. "I'm not asking. I'm expecting. I'm expecting you'll remember that you're first and foremost a professional, that you're paid not at all unhandsomely to do the best job you can on any project you tackle. If the young lady balks, you simply use any means available to unbalk her."

"Hell, Howard, I think I'm hearing something halfway between condescension and a threat."

"Now you know me better than that."

"I sure hope so, because the day I hear whips cracking is the day you get my resignation. I'll be in touch when I know where I'm going."

I hung up. And sat in the booth for a while and stared at the telephone.

And tried to figure out that tantrum. In seven years at *Rowland's* I'd had fifty grillion causes to blow up at Howard Bracken, and I'd always kept my cool, not because I was afraid of him but mostly because coolth tended to be my way to prove a point, particularly if a point genuinely mattered. So how come this fit? What justified it? Bracken's soft-voiced condescensions were nothing new and never bothered me. And he wasn't really threatening me; he wasn't saying Do as I order or else. So?

I left the phone booth. I guessed that *use any means available to unbalk her* was what had done it and what was still bugging me. A good reporter is at least one part whore. The nature of the craft requires a certain amount of deviousness sometimes; to get a one-sentence quote from someone who otherwise isn't interested in giving you a one-sentence quote, you make cooing little noises, never outright promises but little noises about the possibility next week of writing him up in a full-length, praiseful article. But there is whore-dom and there is whoredom.

I was beginning to regret that I'd found Judith, that she was up in that room.

She was asleep on the double bed, wearing my summer robe, lying on her stomach, the sheet just over her hips. The ends of her black hair were wet and her sublime face was totally relaxed.

I drank lots of water because I'd finished the Scotch last night and hadn't gotten around to buying another bottle. I sat on the side of the bed. She stirred, ever so slightly, and wakened a little, and closed her eyes and made an *mmmmmm-mmm* purring sound. I didn't touch her; my restraint was herculean, but I didn't touch her. Presently she came more than half awake, reached out for my hand and said, "Two hundred and seventy-seven thousand dollars for your thoughts."

"They're not all that Jack Armstrong-wholesome."

"All right, then: two hundred and seventy-*eight* thousand dollars."

"Well, there are some choice recollections of you and me performing anatomically memorable acts in Malibu, for starters."

Flustered but cheerful, she sat up and declared, "Uh-oh. I'd better rescind the offer, fast."

"Why?"

"Because I suddenly realize I'm famished. Is that answer evasive enough?"

My call downstairs was just under the wire; the kitchen was about to shut down for the night, but Room Service crankily agreed to deliver two steaks and salads. Judith had slipped out of bed and was rummaging through her suitcase. "What're you looking for?" I asked.

"Traveling clothes."

"For when?"

"When? Tonight. Thanks to Hartley, I have plenty to do back in New York."

"Maybe not tonight. This airport isn't O'Hare or Kennedy."

She looked at me and frowned. "Oh, damn, you're right, aren't you? Would you check it for me? I really am anxious to get back."

I phoned. The next flight to New York was 7:14 A.M.

"Damn!" she repeated. I reserved two seats under the names S. and J. Gallagher, replaced the receiver, and said, "I'd've imagined you'd want to stay on and do some personal detectivizing."

Judith shook her head. "Not yet. Not till I've put some physical distance between me and this lunacy. I'm tired and I'm angry. Not angry—furious. Confused, mostly." I watched her pace, and then the frown was replaced by a sly, wry grin. "If I've changed since Malibu, it's in the stand I take on confusion. In the Malibu days, confusion was my natural birthright; the dumber and more helpless I was, the more I'd be protected against the storm. These days I may be basically just as confused but I don't glide with it, I don't tolerate it."

Was that a double signal? "Um," I said. "What the common jail-bird is telling me is that what happened between us in Malibu was the consequence of confusion and dumbness."

The sly grin broadened. "That's not at all what she's telling you; you were the only one in that chamber of human horrors who took her seriously, who made an effort to unconfuse and undumb her, and she'll always love you for that. No, what I think she's trying to tell you, among other things, is that she's aware of the ways you're looking at her, and she digs you, and she has no intention of sleeping with you tonight."

"She's as subtle as a positive Wasserman."

A nod and another grin. "Yep. That's what makes her so universally beloved."

Room Service knocked, but Judith didn't move. She sat while the waiter rolled the table in and furtively eyed her until I signed the check and waved him out. Still wearing my summer robe, she ate her overcooked steak and wilted salad as if she were dining at Maxim's, and asked me if there was any way, short of killing her *Rowland's* cover story, that I could kill the dredging up of ancient history. "I sound like a painted Barbary Coast madame who's found God and denies everything that went on before revelation day," she confided. "I've never denied anything. I admit that for a while I publicly exploited those old days—'brainless sexpot playgirl gains insights and independence,' that kind of thing. But this is a drastically different ball ga—"

"That's one of the reasons I took the assignment," I said. "To soften the purple stuff. To see that you don't come off as another pretty freak. No, I can't kill the story. But I won't take any advantage of the fact that we're sitting here, that we know each other." Carefully I added, "Unless you change your mind and decide you want me to."

"Why would I do that?"

"Maybe we'll both know when we've learned who tried to ruin you. You may want a gaggle of platforms then, even *Rowland's. Rowland's* isn't *Feminists Forever,* but it reaches a hell of a lot more readers."

"Is the common jailbird being hustled?"

"The common jailbird ought to be smarter than to ask a cat's prat question like that," I said, partially in truth.

We talked. I told her what Snedden and I had and had not tracked down this day. She talked about the arrest, about the kaleidoscope of faces and names and voices inside that jail, about a terrified teen-age runaway named Cheryl who had indeed been treated like a common jailbird, about the sixty or seventy rooters at Andrea Lane's home, about none of them coming forth at the arraignment or after, about disappointment and about dehumanization and about challenge. The trial date was eleven days away. Oliver Starn's name was mentioned from time to time, with pointing fingers that couldn't stay pointed.

"Strange," she said, her voice and verve slackening, "but I kept thinking of Martha Hanaday while I was behind those bars. Of how she might've handled herself if the same thing had happened to her."

"Martha Hanaday? Pistol-packin' Martha?"

"Don't condemn too quickly. Oh, I never really liked Martha, even when I was in absolute awe of her. Does that make sense? When she was clicking on every cylinder, when she was writing and saying all the things that were right square on the button, I could never lose the feeling that she was writing and saying all the right things for a lot of the wrong reasons. 'A woman is more than the sum of her private parts.' Well, fine, stupendous. That encourages thought. But I think where Martha ran into problems was her refusal to acknowledge that we do have private parts."

"*I* shouldn't condemn?" I baited.

Judith smiled. "I know. I hear myself. Blame this rambling on my being so very tired. The unfortunate thing about Martha Hanaday is that if people refer to her at all, they refer to her in the past tense. Me included, too often. Martha lost her way. Somewhere, somehow, she lost her way, but she rang some terribly vital bells and shook up an earthquake full of dust in her time. I didn't like her, but I had tremendous admiration for her. And I was remembering when she was a true, high-voltage dynamo, and I was wondering how *that* Martha would've behaved in that loathsome place . . . My, my, I *am* rambling . . ."

I rolled the serving table into the corridor, returned and directed, "Go to sleep."

She nodded slowly and got up slowly. "Alone. Please, Sam, alone."

"Look: have I touched you?"

"No."

"Despite what you thought I was thinking, have I expressed the remotest interest in sleeping with you?"

"No."

"Has it crossed your solipsistic, ungrateful, common-jailbird confused brain that I find you sexually revolting and the only way I'd consider coming near you is if you gave me two hundred and seventy-seven thousand dollars, cash on the barrelhead?"

"Yes."

"Go to bed. I'll take the chair."

"Sam . . ."

"You heard me."

That arrangement lasted a quarter of an hour, about five minutes longer than I expected.

"Sam . . ."

"I'm sound asleep."

"I'd love—"

Talk about timing. The phone rang. Judith and I looked at each other. I answered and heard a hard, grating voice. "Gallagher?"

"Who's this?"

"Never you mind who's this. You listen." I stood reasonably far from the bed, but the voice was so loud and clear that I was sure Judith could hear most of the words. "We remember you, Gallagher. You got more enemies in Hartley than it's safe for you. You clear out of our town right quick and take that nigger-lovin' Jew whore with you or the next time you wake up'll be in the hospital or maybe the cemetery, both of you. This is no kidding around, you suvvabitch. We say leave right quick and don't ever come back, we mean right quick. You're being watched."

Click.

I hung up and Judith was wide awake. "It starts," she said.

"And probably stops," I said, not too firmly. "Nervous?"

She shook her head, not too decisively. "Not really. I'm getting inured. I've had every kind of anonymous call, from the heavy breathers on down to the patriotic avengers." Then: "Sure, I'm nervous. Cowards always make me nervous because I can never be sure they're not psychopaths, too. Aren't *you* nervous?"

She was sitting up and the robe's sash had loosened or come untied because the folds had parted and inches more of flesh were showing. "Yes," I said. "But not because of the phone call."

She saw where I was looking, and there was a small smile. "Where were we when we were so rudely interrupted?" she asked.

"You were bothering me while I was trying to sleep."

"Oh, yes, now I remember. I was about to offer you two hundred whatever you said on the barrel whatever you said . . ."

The first kiss was an exploratory kiss, a time-measuring kiss. Judith seemed wary for moments, not removed certainly but wary, maybe still shackled to the phone call, maybe gauging who I was,

Sam present or Sam past or maybe Sam nobody, maybe only a pair of arms. I discovered I was a little cautious, too, briefly, wanting her, wanting her with a torrent of passion yet worried that I could lose her forever after this night if I showed too much love or not enough.

Gradually, then abruptly, the mutual caution drained and vanished. The kisses became more concentrated, intense, ardent, both of us voracious, Judith's mouth and body alive and glorious, Judith absolutely innocent of inhibition, Judith the duchess and hoyden, clinging, playing, no longer playing, calling out to me, and then thing didn't receive thing but Judith received Sam, and she breathed, "Sam. Sam. Sam's inside me."

"Loving you."

"Loving me. Yes. Ah, yes, darling, ah yes . . ."

The phone jolted me awake. My watch read seven o'clock. Her side of the bed was empty. A voice, different from last night's, warned that the whore and I were begging for the graveyard if we didn't get out of town within the hour.

And hung up, naturally.

Judith's suitcase was gone from the luggage rack. I looked for a note. There wasn't any.

8

On the flight to Detroit, Norman Hanaday paid the pert stewardess for the Bloody Mary and dutifully wrote *Drink aloft—$1.50* in his spiral notebook. The publicity director at R. A. Storm had urged him to record every out-of-pocket expense while on tour, including doormen's tips. "We asked you to do the promo tour," Andy Masters had said. "There's no reason why you should pay for anything while you're away. Personal things you buy, like a necktie or a hooker, the accounting department mightn't look too generously on that. But be good to yourself, Norm. These tours can be exhausting busters. We've killed fourteen authors on them."

Hanaday had memorized the publisher's itinerary for him, but he read it again now, as if to verify once more that all of it was indeed real. Andy Masters, a hypertonic but friendly young man, had mentioned that he should be prepared to continue on to the West Coast if the tour appeared to be helping the book's sales. Hanaday had argued against any tour, though not forcefully. "Naturally I want the book to be read, but I'm not a performer," he had said. "I know what I'm doing when I talk to students in a classroom—most of the time, anyway—but television, radio . . . I could fall on my face and ruin everything."

"You'll be terrific, baby."

Now, inexplicably and maybe idiotically, he found himself beginning to believe that he just might be terrific. Not terrific, perhaps, but better than adequate. Andy had rehearsed him for three solid days, had been reasonably successful in unstarching him, had played interviewer and fired curve-ball questions at him and taught him how to answer without sounding like an idiot. How bad can I be? he thought. The publisher wouldn't be investing what surely is a sizeable chunk of money if there were serious doubts about me.

That helped. It guaranteed nothing, but it helped.

The Bloody Mary helped, too. The fact that he was a bit of a celebrity, however minor and certainly temporary, continued to surprise and perplex Norman Hanaday—and, increasingly, to please him. He had begun to research and write *How Fascism Won* five years before, at night and on weekends, with hope if not passion that it could be published. Martha had neither the time nor interest to read any of it or listen to him talk about it at any juncture of progress or setback. When she remembered what it was he was doing on those evenings and weekends, she encouraged him to keep at it. With no particular resentment, he understood why: as long as he was in his study, amusing himself, she was freer to juggle her own array of projects.

The father of one of his history students was a literary agent, and Hanaday, normally a very private man, let several hints drop that he believed he had a publishable manuscript. The agent, Arnold Bechler, read it, conveyed reservations about it, but submitted it, and the seventh publishing house, R. A. Storm, bought it. Storm's executive editor, Dan Prostin, worked with him in a tough but good revision that trimmed the fat and tightened the bolts, and at last it was in print. The towering miracle was that *How Fascism Won,* detailing Italian and German gradual acceptance of totalitarian regimes in the years before and during the Second World War, remained the serious work that Hanaday intended yet also became one with popular appeal. The review in *Publishers Weekly* was affirmative. Newspaper and magazine reviews that followed were almost uniformly positive and, he was told, two *Times* reviews, one daily and one Sunday, accounted for a small blizzard of bookshop reorders.

The day before the flight to Detroit, at the Pierre party, Prostin and Masters had introduced him to a raft of people, some of them obvious phonies, many of them apparently genuine and sincere, most of their talk sophisticated and galaxies removed from his bailiwick of academe. At one point, listening to the praise and shamelessly enjoying it, he felt what might have been a breast brushing and then pressing his back. He turned, and it definitely was a breast and it belonged to an attractive young woman named Louise Sperling, the critic who had written one of the most enthusiastic reviews of the book. Minutes later they were alone in one corner of the large room and she said, "You look awfully uncomfortable."

"Does it show? I'm not used to all this."

"Like it?"

"Yes, I think so, more or less. But I suspect an overdose could be fatal."

She laughed. "I've been doing some uninvited peeking and I see you're scheduled to be in Philadelphia next Friday, at the Barclay. I'll be at the Warwick. If you're allowed any free time and if you feel like it, maybe we could have a drink together."

"That sounds fine," he said, flattered.

The plane touched down now at Detroit Airport, and he was met and driven to the Sheraton by Glenn Vanick, Storms' Detroit representative. "I hope you slept on the plane," said Vanick. "You have three interviews tonight—one press and one radio taping, and then a call-in from eleven till one."

"Call-in?"

"That's live radio, *The Phil Haining Show.* There'll be two hours of telephone calls from cranks and insomniacs. They'll ask your opinion on everything under the sun, from your views on suburban aldermen you never heard of to whether you think some lady's husband should have a vasectomy over the weekend. But Haining'll keep plugging the book, and he has an audience of a couple hundred thousand."

Hanaday grinned, for there was nothing else to do. "When I was a kid, I wanted to be a teacher and writer. I should've taken my grandfather's advice and become a drunk."

"It only hurts for a while. The Haining show is over at one, I'll have you back at your hotel at one-thirty and you won't be disturbed till half-past six in the morning. You do a television show at eight."

"Thanks a lot."

The newspaper interview started off as Hanaday had been warned in New York that it, and others, might: He was asked about Martha, reasonable questions about her work in the women's movement, guardedly impertinent questions about the kind of wife, mother and homemaker she was. He stayed cool, spoke well of Martha, carefully said nothing that would even remotely imply any criticism of Martha, pleasantly and he hoped tactfully reminded the interviewer that the subject was his book. The radio taping went well enough—that interviewer assured him his *ers* and *well-uhs* would be erased—with only brief references to the fact that his wife was *the* Martha Hanaday.

The Phil Haining Show began at 11:05 in a drafty, sour-smelling studio. Shortly before midnight, an eternity later, Hanaday had rendered opinions or gently fielded opinions on a miasma of topics, from foreign fascism to domestic communism to sexual promiscuity among the young to his choice for the next mayor of Detroit. Then there was more news at midnight, followed by recorded commercials, during which time Phil Haining assured him, "This'll sell a flock of books tomorrow." Back on the air, the first caller-in said, most politely and softly, "I'd like to hear your views on Judith Harrison. Do you know her?"

"Not really. We've met," Hanaday replied.

The caller-in: "What're your views on her?"

"In what connection?"

"What they've been calling 'Judith's Crusade,' " the polite soft voice answered. "The abortion case. The case where if the atheistic Supreme Court says so, then murder becomes legal overnight in all the fifty states. You go along with that or not, with legalizing murder?"

Hanaday frowned for help at Haining who gave him none. "I'm not quite sure if you're making a statement or asking a ques—"

"I'm doing both. Killing a fetus is murder. Everybody knows that, everybody but Judith Harrison and your own wife. I was just wondering. I've been listening in since this program started. I heard you talk about how the Nazzys killed millions of humans. You don't go along with that. What I'm trying to have you bring out is whether you go along with your wife and that Judith Harrison killing millions of humans, but maybe it isn't the same because they're helpless and unborn. Would you be against murder if the victims weren't Jews, for instance, is what I—"

Haining woke up. "Let's watch that," he scolded. "You ask a question and wait for an answer, or off you go. There's no show on the air as free and open and democratic as my show, but freedom of expression doesn't include yelling 'fire' in a crowded theater, and racial and religious slurs on my show are . . . ."

Christ, thought Hanaday. What am I doing here in this forest of cretins?

"Excuse me," he said, his voice measured and suddenly strong. "First of all, as I understand it, one of the chief arguments for legalizing abortion in every state was that inequities would diminish;

it was hoped that the back-alley butchers would go out of business. The question isn't Should there be abortions? They've always been performed, and they always will be no matter what the law says. The real question is Shouldn't they be performed by legitimate doctors in thoroughly safe and sanitary settings? And shouldn't all women be treated equally under the law, in all the states, as the Constitution seems to have intended? And all doctors, for that matter. As for morality, I see nothing in the proposed law that will *force* a woman to undergo an abor—"

The polite, soft voice: "Well, what I hear about that crazy wife of yours and Judith Har—"

Hanaday sat straight. "All right, that's quite enough," he said. "Neither lady needs my defense. But Martha Hanaday *is* my wife, and under no circumstances will I listen to her being insulted, either by reasonable people or by someone as repulsive as you."

On the drive back to the Sheraton, Glenn Vanick was silent for a while and then asked, "Can I say something?"

Tightly: "Yes."

"I ask because it's out of turn, maybe. I'm a salesman; all I read are order forms and the girlie books and once in a while my kid's report card. But I've met a lot of writers since I've been with Storm, and here's one thing I'm an expert on: Getting all bundled up over shows like that, any shows, is the sure way to go bughouse in a hurry. Ride it out, conserve the balls. The world's full of poor slobs like that one that got you all steamed. Take 'em to heart and you'll never last out these tours."

He was still awake at four, considering a morning call to New York to say he wanted out. I don't belong here, he thought. I'm not a talker. And God knows I'm not a swinger. And here I am, away from the routines of orderliness that I've learned to be comfortable with, pingponging between the urge to go home, where it's lonely but familiar and therefore safe, and the anticipation of sleeping with Judith Harrison.

His eyes opened in the darkened room. Judith Harrison? I mean Louise Sperling. That idiot on the telephone brought up Judith Harrison's name, that's why I—

They had met exactly once, at least two years before, maybe three, in the Columbia Heights apartment. Yet he could see her clearly now, the striking good looks and acute sensuousness, could almost touch her . . .

Insane, mindless rambling, he thought, kicking off the gnarled blanket. Go to sleep. You have to be out of here in a few hours.

Those striking good looks. The rapport between them . . .

They rode the elevator in silence to the lobby after that nasty little scene in the apartment. He invited her to have some coffee, and she nodded, and they walked the block to Broadway and the all-night cafeteria. She hadn't gone to that meeting to cause trouble, she said, although she supposed she should have realized that she was there with a suspect reputation, and maybe her questions ought to have been more delicate. He apologized for the treatment. She shook her head. She had come to admire sincerely much of what the Martha Hanadays were doing, she said, and had gone to learn more, enough perhaps to offer something constructive of her own in time. She wasn't quite sure where she was headed. But the insults had struck several sensitive nerves, had exposed truths about her that she had gradually, grudgingly begun to face up to. She was indeed frittering away the only life she had in one bundle of meaningless sensations after another. And—smiling—why was she now baring all to a stranger? An extraordinarily nice man, but a stranger?

They stayed in the cafeteria for an hour. Now and then he was conscious of people pausing near the table to gape at her, Judith Harrison from television. He was careful to say nothing sweeping about Martha that she might construe as a condemnation. She asked him questions about himself. He said that he was writing a book and she asked more questions, bright and incisive questions, and he was warmed by her.

The night was piercingly cold as they went outside to find her a taxi. Vapor mushroomed from their mouths, and she held onto his arm, and he had the vivid feeling that all he would have to do would be to ask her telephone number, suggest they meet again at a more leisurely time, and she would instantly agree.

He didn't. A cab came, and he opened the door for her.

She looked at him and squeezed his hand. You're a lovely man, Norman Hanaday, she said. We'll see each other again some day, I hope.

He lay on his stomach and clapped a pillow over his head. Put your clothes on and go away, he groaned at her. Please.

Eyes bloodshot and nerves fairly under control, Hanaday did the early morning television show and flew to Philadelphia, where he read about Judith Harrison's arrest. Motel tryst, police, jail . . . It was an outrageous story, and his immediate impulse was to reach her somehow and let her know—

Well, what? She's come a very long way since that night in the cafeteria, from the fritterer she called herself to someone of enormous consequence and worth. She'd remember me, but so what, what help would I be to her? Maybe if I'd phoned her after that night—

Stop it.

There were three messages for him when he registered at the Barclay. One was from Storm's Philadelphia representative, Ursula Pryor, who would be at the hotel at noon. One was from Louise Sperling, with a Warwick telephone number.

And one was from Martha, with a Boston telephone number and the words *Please call immediately. Urgent.* In his room, fearful that something had happened to one of the children, he placed the call and was connected with Martha. The children were all right but she wasn't, she said, and told him of Dr. Wall's sudden death, a tragedy that had left her absolutely, uncharacteristically immobile in Boston. She wanted him to fly to her at once; together they would go home, where she would look after him and he would look after her.

"This isn't altogether clear to me, Martha," he said. "Do you honestly feel you need me?"

"Need? I *want* you. Isn't that enough? Isn't that what you've always complained you never hear me say?"

Norman Hanaday listened and finally heard her. "I'm sorry you hurt, Martha," he said at last. "I'm sincerely sorry. Mostly I'm sorry you didn't hear what I was saying to you the other day."

"We'll discuss that here."

He almost saw her and wavered for a moment, saw both her fragility and total self-absorption, and said, "No, we won't. I'm not going to Boston, partly because I have work to do here, mainly because I've stopped peeling your potatoes. If you want to come to

Philadelphia, I'll be here, and we can talk and maybe even come to something. Otherwise, no."

"I won't *have* you play with me that way!" she cried. "Your place is here with me!"

"Goodbye, Martha," he said, and replaced the receiver, surprised that what he felt was not guilt but relief. We'll see how long that lasts, he thought.

Ursula Pryor appeared shortly before noon, a dowdy lady who impressed and rather amused Hanaday by leaving the door ajar. They went over the revised itinerary together, and when he learned that his final interview that evening would be seven o'clock, he phoned Louise Sperling, who was out, and left word that unless he heard from her he would call for her at eight.

In the Warwick lobby at precisely eight, he was delighted at feeling not at all tired. Louise Sperling emerged from an elevator, prettier and younger than in New York, darkly blonde and well dressed and well built, and her smile was easy and she took his hand. "Well, hello! You're alive!"

He smiled, too, liking the warmth of her hand. "Barely. Where would you like to go? I don't know this city at all."

"Why not stay here? The rain is somehow more depressing in Philadelphia than anywhere else, and the restaurant here is quite good."

She couldn't have been more than a half-dozen years older than his daughter, he decided, with amiable eyes, a prominent cleft in her chin, and an imposingly tight fitting coral dress. She ordered a double vodka martini. Hanaday ordered a Scotch and soda, and she said she had heard him on the Petersen show this afternoon and he moaned and she reached over to hold his hand and declared, "No, no, you were fine. Considering that Petersen can't read and that he somehow got the idea your book was about show biz, you did brilliantly."

Her hand stayed. Her eyes and her attention focused on him. Her breasts stayed inside her lowcut dress, but she leaned forward and close to him often and the unspoken messages they conveyed were wonderful. God, I *am* enjoying this, he thought; I'd almost forgotten the potency of sex games, how pleasurable they can be to the ego as well as the groin . . .

Their conversation, disjointed and frequently vapid, hopped from one topic to another, and she moved away and toward him and away, clearly restless, and ordered a second double vodka martini before he had finished his first single Scotch. She held his hand again, and presently her other hand rested for a moment on his thigh, and he became aware of the exquisite sensation of an erection. She was in Philadelphia for three or four days on a dreary but rent-paying magazine assignment, she said, and she hated this city as she hated all cities, and she stared at him and asked if he was terribly hungry.

He nodded to the waiter for a check.

There were two bottles of vodka in her room, one nearly full, one nearly empty. "I admired your book because it was so sexy," she said.

She received his kiss, passively at first and then greedily, raised her moist hands to his cheeks to help make the kiss more deep-drawn, ground against him, reached down to touch the bulge at his groin. Hanaday held the newness of her, trembling, conscious of her trembling, too, conscious of her breathing as hard as he, marveling at his passion, marveling that he could create passion in someone, that he wasn't old.

"Clothes, all these tons and tons of clothes . . ." she murmured. The clothes disappeared and he began to embrace her and she grinningly retreated from his touch. "There's really no rush, is there, darling?" she said, and regarded his erection, inexplicably embarrassing him. "I happen to be a devout voyeur, and I'm curious about something: How is it that the Smithsonian hasn't claimed that yet?"

"For its age?"

"For its size." Her hand encircled it at its base, and her tongue flicked the tip of it, and her grin was broad and lewd and she directed his hand to her buttocks and said, "Tonight we're going to perform some grand and kinky things."

What the hell was—

She flicked at it again, began to tease it with an increasing intensity, and lithely straddled him. Moments later, the erection failing, passion gone, Hanaday freed himself and sat up. "What's wrong?" she asked.

"Anonymity," he answered. "Anonymity is what's wrong."

Rising, scooping up his clothes, distantly hearing her rush of apologies, he stalked to the bathroom. And examined the fifty-year-old face in the sink mirror as he glared at it. And stalked back to her.

He threw himself on her. He plunged into her—no, not her, it—needing desperately to perform the loveless, mortifying, insanely necessary charade. She understood and cooperated in the abasement until it happened for him; wordlessly she caressed him and wordlessly she watched him dress and leave.

His phone was ringing when he entered his room at the Barclay. "I could blame my behavior on the bennies and the vodka," said Louise Sperling. "Or America with a *k,* or a father fixation so overconcentrated that it's not even stylish any more, or a gang of other alibis. I'm sure the last thing you'd care to hear would be explanations." Pause. "But might we meet again? If I promise to be Mary Pickford?"

"I don't know."

Norman Hanaday, who limited himself to one cigarette a day, and today had smoked two, lit a third. He stripped to his shorts, angry, incomplete, and walked, and walked again. And thought of Judith Harrison for surely the dozenth time this day, and thought of how he had been able to finish the loveless act in the Warwick only with fantasies of Judith Harrison.

And he thought of Martha and resolved, No. No matter what happens from now on, no more Martha, ever. Not ever . . .

9

In the crowded airport limousine to Manhattan, Judith was aware of stares, some covert, some fixed, one almost oily. Completely ignoring them wasn't possible, but she tried, and read the New York morning newspapers.

The Hartley coverage was as she had rather expected it would be—The *Times'* account was reasonably good reporting, as legitimate and balanced as a straight news story could be, with the faint hint of an Olympian editorial to come; the *News,* ever cheerful and playing directly to the gallery of straphangers, winked and giggled. Fair enough, she thought; strip everything that happened in Hartley down to its physical basics, keep the fundamental issues involved turned down low, and it *was* a feast of a story for nosepickers and lonely spinster file clerks who went home at night to their parakeets.

Judith lived, sometimes alone, currently alone, in the upper East Eighties. The address was no longer fashionable, but the neighborhood markets delivered frozen dinners, the two bedroom apartment—which she had seen less and less of over the past year—was comfortable, and she was eager to get to it now, on this late Friday morning, eager to touch something familiar. Alfred the doorman greeted her as she came out of the taxi, gave her her mail and switchboard messages, and rode with her and her suitcase in the elevator.

The normally breezy and gabby Alfred was oddly subdued as they rode up. Judith supposed she understood the awkwardness and said, smiling, "Well?"

He blinked at her. "What?"

"You're busting to hear the details, aren't you?"

Alfred smiled, too. "Well, 9-J's kind of interested."

"Okay. You're hereby authorized to report to 9-J that I wasn't with one man in that motel, I was with seventeen—seventeen and a half if we count the Alsatian transvestite—and the orgy lasted till I exhausted every last one of them."

"I get it. In other words, bug off."

"You're a poet, Alfred."

The old but graceful apartment had large, airy rooms and comparatively few personal possessions—the Bracque and the two Cezanne prints were important to Judith, as were, for the sheer corniness of it, the collection of ashtrays friends had swiped for her in hotels and restaurants throughout Europe. The rest was impersonal, for she was by impulse and nature a traveler, impatient with the ownership of things. She moved quickly through the flat, reacquainting herself as though she had been away for months rather than days, and glanced at her messages as she drank orange juice in the kitchen, and placed a person-to-person call to her attorney and onetime lover, Ray Pallino. He was in Columbus, Mississippi, of all non-Raymond Pallino places, and Judith was amused at the image of him there, urbane and luxury-loving Ray. "I'll run to defend any penniless bastard if the case has real balls," he'd told her one evening at Pavillon. "But why do they all live on Tobacco Road so that I have to sleep at the Crabs Hilton? Just once in a while, why can't these indigent human rights cases live at the Fontainebleau?"

Ray wasn't in his room. A drowsy voice at the Columbus hotel promised to give him the return-call message.

Waiting, slipping off her shoes, Judith examined the messages and mail that seemed most important. She came upon a message that her mother had called at 7:04 this morning and another message that Mrs. Brustelli had called at 10:15 this morning. Both messages contained telephone numbers.

Something's wrong, Judith thought, tightening, something that has nothing to do with Hartley. Someone's ill, or someone's died. Mama's never phoned me here before.

She thought of Tut, her father, whom she had not seen nor talked with nor heard from in twelve—no, thirteen years.

Tensing more, staring at the papers for a time, she dialed her home—no, *their* home—and got no answer. She remembered who Mrs. Brustelli was, the family's next door neighbor on Spruce Street, a stout, warty, vastly warm lady, the comic-strip stereotype of the Jewish mother, only accidentally Sicilian. Judith regarded both messages, and decided to find her sister Esther's number and try her. Esther didn't answer, either.

Mrs. Brustelli did, though. Tut wasn't expected to live through the day. Mama had told Mrs. Brustelli to call here, hoped that Judith could get to the hospital before Tut passed on.

"You onna line?" Mrs. Brustelli asked. "I no hear you say nothing."

I don't know how you say *chutzpah* in Italian, Judith wanted to roar; you can tell them I have absolutely no interest in watching that hateful, spiteful man gasp his last.

Instead, she asked, "Is Esther with my mother?"

"No. Esther and her family, they go on a vacation last night. You' papa take sick maybe three, four o'clock inna morning."

"Thank you, Mrs. Brustelli," Judith said evenly. "Tell my mother I'll be there, will you? Thank you for everything."

"What 'thank you?' You' mama and you' papa, to me they just like a brother and a sister. Don't say no thank you."

"I'll be there," Judith repeated, and replaced the receiver.

And walked. Damn. *Damn!*

Of course he's not spiteful and hateful. Of course he did the spiteful, hateful thing he did, and stuck fast to it for thirteen stubborn years as though it were some screwed-up kind of holy covenant, because he's a limited, proudly limited, frightened, spineless man.

But the hyprocisy, the damned hypocrisy! Do they truly expect me to go that hypocritical route myself, drop everything and fly to his side, play-act grief, exchange soggy globs of mutual forgiveness, pretend he was Schweitzer and Solomon when what he really was was a limited, frightened, spineless man who cracked the whip over his family of women while he begged the rest of the world, all male, to kick him and keep kicking?

No. I won't go.

I told Mrs. Brustelli I would. Yes. I learned spinelessness from Tut.

Ray Pallino phoned as she was unpacking and debating whether to repack.

"Tony reached me here," said Ray, quick, kinetic, all immediacy, a master short-order cook with ten different meals to prepare in four minutes, completing them wildly but perfectly in two minutes. Tony was Ray's brother, the quiet half of Pallino and Pallino, Counselors at Law, the brother who stayed behind his desk in New York and made the firm prosper with civil cases while flamboyant, brilliant Ray, wearing his pin-striped gladiator suit, rode his snorting dragon up and down the country, propping up heroes and smiting villains, a tenaciously tough man, dynamic, full of tricks and fierce conscience. "I would've flown out to you, but this case here's just winding up. I did have a long distance conversation, though, with your eminent legal representative, Lester Farr. I absolutely refuse to believe there isn't a *t* at the end of his name. He strikes me as a lawyer who advertises in public toilets. You all right?"

"Probably."

" 'Probably.' You're almost as scintillating as Lester Farr with a *t*. Now what I want you to do is tell me everything that happened, from the instant you stepped off the plane in Hartley. No probablies, none of your famous half-ass psychological evaluations, but just what happened."

Judith told him.

"All right. The trial date is the nineteenth. This is why I went to law school: so I can enjoy working from time to time. This, you nympho spadelover, is one case I intend to *thor*oughly enjoy. Those wahoos haven't read the Constitution; they've been too busy wiping their tails with it. Today's Friday. With any luck I'll be back out of this steambath by the middle of the week—their idea of air conditioning in this hotel is for the bellboy to blow through the keyhole once a day at vespers. In the meantime, I want you to start pitching, beginning now. Call that fairy who handles your bookings and have him put you on every show he can. That should be a cinch, even for him; your name, especially now, is hot as a pistol. Wring every drop of pre-trial publicity out of it. And don't worry about the ethical-smethical of discussing it in public before the trial. By the nineteenth of this month I want those Hartley shits to be household words."

"I'd better tell you something, Ray. I had a call a little before you called. My father is dying, and I'm going to fly home."

The rat-a-tat Ray changed instantly. "Oh, I'm sorry, kid. Naturally you go there."

"It should be for only a few days," she said, and read him the Regal City telephone number where she could be reached.

"Wait a moment. Don't I remember your telling me he tossed you out of the house when you were seven?"

"A bit older, not much. I don't want to go. I really don't want to wade through those barbaric tribal dances I have no feeling for, and those barbaric relatives, and the Rotary Club locals who'll be sure to cluck at one another and say, 'Here comes Hester Prynne.' But I think I pretty well have to go."

"Sure. You have your flight set?"

"I'll take care of that now."

"You want me to have the office do it for you, have somebody drive you?"

Mercifully, the sense of humor and balance returned. "Just listen to the voice of instinctive male chauvinism! There are certain simple acts of responsibility I can perform, even if I am only a female."

Ray, dear, good Ray, caught the soft ball. "All right. Be patient with us pigs, all right? We're still reasonably new to this uppity stuff, and lately we sweat a lot. You take care, loov. If I need you, I know where to find you. We're gonna drop some mighty loud bombs in Hartley."

The next flight to Pittsburgh was 3:55, from LaGuardia. Judith packed only essentials and took a cab to LaGuardia because the prospect of riding an airport limousine twice in one day was somehow burdensome.

Halfway there, she realized she had enough money to pay the driver but not a great deal more, and hoped someone at the airport would cash a personal check. She disliked credit cards, although she owned too many of them, disliked admitting that she was still a lettucehead in the business of handling money, understanding it, choosing sensible amounts to see her through a day or two days or ten. Last year she had earned $61,000 for appearances and articles, and had given much of it away. This year, although she was in greater demand, she supposed she would earn less than that, largely because she was developing a pattern of turning back half and frequently all of her fees to this ambitious cause and that worthy

89

organization that had hired her in the first instance. She occasionally had to be sneaky about it because of Ray Pallino. Nosy Ray had read the last income tax return that Tony had prepared for her and had scolded her: "This glowing altruism of yours can land you smack in the poorhouse!"

"You're a fine one to talk," she'd said defensively. "Your whole career is one big freebie."

"Like hell it is. I can afford to be the noble prince nine months a year because I work my handsome dago ass off the other three months screwing the fat money boys out of their checkbooks. Nobility's fine in its place," he said, stabbing his finger at the name of one organization. "But hell, *this* outfit could've paid your fee with the greatest of ease. You obviously let the word get out that you won't take money from paupers and they saw you coming. And *this* outfit, here, you should've had your fairy booker charge quadruple. I thought you sheenies were supposed to be so bright!"

"But they—"

"The first rule of pragmatic liberalism someone failed to teach you is that people aren't deserving of free or cheap rides simply because they're black or women or black women Puerto Ricans or midgets with abnormally large peckers. The Dickensian gag that poverty and disadvantage are synonymous with ennoblement of the human spirit is a field of bovine deposit. Help the genuinely helpless, sure. But go on the cheap and you become Anytime Annie. Anytime Annie makes it with anyone for sixty-five cents, and the fellas start to lose respect."

Ray was right, of course, and she hadn't resisted when he delivered a bullying order to gentle Jerrold Fayne, her agent, to collect from that moment on all Judith Harrison fees in advance, deduct his commission, and forward the remainder to Pallino and Pallino; sometimes Jerrold obeyed, sometimes she talked him into disobeying. Judith appreciated their good intentions no matter how chauvinist their attitudes might seem. What she did *not* appreciate was the fact that they were right, that she simply could not get the hang of managing money. I'll either undertip or overtip this driver, she thought. What's fifteen or twenty percent of whatever?

Fifteen or twenty percent of whatever. That's what sexism is all about, damn it. *Don't muddle your girl head with man matters, doll baby. You tidy up the cave and I'll tend to running the world.* And conditioned from the cradle on, we fall into the assigned role.

The tip was realistic, she gathered, because the driver didn't look surprised as he accepted it, but neither did he seem surly. At LaGuardia, she paid for her flight with a credit card, and the lissome Oriental girl behind the counter burbled, "I'd've known you without reading the name, Miss Harrison. All I want to say is, you have a lot of friends and supporters behind you." Judith thanked her, arranged for a rented car to be waiting for her in Pittsburgh, and cashed a personal check. She and the other passengers couldn't board the 3:55 until 4:40 because weather conditions were worse in Pittsburgh than here, and the half-filled plane delayed its takeoff another three-quarters of an hour after taxiing to the runway.

Her seatmate, a young Navy lieutenant, offered her chewing gum, which she politely refused, and wanted to chat, which she politely discouraged, for she needed to get herself together, needed to find some firm semblance of herself within the fragmented accumulations of these past days. She thought about Sam Gallagher. *I didn't want him trailing me but I shouldn't have tiptoed off*, she thought. *With any character I would have at least left him a note.*

But written what? That he is kind and the sex was good and the warmth was sweet but th-th-th-th-that's all, folks, because neither of us was doing much more than using the other? That traveling as a loner has its inherent pitfalls, but a loner is what I am and may always be? How do you write that in a morning-after note to someone as good as Sam?

I like Sam. And Sam is precisely what I don't need.

Do I need anyone?

Yes, someone. Someone who must matter very much. Maybe that's why there've been so many Judiths: because there've been so many Sams. Before and after Peter, I settled for transients. No, not settled for; too often welcomed, too often demanded the Sams, strong Sams and weak Sams, always conveniently temporary caretakers. That's not good enough any more . . .

Airborne, she stared out at the dark, driving rain, thought of her father, and wondered at her absence of feeling.

There were memories, certainly, crowding in and unsorted, but no real feeling she could hold, no feeling about Tut, not love, not hate, not even simple sadness that he was dying or dead.

I can't even dredge up an image of what he might look like now, she thought; I can barely get a clear picture of what he looked like then. Odd, the trickiness and manipulations of memory. Odd, that I can remember vividly everything about that last day, everything except his face . . .

She had gone to Pittsburgh, a half hour's bus ride from Regal City, on that July day, her seventeenth birthday. Don Lovell, twice her age and utterly gorgeous, met her at the bus station, and she walked with him to the William Penn, waited what seemed hours in the cavernous, busy hotel lobby while he got his key, and together, silently, almost morosely, they went to his room. Scarcely a moment after they were alone she realized she didn't love him after all, partly because what had sounded and felt so natural and right on the telephone was suddenly unnatural and wrong, partly because he was in far too much of a hurry to undress her. But she pretended love, and lust, wishing she had the courage to say, "Let's talk first."

Then he was done. She clutched at him, waited for this perfect man to be perfect, to caress her, to do something, say something to assure her she was more than a collection of organs. But he was done. The shared cigarette and his kiss at her cheek were perfunctory. He read his wrist watch. He grinned at her as he rose from the bed and explained, not facing her, that he hadn't had the heart to tell her when she'd got off the bus but there was a terribly important business appointment he would have to keep within the hour, in Oakland. He hummed "I'll Get By" as they dressed, and then they were back in the lobby again. "You'll be just fine, right? I'll be in touch," he said, and sped away.

Blank, wounded, dazed, again blank, she walked from Pittsburgh street to Pittsburgh street, and then there was nothing to do but go home. Mama was in the parlor and slapped her face, hard, and cried, "God forgive me!" in Yiddish. Tut demanded of Judith, "Who is that man?"

"Man?"

"In the hotel, that man."

Her Uncle Charlie, Mama's sister Sophie's husband, had been in the William Penn lobby, had seen her and the man go into the elevator, had telephoned here.

Tut, the world's most passive of men, never so upset as at that moment: "You will answer your father. Who is that man?"

"I don't know what you mean. I was at work today."

Did Tut glare at me? Did he roll Heaven-imploring eyes? I can see the back of him, his round, slumped shoulders, I can see him leaving the parlor. Vividly, vividly, I can see everything in that room, the flowered wallpaper, the China bulldog, the summer window curtains, Mama's unbearable pain. I can't see Tut.

Judith rushed to her bedroom, the bedroom that was hers alone since Esther had married and moved away. She shivered in the agony of what she had caused and what it surely would have to cost, burrowed her face into the bed pillow and waited for Tut to come, to forgive, to punish, to punish and forgive, to come, simply to come to her.

He didn't. Mama did. "You stayed out of your job today. How do you lie, where did you learn to lie? Right away after Uncle Charlie called on the telephone, I called your work and Mr. Sobol said you called him up on the telephone at eight o'clock and said you were sick and had to take off the day. What you did today was kill your father."

"Mama—"

"Whore. Liar. You disgraced your family and your people and yourself. The best thing is you leave."

Hearing, not understanding; Mama made threats, rarely idle ones. "Leave?" A horrid pause. "Do you mean that?"

"I mean that," Mama said, hoarsely but softly, the pain still very visible, the anger now missing.

"I—Do you really want me to go, Mama?"

"Your father wants it."

"Tut? Tut wants me to leave my home?" Another pause, more dreadful. "Where would I go?"

"Anywhere. Go to your hotel bums. But your father won't have you here."

"Why doesn't he tell me?"

"He doesn't have to tell you anything. He told me and I told you. Enough."

Now he was dying. Or dead. Tut, whose most outsize calamity in life was that he had never sired a son. Gentle Tut, weeping, actually weeping tears of joy the day the school principal, Mr. Quinn, personally phoned him that Judith had just won the county's third-grade spelling bee, a huge local event, and her teacher believed she could read and comprehend on a seventh-grade level, and he and Mrs. Hershkowitz ought to be mighty proud of their little girl; Tut festooning her with kisses, sweeping her off the ground, furiously swinging her around and shouting. "Whoop! Whooo-*oooo-ooop!*" kissing her and kissing her and kissing her.

Tut. How do you sustain rage at a complex man, a constricted and helpless man, the very giant oak of a certified *nebbish* who would tell the brute scum pushing him into the gas oven, "I understand. You're just following orders"?

Nothing, she thought. I feel nothing, next to nothing. I've done some growing in thirteen years. I've frittered away energies, loved unwisely, wasted time trying to reverse irreversibles, but I've grown up. Now I go home—yes, home—where I'll be expected to fall into a family niche no part of me fits. There will be thirteen-years-older Mama, decent and robotized Mama, programmed from birth to regard all of life as two sets of dishes to be constantly washed and dried, and one man to cater to. There will be thirteen-years-older Esther, equally decent and robotized Esther but a greater Yiddish tragedy than Mama because Esther tried to resist the perpetual dishes and catering and then, in the moment-of-truth crunch, gave up and gave in.

I feel nothing, Judith repeated to herself as the plane set down in Pittsburgh. Not hollow, not empty, just—nothing.

Hateful feeling, she thought. Hateful and scary.

The rented car was waiting. She dialed her parents' number. There was no answer.

The heavy rain made the dark evening darker. Judith had not learned to drive until she had been well into her twenties, drove infrequently because the need was infrequent, and she was pleased at her comfort behind the wheel. Esther had once announced a desire to take driving lessons. Tut had shaken his head in disapproval but, as usual, had left the interpretation of that disapproval to

Mama. Mama, the model of symbiosis, had caught his signal, would have caught it instantly if he had been at the opposite end of the globe, and the quick verdict was a resolute no: "machines" were dangerous, especially with all those lunatic college kids driving all over the road. That there were no college kids in or around Regal City, lunatic or otherwise, was, by family logic, entirely beside the point.

The roads out of Pittsburgh were good but became narrow and bumpy as Judith got nearer to Regal City, passing coal towns and mill towns that were even uglier and smaller and gloomier, if possible, than Regal City. The realization that she could find her way, despite the weather and the years, was good. The realization that her stomach was knotting and her palms were sweaty was not.

Regal City Hospital, a monstrosity of dirty black brick and foreboding, groaning with age, stood, leaned, on the outskirts of the town. Judith had been inside it once, to visit Zayde, Mama's and Aunt Sophie's father, and she remembered standing close to the door of his ward and seeing the doctor prance into the corridor, shake his large head and growl to a young doctor who had come out with him, "God must've invented the Jews and insulin shock on the same afternoon. If I *have* to treat these ward patients, give me the quiet coloreds any day in the week. They at least know their place, most of them." She parked the car now, entered the building, which clearly hadn't been aired out over the intervening years, and spoke the name of Rabbi Hershkowitz to the desk nurse. The nurse checked and told her that Mr. Hershkowitz had died an hour ago.

She found her mother and her mother's sister Sophie in a room off the lobby, huddled together in a wicker sofa, under dim lights, like two gray and puffy children orphaned by storm. She walked to her mother, passing a magazine table and almost expecting, from the tail of her eye, to come upon copies of *Woman's Home Companion* and *American*. Sophie saw her first. "Look," she said. "It's Judith. She's here."

Mama looked, and wept.

Judith sat and cradled her and wanted to weep with her, if only because some display of emotion might have comforted her as much as the embrace. "Your father's not here any more," Mama said, her voice small, cramped, wistful.

"I know, Mama. I just heard."

"Mrs. Brustelli said about you calling up. A good trip you had on the airplane? I was so worried, the weather."

I was so worried, the weather. But you're not Molly Goldberg, Mama, Judith did not say. You were born and raised in New Jersey, remember? she did not say.

"It was fine, Mama," she said.

"She doesn't want to ask nothing?" Sophie declared. "What time your Yasif passed away, nothing?"

"Maybe an hour, longer," said Mama. "Uncle Charlie is talking to the funeral people."

"Why are you still here?" Judith asked gently. "Why aren't you at the house?"

"Charlie said to wait," Sophie answered. "Charlie's got the machine. We can't go till Charlie gets back."

Incredible, Judith thought. There has to be a taxi, even in Regal City. Or someone who would have driven them to the house. Sophie's husband Charlie couldn't have considered that, couldn't have arranged something so that my mother wouldn't have to sit here like a marooned sheep? The immovability. The passivity. The dependency, no questions asked. Incredible.

"I have a car outside," she said tenderly, warmly. "Come. I'll take us home."

"But what if Charlie comes?" objected Sophie, an intolerable woman less than a year older than Mama, but Mama's rock when Judith was a girl, and now.

"I'll tell the nurse at the desk to tell him when he comes, Aunt Sophie."

"I want to go home," Mama said.

"Yes," Judith said, and helped her up.

"I'll stay here," Sophie announced. "Maybe Charlie wouldn't get the message, he wouldn't know where we went."

In the parking lot, in the rain, Mama marveled, "Such a fancy machine. This is your machine?"

"I rented it at the airport."

"America," sighed Mama, who had always lived in America, an inch and a half of it. She mentioned qualms about riding on the Sabbath, but merely mentioned them. They rode in the direction of the abominable house on Spruce Street. Mama's feet barely touched the floor of the car. She was a work-swollen, spotless woman with nothing about her that suggested beauty, though Judith had seen photographs of her as a girl and she had been wholesomely, unaffectedly pretty. Mama explained that Esther, Myron, and their children were on their way home; they had driven through the night to Atlantic City, had just checked into their hotel when Uncle Charlie called them, and checked out again. Mama remained silent for the remainder of the ride, so Judith remained silent, too.

They hurried out of the car and the rain. There was a basin of water on the front porch, and Judith, years removed from their religion cluttered with superstitions, immediately remembered this one: a basin of water protects the visitor entering the home of the recently interred from contamination with the dead. Mama kissed her fingers and touched the *mezuzah* slanted on the doorpost. Judith automatically did the same.

They entered the lighted house which, despite the town's unceasing avalanches of soot and dirt, Mama always kept compulsively clean. The parlor smelled of age. A sheet covered the wall mirror so that the survivors of the dead would not only not see their reflections but avoid seeing the still-visiting Death. The chairs had already been replaced by low wooden boxes, to symbolize lowliness in this period of loss. Otherwise, Judith observed, everything that had been in this parlor the last day she had been in it was here, dusted but unmoved: the China bulldog, the flowered wallpaper, the green ferns, the long, narrow painting reproduction of the imbecile woman wearing a Martha Washington costume and holding a rose. All that was new was a small television set. On the set was a dime ashtray and a faded photo of Esther, aged three, astride a fake pony.

The house was empty of Tut, and Mama wept again, but controlled herself and murmured, "Shabbes." Judith understood that as well; the Sabbath of Friday sundown to Saturday sundown was a weekly celebration and that celebration properly took precedence over sorrow. Mrs. Brustelli, heavier and grayer but remarkably no older, waddled into the parlor from the kitchen. She looked at Mama, and Mama simply nodded, and they embraced. Then the Italian lady and Judith greeted each other, and kissed, and the lady asked, "Judith, you talk to you' papa before he die?"

"No."

Mrs. Brustelli sighed something philosophical or religious or both in Italian and then said, "I make supper. You wanna eat, no wanna eat, it's ready when you want."

"You're hungry?" Mama asked.

"No, Mama. Are you? I'll get you something."

"No. Maybe I'll lay down a little while."

"Of course."

They went upstairs. Mama, suddenly very old, said, "Don't unmake the bed. I'll just lay down on top." Judith propped two pillows. Mama sat on the bed. Judith knelt to take off her mother's shoes, and her mother gazed at her as if trying to place her, and then extended her arms and mother and daughter embraced. "My Judith, my baby," she mourned in Yiddish.

Judith said nothing, could think of nothing to say, felt contempt at feeling nothing, held this woman who held her and could say only, "Sleep, Mama."

"I won't sleep. You'll wake me up when the family comes?"

"Yes."

In spite of carpeting, the hall floor and the stairs made hollow sounds as she walked on them. In the kitchen she helped Mrs. Brustelli, who had been phoned earlier by Uncle Charlie to see to the front porch basin of water, the covered mirrors and the wooden boxes for after the funeral. The boxes hadn't been a problem on such short notice; her sons Ralph and Mario owned a grocery store, so she got them immediately. Then she covered the mirror and put the basin of water on the porch, all before it was really necessary. "So how you been, Judith? Pretty like always. We no see you in a long time."

Is this dear, guileless woman preparing a lecture? thought Judith. Maybe she believes she has the right. By some old neighbor code, maybe she does have a right; Mr. Brustelli was ill for an entire year when I was about fourteen, and Mama, who drove me up the wall by categorizing all Gentiles as either *goyim* or *fineh goyim*, spent more of that year next door than here, cooking meals for Mr. Brustelli, sitting up with the worried and sometimes hysterical Mrs. Brustelli, caring for Ralph and Mario and Lina and Paolo and Angelo. Will there be other lectures while I'm here, arched eyebrows, ugly words, open hostility, high-fevered tempers?

I'll leave if there are. I owe nothing to these people and this place.

"I've been all right," she answered.

" 'At's good. Long as you' all right. You hear my Paolo get marry?"

Paolo . . . Which one was—Oh, yes. Paolo was the lame boy, shy, always just a little dense. "Really?" Judith said with enthusiasm. "Isn't that wonderful! Would I know the girl?"

"She's'a from McKeesport, a schoolteacher. She's relate' to Enrico Fermi. You know who's Enrico Fermi?"

Paolo led to Lina—Lina was Judith's age, unmarried, a nurse in Sewickley—and Lina led to more questions about who from the past was where, and Judith discovered herself caught up, fascinated to learn that her school principal, Mr. Quinn, had committed suicide, and that Mr. Thrope the mailman had had to retire because of rheumatism, and his daughter Geraldine had married Fred Long-dorf and had two sets of twins. There were only passing references to Tut. There were, thankfully, no references, even guarded ones, to Judith the thoughtless, Judith the sinner. The talk was good because the recollections were selective and she was almost sorry when Mrs. Brustelli presently said, "I gonna go on home now. You' family, they be here soon."

"Stay, if it's convenient for you. You're family."

The woman shook her head. "I go. Anybody want me, I come back to help."

"My mother is very lucky to have you as a friend, Mrs. Brustelli."

"Judith, I say one thing. I never get in no trouble because I no tell nobody except my children what to do. But I tell you one thing. You be good to you' mama, don't start up. You' Mama, she cry to me maybe a million time, she say the most bad thing in her whole life was when she make you go away, she never gonna forgive herself. You act nice, you hear?"

"Yes. I hear."

Alone, once again alien, Judith tidied the perfectly tidy kitchen and waited. To forgive or not to forgive—"You act nice, you hear?"—was scarcely a burning quandary at this late date. She and Esther had never been especially close, partly because of the nine-year age difference, but she kept up with the happenings and nonhappenings at home through Esther. They talked by telephone fairly frequently, and Esther visited her every other year or so in

New York, and with minor variations the forgiveness dialogue was always the same: "Mama would have you home in a minute, but Tut still—" "Try to understand, Esther. I don't *want* to go home. You say she'd do anything if I'd forgive her, and I believe you. I forgave her a week after I left." "Maybe if you'd write to Tut or call him . . ." "No." "He's a stubborn man, Judith, that's all. If you'd reach out to him just a little, he'd be the happiest man in the world." "Has he said that?" "No, but I know he—" "How's Myron, Esther? How are the kids?"

She had seen Mama a year before. She had gone to Pittsburgh for a television interview, and Esther had brought Mama to the Chatham. The short meeting had begun with awkward but genuine displays of love and had degenerated speedily into a messy, boorish disaster. Tut didn't know Mama was coming here; he wouldn't have allowed it. Was Tut *truly* still Stonewall Hershkowitz because of what Judith had done in the dark ages? Yes, but more upset over what she had become. What had she become? An everlasting burden and shame to him; she lived with men out of marriage, with *goyim*, she behaved like some jungle animal without conscience. And what were Mama's views of his everlasting burden and shame? It wasn't her job to correct Tut's religious beliefs.

Enraged, trembling, Judith sprang to her feet. "Not your *job*?" she cried. "Not your *job* to have an opinion or a feeling of your own? You're more pathetic than *he* is! He's just blind, but you're worse, you have eyes and you follow the blind! He wouldn't have *allowed* you to come here? Who's *he*? God? If he's God, then he'll find out, won't he, and you'll be punished for disobeying God—"

"Judith!" Esther gasped.

"Get out of this room. Get out of my life and I'll gladly get out of yours, once and for all. I don't need a mother who sneaks love to me through the back door. Go on back to your lord and master; go on back to your happy slave quarters! I don't need *any*thing of yours!"

I'm sorry, Mama, Judith thought now, hearing it and hating it. She straightened the couch cover, for the relatives would be here soon.

10

Gallagher here.

Friday morning, seven o'clock. Still trying to take in the fact that Judith's suitcase was gone from the luggage rack. I looked again for a note. There wasn't any.

Being wakened by an anonymous, threatening phone call—"You two're begging for the graveyard if you're not out of this town in an hour"—isn't the most salubrious way to start a day. Of course it bothered me. To say I was more irritated than frightened isn't to say I'm a two-fisted, trenchcoated pinbrain who chortles at danger, ho ho ho. But I'd heard and read threats before, in connection with one story or another of mine that made someone mad or nervous. All it takes to attempt to silence a reporter is the price of a telephone call or a stamp.

That doesn't mean I was blasé, either. I wasn't about to certify those callers as harmless cranks. Someone didn't approve of my having returned to Hartley, and maybe that someone and his army of the anonymous did plan on vengeful games if I didn't tuck my tail in my pocket and race home to safety. At the same time, a pro who scares all that easily is much better off covering Shaker Heights flower shows.

What bothered me a lot more was that empty luggage rack.

Her leaving me was one thing; her stealing away was quite another. The empty bed, the empty rack, the room empty of Judith only hours after it had been filled with her—it all added up to a tacky neon sign blinking *Transients transcience transients transcience welcome we close at dawn.*

Okay, now it can be told: I'm Louisa May Alcott's illegitimate son. I was stolen by gypsies who taught me to smoke cigarettes and to ascribe neither morality nor immorality to the act of sex, but I'm still Mummy's boy. I've never been especially good at screwing on the run. I'm even worse when it comes to those who screw me on the run. For whatever reason Judith had for disappearing—and she may have had what she considered a bushel of valid ones—skipping off like that left me angry. And hurt.

I phoned down for coffee and the *Statesman-Patriot*. I was halfway through my shave when the telephone rang again. This jasper sounded older, less B-movie thug than the others. He thought I ought to know there were folks around who were ready to bust my arms and legs if I stayed and stirred things up.

"Stir up Mr. Starn, do you mean?" I asked, just grabbing.

"Mr. Who?"

"You know my name," I said. "What's yours?"

"I'm just passing on some good advice to you. My name don't matter. What matters is there's folks watching you."

"What folks? Do *they* have names?"

"Certain folks. You just better believe they mean business, friend. Your best bet—"

Something snapped. "Hold it there," I said, louder than I intended; he came on as a schnook messenger boy, not as a vigilante leader, but enough was enough. "*Your* best bet is to spread the word to those certain folks that I don't knuckle, certainly not for a bunch of ignorant farts too scared to have names."

I slammed that receiver. And sat. And studied my cold fingertips, and laughed. Laughed at Six-Gun Gallagher. Heard young Captain Guts declare, "*All right, boys, I'll take you on but let's fight fair, only fifteen of you at a time, you with your torpedos, me with my bare hands and raw courage.* It was the gospel according to St. John Wayne, infantile and showy, and I'd played it straight, braver than brave, no stunt man needed for this shot, C.B. Awfully humorous. Har har har. Har har har because maybe I'd just invited the Godzilla family to come out and play.

What I didn't plan to do was make a career of waiting around for more such calls. Lather still on my face, I phoned the motel switchboard and said, "I'm accepting no more calls unless the party identifies himself and his business." I finished shaving and took a quick shower and hoped there was no reason to worry about Judith's being safe. I reassured myself there wasn't; we'd been tailed here, and it was conceivable that she was tailed from here to the airport, but roughing her up made no sense, even Godzilla sense.

The coffee and the *Statesman-Patriot* came. Did I make sure the waiter was the waiter before I let him in? You're damned right I did.

The front-page Judith story was sheer genius. There was a picture of her, between two cops, climbing the courthouse steps. The genius of the photographer was that he made her look floozy-tough. The genius of the story was that, with sprinklings of "was alleged"s and "was asserted"s splendidly placed, her crime was infinitely graver than the bombings of Pearl Harbor and Hiroshima combined. Luther Cobb's skin color wasn't mentioned, but you'll be fascinated to learn he was a member of the Black Abyssinian Church on Cliveden Avenue. Oh, yes, and Judith Harrison's father was a rabbi. It was a long and magnificently executed story, a marvel of character assassination, the raising of innuendo and quarter-truths to the level of high art. As a guy who occasionally can still seek and find goodness in his fellows, I was nauseated. As the kind of reader into whose fan this shit was directly aimed, I wanted the Judith Harrisons Stopped Before It Was Too Late.

While I was dressing and trying to figure the next move, the phone rang. The switchboard girl said the caller wouldn't give her name but was a friend of Mrs. Lane. "Put her on," I said.

The lady and her husband had been one of the couples at Andrea Lane's home at the time of the arrest on Wednesday night, she said. Did I know that Andrea had immediately retained Noah Walters, not Lester Farr?

"No, I certainly didn't know that. How did Farr get in the act?"

"All I can do is guess. We were there when Andrea phoned Mr. Walters. She hung up and said he agreed to take the case, then and there. What I think happened is that Carl came home later, after we all left, and heard the whole story, and got on the phone and dismissed Mr. Walters."

"Carl?"

"Andrea's husband. He's a builder here, a very successful one. He's always indulged Andrea in her different pursuits, but he probably decided this time, with the police and all, that notoriety was something he didn't need."

"So he cans Noah Walters. Who hired Farr?"

"Again, I'm only guessing. Carl did, I think, for Andrea's sake. No legal representation at all might've made it look like she was abandoning Judith Harrison entirely. Lester Farr can be directed, pushed around. Noah Walters is old and ill, but he would've taken complete charge."

"Why won't you tell me who you are?" I asked.

Pause. "Because my husband's in business here."

"But you and he went to the Lane home that night. I gather from that that you and he were planning to attend the three-day seminar, out in the open."

"Yes, very much so. Most of us did. But it didn't occur to us there would be trouble—anything like this . . ."

"Oliver Starn trouble?"

A little pause. "Yes. One way or another, yes."

"What does 'one way or another' mean?"

"He's—who he is. In one way or another, he holds the reins over people who live and work here. That's an awful thing to admit, in this day and age, that one human being will fall to his knees in fear of another human being—but that's how it is. My husband and I are the most liberated and independent couple on earth, and it turns out we're not. Any more than the Lanes are, any more than all those other liberated and independent people who signed up for the seminar are."

"This fear you're talking about—"

"All right, it's indefensible. But what're we supposed to do? Our roots are here. Should we speak up, say what we know, and then move? Move where? From what to what? We've built a $67,000 house here. We have family here. Our friends are here. Our children go to school here, have *their* friends here. Moving isn't that easy."

"Is living on your knees that much easier? *Please* meet me," I said. "Let's talk."

"No. The one to talk with is Noah Walters."

"I promise your name and your husband's will be protected. Starn's never going to be whipped without help from you, people like you."

"I'm sorry, Mr. Gallagher. We're fresh out of heroism," she said and hung up.

I found Noah Walters' home number in the directory and called it. Mr. Walters did indeed know who I was, Mrs. Walters said after checking, and he would be glad to chat with me there in their house if I wouldn't mind waiting till later on this afternoon. I thanked her and finished dressing. There were more calls to be made, but not from this motel room, which was fast becoming Cell Block Eleven.

I was halfway out the door when I stopped and went back to answer yet another call, this one from a Honey Bester. Honey Bester was Mrs. Lyman Bester, and Lyman had told her about my thousand dollar offer. He was sleeping now, but if I would come to their apartment at noon he'd be up and she would see to it that he told me everything. Only a thousand was no good. The price was two thousand, in cash, or nothing doing.

"Exactly what will I get for that kind of money?" I asked.

"Everything you're looking for. I guarantee that." She gave me the address and warned me to come alone and I heard a click.

I phoned Burt Oehlrichs and explained why I wanted two grand in cash delivered here as soon as possible. Done, Burt promised. I described my other calls, the crank ones. "I'll send someone to run with you, Sammy," he said. "No story's worth getting chopped up for."

"Forget it, pal. I'll watch out for traffic and be in touch with you later."

I reached the Bester flat at noon on the nose, having spent the morning in trying to track down the Cobbs, Andrea Lane, anyone who would own up to having been on Three Oaks Drive on Wednesday evening—all that driving around with a spectacular absence of luck. One stop was back at my motel. The envelope with the money was there. Nothing else in the box, not even one measly death threat.

The Bester address turned out to be around the corner from the Polo. Apartment 37 was got to by climbing an endless flight of wooden stairs attached to a grimly grubby rooming house. The door was ajar. I knocked. And waited. And knocked again and waited, and peered through the window and saw an overturned chair in what otherwise seemed a neat enough living room.

I knocked a third time. And reflected on the law that says you're not allowed to enter a private dwelling without permission, and broke the law, covering myself by calling out, "Hello?" No one answered in either of the flat's two rooms. A floor lamp was lighted near the overturned chair, but they, plus the slightly opened door, were the only signs of anything remotely diskosher.

Something was very diskosher, though.

I left. At the bottom of the stairs, a fat man was rolling a garbage can toward two other garbage cans, and I asked him if he'd seen Mr. or Mrs. Bester around. He stopped rolling and rubbed his nose. "I seen Bester's missus, maybe half an hour ago," he said. "Come runnin' down those steps like a bat outta hell, and then she kept on runnin'. You here collectin'?"

"That's right," I said. Why not?

He shook his head. "Good luck. They owe everybody under the sun, that pair. Fight like cats and dogs, you can hear her the other end of town. Very common types."

"Did you happen to notice anybody go up to their apartment or down today?"

He looked at me and switched off; it wasn't a bill collector's question. He shook his head again and went back to his garbage can.

I decided to go and come back rather than hang around, stakeout-fashion, for what could be a long waste of time. Driving in search of a drink and a sandwich, my rear-view mirror showed a four-year-old green Chevvy hardtop behind me, two men in it, and I became aware that I'd seen that same car behind me several times today.

Or had I?

Let's find out, I thought.

The Chevvy stayed behind me for a half-dozen blocks. I spotted a liquor store and a parking space up ahead, and slowed down and parked. The Chevvy kept going. I bought a quart of Scotch and came back to the car. No Chevvy, anywhere.

But there it was again, a few blocks later.

You know what I decided? I decided I was scared. Yeah.

11

The Regal City rain slackened by the time Aunt Sophie and Uncle Charlie came. "Where's your mother?" demanded Sophie, tall and bigboned and more attractive than Mama—and a devoutly stupid woman whom Judith had once described to Esther as the single greatest argument for the women's movement. Sophie and Mama shared the same sense of imminent apocalypse: airplanes fell, trains derailed, cars crashed, crossing streets was dangerous, living was a perpetual risk. The only difference between them was that Mama cowed easily and occasionally read a newspaper, whereas Sophie traveled at the top of her lungs and flaunted total ignorance of everything outside her family as proof of womanhood.

"Mama's resting," Judith answered. Sophie strode to the stairs. "Let her rest," Judith said. Sophie went up the stairs.

"All I had to eat all day was a hard-boiled egg," announced Charlie, lumbering to the dining room table. He stropped mustard on a slice of rye bread, picked up some corned beef with his fingers and said, "You want to fix me up a plate, a little of everything but no chicken? I've had chicken three times already this week. I'll turn into a chicken, like they say."

Judith surprised herself by obeying. Charlie Rosen, with the space shoes and the bushy mustache and the denture breath and the belt-plus-suspenders, sold paint supplies and lived with Sophie in Pittsburgh's Squirrel Hill, fourteen miles from Regal City. They had one daughter, Rosalind, roughly Esther's age, whom they had raised to be an enchanted princess, beloved and brainless. They had doted on her, taken her everywhere, given her everything; everything except room to grow up. According to Esther, her parents had talked her out of three announced engagements, and others unannounced, because they knew she could do better. According to Esther, Rosalind, nearly forty years old, was living at home when she wasn't taking swingles cruises in search of Mister Right, whose Rightness would be confirmed or denied by her parents. She didn't work, because office work was beneath princesses and professions had a prejudice against people with "enchanted princess" as their sole credential. Charlie Rosen was a windbag of platitudes and a blowhard horror, and he and Sophie richly deserved each other, but Judith recognized that he was every family's Mr. Dependable, who responded instantly when needed and who shouldered the unpleasant and necessary responsibilities. She disliked him, but was glad there was a Charlie Rosen now.

He didn't thank her for the filled plate. He barely glanced at her as he accepted it, and he ate, rapidly and robustly, standing, and remarked, "Well, your Dad's out of the picture. Tsk. A nice man, wouldn't hurt a fly, everything to live for, whole life ahead of him, but what're you gonna do? Worked like a dog. I told him and told him and told him he was letting everybody walk all over him, that's the fastest way to the cemetery, God forbid, and he says yeah, yeah, and it went in one ear and out of the other, like they say. But a *mensch*, you know what I'm tryin' to bring out?"

Patiently, tolerantly: "Yes."

"So you're back home."

Unaccountably eleven years old: "Yes."

He wolfed his boiled potato. "You plan to stay how long?"

"I'm not sure."

"We've been reading all about you there in the daily papers."

Here it comes, as welcome as mud at a lawn party, she thought, pouring tea, and carried the cup through the opened double doors to the parlor a few feet away, wishing it were the next county, the next continent.

He followed, still eating. "You like to know what I think?"

"No."

Bushy eyebrows lifted. "What?"

"I said no."

"I'll tell you what I think. You were always a wild kid. Your Dad, *alav hasholom*, he used to come to me with tears streaming down his cheeks, like they say, and he'd say, 'What did I do wrong, she's so wild? How is it your Rosalind and my Esther are one hundred percent and this other one's so wild?' Like that. You want my advice?

108

You should get down there on your knees and thank God that your Dad was already in the hospital and too sick to hear number one that you were arrested and number two you were doing it with a *shvartzer*. You shortened your Dad's life as it was. If he knew about this, he'd've dropped dead right there on the spot, God forbid. Listen, I'm as modern and broadminded as the next—"

Judith set her cup down and picked up her suitcase. "Where you going?"

She left him without answering. The door to Mama's—and Tut's—bedroom was open, and as Judith walked past it she saw Sophie, heard Sophie say, "The main thing is he didn't suffer, thank God." Her own bedroom was strikingly smaller than she had remembered it but, like the rest of the house, unchanged. Her books, thoroughly dusted, were intact. The Raggedy Ann doll Tut had bought her when she was little sat at the head of the bed. The bedroom window directly faced the next house's bedroom window, not the Brustellis' but the Goldmans'. That room had been Herbie Goldman's. She hadn't thought of Herbie in ever so long, and undressing now and opening her suitcase, she wondered how he was, wondered if he had pursued his dream to become an actor or if he had gone into his father's dress shop business. God, but I was a brazen kid! She remembered, amused, mildly embarrassed, that summer they had been sixteen. He and his family had just moved next door, and it was a hot summer, and she had kept the window-shade up and a tiny light on, and she would drift past her window, in underclothes at first, eventually in nothing, pretending to be looking for something, pretending she was completely unaware that he was huddling in the dark. Poor Herbie, poor Nice Jewish Boy Herbie, fantasy victim of the fantasy vampire, she thought. The unforgivable vulgarity was that I didn't even like him much.

She found clothes still in the bureau and the closet, tried on one of her old party dresses out of curiosity and found she had been the same size at fifteen as she was now at thirty. Changing into a subdued summer dress she had brought, she caught sight of the Raggedy Ann doll again. She went to it, touched it, soon was cradling it, and her patchy memory traced it to a small town much like Regal City, in Minnesota, when she was eight years old. The town's name was Clairton. Tut had had one of his short-lived congregations there, but what did that have to do with the doll? Oh, yes, wait, now she knew . . .

> *The fuss over me was heady stuff for an eight-year-old. The ambulance clang-clanged me to the hospital in the middle of the night and I was put in intensive care. Pneumonia, and I was going to be just fine. All that scared me was that everybody kept assuring me I was going to be just fine, over and over and over.*
>
> *Tut brought me the doll. He wasn't supposed to get too close to me but he hugged me—I could feel his skinny arms trembling—and he said, "A little dolly for my special dolly."*
>
> *I was taken home the day before Passover and put to bed. Tut's seders were always unendurably long; he wouldn't leave his seat at the head of the table until every last t was crossed and every last i was dotted. That seder, though, he must have interrupted himself a half-dozen times to run upstairs and look in on me. He even conducted some of that seder at the bottom of the stairs, so that I could hear. I fell asleep. I woke up and he was in the chair near the bed. I still can't see his face, but his lips were moving in prayer. I was clutching the Raggedy Ann and he came to me and pretended to try to take it from me. "Give me the dolly," he teased. "I want to play with the dolly."*
>
> *I giggled. "Tut, you're silly!"*
>
> *"That's a nice name to call your father? Give me the dolly or I'll take a strap and give you a putch-putch-putch you know where."*
>
> *I laughed and I squealed. "No, you can't have it!"*
>
> *He sighed. "Ah, to think. To think a little girl wouldn't even give her own father the dolly to play with."*
>
> *I got well slowly and looked for him to be silly with me again, but it didn't happen . . .*

Mama and the Rosens were in the parlor when Esther arrived. She had put on weight, Judith quickly noticed—not mounds of it, but her hips had grown larger and her pleasant face was fuller than it had been last year. Judith kissed her, watched the automatic and genuine displays of love between her sister and mother, listened to the details of Tut again, heard the legitimate sorrow, and continued to observe plays of feeling from a hazy distance with little feeling of her own. Myron was driving the children home because they were tired and cranky from the long trip, and then he would come back, Esther said. They would have been here sooner but there had been an awful traffic snarl on the turnpike.

The two sisters found a private corner of the house, and Esther rained questions about Hartley. Judith answered, careful not to overflavor the details with melodrama, as careful not to sound pompous about the principles involved. There were more questions, and there were no signals of approval in Esther's eager concern, but neither was there the hint of censure. "My baby sister, with the runny nose and the skinned knee," Esther clucked. "My baby sister with a prison record."

"Shocked?"

"After all these years? What could you possibly do after all these years that could shock me any more? Except that you came home to be with Mama. That's the shocker of the century, and I love you for it. Come on, we ought to go back in."

Coffee was sipped, food was partially eaten, sighs were sighed, Judith stayed removed and uneasy. Mama never talked on the telephone during the Sabbath, so Judith and Esther and Charlie took turns at accepting condolence calls from people who probably had ignored Tut when he was alive. One caller, a Mr. Eisenberg, asked Judith if she was Esther, and when she told him who she was, he began a soft sermon on what a pious, selfless father she'd lost and how she ought to be ashamed of herself for what was on TV and in the newspapers about her. She quietly replaced the receiver. Charlie yawned and scratched his barrel of a chest and said, "I better go home. Did I have a day? I had a day," and pointedly said good night to everyone but Judith and left. An elderly couple named Kabler came to pay their respects and glanced nervously at Judith the convict as they drank coffee and ate sponge cake, and then they departed. Esther's husband Myron arrived. Myron Glantz, of the poached-egg eyes and sagging chin and angelic disposition, was openly and sincerely welcoming to Judith, the only person except for Esther who had been, and that helped. He stayed only a short while because Esther, who would stay the night, didn't want the boys left alone for too long. Judith walked with him onto the porch. The rain had stopped. "Are they giving you a rough time in there?" he asked.

"I'll survive." She smiled.

"Sure you will. And you'll even survive tomorrow, too—you'll be running into a lot of the kinds of folks you wouldn't exactly call the sophisticated set." He patted her arm. "Head high, okay, Judith? If anybody tries to make *tsoris* for you, Esther and I'll be around to beat them off with a stick."

"Thank you, Myron. You're a darling," she said and watched him go. He had been less uncomfortable with her this night than he usually was, and Judith hoped that meant his discomfort was gone for good. She had often had access to large sums of money from the time she was twenty years old, and she had sent checks to Mama. Mama had never deposited them. Judith finally persuaded Esther to accept a fixed sum every month and give it to Mama, specifying that it was from Myron's pharmacy profits. Myron had resisted the conspiracy at first, hesitant to take credit for gifts he could not afford to match, but finally he had given in.

At last the endless evening was nearly ended. Mama went to bed, and then Sophie looked at Judith as if seeing her for the first time. "What're you doing here anyway," she seethed. "A bum tramp, that's all you are with all your fancy ways; a tramp, that's all she is that's all she'll ever be—"

"Aunt Sophie," Esther cautioned.

"Just being a bum tramp's not good enough for you, oh no, you have to go on the television and tell the whole world you're a criminal in jail like that's what to be proud of and then you have the gall, the tramp *gall* to prance in here like you're the Queen of the May—"

Esther again: "Aunt *Sophie!*"

"No, I'm not finished. You! You killed your father, he should only rest in peace. You're not satisfied? What did you come back here for, to kill your mother off, too? Bum, tramp, that's all you know, you couldn't send your parents one red cent—" She waved Esther away. "I said I'm not finished. Your cousin Rosalind, maybe you laugh out her because she's a decent, refined—"

Judith rose. "You *are* finished," she said quietly, evenly. "I realize you've had a difficult day. I realize you love my mother and want only good things for her. But you're a miserable and ignorant woman, Sophie."

Sophie gaped at Esther. "You hear how she talks to me?"

"I'll leave if that's what my mother wants," said Judith. "I came here because that's what she wanted and I'll go if she tells me to. *She*'ll tell me, not you. I can't resent your being a dumb woman but I do resent the pride you take in being a dumb woman. Now let's stop all this."

"You hear how she talks, how they all talk these days?" Sophie asked no one, and shook her head, and went upstairs.

The two sisters cleared the dining room table. "You must be exhausted after all that riding," Judith said.

"Not really. I just sat," Esther answered, glancing toward the stairs as she lit a cigarette; smoking was forbidden on *Shabbes*. "Myron's the one who's falling off his feet."

"Sweet, solid Myron," Judith said. "I like him more every time I see him."

Esther nodded. "I think he's taking this harder than he lets on —about Tut, I mean. Tut passed out in *shul* the other morning. Myron was there and wanted to take him to a doctor, but he seemed fine after a couple of minutes. We were going to cancel the trip to Atlantic City because of that, but we went because Tut kept insisting he was all right. Poor Myron; I think he feels partly responsible. Driving home, he kept saying, 'If I'd taken him to a doctor, if I hadn't listened to him . . .'"

"It's a good thing Myron's a man. If he were a woman and talked like that in front of Sophie, she'd have him charged with first degree murder."

Grinning, Esther said, "Good old reliable, predictable Aunt Sophie. You stood up to her beautifully. I wouldn't've had the nerve."

"Why not?"

"I'm the born peace keeper, remember? I've always been the one who hides under the covers when the voices raise."

They took warm coffee to chairs in the parlor, and Judith asked, "Why, Esther?"

"Why what?"

"Why was it so important to keep the peace? I remember that the one thing you read, ate, drank and slept was biology."

"That again."

"Yes, that again. What was the name of that teacher with the Harpo Marx hair?"

"Elsie Spindell. All right, Judith . . ."

"She called Tut to school and told him you had the most brilliant future in biology of any student she'd ever had. She offered to move heaven and earth to help you get a scholarship to Northrop. You were ecstatic, you were walking on air. What went sour?"

Esther stirred her coffee reflectively. "It's funny—Tut was ecstatic, too. He came home and he couldn't stop raving about all that praise from Spindell."

"But?"

"A biologist, he could see. A female biologist, he could sort of see. But a daughter of his in that profession—any profession—that was just too much for him to grasp. I was only eighteen years old, and Northrop seemed halfway around the world." She looked at Judith. "All right, a week doesn't go by that I don't think about it. But I didn't fight, and the milk's been long since spilled. I took a job, I stayed close to home, and I met Myron, and married him, and we had Michael and Barry. So I didn't become Darwin or Mendel, but that was a disappointment, not a catastrophe." She smiled. "No more raking coals, Judith, okay? If you don't lecture me about what should have been, I won't lecture you."

Judith smiled, too, and nodded. "Okay, a deal."

They continued to talk in the dimly lighted room, both of them tired, Judith recollecting names from the past, asking who had moved away, who had stayed. Buzz Wyler's name came up. "Oh, he's still here," Esther said. "And handsomer, if that's possible. He married Doris Ostersen and they moved into the old Hycliff house after his mother remarried. They say Buzz is making money hand over fist these days, more than his father ever did, but you ought to see him. He comes into the pharmacy now and then and he still dresses like he's on relief. He knows me, and he always asks me about you. You had a crush on him there for a while, didn't you?"

"Something like that. Doris *Ostersen*? He married *Doris*?" Esther nodded and Judith exclaimed, "My God, that must've been a royal scandal around town, a Wyler marrying the other side of the tracks!"

"You and she had some kind of falling out, as I—"

"Mmm, you're putting it mildly," said Judith. "That was my very first crisis—it could've happened yesterday, it's so clear to me. We were really close, Doris and I. We walked to school and home together, we shared our packed lunches, we talked on the phone together at six o'clock because we hadn't seen each other since five-thirty. Then I borrowed movie money from her one day and for some reason I didn't have it to pay back on the day I promised, and she said, 'That's the kike in you. When are you kikes ever going to learn to stop taking advantage of people?' " She paused. "Strange, to remember that moment so vividly. Maybe not so strange. The friendship to the death ended right then and there. I went to pieces . . ."

Then: "Why don't you go to sleep, Esther? You look absolutely bleary-eyed."

"Yes, I guess I'd better. How about you?"

"Soon. I'll stay here for a few minutes."

"Be sure it's only a few minutes," Esther cautioned at the stairway. "We have *shul* in the morning."

Judith unbuttoned the front of her dress and searched for small chores to do, unaccountably postponing the end of this long, unclear day. At the kitchen cabinet she discovered a pint bottle of Four Roses, and poured a little of it into a water tumbler.

Buzz Wyler . . .

The Wylers were the Mellons and the Carnegies and the Rockefellers in Regal City when I was sixteen and Buzz was seventeen. They lived in the estate in Hycliff, three miles and thirty galaxies from Regal City, and they were into banking and real estate and insurance, not millionaires but wealthy, and monumentally separate: private schools; summers on the Cape; Christmases in Palm Beach; Mrs. Wyler—white-gloved aristocratic Mrs. Wyler—appealing in her Wellesley tones for Red Cross contributions; Mr. Wyler—Spencer Wyler, Sr., and what Hollywood writer could have invented a more imperial name?—boatsman and rifle fancier, found dramatically dead one morning in his Hycliff study with a gun on his chest and a bullet in his head.

Every girl knew who Buzz Wyler was, that summer I was sixteen. He dated the proper Wasp daughters whose fathers owned the mills and foundries between here and Pittsburgh, and we were envious, not because they were pampered Wasps but because he took them out and probably made passionate love to them. He was gorgeous. He saw me that summer, and he pressed, and pressed all the harder when I wouldn't go out with him. I couldn't tell him the reason was

115

that my parents might find out I was with a shaygets. *I played it teddibly Audrey Hepburn, the cool, elusive goddess, and said I had a boyfriend.*

My boyfriend that summer, Lord look down on me, was Herbie Goldman.

Buzz learned I had a summer job at Sobol's Market, and whatever term they used for the rush act that year began. He would be there in his sports car when I finished work. I let him drive me a few blocks from home. The third time, we stopped for a while at one of those soapy-windowed bars on Maple Street—a beer for him, a chaste Coke for me—and I told him the truth, about Tut and Mama.

We agreed to meet that Saturday, in town. Tut never allowed work on Saturday. Buzz drove me to the Hycliff house. His father was dead and his mother and the servants were away. They had a swimming pool. I refused to go in nude, and he laughed tolerantly at the tense prude. We went looking for a bathing suit, and he kissed me and I flew into a million fragments. I wasn't a virgin, which seemed to surprise him, but he was affably gentle, anyway. Gentle and loving.

I fell crazy in love with Buzz Wyler. Everything about him was right. Everything. He called me Joodee-Joodee-Joodee, Cary Grant style. He had that air of extravagant confidence, even cockiness, but he had keen perceptions, sharp intelligence. He made me feel I was the most important thing that had ever happened to him. We saw each other every day that August, stealthily, sometimes only for moments, always alone; we couldn't keep our hands off each other.

His mother came home from Cape Cod. He introduced us. She couldn't have been more gracious, and then the name Hershkowitz hit her squarely between the patrician eyes. She stayed gracious, and Buzz drove me to the block near my house, full of plans and devotion, and I never heard from Buzz Wyler again . . .

Judith sipped the Four Roses. It tasted horrid. She emptied the tumbler into the sink, washed the glass and dried it. She locked the front door and switched off the lights. Esther was asleep. She undressed and slipped into the bed beside her sister, to wait for sleep and morning.

12

"I won't have you *play* with me that way!" Martha insisted. "Your place is here with me."

"Goodbye, Martha," Norman said, and hung up.

The line went dead and Martha Hanaday finally returned the receiver to its cradle, devastated by the shriek quality in her voice, by the ugly way she had denuded herself to Norman. She phoned the number of Jan Atwell, the Sisters of Sappho contact. A voice answered, neither female nor male, and said that Jan wasn't in. Martha recited her name and asked that a message be delivered: "I became ill just after I arrived in Boston. I had to see a doctor. It was a touch of ptomaine, and I'm much better now, but I'm afraid I'll have to go back to New York today. Would you please tell Miss At—Jan—that I'm terribly sorry for any inconvenience I might've caused, but that I'm not really feeling well enough to stay on?"

"I'll tell her. I'm sorry."

"Thank you."

The other bed was a maze of things she had spilled from her purse the day before in search of Valium. There was the vial of yellow tablets, near the pillow, as obvious as could be, and she swallowed two with water. She had reached Norman from his itinerary, which she had found in her briefcase. The maddening thing was that she remembered thrashing through this case yesterday for the itinerary and not being able to find it.

The day was Friday, the hotel was in Boston, and Dr. Stephanie Wall was dead.

Martha began to repack her suitcase, sorely aware that the nightmare that had been yesterday was madness, too, some inexplicable playing out of disturbance. Obviously, not excusably, it had been touched off by Stephanie's death. She imagined Jan Atwell would be angry, properly so, but what mattered now was to leave, to look after herself first. Eventually, in her own familiar quarters, she would piece everything together, sort out, make sense, evaluate the nightmare in perspective, interpret it in a healthier setting and benefit from it. There had to be logical explanations. She would discern them, and profit.

She phoned the airport and had her return flight to New York changed to one in two hours from now. Calmer, satisfied to have made the reservation change without fumbling, she finished packing and called down to the desk to have her bill ready and to have a bellhop sent up for her luggage. The view of the lagoon from her window was bright, peaceful. The flying weather would be good.

She went into the bathroom to inspect her face and hair before leaving. At the mirror, she noticed a blotchy blue mark on her chin, slightly swollen. It hurt, not painfully, when she touched it, and she tried to remember how it had happened.

Suddenly, totally unrelated to the swollen chin, she remembered the . . . object. The grotesque thing, the phallus.

She rushed to look inside the opened and empty desk drawers, under both beds, throughout the room. She phoned the desk again and said, "I'll be here a bit longer than I expected. Would you catch the bellhop and ask him to wait?" Desperately she checked every inch of the room and bathroom, once and then once more and then one more. She heard herself breathing. *Where is it? Does it exist? No. I dreamed it. I fantasied the whole thing. There's nothing here. I fan—*

In the waste basket. the basket she had just gone through repeatedly, was the oblong box and the festive striped paper. Here was the card, torn in quarters, that began *Hi Martha. Read you were coming (ha ha ! !).* Torn in quarters . . . *I flushed it down the toilet. Didn't I? Didn't I?*

She carefully flushed the four quarters, watching as she did, conscious of nothing else, meticulously conscious only of what she was doing.

The object was nowhere to be seen. At last she phoned for the bellhop. I'm overworked, I'm overwrought, she thought. Everything will fall into place as soon as I'm out of here. I'll be myself again.

In the rocking bus to Logan Airport, feeling better, she began to have misgivings about leaving Jan Atwell in the lurch, about setting out in good faith to lead others in a cause and then reneging. I wish I'd met this Jan Atwell in person, she thought. The woman had sounded intelligent and rather sensitive. If I knew her, I would telephone her from the airport and tell her that ptomaine story had been only that, a story, a protective one. That I'd experienced a certain emotional setback, a temporary retreat, and until I was fully in command of myself again it was grossly unfair to her and her people for me to offer them less than my best. But that kind of strict honesty merely compounds fractures. Honesty raises eyebrows. Which is sad. How much simpler and how much nicer living would be if a person could touch another person and say, Please wait a bit. Please wait for me just a little longer . . .

The side of her chin hurt.

The man seated next to her, a proper looking middle-aged man in a well-cut business suit, smiled at her over his newspaper; either he recognized her or was just being bus-cordial. His leg accidentally brushed hers—not purposely, certainly; there was nothing about him that even faintly suggested uninvited forwardness—and he quickly righted himself.

Talk to me, she begged, looking through the bus window. *Offer to buy me a drink when we get to the terminal. Please. Take me with you. Be kind. Be related. Relate to me. Talk to me.*

Where to, lady?

What?

Where to? Inside her head, a growly voice, impatient, not at all Bostonian. Who? Images began to shift and take shape in her mind . . .

Martha sat up sharply. *Where to? You sittin' there, the back o' my cab a whole half a minute, you don't say nothin'. You want I drive you someplace? Talk to me, lady. It's two a.m. in the morning and I got me a head cold. Where you wanna go? Talk to me.*

Talk to me . . .

She'd phoned the desk and asked the time.

"It's three minutes past twelve, Miss Hanaday."

"Twelve o'clock midnight?"

"That's right. Would you like to leave a wakeup call?"

"No. Thank you very much. Good night."

At two A.M., wearing her coat, clutching her purse, she had ridden the elevator to the nearly deserted lobby, walked on the balls of her feet to the deserted corner, shivering in the June night air. A taxi stopped finally. She let herself in

"Where to? Talk to me."

"Let's—drive around."

"This time o' night?"

"Yes."

The meter read an even two dollars. At a red light, the driver addressed her through his rear-view mirror. "Keep drivin'? How long you wanna keep drivin'? Boston's a pretty good size city."

"Are you worried about getting paid?"

"No. But this can set you back, lady. Long as you know that, I'm set to push this hack all night."

"Are there exciting places you could take me to? Somewhere lively."

"Like what'd you have in mind? What's open now is mainly strip joints, like that." She saw him look at her directly, saw him observe a lady. He was young, early or mid-twenties, her son Richard's age, with wild Brillo hair and an outsized handlebar mustache. "You want strip joints?"

With dignity: "Nothing that—blatant."

"You lookin' to play house?"

"I don't understand."

"That makes two of us."

"I don't appreciate such impertinence."

The red light turned green. "Fine with me," he said, facing forward. "We'll drive."

"Somewhere quiet."

"Second ago you said someplace lively. Make up your mind."

"I meant to say quiet. Are there quiet places?"

"What's not quiet, this time o' night?"

"Near water."

"Near water," he repeated. "There's the Charles River, back near where I picked you up. But it's dark there. This is the muggers' workin' hours."

"Let's go there."

"The middle o' the night, water," he sighed, and drove.

They walked together to the water's edge, her coat unbuttoned to the fresh wind, no longer cold. He had parked and locked the taxi after turning off the meter, grumbling about screwy ways to make a living, but he joined her willingly enough, as if he, too, were seeking an adventure. The place wasn't dark at all. The moon was full, lighting the night, and he stood beside her as she watched the water, watched the dips and ripples and erotic lickings at the shore. "Where are you from?" she asked.

"The Bronx."

"Why are you in Boston?"

"To drive ladies around in the middle o' the night, that's why I'm in Boston."

"My, you're crabby."

"Nahh-hh." He wore a leather jacket and he looked primordial; this is a mindless, maybe dangerous thing I'm doing, she thought, yet he's smiling under that preposterous mustache and that gruff exterior. He's gentle, and he likes me. He would have refused to come with me, otherwise. "What's the hot flashes about hangin' around and lookin' at water?" he asked.

" 'Consider the sea's listless chime,' " she said. " 'Time's self it is, made audible—/The murmur of the earth's own shell.' "

"Is that so?" he said, and she said " 'Secret continuance sublime,' " and he put his hand on her groin.

She jolted away. "How dare you!" she gasped, shocked.

"You got problems, lady, anybody ever tell you that? You didn't bring me here to listen to you recite cockeye poems. You want fixed up."

Her head swirled. "That's disgusting. I want . . . tenderness."

"That's my middle name. Where you *goin'*?" Her purse fell as he reached for her, not brutally at first, and she fought him and suspected he might harm her, maybe even kill her, if she cried for help. "Where you *goin'*, I said! Ritzy ladies like you, you spiel that poetry bull when what you're really lookin' for is this, and you don't even have the guts to admit it. You admit it now. Ad*mit* it."

"You're hurting me . . ."

"Hell I'm hurtin' you. Come on, ritzy stuff, admit this is what you're lookin' for!"

"Be gentle to me," she whispered mournfully.

He forced her to the cold ground, harshly, and raised her skirt high and chortled, "That's you ritzy ones, awright, poetry talk and no pants on underneath." Then no time passed and he was pinioning her and plunging that hateful, unreal, loveless indignity into her, and she tried to scream, tried to form words that would help him understand she desperately needed not this but tenderness, compassion, respectful tenderness, and she was ill with the abuse, the impersonal abuse of him, and agonizingly endured the oppressive weight and greed of him, and then he was up and closing his zipper.

"Let's go," he said. "I'll take you to where I picked you up at."

"You—*scum*," she breathed.

"Whoo-ey, what's that, your poetry bit again? You dug it more than me."

"Vicious, contemptible."

" 'Vicious, contemptible,' " he mocked. "You damn near bust my back, wrappin' them legs around me like I was gonna get away. And them dirty-word orders you were yappin' at me . . . Lady! I never heard such language! You oughtta be ashamed!"

"Lies. Filthy lies. I won't hear such disgraceful lies."

"You gonna get up so I can take you back?"

"I wouldn't go anywhere with you," she whimpered.

"Whatever you say, ritzy lady." He retrieved her purse from the ground. She scrambled frantically for it but he snapped it away. "Don't get nervous," he cautioned. "I snatch snatch when it's offered to me, not pocketbooks. I figure twelve bucks is about what the meter would read right now if it was on. I'll just help myself to that and no more, not even a tip, so you're in double luck tonight. Hey now, happy hallelujah, whadda we have *here*? The ritzy lady owns herself a dildo!"

He brought the grotesque object from the purse. She gaped, stupified. "Say, maybe you don't have problems after all, ritzy lady," he teased. "You take your pocketbook outta the house all prepared: wallet, pencil, pen, comb, lipstick, and dildo. Gee, I apologize if I didn't talk refined enough for you, ritzy lady. I can see now you're real high class."

With a roar of outrage she leapt at him, slapping his body, trying to scratch and hurt him, and he punched her face and gripped her wrist. "You shouldn't make me hit you," he scolded, not unkindly.

"I'm a lover, I'm not a hitter. Don't ever hit lovers, okay?" Letting her go, he retrieved her wallet from the purse, flicked a cigarette lighter to see by, and counted bills aloud. "No singles. Figures," he snorted. "Okay, here's what I do. I leave the twenty because twenty's too much, even with a good tip. This ten's not enough. So I take this ten and this five. I'd write you out a receipt but I forget how you spell 'For services rendered.'" He plunked her belongings into her hands and said, "That's a shame you don't wanna be more friendly, ritzy lady, but whatever feels right, do it, dig? I don't like that you made me hit you, because you call me names but I'm really a very nice guy. You sure you wanna stay here all by yourself?"

"Go away."

He shrugged, and the night swallowed him. She pitched the object into the water, as far as she could throw it. Her head swirled again. She recited more Rossetti, coolly asked where he was from, heard silence. Where was he? Was he hiding, had she been cruel to him, said something unkind? She didn't know his name but she called to him, walked to find him, walked and walked and walked, sat to rest and then walked again, huddling inside her coat, grateful for the clean air, for everything clean. Presently she saw the name of her hotel in great lights, a beacon, a bright, welcoming beacon, and she found her way. The lobby clock read 5:40. A man behind the front desk glanced at her. She calmly asked for her key, remembering her room number without an instant's groping, and was given the key. In the room, she methodically prepared for bed, suddenly humiliated that she had bought a Fudgicle at the Good Humor truck and hadn't had the twenty-five cents to pay for it.

The airport bus pulled into Logan. She walked with her head high to check in. Everything was in order; boarding would begin within ten to fifteen minutes; the weather outlook was perfect. The nice young lady took her suitcase, gave her a boarding pass, and she carried the pass and her purse and her briefcase to the waiting area and sat, pleased by the bustling activity of people in movement.

The loudspeaker squawked that the flight was ready for boarding. Everyone rose and filed. A uniformed man asked her to open her briefcase.

"Whatever for?"

"A spot check, ma'am," he answered, no answer at all, and he said something or other about hijacking.

"Are you serious?" she demanded haughtily. "Am I suspected of being a hijacker?"

"Ma'am—"

"This company will certainly hear from me!" she declared, and imperiously stalked away, down the ramp, clutching her case and purse. The idea. The stinging insult.

She entered the first unoccupied phone booth she saw and closed the accordion door. She fingered through her little book of names and addresses and numbers for someone who would help her get to Stephanie Wall.

She found Jan Atwell's number and dialed it. Jan Atwell answered.

"This is Martha Hanaday," she said evenly. "I'm at the Boston Airport. I don't know whom else to call. Would you come and get me?"

13

Sam Gallagher, the people's choice.

Noah Walters had the lean, firm face of a Roman senator, its nobility marred less by gnarled neck muscles than by powerfully heavy eyeglasses, which magnified his eyes to nearly twice their size. His full head of wavy hair was an argent white, his manner was strong, his smooth and beautiful hands were expressive, and he was, incredibly, seventy-seven years old. Sitting with him on his front porch that late Friday afternoon, I must've come on at first as a nauseating forelock-yanker because of the trouble I had keeping the awe out of my voice. Well, I *was* in awe of him. I'd read his book, *The People, Maybe,* when I was in college, and I was a Walters-worshiper from then on. This was the civil liberties giant who wrote that everyone owned seeds of moral courage and heroism, and who made it all persuasive. This was a great man, and I told him so.

He grinned and chided, "Sorry you said that. I was just about to tell you how very sincerely I admired *Saigon Journal.* No, it was *Saigon Diary,* wasn't it? That'll teach you to praise contrary old cusses before they have the chance to praise you." Mrs. Walters had brought us two glasses of sherry and a plate of gooey cookies. "I'm sure you'd much prefer something harder than this soda pop, young man," he said when we were alone. "So would I, but Mrs. Walters and my doctor are in some kind of conspiracy together and this soda pop is all there is in the house. They're under some peculiar impression that bourbon is bad for my heart." I assured him sherry was fine, and I told him why I'd come to Hartley and what had happened since I'd come and why I'd asked to see him. He folded his arms across his chest. He had a brace of misgivings about *Rowland's* on principle, but he'd liked my Oliver Starn story, he said generously, and he would fill in whatever blank spaces he could.

Yes, he had been retained by Andrea Lane for the Harrison

defense, and yes he had been dismissed by Carl Lane that same night. No, he hadn't a drop of doubt that Starn was behind everything, including those phoned threats on my life.

"I've been a Starn watcher and a Starn shin-kicker for more years than either of us would care to remember," he said. "We never see each other any more, but I think we have a sort of mutual respect, Ollie and I, the kind that two boxers who've been trying to punch each other out of the ring for thirty years have. Neither of us has succeeded, but that's not for lack of axle grease. Yes, he's capable of willful destructiveness, and he's best at it when he puts on his crusader hat. Any man with as many tentacles as Ollie Starn has is capable of a very great deal of destruction." He surveyed me through those huge glasses. "But I don't have to set you on my knee and tell you that power corrupts, young man. That's what you were writing about in your war book and your magazine piece on Ollie."

"What did I miss in that magazine piece, Mr. Walters?" I asked. "For all the work I did, all the doors I knocked at, I've always had the nagging feeling that it was far from complete, that the core wasn't there."

He nodded. "You knocked at the doors of frightened people. Frightened people have a funny way of not answering questions very directly or honestly. No, you got your facts straight, the ones you were able to get. If there was anything missing, I'd say it was balance. Sure, Ollie is an evil man. But he's one of the frightened people, too, and that means he's human."

"I didn't get much evidence of that," I said. "I heard dozens of canned testimonials, but they were transparent as air. What's human about him—that he's anti-vivisection?"

"That he's complex, as most evil people are. I'm nine years older than Ollie. We both of us were born and reared here in Hartley, and I watched him grow up. He had tremendous promise once. Inherited a flood of money, could've been one of those polo pony playboys for the rest of his life. He looked up to me—my hunch is that was because I seemed to be the only fella around town who read books I didn't *have* to read."

Grinning, he went on. "Maybe Ollie was working to punch me out of the ring even then, when he was in his teens, but I don't think so. He'd come to me for books to read, and he'd read 'em, and one week he was going to be Spinoza and the next week he was planning to be St. George. I spent a lot of time with him. It wasn't just that I was flattered—hell, I was a running paladin in those days, out to save the world by nightfall, and time wasn't something to squander. I saw a lot of potential in young Ollie. An excitement about him, endless curiosity, a first-rate mind."

"What happened?"

"A combination of things happened. He marched out into the big world to serve bleeding humanity, and what he learned after a few years of that was something the books and I had unfortunately neglected to tell him: that most of the folks who make up bleeding humanity are a dismal lot who smell bad and can't always be counted on to appreciate the selfless things you're doing for them. Coming back home, coming down to earth and reality happened. Genevieve, the girl from the good family his parents manipulated him into marrying, happened. Their first two babies, sons, were stillborn. Genevieve came from a religious family, the type that hears of a plane crash with no survivors and knows it was divinely inspired because there'd been a well-known atheist on board. After she lost that second baby, Genevieve became a religious nut, a God-smites-all-transgressors nut. Their third son lived, that was Roger, but he started giving Ollie grief the minute he quit diapers—drank like a salmon, cracked up cars—even cars that he stole—wrote bum checks, dated black girls because Ollie and Genevieve despised blacks, the whole shebang. They kicked him out of the house, disowned him."

Noah Walters rubbed his nose. "Life was an awfully frustrating business for Ollie Starn. He must've gradually come to believe that he'd been doing right by everybody—the bleeding humanity out there, the parents who made him marry a girl he didn't love, the wife who moved into the bosom of Abraham, the renegade son—and nobody was giving him anything back. He turned into something of a religious nut himself. You were proper or you were improper, you were white or black, you were right or wrong, with no court of appeals—that kind of religious nut, I mean. From that position, it isn't hard to rationalize your own sinful actions and passions."

"There was a daughter, wasn't there?" I asked.

"Yep. Harriet. She lives at home."

"Starn had me out to the house while I was researching the story. I wanted to meet her, but he said she was in delicate health and that was the end of it."

He picked up his sherry glass and stared at it for a long time. He sighed. "Harriet Starn," he said slowly, "had an illegal abortion ten years ago."

A lightbulb, maybe *the* lightbulb, switched on over my head. Poor eyesight and all, he saw the lightbulb.

"Hold those horses, young man," he cautioned. "I'm opening this can of peas against my better judgment, and I'm going to trust you to be as judicious as you can."

Harriet, he explained, was born a year after Roger. As Roger promised to become less and less manageable, an embittered Starn commanded that his daughter be more and more so. Selected playmates, no boys, frequent descriptions of the wages of sin. Her nervous breakdown at twenty was called rheumatic fever. Her "career" after graduating from a proper young ladies' proper college was to stay at home and handle her father's correspondence in his study. When she was twenty-three, her father found some verses she had composed and, without consulting her, mortified her by proudly publishing them in all his newspapers—mortified her because she had written them for herself and because she knew they weren't good. At twenty-six, she admitted to her father that she was pregnant. She would not tell him who the man was, only that she felt happy and purposeful for the first time in her life and had every intention of having the child, with or without parental blessing. The bedazed Starn hustled her to his personal physician who tested her, assessed the fetus to be fourteen weeks along, and infuriated Starn by refusing to remove it, large fee offer notwithstanding. Harriet was bedazed as well, for the Starn newspapers were unceasing in their editorials that abortion was human murder, absolutely never justified. She could have left her father's house for good—but she didn't, and an abortionist was found quickly, at Starn's resolute insistence and direction. The job was performed, in a tenement room over a barber shop in a seedy neighborhood miles from Hartley, a job done so clumsily that Harriet nearly died. Oliver Starn eventually learned who the man was who had degraded his daughter: his chauffeur of five months, the slight, shy Mexican who had been hired on glowing recommendation as a splendid driver and respectful greaser. He was replaced by a white grandfather. The Mexican disappeared. His wife reported him missing. He never turned up again.

I shivered, smiling to let him know it was playacting. "That's some horror story to hear on one glass of sherry," I acknowledged. "Am I hearing what I suspect I'm hearing—that Starn ordered up a killing?"

He shook his head. "That's the dangerous thing about Ollie," he said. "He's a caliph. He doesn't have to lower himself to be that direct. Over the years he's built a network of highly paid loyalists he's trained to read his mind. It would've been completely out of character for him to say, 'Have that man killed.' What more probably happened was that he grunted his displeasure to one of his upper echelon boys and the matter in time was disposed of—the matter, of course, was that driver. But I can't *prove* that the driver was done in, and till I, or someone—and there will be someone, someday—can make a legal case that Ollie is an outlaw, he has the same right you and I have to run around free.

"Point of telling you all this," Noah Walters continued, "is that Ollie could've kicked his daughter out, same as he did his son, for letting him down, for not behaving the way someone he owned was expected to behave. I think he believes to this day that she got herself pregnant for only one reason: to embarrass and hurt him. Maybe, deep down, that was her intention. Well, she did hurt him—she'd been the one sweet constant in his life, she was always going to stay seven years old and fuss over him and make him the center of the universe—and the way to hurt her in return was to pen her in for life, never let her forget that she'd paid her loving, trusting father back by conceiving an illegitimate colored tot and leaving him no option but to arrange for her to destroy it."

"So his having Judith Harrison arrested—"

"—is connected. Of course. That young Miss Harrison's started to clear too many clouds away from the dumb, uneven abortion laws in this country. When she claims that the decision to abort should be between a woman and her conscience, and when she gets more and more people to consider that as an alternative to overpopulating the world with children they're not able or ready to rightly take care of, that's a snowball that Ollie's got to stop from doing any more rolling. Because he really believes abortion is evil—for other people. Slay the apostles who stir up the natives. *They* are responsible for sin. That's pure Ollie cause and effect logic. If he can show that Miss Harrison is what we used to call a sportin' lady, it naturally follows that anything she's identified with is *ipso facto* leprous. Sometimes it works. Ollie's played some lucky games with his tarbrush."

"Why did you say that telling me about Harriet is against your better judgment?" I asked.

"Because she's a tragic little thing, cowed as a whipped kitten. If that story ever got out, it mightn't be the end of Ollie Starn but it would be the end of him as the arbiter of other people's morals. I'm all for that. But it could send Harriet over the brink, too, and I wouldn't be for that." He sat forward. "On the other hand, if *she* went to Ollie with a blackmail proposition—'You call the hounds off Miss Harrison or I blow the whistle on you . . .' "

"What're the chances of that?"

He sat back. "I'd say roughly one in thirty million. I would've tried to see her if I'd stayed on the case, see her and explain what her father was out to do to someone as decent as she is. It wouldn't've worked, most likely, but it would've been worth a try."

"Judith Harrison wants the trial, though. If she loses that forum, Starn wins."

Noah Walters nodded fiercely. "Absolutely. And she should have it. What I'm talking about is an ace in the hole. Your friend Miss Harrison has a lot going for her, but if she or her lawyer thinks that courtroom's going to be nothing more than a stage for her to play Portia on, she'll need some educating. Starn's no creampuff. He'll pull out every stop to have his boys show her up as plain dirt. Forget the fact that if the trial goes against her she can win it on appeal. It's going to be tried first in Hartley, inside Ollie's vest pocket, and exoneration later on seldom wipes the original dirt out of people's minds. This case should be won here in Hartley, because there are some mighty important principles involved."

"What if I got to see Harriet Starn?" I asked.

"You? Why you? What credentials would you take—that you write for a magazine?"

"That I'm interested in justice. Would I have your permission to tell her about this talk?"

Noah Walters did some lip nibbling. "Yes," he answered finally. "Matter of fact, yes. If you went about it the right way, if she sized you up to be the decent young man I size you up to be, you just might get somewhere." And he added, "All you have to do is get in to see her. That shouldn't be any harder than talking the Pope into flying over tonight to go nightclubbing." He chuckled. "But my permission? Here it is."

Mrs. Walters, pint-sized and a charmer, came out on the porch. She'd asked me in private not to stay too long, because her husband had far less energy than he might appear to have. "That was your office on the line, Mr. Gallagher," she said—the signal we'd agreed on to get me out, without making him suspect there was concern over him. "They'd like for you to go there now."

"I didn't hear the phone," Noah Walters said.

I thanked them both and asked one last question. "Sir, do you know Luther and Rosetta Cobb?"

"Just from reading the complaint."

"Why would they be in on this—assuming the charge is as phony as Judith Harrison claims it is? For money? This is pretty raunchy stuff for a quiet cabinetmaker and his church-going wife, even for big money."

He shrugged. "Why did that hotel clerk's wife say he'd be home to meet you and then he wasn't? Why didn't that lady who called you this morning give her name? Why do all the Carl Lanes, who ought to know better, shiver and shake? Fear comes wrapped up in different packages, big ones and little ones, but it keeps a lot of folks galloping. You find out why there are shiverers and shakers and you tell me. I've been trying to find an answer to that one all my life." He stood to shake my hand. "Luck to you, young man. If you repeat what I've told you about Harriet, I hope it's to someone thoughtful. I think you understand what I mean."

"My word on that, sir."

"You have a nap to take before supper," Mrs. Walters chided him.

He grinned at me. "What you may not know you're witnessing is fear in action. Just the thought of not obeying my wife's orders sends ice up my spine."

I drove toward the Starn family estate, on a nearly guaranteed goose chase. I'd been guardedly welcomed there at the time of the *Rowland's* piece, but that was before the article ran. In a small knot of thoroughfare traffic on the way, I saw—I think I saw—that four-year-old green Chevvy hardtop. Maybe I imagined it. Nevertheless, I changed my route at the first side street, just in case Godzilla and company were toting a crystal ball, and drove in random circles for a while, and thought about Harriet Starn.

What if I'd learned the truth about her, my first time in Hartley, had been able to pin it down as truth? Would I have printed it, without her okay?

No, I'm sure not. I could have warmed my hands over such a story then. But no, that kind of clanking family skeleton stuff, with someone innocent serving as the football . . . no, I'm sure not.

Then, anyway. What I was after now was a leadpipe cinch: to have Harriet Starn right there to roll out the red carpet for me and tell me yes, yes, she was an eternal recluse because anti-abortion Daddy had forced her to kill her baby and chained her to the newel post for all time as punishment. And how many lumps of sugar will you have in your coffee, Mr. Gallagher?

My circuitous driving was, I was realizing, symbolic of most of my hours since I'd come to Hartley. Before the visit to Noah Walters, I'd tried the Besters again; no Honey, no Lyman, no sale. I'd gone to the Cobbs' again; again no sale. I'd been in telephone touch with Burt Oehlrichs; the only substantial help Burt furnished was to advise me he'd had a long distance call from Howard Bracken, who commented that I'd been unduly sharp with him on the phone and that he wasn't used to being hung up on. Big deal.

See? Everybody was out to give me a hard time.

One person most of all. Judith. Yeah, I was still smarting over that. There she was in my arms, rhapsodizing that we'd found each other again, and then poof, vanished.

Judith, you back-in-my-life bitch. How come you do me like you do-do-do, twice in ten years?

132

I planned various ploys that, with a pinch of luck, would get me in to see Harriet Starn. Driving a straighter line toward the estate, with no green Chevvy anywhere in sight, I told Harriet Starn to wait, because Judith kept interrupting.

Judith of Malibu. Ten years ago . . .

I was working in Hollywood, at what remained of the once-mighty Grafton Studios, writing publicity releases for such Grafton epics as Teenage Rebel *and* Blanket Party *by day, and writing* The Novel, *shamelessly borrowing style and content from* Day of the Locust, *by night. And in between grinding out speculative original screenplays that my agent called Oscar-copping material and couldn't sell.*

Tinsel Town, in that period of the early 1960s, was approximately as glamorous as a deserted mine shaft with strobe lights. Unemployment was becoming the fashionable profession. People couldn't be coaxed to go to the movies and pay to see garbage when they could see garbage on their home screens for free. I at least had a job. I'd send cheery letters to my folks to the effect that my big break was just around the corner. My Ohio storekeeper father answered that he'd been married and settled down in his own business at twenty-four, my age. Privately I was giving myself two months more. That would round out one full year in the Blanket Party *vineyards, and I would then pack up and tread on to the next Eldorado.*

Then word came that fresh money was being injected into Grafton's wizened veins, that Grafton was going to be mighty as never before, that properties were being eagerly sought. That was the old-time Hollywood overstated language, but my agent re-submitted a couple of my screenplays to Grafton, and they did pick up on one, Street Dancing. *The money choked no horses, but it was a movie sale, and it promised a screen credit, and I phoned my father with the news and assured him that limitless fame and fortune were on the way. He demanded to know why I hadn't waited until six o'clock to call, when the rates were cheaper.*

Grafton's Santa Claus turned out to be W. W. Molenkamp. There may have been wealthier men than W. W. Molenkamp, but awfully few came to mind. Amsterdam-born, universe-based, he owned or controlled steamship lines, an international chain of hotels, paper mills, evidently everything except my father's hardware

*store. No one had ever actually seen W. W. Molenkamp, who
traveled, if the mountains couldn't come to him, by stealth of night;
the Vine Street scoop was that he made Howard Hughes look like a
hand-clapping Catskills* tummeler.

*Why Molenkamp money to float Grafton? Because Grafton that
year still had a reputation for manufacturing its product with
relative care and quality yet was hungry enough to take orders
without question. Someone in the Molenkamp hierarchy had chosen*
Street Dancing *as the suitable vehicle for Judith Harrison's first
role in pictures.*

*I didn't know who Judith Harrison was. No one did. We soon
found out. She was Molenkamp's mistress—the term could still be
spoken in those days without breaking up—but that was quite beside
the point. She* had *to be, no contest, the most beautiful thing ever to
have come to town, face utterly flawless, figure superb, no sharp
lines, nothing underdone or overdone, mammoth green eyes and
regally lascivious mouth that made instantaneous horniness a
matter of simple good taste.*

*I wasn't invited to the executive conferences, or to the pre-shooting
rehearsals. The first verdict I got was from Jack Weinzimer, the
assistant director: "For all this is costing, that chick's gotta be the
greatest lay in history. She sure can't act."*

*I was allowed on the set, on the understanding that, as a lowly
screenwriter, I'd keep my mouth shut. I was introduced to her, as
were some of the other little people, the little people being the
anonymous group sometimes publicly thanked by the stars in their
Academy Award acceptance speeches. She gave us a Queen Mother
nod.*

And she was *a lousy actress. Not only a disdainful bitch but a
glaringly incompetent actress. Bill Fisher, the director, blinked at
Jack Weinzimer, and Jack blinked at Bill, and then it was the
seventeenth time to try the simple scene. I felt sorry for her.* Street
Dancing *was about an embittered young war widow who descends
through a series of increasingly ugly affairs and is near collapse
before she discovers that life is worth living, after all. If it sounds
like sludgy soap opera that's because it* was *sludgy soap opera,
although I was Alexander Tolstoi while I was writing it. Sludgy or
not, it required an actress if it was going to work at all, and I*

134

watched this glorious creature called Judith Harrison fall on her decorous duff each time she said, "Good morning, Mr. Parks," to the mailman, and I had the sweaty impression that this was one movie that wouldn't be completed. Unless the part could be changed to make her a deaf mute sitting still in a chair for nine reels.

The shooting was in its fifth day when I learned that the non-existent W. W. Molenkamp had been in the vicinity, a Malibu beach house, all along. That was more than I cared to learn. I stayed as far as possible from the sound stage. Jack Weinzimer would bring me orders from on high to rework this scene and simplify that one, and it reached the point where his only comment on the picture's progress was to roll his eyes Heavenward. I had visions of going into partnership with my father in the hardware store.

At the end of the picture's second week of shooting, a limpid Saturday, I went to the Malibu beach house to hand-deliver a chunk of script changes she was to learn by Monday morning. She was on the terrace above the beach, gazing at the Pacific and nearly spilling out of her half-ounce bikini, a copy of Anaïs Nin spreadeagled on her lap. She greeted me by name, but was neither friendly nor unfriendly. We'd never really spoken to each other before, but the guardedly imploring way she looked at me as we talked now about the script told me we had one knowledge in common. She was expected to be Marilyn Monroe and Sarah Bernhardt, and we both knew she was consummately hopeless.

"Are you in a hurry to go back to wherever it is you'd go back to?" she asked.

"A bit of a hurry," I said. What I had to go back to were an orange-haired carhop named Cindy, who would be off work at midnight and who had it in her head that I could get her into the moom pitchurs, and my one-room Yucca flat with a stack of cups and spoons and dishes in the sink that would one day have to be taken out and washed.

She asked me to fix her a screwdriver, and anything I liked for myself at the bar. We sat with drinks neither of us touched. "Moley's in the East for the weekend," she said. "Three thousand miles to get there and three thousand miles to get back, all in the same weekend. The mind boggles."

"Moley," I said, "would be short for Molenkamp."

"How quickly you catch nuances," she ridiculed. I sat up and placed my drink on the tile floor, nuances she caught. "Let's erase that, can we?" she said quickly. "I've been studying to be a harpy. I'm showing off, because I find I'm better at that than I am at being an actress."

"You're not profoundly convincing at either," I said. "Why work so hard at jobs that don't matter all that much?"

She must have judged that I wasn't looking to hurt or exploit—the natural Hollywood instinct, running equal with the instinct to breathe—and the rapport began there, an uneasy rapport but a rapport. Could I keep quiet? Yes, I could keep quiet. She didn't want to be in the movies. She didn't want to do anything she couldn't do well. She knew she was a caricature, a rich man's rent-a-girl, all the more a caricature because the only difference between it and two-dollar hookerdom was this beach house and all the residual comforts like this beach house, and she disliked it and she was prepared to leave none of it. "Dull," she said. "There's nothing duller than a cheap broad qvetching that she has everything money can buy." She sipped her screwdriver, and contemplated the ocean, and looked at me and asked, eyebrow high, "Will you stay a while? Want to screw?"

I got those kinds of offers, from gorgeous women in palatial settings, hourly. I saw she was serious. What she was asking me was would I concretize the fact that she was worthless by taking her over my knee and spanking her. "I don't screw cheap broads," I said, trying to sound convincingly disinterested despite the fact that my tongue was hanging out. "You want a friend, here's a friend. You want a stud, I'm sorry but I swore to my mother I wouldn't fool around with cheap tramps."

I spent that Saturday afternoon with Judith, certainly not with anything resembling a tramp. We made love on the beach. Love. I try not to use words like ecstatic, but ecstatic can be the only word to describe that afternoon on that beach. We did everything wrong and clumsy in the beginning, as if trying to digest a compendium of sex manuals all at once, but my non-Hollywood fumblings and her non-Hollywood awkwardness made it all ludicrously, supremely right. What was right about it was that waves did not crack at the shore, firecrackers did not go off on cue, we were panting like minks

136

and something miraculous happened for each of us, both of us, but so earthbound-miraculous that we agreed, no words needed, that there would be more, and more.

The imperfect thing I did that Saturday was to say, "You're beautiful."

She moved away from me for a moment, angry. "God, I hate that," she complained. "Beautiful? So what? I've heard that all my life. It's like complimenting you for having a belly button. What's the accomplishment; what did I do to deserve that compliment? Beauty. Beauty is a deformity if that's all there is."

"Homely people might not agree."

"Homely people can go to hell," she snorted. "Homely people aren't homely because they have crooked noses or small chins or flat chests or fat legs or pimply skin. They're homely, they're ugly because they wallow in what they look like. Don't you ever tell me again what I look like, or this is definitely, distinctly the end. Is that definitely, distinctly clear?"

How do you save face, face that's had an omelet thrown in it? "Let go that imperious tone," I said. "Both of us have important things to learn from each other. And while you're high dudgeoning, let go of this, too," I said, indicating the death grip her hand had on what those sex manuals antiseptically referred to as my male member. "I can't learn much of anything if I'm going around gasping."

She laughed louder, more genuinely, more melodiously than anyone had ever laughed.

The picture slogged along, but Judith and I raced. We met over the next weeks, at every conceivable and inconceivable opportunity, risking the calamity of being caught, risking it because we were downright batty about each other. Once in a lifetime, possibly oftener though probably not, the chemistry between two people is so mutually spontaneous and all-envelopingly perfect that even the most obvious risks are well worth taking. The great line in the Cole Porter song about intense love affairs being too hot not to cool down applied to other people, not to us. We were deliriously intense, wildly happy. The marvelous sex, the giddy fun, the sweet kisses, the sharing of thoughts, back to sex again, inevitably back to sex again—we were ravenous lovers, running a single stratospheric fever.

And we sat one night in Lambatelli's, a dark little spot just off the Strip, the kind of joint a Molenkamp wouldn't know about unless he had extremely good reason to. He came to us, W. W. Molenkamp, with a sleek-looking gent at his right and another at his left. He wasn't a big man, but he had big presence. He pointedly ignored me. His attention riveted on her and he blazed, ever so softly, "Get up."

"Moley . . ."

"You know how I dislike repeating myself. Get up. We will leave now. Get up now and I won't have your two-penny pig sweetheart torn apart." He looked at me and smiled a chillingly gracious smile. "You understand, little boy. You played with a toy that wasn't yours. Now I take the toy back. You're a nice little boy but you're a stupid little boy."

Judith sat there, wide-eyed and glacially still. I started to say something. He grabbed her hair. She let out a little yelp and I shot up and zapped a fist into the belly of W. W. Molenkamp. He went "whooofff" and doubled. His flunkies came at me. Judith yelped some more. I fought and kicked like hell. A bunch of men pulled the flunkies off me. I mustn't have hit Molenkamp as hard as I'd meant to, because he was standing erect soon enough, brushing his shirtfront with his hand, his smile a masterpiece of composure and control. "How stupid of you, darling," he said to the still-recoiling Judith. "Curious. We'll leave now?"

"No."

He bowed. " 'No.' A very expensive 'no.' As you wish." The flunkies followed him out.

I took Judith to my cozy shambles of a flat on Yucca. "Daddy Warbucks was right," I said. "That was the most expensive 'no' since—"

"Spare me the similes," she said tonelessly, unbuttoning her dress. "I'm home now. Similes are the last thing I need."

Street Dancing *was canceled. Grafton, of course, tossed me on my ear. Judith was distressed, not by her abrupt change of fortunes but by my loss of a job. I can't say I was riotously overjoyed at being out of a job, either; writers' jobs were hen's teeth as it was; Hollywood, an incestuous little company town, would learn fast that I wasn't Molenkamp's favorite wordsmith and I'd be lucky if someone hired me to write* Men's Room *on doors. But it wasn't all that serious. I had two hundred and seventy dollars in the bank, and I had Judith.*

I had Judith for four days and nights after the shootout at Lambatelli's. I came back to the flat one afternoon—we were going to drive to Big Sur for the weekend, to drink wine and swim and walk a lot and talk about The Novel—*and the only thing of Judith's that was in the flat was a long, long letter, from her to me.*

Leaving this way was cowardly, she wrote, but she was afraid to face me, for fear I'd talk her out of her decision to go. She was hopelessly mixed-up, she wrote, in love with me but not enough, repelled by the Moley kind of life but not enough, securely aware of nothing except that she had an ongoing, dismally low estimate of herself and was repelled most of all by that. She repeated that she loved me. And wrote that I deserved better than to be used by an addled, schizophrenic, basically hollow brat who basked in the love and goodness of a Sam and who wasn't in any way ready to turn her back forever on the extravagant creature comforts offered by the Moleys. She was done with Moley—in honesty because he was done with her, she wrote—but there were other Moleys around some-where, and her mixed blessing-affliction called beauty would fade and die before long and she would barter it while she could; that was really all she was good at. She hoped I wouldn't hate her for mak-ing me believe she was a nicer person than she was.

I went looking for her. I drove on three wheels to Malibu, where the caretaker told me he had instructions not to let her in. I kept looking. Half a year later, working as a junior-junior editor at Rowland's *in New York, I came upon a UPI picture of her, the antithesis of the independent woman she was to become, and a few other bikinied beautikins, frolicking on the private yacht of that year's Daddy Warbucks. I wanted to knock her in the eye. I wanted to knock myself in the eye for my gullibility and for still being batty about her, make her see herself in that yacht-frolicking picture, see the puzzled, sad eyes above that obscenely plastic smile.*

Instead, I worked to climb the Rowland's *ladder. I tripped on some rungs, but I climbed. I went to every party in town. I romanced a lot of ladies, occasionally with concentration. I even got married, a*

dynamite marriage for the five years it lasted, one year together, four
years more or less estranged. There were intervals of time when I
didn't even think about Judith . . .

The Starn estate, at the farthest point of Rachel Drive, was relatively modest, considering its mandarin's wealth and the emotional
splashiness reflected in his newspapers. There were acres and acres
of grounds, to be sure, but the house itself seemed to belong, say, to a
well-to-do small-town stockbroker who had a few years of reduced
income and hadn't quite kept up repairs. I parked the car and rang
the bell. A lady not much larger than a Fordham tackle, wearing a
nurse's dress and space shoes, opened the door and viewed me
without a pandemonium of hospitality. "I must see Miss Starn. It's a
matter of the greatest urgency, concerning her father," I said, wondering if Laurence Olivier could speak the line any more persuasively.

The Fordham tackle wasn't biting. Olivier would have done the
line better. I got slammed out.

I walked to the side of the house and around it. Okay, it was
dumdum hawkshawing. When Mike Hammer walks around a house
of mystery he never fails to find something—a blonde all over, at
least. I don't know what the hell I imagined I'd come upon. A bottle
on the ground with a note in it leading me to her? Harriet herself
passing her upstairs window, spotting me and motioning for me to
climb the trellis? I finally returned to the car and drove off, feeling
like eight kinds of a fool.

Which was exactly what I was. One kind of a fool is the kind who
forgets that he'd been scared earlier in the day and had had every
right to be scared. That was the kind of fool I was most of, because a
few minutes away from the Starn house, on a quiet road heading
toward Hartley, the four-door green Chevvy hardtop came zooming
from behind, overtook me, and blocked me so that I had to screech
to a stop. I had the reflexive sense to press the lock buttons on both
my doors.

I'd seen two men in the Chevvy earlier. Now three barreled out,
Godzillas all but infinitely faster of step. One I could take on, I
thought, certainly not three—but these apes are going to have to
work for their pay.

They yanked at the locked doors, rocked the car, and for a minute it seemed as if they were trying to push it over on its side, all of it fast, so fast that I, damn-right scared, couldn't get a clear image of their faces. One of them got smart. A rock came crashing at my window, not breaking it but cracking the outer pane. Then there was another heave, harder this time, and the car was pitched over, me in it, and no I don't know how they got a door open and got me.

But they got me. I, the brave fire-eater who was going to throw the first punch, didn't get the opportunity. I was dragged out by my hair and kicked in the face, in the groin, in the face again. Something else I don't know is how I rolled away and leapt up. I tried to run. A sledgehammer of a fist caught me at the back of the neck, and I wheeled and rammed a fist into the nearest ape's eye, and what sank me was the world's heaviest sledgehammer at my kidneys. That was when the stomping began in earnest, my body a stage for flamenco dancers, and the other thing I can't tell you is how I stayed conscious.

It wound down, and it ended. I couldn't see anything but I was breathing, because I could hear wheezes rattling out of me, and one of the apes was close to my ear and he said, "Couldn't mind your own business, could you, you suvvabitch? Mebbe now you and your Jew whore'll learn not to go where you ain't been invited."

The Chevvy went. My mouth was full of blood, but I could barely open my mouth, much less move my head to let the blood out. I heard a dog bark. And bark and bark and bark. Pain would have been welcome. I felt nothing, no sensations, nothing. All I can remember thinking before I passed out was, *Got to reach Judith, got to tell her to stay away, she's not safe, nobody's safe.*

14

An orthodox Jewish synogogue service requires that women and men be separated. The tradition was archaic nonsense, Judith believed resentfully—she considered the explanation usually offered, that separation symbolized the uniqueness of the respective roles of the sexes, to be a deceitful, hypocritical cop-out—but she climbed the stairs of her father's grubby little *shul* with her mother and sister and aunt at eight-thirty on Saturday morning.

A very old lady had preceded them and held what seemed to be an equally old prayer book close to her obviously nearly blind eyes. Judith knew the synagogue well, remembered every endless Friday night and Saturday morning and religious holiday in this same row of benches, remembered the fetid smell, remembered her bewilderment at being taught to read Hebrew but not taught to understand what she read. It was enough that females learned the letters and pronunciations; comprehension of the language was for the men.

Twelve men, most faces seamed, were gathered downstairs, and presently Myron Glantz called out, *"Boruch atah Hashem,"* and the service began, not to honor Tut but the Sabbath. Remarkable religion, Judith thought, watching pharmacist Myron preside over the worship. No man was better than another man in Judaism. A rabbi was a scholar and teacher, with no more authority to conduct a service than a fruit huckster, a janitor, a pharmacist. How seemingly democratic and how manifestly inconsistent and two-faced, she thought; everyone is equal in the sight of God—including us darkies up here at the back of the bus. Yet she found the sequence and followed the service in the prayer book with ease, pleased that the letters and words automatically came back to her after so many years away, childishly proud that she could close her eyes from time to time and silently recite long passages from memory.

One of the dozen men, his face familiar, was looking at her, greeting her with a sober nod. She nodded, too, and then brightened and smiled when she suddenly placed him, placed Herbie Goldman, the boy next door on Spruce Street. They exchanged a restrained sign language, agreeing to meet after the service.

She regarded Herbie. They were the same age but he looked older than thirty. Maybe it was the high hairline; maybe it was the fleshiness around the chin; maybe it was simply the look of someone who had settled in and for Regal City. She regarded him and remembered the mischievous joke, the law as set down by Mama and Tut: Gentile boys had Only One Thing on their minds, whereas Jewish boys had far loftier thoughts and aspirations. Her parents had encouraged her to be nice to shy, refined Herbie Goldman. Hello, Herbie, she said now, you shy, refined hymen-breaker, you.

She stood with the others as Herbie and Myron helped Charlie Rosen remove the Torah from the arc, Uncle Charlie who had pulled the strings that had brought Tut and his family of gypsies to Regal City. He had meant well, of course, Judith thought, remembering.

I was nine years old and Esther was nearly eighteen when we moved here. In the first eight years of my life we'd lived in five different houses in five different communities around the country, because of Tut's uncanny gift for irritating members and losing congregations. In his nebuchel *way, certain of nothing except that everyone had an obligation to be as pious as he, he would telephone the wrong members out of sound sleeps to please come and help make up morning* minyans. *He would timidly, without invitation, tell specific members, almost invariably those who held his contract renewals in their hands, that it was a sin for them to drive to Sabbath services even if they parked their cars a block away. He would court disrespect by asking for five-dollar salary increases as if hoping to be turned down, which he usually was. He would mean only the best, and he would unfailingly say it wrong, do it wrong. There was always at least one member of each congregation who liked him or pitied him, who would take him aside and warn him that it was every bit as important to be a politician as God's servant. It was advice he never understood. And so we kept moving.*

I heard Uncle Charlie tell him, the first day we moved into the house, that dreary house in this dreary ghost town, "Your big job now's to mind your p's and q's like they say. My Sophie's naturally glad the family's gonna be close by, but what I don't want you to ever forget is I went out on a limb, selling you to the board here. You're lucky I'm such good friends with the shul's *president. But you go making enemies, you even say boo when it isn't necessary, and it's a black mark against me because I stuck my neck out for you, like they say. For my sake, for your sake, for everybody, do what the members want, don't get them down on you. It's a job. We're all in one bidness or another to keep the customers happy, right? Be smart. You're no Stephen S. Wise and you're no spring chicken any more. How many more years you figure you can go on* schlepping *your family all over the world?"*

Tut got the message. He learned to shuffle.

"It's wonderful seeing you again, Judith," said Herbie Goldman, palm damp, eyes darting. "Not under these circumstances, of course, but then that's the way it goes."

"It's so good to see you, too, Herbie," Judith said. "I've thought of you often. Where are you living now?"

"Oh, here. I never did make it to the Great White Way after all. I started to, I mean I planned to, but then Uncle Sam put me in a soldier suit for eighteen months, and then I went to Carnegie Tech, and before I turned around I was an old married man, working with my Dad."

"Would I know your wife?"

"No, I don't think so, she's a foreign girl, from Manchester, England. Say, it's really *won*derful seeing you again! We've been reading ab— Ah, you'd love Rita. My wife. Maybe we'll come by tomorrow, afterwards, and pay our respects . . ."

"Thank you, Herbie. That would be awfully nice," she said, and he went to Mama, who seemed strangely numb, as if on the threshold of genuinely facing the enormity of her loss, and he quietly spoke a condolence to her in Yiddish.

She and Esther and Myron walked the morning-shadowy streets of Regal City toward home, behind Mama and the Rosens. "Nervous Herbie," Esther remarked, not unkindly. "He was certainly sweet on you that one year, remember? Mama had it in her head that you two would get married."

"Mmm," Judith nodded. "Mama was great for getting me married. It used to make me so mad."

"She'd say, 'Wait till *you're* a mother and you'll understand.' "

Judith nodded again, and recalled with mingled regrets the anguish she'd caused Mama, not the neurotic, self-indulgent anguish ("Where were you till ten o'clock at night? I wore out this carpet back and forth, I was ready to call up the police") but the comparatively appropriate fits of worry. Esther, plain, sensible, studious, obedient, had always been a smoothly manageable daughter. Judith, both pretty and restless and inexplicably ambitious, wrote poems and talked early of devoting her life to feeding the hungry in China or Africa or both. She was outgoing, she was inquisitive, she was popular, she was different, and she perplexed Mama, safety-first-and-last Mama who knew there was safety only for those Jews who didn't venture out.

Her body was a woman's before she was fifteen, and the boys noticed her and Mama saw the boys notice her and fixed the future. "To meet a respectable man and marry young isn't the worst thing," said Mama, a bride at seventeen. "The world you want to see, Miss Fancy? A good husband and a family, that's the world. You show me anywhere in all those books you read where it says there's anything better for a woman to be than a wife and a mother. You'll never show me because you wouldn't find it."

"What if you had a son? Would you tell a son that's all there is, to be a husband and father?"

"Don't ask what you know. A man is different. I pray to God every night I should only have the *naches* that Esther would find somebody nice. A fine girl like that, sitting home in the rocking chair, we should've had grandchildren by her already. Don't you make me arguments. The most important thing for a girl is to make a good home for a good husband. *I* don't only say that. The Bible says it. *God* says it."

The cheeky question: "Then why did God give women a brain and not expect us to use it?"

The Mama answer: "Enough with that! God forbid a million times a girl could end up like the Spitz girl, that's why you'll finish your high school and get married! Don't ask so many questions! *Genug!*"

"Who's the Spitz girl?"

"That's enough, I said!"

She asked Esther who the Spitz girl was, and Esther hesitated and finally told her. The Spitzes had lived in Regal City till about ten years before, respected people, religious people, whose daughter Henrietta, eighteen, was made pregnant by the Polish boy they had forbidden her to see. The pair stole money from both their fathers and vanished. The boy's father turned his humiliation and rage into an anti-Semitic crusade by shouting to everyone who would listen —and Regal City listened—that The Jews had made his son a thief and a runaway. He and some friends got drunk one night and marched to the Spitz house across town and stormed their way in and broke furniture and the boy's father knocked Mr. Spitz to the floor and was arrested the next day. The Spitzes sold their house and business and moved away. There were people in town still talking about it all.

"Be patient with Mama," Esther said. "Listen to her. You don't have to go along with everything but you don't have to fight, either. She has blind spots, she has her limitations, but some of her worry is understandable. You're not like the rest of us, Judith. You're heading somewhere, you're not going to get lost in the woods. But this is where Tut is. Don't do anything foolish here, where there're people with nothing to do but wait for any of us to make the slightest false step. That's really all Mama's saying. You're beautiful and you're smart and you're popular. Don't give us any reason to be ashamed of you."

Good friends drifted into the Spruce Street house, stayed for a time, and drifted out. Judith worked at being the gracious, welcoming daughter to those who addressed themselves to her, and even to those who didn't, those who seemed puzzled about how to behave with this semi-Martian. The hell with it, she thought. I don't have to have them accept me. They see me as something strange, something not quite clean. So be it. I can't blame them for that. I can be civil without truckling or battling or coming down with the sulks. I'm here because of Mama.

Rosalind, Sophie's and Charlie's enchanted princess, arrived as one cluster of visitors was leaving, at roughly the time that Judith's urge to escape into the rented car and drive, just drive, began to grow inordinate. She watched Sophie help the expressionless thirty-nine-year-old child out of her raincoat, saw Sophie's love and Rosalind's bored expectation of love and simultaneous rejection of it, and felt a brief wave of pity for Sophie, who must have had her hands full over the years as the mother of an enchanted princess. Judith hadn't seen her cousin in a very long while but imagined she would have recognized her anywhere. The continual spoiled brat poutiness about her hadn't changed, nor the expensive-cheap over-dressing, nor the sign behind the aging-child face that read VACANCY.

The parlor wasn't that crowded, but Rosalind took her enchanted princess time in wafting royally toward Judith. Judith greeted her. With a phony smile, showing a blizzard of capped teeth that surely had cost Charlie four million dollars, she greeted back, "Well, long time no see, stranger."

They sat on the sofa. "I'll bet it's been a dog's age, like they say," said Judith.

"At least. Well. I must admit it's a shock and a surprise to see you back at the old homestead, Judith, considering. It's too bad you couldn't find a few minutes to come see Uncle Joe while he was alive, but we realize how busy you've been." A smile. *"C'est la vie.* That's life."

Sophie brought her orange juice, coffee, and a sandwich. She accepted the tray without glancing at Sophie.

"What're you doing these days, Roz?" Judith asked.

"Doing?"

"Doing. To keep busy."

Rosalind blinked. "Oh. Well, I'm always keeping busy. I'm taking Yoga. And a film course at Pitt, Tuesdays and Thursdays. There's this marvelous instructor who teaches you what to *look* for when you go to a movie. Most movies are trash nowadays, but we're learning there're all kinds of things you can learn even if it's trash. Let's see. I'm sailing the end of this month, if all's well, for my annual trip to Europe I take every year."

"That's very interesting," Judith said, hoping there was no con-descension in her voice. "What do you do every year in Europe?"

"Do?"

"Do. What do you do?"

Rosalind blinked. "What does anybody do? I *go* there. I re-live history, I meet people, I eat in different restaurants and go to different hotels. What does anybody do when they go to Europe? I don't sleep around and have sex orgies, if that's what you're driving at."

Softly: "No."

147

Softly: "What're you, looking down on me? Feeling sorry for me because I only stop at the best hotels and my father's paying for it instead of some sexy degenerate? You don't have to bother, thank you. A sophisticate maybe I'm not, a whaddayacallit a liberated woman I'm not. But one place I've never been to is in jail, so all of those superior looks you always give me I honestly don't need, thank you very much."

Uncle Charlie appeared. "You fed the cat before you left the house? I left so early, I forgot," he said to Rosalind.

"I'll do it when I go home."

"Go see your Aunt Frieda. She's in the kitchen."

"Why's she in the kitchen? Why doesn't she come out here?"

"Who figures what? She likes to sit in the kitchen. Your mother's there sitting with her. Go, *ketzaleh*. Go say hello to Aunt Frieda."

"When I'm ready, all *right*? Can't you see me drinking a cup of coffee? I had a hundred things to do today, but I got dressed and drove out here. If she's dying to see me, tell her I'm here. I'll say hello when I'm *ready* to, you *know*?"

He padded away.

Rosalind glowered at Judith. "What're you looking at?"

At someone terribly sad and suffering, Judith wished to say. And whispered, "At a nothing. At an absolute nothing."

She decided against the car and walked the half-dozen winding, hilly blocks toward "town," Regal City's two-street business district, walked fast, appalled that she could have talked that way to Rosalind, to anyone that adrift, that helpless. I'm supposed to be the one who preaches that you don't begin to change assigned roles by attacking the victim. I do feel contempt for them, the Rosalinds, the Sophies, the Mamas, the treadmillers who blandly settle for third best—maybe mostly for the Esthers, who peer hungrily at alternatives and then scurry home safe.

Big Deal Harrison, the fount of wisdom, the parter of social waves, sees all, knows all, understands all . . . Laugh here, as we used to say at Regal City High. I look down my royal Hershkowitz nose at the treadmillers, and in the meantime I'm as adrift in my way as they are in theirs. He was my father and she is my mother. Prehistoric wars between us aside, fancy-shmancy psycho-social interpretations of their shortcomings and hangups aside, he was my father and she is my mother, people who loved me, people I loved, a huge part of my life, and the only conscious feeling I can summon is mild contempt.

So why did I come home again, when the book clearly says you can't? To look around for my navel?

She reached Poplar Avenue, still pretending she was on her way somewhere. The Farrell Funeral Home, the town's only one, was on the north corner and she neared it, slowing her steps. Old men from the *shul* would go there tonight, to say psalms and wash Tut's body and cut his fingernails and make him presentable enough for his soul to rise. They would stay with him through the night, never leaving him alone in the dark, lest demons steal in and rob his soul.

Probably no one was there now.

She paused at the front door. And walked on.

Here was the Lyric Theatre. *Tomahawk Canyon,* starring Randy Grant, plus—today's matinee showing only—five animated cartoons. *(Ah, Lyric, Lyric, glorious oasis, how I cherished you. I'd sit in the third row aisle seat, always the same seat, and watch the flickering wall, and you'd tell me tall, heavenly tales about humble beginnings and triumphant endings, we'd work our wizardries together and I'd be up on that wall, beating out Elizabeth Taylor for Rock Hudson's affections, every girl's ultimate dream.)* Here was Goldman's dress shop, Herbie's and Herbie's father's business, larger than she had remembered it—odd, because the other stores and shops on Poplar Avenue seemed smaller than she had remembered. *(I treated you unconscionably, dear Herbie. You never knew that, but that hardly justifies it. I paraded nude back and forth at my bedroom window, like the exhibitionistic dirty rat that I was, always scrupulously careful not to look toward your bedroom window next door where you were watching with the lights out. And then we met in daylight, you gulping, I batting my lashes exactly like every Lady Innocent on the Lyric screen. I let you take me to that July dance because you were the only Jewish boy over eight that summer, and my parents liked your parents, and my obeying them was better than not going to a dance at all. And when your shaky hand made that exploratory trip under my dress, I murmured bloody murder, and you were so profoundly apologetic, and you stayed comatose with guilt until—how many dates later? —when it was all the way for the first time for both of us. Unconscionable, dear Herbie, because I purposely set about to make you believe you'd done something irremediably wrong, when the vulgar truth was that I'd orchestrated the main event from the start. Forgive me, dear Herbie. And thank you.)*

"Joodee-Joodee-Joodee!" she heard, instantly remembering Buzz Wyler, even before she turned.

She was right, and suddenly enormously happy. Buzz Wyler brought the world's most expensive sports car to a sharp stop at the curb and flew out, laughing, arms wide, and stood, simply stood, as Judith exclaimed his name and herself stood, simply stood, until he tore at her and they embraced. "Joodee-Joodee-Joodee!" he bellowed, lifting her inches off the sidewalk, hugging her hard. "Where'd *you* drop from, since when was it, 1776?"

"Buzz, you maniac! Hello! And put me down!" she squealed, loving the exuberance of him. He swung her around, still laughing, babbling ferociously about how terrific it was to see her, how terrific she looked for an old bag, and she laughed and babbled, too, and passersby stared and it didn't matter. She remembered how abruptly they had ended in 1776, and why, but that didn't matter, either.

"Where're you bound?" he asked, broadshouldered and—Esther was right—handsomer than ever. The 1950s style blond crewcut made him look boyish. The sweatshirt and dungarees, his 1950s style uniform, hadn't changed, either, nor the enthusiasm, the electricity.

"Nowhere, really. I was walking around, looking at the big-city sights."

"Put it in here," he demanded, guiding her to the car. "I was on my way home. We'll go there and drink some drinks and catch up."

"Well . . ."

"No sassing back. You know I never liked my women sassing me back."

"Well, in that case, I guess I'd better do as I'm told."

Inside, the doors closed, Buzz bearhugged her again, kissed her mouth hard but swiftly, quickly and crudely squeezed one of her breasts. The grab was too clownish to be sexual, but Judith said, "Buzz, this feeling me up is extremely flattering, but we're on the main street in the middle of the day. What will the neighbors think?"

"Neighbors? These rubes? If I worried more than a minute a year about these scabby mothers, I'd need them instead of the other way around, right?"

He gunned the motor and sped off, as if he owned Regal City, and probably did. He wore wizened moccasins, no socks. "What brings you back, Joodee-Joodee-Joodee?" he asked. "Last time Doris and I saw you on the boob tube—yesterday? the day before before yesterday? I can't keep time straight any more—you were coming out of the hoosegow on one of those civil rights deals of yours. Do you remember Doris from way back when? She remembers you. Doris Ostersen?"

"Sure. Doris and I used to swipe things at Woolworth's after school."

"No joke? Doris? The mother of my kiddies a klepto? I'll have to beat her bucket for that." He guffawed, a Rotarian one-of-the-boys guffaw. "So what brings you back? You hiding out from the coppers, Bugsy?"

She told him about Tut.

He was sorry.

He also was Buzz Wyler, though curiously not Buzz. It's forever since 1776, to be sure, she thought, and people grow, people change. And it's unfair to make character judgments this fast. But this doesn't seem to be Buzz at all, the Buzz Wyler who read Villon to me after lovemaking . . .

He asked her about Hartley, and she told him. He wanted details about the night in jail, fair enough, and she told him that, as well. "That must've been a barrel of laughs," he said, grinning. "I've never been in the jug"—he didn't quite add *That's because nobody around here is big enough to arrest me*—"but Doris was, a couple of years back. She was driving someplace in Kentucky and they picked her up for speeding. All she had on her were two hundred credit cards and about ten bucks in cash. They stuck her in the cooler for six, seven hours while they were trying to find me." He laughed. "Those six, seven hours behind bars cost me whatever the fine was *plus* taking her to the Virgin Islands to recuperate. Doris always has terminal claustrophobia. I don't think she's recovered yet." And affectionately: "Nutty broad."

As they approached Hycliff, Judith suddenly said, " *'I am not, I'm well aware,/An angel's son in a diadem,/Of Stars or constellations.'* "

Buzz's brows met. "What's that, a Burma Shave sign?"

"François Villon."

The bell rang. "Christ Almighty! 'The Testament,' right?"

"Right."

The ruddiness in his face deepened. "Man, talk about 1776! How do you remember all that?"

"I had a first-class instructor."

He shook his head, beaming. " *'Be it Paris who dies or Helen/Whoever dies dies in such pain . . .'* "

Together they recited, " *'The wind is knocked out of him,/His gall breaks on his heart.'* "

"Christ Almighty," he repeated, softly this time. "Where did all that go? You know the last thing I read? A balance sheet, and a book on marlin fishing. Hell of a thing, the way you forget . . ."

The Hycliff estate was somehow colder in feeling than she had remembered it, more pretentious, style absent, overseer's love absent.

In the huge hall, Buzz boomed, "Hey, Doris, you outside? Guess what celebrity I brought home today!" To Judith he said, "I'll be back in half a sec. I've gotta prepare the old woman for *this*!" and was gone. The mammoth front room off the hall was now an immediately jarring inconsistency of modern furniture and surely overpriced chromo trash. The room had once exuded comfort; now it billboarded only wealth and tastelessness; except for a deep, old-fashioned armchair under the stained glass window and an elegant oil painting of Buzz's elegant mother above the fireplace, every object seemed to be competing, gaudily, with the object next to it. The yellow and black gooseneck lamp, modern in its free and simple lines, was strikingly out of place here. The glass-top, wrought iron end table didn't belong in this room which now contained —eyesores of nose-thumbing eyesores—carved wooden cherubs and iron figures with the breasts of women and the beaked heads of birds. And the largest television set she had ever seen. And a wall bookcase with more bric-a-brac than books. Things, dozens and dozens of things, possessions, acquisitions, bought and paid for Things. It's their business if they're not offended, she thought, hotly offended; it's their business if they want to go hiring an interior decorator who ought to lose his citizenship.

"Judy!" she heard, and Doris That's-the-kike-in-you Ostersen Wyler came lunging at her, all welcoming arms and joy, and Judith, never used to the name Judy, was welcoming arms and joy, too, even sincerely so. They babbled about how much time had gone by, much as she and Buzz had done on Poplar Avenue, and Doris pointed to Buzz, near them, and declaimed, "Leave it to Sir Walter Raleigh here to leave you standing around all by yourself in the living room. Come on out to the pool. Lynne Evans in there. You've got to meet her. The weather's been so crappy lately, I run outdoors and live there at the first sign of sun. Buzz, get more ice, we're very low." To Judith, arm around her as they walked to the terrace: "I pay our maid ten times what she's worth, and she can't even remember to move off her black fanny to make more ice cubes than absolutely necessary, so we're always running out. You look just great, Judy! What's this crazy jazz we're hearing about you on the television? What is it, a gag or what?"

"No, it's for real," Judith replied, abruptly aware that she would almost rather be at home on Spruce Street than here. Doris Ostersen's mother had been a maid, though her fanny had presumably been white. Pretty Doris Ostersen Wyler, in her two-piece red swim suit and two-ton diamond ring, had clearly come a fair journey, all right. Stay loose, Judith warned herself.

A young woman, perhaps two or three years younger than Judith and Doris, was sunning herself on the terrace, wearing a flowered swim suit and dark glasses and a plastic nose guard, holding a drink in one hand and a copy of *Vogue* in the other. Three small children were splashing one another gaily and violently at the shallow end of the pool. Doris introduced the young woman, who removed her glasses and stood, an attractive, pudgy young woman with orange hair and one hoop earring. "Lynne Evans," said Doris, "I'd like you to meet . . . Whad'ja say your name was?"

"Minnie Mouse," Judith said, smiling approvingly, and extended her hand. "Hello, Lynne. I'm Judith Harrison."

"I certainly know that," Lynne Evans declared, taking the hand, her own smile a shade too serious. "I've been your biggest fan since I used to see you on *Judith's World*. That was a marvelous show. I even wrote you a fan letter once."

"You did? I hope I answered it."

"Well, it was one of those form-letter thank-you things."

"Ouch. Forgive me."

"Name your poison, Judy," Doris said, indicating the copiously stocked portable bar, and Judith asked for a light rye and ginger ale. Doris began to pour, yelled, "*Buzz!* What the hell gives with the *ice?*" and suddenly seemed too concentratedly steady on her feet, as if she'd begun drinking early, and confided, "Lynne here and her husband Jamie—Jamie should be along soon—moved here to town around New Year's, wasn't it, Lynne? When I told her you and I grew up together, we were bosom buddies, she nearly keeled over. *Buzz, ice,* goddammit! Oh, by the way, Judy, Buzz mentioned that your Dad just died the other day. I'm very sorry. *Buzz,* goddammit!"

"Jamie and the baby and I lived in Philadelphia till he got transferred here," said Lynne Evans. "Not Philadelphia, actually; Upper Darby. I was almost ready to head for Reno when I heard we were going to be buried alive here. Not that Philly is any great paradise, except for a few really fine stores, but the one good thing about Philly, that made it bearable, was they have legitimate theater there. I can't go to plays often enough. That's the one thing I would've given my eye teeth for: to be an actress, to be in the public eye. I'd watch you on *Judith's World,* interviewing all the famous celebrities, especially the actresses, and you and they were always so *special looking* . . ."

"That's awfully—" Judith began.

"*Buzz!*"

"*Coming!*"

"I did some little theater work in Philly, till the baby came," Lynne Evans said. "I was in *The Show-Off,* and I did the nurse in *A Streetcar Called Desire.* My stage name was Lynne Joye, with an *e*; you wouldn't've heard of it. I did a TV commercial for Wanamaker's for panty hose, but that was for the bread, that's not theater. You had Tallulah Bankhead on your show before she passed away. Was she as foul-mouthed in person as they say she was?"

Mercifully, Buzz appeared. Mercilessly, he announced, "The iceman cometh."

"And none too soon," Doris acknowledged, "I'm all in favor of a man who comes."

Lynne Evans giggled. "That's the first time I've ever been accused of coming late," Buzz said, winking at the women and taking aggressive charge of the bar.

"Mama's always grateful for small favors," Doris drawled, and sank into the chaise next to Judith. "Well, let's not say small, let's say small to medium. Ooops, that's letting out family secrets. Too bad."

Buzz glowered behind the bumptious grin, and Lynne Evans giggled again, and Judith smiled because it probably was expected of her, and she listened to a few moments more of smirky, infantile, implicitly hostile sex dialogue between them, and sensed the ominous tension, and broke in as soon as she could to ask whose children belonged to whom. Joye-Ellen, aged five, was the Evanses'. Buzzy, aged six, and Deedee, aged four and a half, were the Wylers'. "They're lovely," Judith said. "I'm fond of children. I wish I could be more relaxed with them."

"Have a couple of your own," Doris advised.

"I was in labor with Joye-Ellen for fourteen solid hours," said Lynne Evans. "I kiss the ground she walks on, but I wouldn't go through that again for the keys to Fort Knox."

"Why haven't you ever had any kids, Judy?" Doris inquired calmly. "You've done just about everything else."

Good, bitchy question, Judith thought. Buzz started to protest, but she waved the protest away. "The most practical answer that comes to mind is that I've never been married."

"Why would something that conventional stop you?" Doris baited. "When did you ever do anything by the books?"

Buzz, testily: "Okay, honey." To Judith, smiling: "When my duchess starts mislaying her manners, that usually means she's had half a belt too many."

"What're you, apologizing for me?" Doris objected.

"No, but—"

"Fair is fair," Judith conceded. "If I had a child, it would be because a man and I were ready to commit ourselves to the responsibility of it. If we had a child because a culture said it was expected of us, that would be unfair to the baby *and* to us."

"Isn't that sort of a selfish attitude?" Lynne Evans asked.

"Of course it's selfish. But if there was more of that kind of selfishness, there just might be fewer unloved and uncared-for children, and more space and time and freedom for people to pursue the fullest lives possible."

"Jamie wanted a boy," Lynne Evans said. "But it would bring tears to your eyes, how crazy wild he is about Joye-Ellen. When he's acting silly, he says he plans to marry her off the first time she gets the curse so she can hurry up and give him a grandson."

"Where the hell's my drink?" Doris complained.

There were more drinks, and questions about Hartley, and direct, unelaborate answers, and Judith was dismayed that what they kept asking, in politely couched evasions, was: If you were all that anxious to sleep with a colored man, why couldn't you have done it somewhere private so that no one would know? Why do you go looking to rock boats? Buzz discreetly changed the course of the lazy afternoon talk around to the safer seas of chitchat. She rehearsed excuses to leave, yet stayed, repelled and fascinated by the repeated references to owning things, by the compulsive double entendres about genitalia that Doris instigated and Lynne giggled at and Buzz rather refereed, by the determined emptiness of their chatter. How did you settle for all this, Buzz? she wanted to ask. You, sitting there, imbecile-grinning and encouraging the smutty gunk about going down and getting in and ripe bananas, making a public advertisement that you and your wife share an inadequate sex life; who are you, Buzz, why can't I see you in anything resembling focus, how dare you be D'Artagnan at seventeen and Comfy Klutz at thirty-one?

Lynne Evans and Buzz swam. Doris, drinking steadily, now chummy, now randomly querulous, words occasionally slurring, no longer bothering to conceal the fact that she was beyond sobriety, took Judith on what she called the forty-cent tour of the house, and Judith offered no hint that she knew the house well. "The minute Buzz's ballbuster mother got married again and moved out of here, I had the whole place done over," Doris informed. "We kept some of her junk around because Buzz got heavy about that, but you wouldn't believe what this dump looked like till I went to work. It gave you the spooks. It was like serving a sentence in a museum." Room after vast, color-splashy room was almost relentless in bordello taste, but Doris was obviously proud of her empire. "Not bad for Hattie Ostersen's little girl from Glidden Road, huh?" she preened.

"It's spectacular," Judith said. "How *is* your mother, Doris?"

Doris blinked, as though trying to recall. "She's in Arizona with asthma. We don't see each other much. C'mon, I'm gonna show you the Taj Mahal of toilets. You'll flip."

The main bathroom's walls and ceilings—Belle Watling-baroque—were mirrored. There was a giant television screen built into one of the walls for viewing while in the tub. The tub, colored a shiny black, with steps leading up to it, was roomy enough for a party of four. "My big appointment of the day is from three o'clock till four, Monday to Friday," Doris said. "I soak in there and watch *General Hospital* and *Secret Storm.* Nobody can come near me then. That's the holy hour. How about all this, Judy?"

"It's very grand," Judith allowed, and continued on the plush honky-tonk tour, and finally asked, "How did you and Buzz find each other, Doris?"

"Um." In the comparatively small sewing room, Doris brought a bottle out of a deep drawer and stiffened her drink. "Boy, that's a long time ago. I was working at the bank—his mother and uncle were running it after his father shot his brains out. There was this talk that old man Wyler was a weekend fag, did you ever hear that? Buzz was finishing up college at Pitt and doing this and that at the bank. He'd walk by and we just met. He saw me at the teller's window a couple of times, and we went out. He was the horniest kid that ever drew breath." She snickered. "Tried every which way to slip me into the sack. Well, *I* didn't go to Pitt or even past high school, but you're talking to the smartest artist in captivity. No tickee, no washee, you know? I wasn't that crude, but I got the message through loud and clear: no wedding bells, no nookie, cookie. And I played it like a genius and I got the wedding bells. The Wylers were fit to be tied. They tried everything; I wasn't classy enough for their classy prince.

"Be eight years in August," she said in Deedee's bedroom that contained vigorously busy Disney-populated wallpaper, a clothes closet chock full of clothes on silk hangers, and a color TV set. "I don't think he still knows what hit him, but I've got him trained. We do okay. Hattie Ostersen's little girl from Glidden Road is doing *very* okay. When you and I were kids, did it ever once enter your head that some day I'd own *two* minks?"

She wanted praise, seemed to need some assurance that she indeed had engineered herself to the helm of the best of all possible worlds. Judith couldn't bring herself to that, but granted, frammis-fashion, that it was all something to see. Doris drained her drink in a quick series of swallows. Unasked, she insisted that she enjoyed her life just fine. Buzz, who'd nearly flunked out in business administration at Pitt, surprised everybody by buckling down and becoming a dynamite businessman overnight. He still worked hard, worked long hours, and he didn't bother her much.

The tour went on through endless rooms filled with ugliness, and the monologue continued in a voice that seemed to grow shriller and more defensive by the minute. The drink was magically refilled, from a bottle in some bedroom, and again gulped. She explained that her kids were to have everything, but they were to be raised right. Little Buzzy would play football and baseball to insure in advance that he wouldn't end up a fag, and he would go into the family businesses and marry the creamiest of the crop around, and Deedee would be watched over, so she grew up pure and married the right kind of man. "She ain't about to get caught screwin' the coloreds," Doris added, her voice slurring badly.

Judith flinched from the nastiness in the tone. *Pretend it's a joke,* she cautioned herself. "Better keep her away from Hartley, then," she said, hoping for the sound of gaiety.

Doris gave her a scornful smile. "You only screw them in Hartley, huh? That's not what I heard, Judy-baby."

The nastiness was open. Judith said, "Oh, come on now, Doris."

" 'Oh, come on now,' " she said in a nasal mimicry. "*Shit.* You been walking around here all day, in my *home,* like you smelled something bad or something. You think I'm *common,* don't you?"

"Doris—"

"You've always had this notion about yourself that every time you go to the toilet, out comes ice cream. You're better than everybody else. Your folks didn't have three nickels more than my folks did, but you were always putting on airs like you were some queen and I was dirt. Go ahead and deny it. The Glidden Road folks were dirt."

"Doris, you know that was never—"

"Yeah, correct Doris, set lowlife Doris straight. Why'd you come here, to gloat? Whadda *you* have to gloat over, that you get your name in the paper because you go around frigging niggers? *I'm* the one to gloat, you fancy shithead kike! Where're you better than me? I earned *my* minks and everything that goes with it the decent way, through marriage. But you wouldn't know anything about decent, would you, you—"

Appalled, Judith hurried down the stairs, missing steps, Doris bawling after her. She emerged onto the patio. A thirtyish man she assumed to be Lynne Evans' husband, wearing confidence and success, was accepting a drink from Buzz, and saw her and stopped whatever he was saying and effusively greeted, "Say, you *are* you, aren't you? These wise guys said you were here and I was positive they were putting me on." Buzz, wet in swim trunks, looked from her toward the house with troubled eyes, but he introduced Jamie Evans. Jamie Evans spoke of how tickled to death he was to meet *the* Judith Harrison. She interrupted him.

"Will you drive me to town, Buzz? *Now?*"

"Now? Why don't—"

"Now. I don't want to wait for a taxi."

"Well, sure, all right . . ."

Doris appeared, smiling. "Oh my, did we hurt its wittle feewings? Did high society decide she had enough slumming for one day?"

The Evanses looked bewildered. Buzz looked mortified, and rumbled, "Damn it, quit making these goddamn scenes of yours."

"What scenes?" Doris purred, feigning injured innocence, and sweetly addressed Jamie Evans. "Jamie, you should've been here earlier when high society Miss Harrison was lecturing us riffraff about honesty. You know what my maiden name was? Ostersen. I used my name till I got married. I wasn't ashamed of it. I'd call that honesty, wouldn't you? But my high society girl friend here wasn't named Harrison back—"

Judith hastened from this house of horrors to Buzz's gleaming car.

Driving, Buzz said, "Sorry about Doris, Joodee-Joodee-Joodee. Certain days she hits the sauce with a vengeance. Some days it makes her cute as hell and other days it makes her a mess. Today was mess day. It started about a year ago. Basically she's a good kid. What the hell, you're big enough to let that kind of thing roll off your back, right?"

What made you marry her? Judith wished she could ask. And asked, "Does she know about you and me that summer?"

He shook his head, his jaw set. "No way. You and I just knew each other, that's all she knows. Goofy thing about Doris: she's the squarest thing that ever lived, in spite of that dirty tongue. You're the psychologist, you figure her out; I've stopped trying. Lynne, for instance, Lynne balls any guy that lopes down the pike. I know that, and Jamie suspects it, but Doris knows from nothing. If she did, she'd drop her cold."

He was sullenly silent for minutes, and then he slowed the car and braked it to a stop on a dirt road surrounded on either side by voluptuous wheat fields. He stared at her, as if pushing back time, and said to her, his eyes serious, "Be nice to me, baby . . ."

O God.

"You remember what we had. I remember. I've remembered every day. It isn't the same with Doris, with Lynne, with anyone. I was in Atlanta, wherever it was, a week ago, ten days ago, I had a girl, one hundred dollars, she looked like you almost down to the ankles. One hundred dollars and she wasn't you, anything like you, come here, baby, you remember, I remember, let's make it here, please, I haven't said please since ever, please . . ."

Judith felt his hands with the alarm of pity; fleetingly considered philanthropy, as fleetingly rejected it. She tried to free herself, tried to form a smile that would show both understanding and disapproval, and said, "Start the car, Buzz," relishing not at all the directive tone in her voice. "I hate wrestling."

"I remember—"

"What you remember is 1776. *Don't* have me do stupid things like slap you and walk home. *No,* Buzz, it's my turn to say please, you're not some moron strongarmer—"

"You're all crazy with that kind of talk, this is *Buzz,* you don't forget what we had!" he croaked, grabbing her, all too gravely serious, ferocious and unloving hands everywhere at once. Judith fought him, less frightened than angry when she saw that he was indeed a moron strongarmer, desperate to defile them both. Fear became real when he slapped her hand brutally as she struggled to open her door, and she gasped, aware suddenly that rape wasn't some quaint abstraction but something very possible, fear was real and loathing was real, and she struck his face as hard as she could, stunning him, and the fear was gone.

"All right!" she cried, erupting in fury. "Come on, let's screw the broads, that's what they're for, right? If they don't want to come across, that makes it a little tougher but it doesn't matter, we just slug 'em and ram it into them, we have the right because we're boys and they're tail—"

"Jesus, Judy—"

"No, that's wrong, calling us by name spoils it, we're not people, we're service stations. Come on, get cracking, mustn't let your manhood be in doubt for a second, right? Right?"

"Jesus," he repeated softly. There was an awed silence for a time, and finally he turned and switched on the ignition.

At Poplar Avenue she said, "I'll get out here."

He obeyed. "I'm sorry you made me out to be a creep back there," he said. "Okay, I shouldn't've been so roughhouse, but you know I'm not a creep."

She opened her door.

"Let me see you again before you leave town," he said. "We'll have a drink somewhere and talk. We have a lot of things to say to each other, Joodee-Joodee-Joodee."

"Goodbye," she said.

She walked until she felt some semblance of composure, and entered the front door of the funeral home and spoke Rabbi Hershkowitz's name when a man came to her. "Are you one of the bereaved?" he asked.

"Yes."

The man took her to a simple coffin in a room with two other coffins, both of them statelier. He left. Judith hesitated and then deliberately raised the top.

Her hand shook, though only for moments. She studied Tut's face, and marveled at the stillness. She had never seen anything so white as his face, nor so full of peace. The harassed look was gone. He was younger. She saw the gold wedding band on his finger, and touched his hand and shuddered, for nothing in her experience, even icy twigs she once had touched in the woods, had ever been so cold. "Tut. *Meine tata,*" she said aloud.

Then Judith Hershkowitz closed the top and dashed from the room and the building and walked fast, puzzled that she had thought for a moment she might find answers there.

15

Your friend and mine, Sam Gallagher.

It was daylight, just a fleck past dawn, when I came to. I said earlier that when those three apes had quit playing Jose Greco on me, I felt nothing and would have welcomed pain. Well, that was then. When I came to—a dog was barking somewhere, maybe the same dog, as if confirming everyone else's opinion that I shouldn't have come to Hartley—I had enough varied and assorted pains to furnish the Marquis de Sade with a month of nocturnal emissions. Inventory was very slow. I couldn't stand; I made trojan attempts, and couldn't swing it. One eye was completely shut. The other eye saw just enough to tell me it was daylight.

I hurt. To repeat: I hurt.

My wristwatch, possibly the only thing not broken, read somewhere between five and six o'clock. There was a woodpecker convention going on inside my head. I crawled with mighty effort to the overturned Plymouth. Righting it was one of the innumerable tasks I wasn't up to. So I crawled. At times I did get partially to my feet, and stumbled, and nearly stood, and fell. Mostly I crawled. In no particular direction.

And passed out again.

I woke up in a hospital bed—a ward, because I remember other beds. Then I blanked out once more and woke up in another hospital bed, a private room. A young doctor was taking my pulse. I felt pounds of bandages around my head. The shut eye was still shut, and deep breaths were hard to negotiate, but otherwise the pains weren't as great as before. Sedation, the doctor explained, and catalogued my reasons for being where I was, starting with cracked ribs, general body bruises, a busted wrist, and onward and upward to a mild concussion. They were watching my liver, he said—an opening for a gag line, which I was in no mood to provide.

What day was it? I asked. Sunday; I'd been unconscious for most of the thirty-five hours I'd been here. Was I up to talking to the police? he asked. You're damned right I am, I answered, and he nodded to a nurse I hadn't seen, and she left the room. How had I got here? A farmer had found me and called for an ambulance, the doctor said. Admissions had looked for identification in my wallet, read Howard Bracken's name as the person to contact in case of emergency, and a Mr. Oehlrichs had had me moved from a ward to here. How long will I be here? I asked. His lips pursed in contemplation and he said, "That depends on what some more tests tell us. Except for that beauty of a beating you took, you're a healthy man, and that's all to the good. If we get a good report on the liver, and if your urine and bowel functions stay reasonably normal, I'd think we can shoo you out of here in about a week, a day or so either way. We're going to take you down for a few of those tests now. The police should be here by the time we're done, and so should your friend Mr. Oehlrichs. I understand he's been here several times. He left word to be called as soon as you were back among the living."

Two orderlies came. As they lifted me onto a table on wheels, and I winced, the doctor asked, "How do you feel, all in all?"

"Mad," I said.

"Physically, I mean. Is your head—"

"Mad," I repeated, and I was wheeled away to be examined. When I was brought back, about a half-hour later, a man and a young woman were in the room, an expressionless cop who identified himself as Langford, plain clothes and lumpy, and a stenographer in a lady cop's uniform. Hunch, nothing more than hunch, told me this guy wasn't a member of the Sam Gallagher fan club. I told him everything that had happened, step-by-step. The stenographer took it all down. Not only did he stay expressionless; everything about him came on as totally perfunctory. That added to my anger, which I was working to keep on a low, low burner.

"You ready to describe your assailants?" he asked. The way the Camus character must have droned, *Mother died today. Or maybe yesterday.*

"It went awfully fast, as I said."

"Umm. You claim there were three of them. Were they Caucasian or colored?"

"White."

"You're sure about that."

"Of course I'm sure."

"Describe them."

"They were big."

"Uh huh. Big. Tall-big? Broad-big?"

"Burly."

"All three of them?"

"All three of them."

"Uh huh. Wouldn't call that very specific. You know they weren't colored. Is that all you saw, that they weren't colored? One of them must've had something that distinguished him. A mark, something out of the ordinary."

"There wasn't anything out of the ordinary about them except that they were all somewhere between thirty and forty years old, as I said, and they were burly. It wasn't nighttime, but it wasn't all that light, either. And everything was quick. I was scared. Wait. I got one of them. I got him straight in the eye. Some burly guy somewhere is sporting a king-size shiner."

"Did you get the Chevrolet's license number?"

That ripped it, that finally got the blood percolating for real, that certified that my hunch was smack on the button. "No, officer," I said. "It somehow didn't occur to me to read a license number while I was having my balls jumped on."

The stenographer dropped her pencil. Langford darkened and rumbled, "You're in mixed company, young fella."

I conceded that with a slight nod.

"Now, then," he said. "Let's go over again why you seem so sure your assailants were local folks. They could've been outsiders, right? From anywhere, right?"

I sighed. I repeated everything, from the anonymous telephone calls to the one gorilla's you-and-your-Jew-whore speech. Incredibly, even for him, Langford said, "Mize well tell you here and now you aren't giving us much to go on. Most of what I can make out of what you're saying is that you came here from out of town looking for trouble, and—"

"Okay!" I said angrily. "Let's cut the crap, Langford. I had the shit kicked out of me and you're telling me it serves me right." He went furious-white. "Take all this down," I directed the lady cop and looked at Langford. "I think you're somebody's bootlicker. I think if you represent the law in this town, the safest and nicest thing I can say about myself is that I don't live here." Boiling harder, to the stenographer: "Make sure I get a copy of this transcript, miss, word for word, especially the part where this tinhorn mentioned my coming here to look for trouble." To the quiet-blazing Langford, I blazed, "Don't give me that hick-town glare, copper. I think you're a bum. I don't think you're working for Hartley. I think you're running errands for Oliver Starn." To the stenographer: "You getting all this down, miss?"

Langford's voice was low and ominous. "You're pretty big with the lip, boy."

I ached. "Oh, gumshoe out of here," I ordered. "You have as much interest in finding who clobbered me as I have in nominating you and the rest of you Hartley cops for this year's integrity award. Out. You're stenching up the room."

Burt Oehlrichs, fat and dapper, visited me that day. I summarized the lovebird exchange with Langford, and he wasn't amused.

"I'm surprised at you, Sammy," he chided. "Blowing up is no way to learn anything. Isn't that why you're in Hartley—to learn something?"

"No, I'm in Hartley for a rest cure. What're you laying on me, a first semester journalism lesson? Look at this goddamn eye! And this goddamn once-heroic body! Jesus, you know what the Langfords and the Albrights are probably doing this minute? They're probably gathering evidence that I stole the Plymouth I rented. How many years would the head of an international car thief ring get around here? God*dam*mit, but I'm mad! Mad because I'm here on my prat while scumbums are running loose!"

Saying it made me remember Judith. My fear for her safety seemed a little less rational now than it had at the time of the beating, but I asked Burt to get her New York telephone number for me; *Rowland's* kept up-to-date records of private numbers and addresses. Burt agreed, but asked, "Who'd go after her all the way to New York, Sammy?"

"Scumbums, that's who," I snapped. "The world's full of 'em."

Hysterical? Yes, when I said it. Then I learned that Lyman Bester, the Polo desk clerk, was a patient on the next floor, the victim of a brutal beating by unknown assailants. Who'd go after Judith all the way to New York? Cousins of unknown assailants. Logical question, logical answer.

16

On Sunday morning, in the synagogue's sanctuary, Myron Glantz spoke of Joseph Hershkowitz, although Tut had many times over the years expressly instructed that he wished no eulogy. Myron made no attempt to suggest that Tut had walked in greatness, but Judith was touched by the obvious affection her brother-in-law felt for the man who would be consigned this day to the earth.

The morning was surprisingly bright for Regal City. Women and men sat together in the crowded sanctuary, because the service was not a religious one. Mama sat between Judith and Esther. She had broken down once today, just before leaving the house, on seeing Tut's empty reading chair near the front door. Now she wept as Myron spoke, wept and squeezed Judith's hand. Judith, sitting rigid, experienced a dryness, a tightening in her throat. It had nothing to do with grief, she was sure, for she felt none. A once-removed empathy with Mama's grief, perhaps. An appreciation of Myron's simple sadness. Maybe it was the ritual itself, this one and the rituals to come, abiding and unchanged through twenty-five hundred years, both old and fresh. Maybe that, she thought.

At the brief pre-burial service, an old man with scissors cut the small strip of black ribbon each family member wore, and performed the *kriah,* to dramatize the tearing of the heart. At the cemetery, Charlie Rosen spoke the *kaddish* near the coffin of her father, and Judith Hershkowitz's eyes filmed unexpectedly, and sobs broke from her throat, and she held her mother and sister and sobbed without constraint for many minutes, unable to stop, glad not to stop, sobbed at their loss and her loss, her very special loss. Esther comforted her. She called her father's name, her choked voice loud, imploring.

In the house, Mama asked, "You can stay a few days?"

"I ought to leave today, Mama. I have a lot of work to do." Hoping—childishly, she suspected—to be dissuaded from leaving, she added, "But if you think I can help in any way by staying . . ."

"Work comes first. I'm all right. Do what's right for you," Mama said, without a hint of having been injured.

They were alone. "That business with the policemen," said Mama. "Tell me about it."

"Mama . . ."

"I wouldn't bawl you out, I wouldn't say a word. I promise. But there's trouble for you? God forbid, you could go to jail?"

"No, it's nothing like that," Judith answered, not at all certain it wasn't, and explained Hartley, not expecting her mother to support or wholly understand the circumstances and principles, guardedly gratified that Mama was listening, was trying to understand. Then Judith was done and Mama spoke. "I wouldn't say a word. But maybe if you told them you didn't do something wrong, you didn't mean to start up, you wouldn't do it again . . ."

More people came and went during the afternoon, and Judith decided she would go after the final service, the one held in the parlor at sunset. One of the visitors was Herbie Goldman, spectacularly uxorious as he introduced her to his wife, Rita, a hair-teased Manchester girl with the sullen disposition of someone who had been taken away from a Mah-Jongg game. While she was in earshot, Herbie characterized himself as the luckiest man in the world for having Rita, great wife, great friend. When she was out of earshot, he confided that he was going to New York on business one of these days—alone, he emphasized, all too transparently—and how could he reach her there?

She gave him her private telephone number and added, "I hope you'll come soon. My fiancé would like to meet you, I'm sure." Herbie was stung, and seemed to lose interest. Well, you tried, Herbie, she thought, rather more incensed by this vulgarity than by any other since she had come home. You had visions of safely separating from your perfect marriage for a few nights with a free whore, didn't you? Ah, that's immoral, Herbie, luckiest-man-in-the-world Herbie. That was awfully insulting of you.

At last it was time to leave. She spent a few moments with Esther, glanced covertly at Mama, troubled and hurt once again that Mama hadn't urged her to stay on. As Myron carried her suitcase to the rented car, she went to her mother, who raised herself heavily from

Tut's reading chair. Mama said, in Yiddish, "You cried at your father's grave."

Judith nodded.

Mama nodded, too, and for the last time extended her arms and they embraced, this time so feelingly that Judith feared she might cry again.

"You'll dress warm," Mama said. "You'll watch yourself up in the airplane. You'll write here a letter sometime."

"Yes, Mama."

Behind the steering wheel, scarcely a block away from Spruce Street, she began to weep once more. The tears came easily, but the reasons did not. She switched on the car radio. A cheerful, lively polka was playing.

Halfway to the airport, she nibbled on the idea of not flying back to New York just yet. Frivolous, maybe, especially with so much unfinished business waiting for her, but the prospect of checking into a hotel and sorting herself out for a few hours grew more and more inviting. She dismissed the idea as too frivolous. And saw the sign pointing to Pittsburgh, and headed there.

And remembered Don Lovell, her William Penn Hotel lover who was responsible for her becoming Judith Harrison too young, before she had been ready to quit being Judith Hershkowitz.

He had been about thirty-five then, would be roughly forty-eight now. Was he living in Pittsburgh, with a wife and mortgage and 2.1 children? she wondered, keeping the radio blaring at top volume. Was he as dazzlingly handsome?

I met him only a few weeks after the end of the world, that doomsday realization that Buzz Wyler would never call me again. On Sundays I took a class in modern dance, a mishagas that Tut and Mama tolerated only because it was sponsored by the Jewish Y in Pittsburgh. The instructor was Don Lovell. He was a Gimbel's haberdashery department clerk by trade, a famous choreographer by ambition, and he picked up extra money on Sundays by trying to teach teen-age oxen how not to stomp on their own feet. I was one of the non-oxen. I might have developed into no more than an average dancer if I'd stayed at it, but I was light on my feet, with a sense of grace. And I became teacher's pet.

He knew I wasn't quite seventeen years old. We got into a habit of his walking me to the bus stop after class, sometimes stopping on the way for coffee, and he would look at me so intently and say I couldn't be that young, that I was much too sophisticated and mature— preposterous talk, of course, and of course I lowered my eyes and ate it all up. Looking back, he was an anthology of clichés— his trap of a marriage to a clutching, frigid wife who was holding him back from following his destiny, his need for constant reas- surance, his hunger for affection—but they didn't come out as platitudes, and I, sophisticated and mature, absolutely believed every spoken and unspoken word.

Then came June, my seventeenth birthday in the William Penn Hotel. We'd planned it over several Sundays, at first by double message jokes, gradually by guiltily examining the wrongness of it, finally by agreeing that we were too profoundly in love to be restrained by outdated social strictures. And Uncle Charlie saw us enter the elevator, and from Regal City I went to New York City.

I went to New York because New York seemed—logical. I'd never been there and I knew no one there, but it was nearer than Africa or Asia. The vastness and wall-to-wall impersonality of Manhattan petrified me. I telephoned Esther, collect, from my first lodging, the YWHA (how's that address for a fallen woman?), and Esther was still shocked by what Mama and Tut had done, and she promised to smooth things over so that I could come home where I belonged, and she wired me a hundred dollars. She called me two days later. She hadn't yet been able to smooth things over. She was worried about me. She would bring the folks to their senses. "It's all for the best," I said, voice steady, upper lip stiff as putty. "I'm hardly unpacked and I'm already getting offers for good jobs. Thanks for this loan, Esther. It'll be paid back before you know it."

What does a pretty, witless, directionless girl do when she arrives in New York in the 1960s, besides cry a lot and stay scared a lot? She gets a part-time job to pay the rent and she makes the rounds of all the theatrical agents, one of whom will transform her into a Broadway star by next curtain time. I had neither talent nor much interest in the theater, but that was beside the point. I had looks. Nothing much to say, but plenty of looks. You're not like the rest of us, Judith, *Esther had once said to me.* You're heading somewhere, you're not going to get lost in the woods. Sure. In those first weeks in New York, no one offered me work—well, there was one firm offer to* star in art films, real feelthy peectures, and I ran all the way back to the Y, so that doesn't count—but everyone offered rosy predictions. With that face and figure, little lady, you're damn tootin' not going to get lost in the woods. No one seriously recommended that I learn how to do something other than thrust the chest forward and look beautiful. Oh my, here I go sounding like a sinned-against, storm-tossed waif. I wasn't. I could have learned how to do something useful. No one stopped me. No one but me.

My name became Judith Harrison because one of the epicene young actors I met on those masochistic rounds convinced me that Hershkowitz just wouldn't do on a marquee. I occasionally still regret that I took the Harrison copout—I, who've always felt reasonably content to belong to a people who wrote the Twenty-third Psalm and the Ten Commandments—but it seemed right when I did it; it was a bridges-burning act, a once-and-for-all liberation from Regal City. The pain of that liberation didn't go away, but the often numbing loneliness began to recede. The epicene young actor introduced me to his friends, who introduced me to their friends. I moved into the Bleecker Street rabbit warren of an at-permanent-liberty actress to cut down on rent, and there were spaghetti and Chianti parties most nights, and we would all sit around and talk lavishly of our impending success.

I sat around with them for two years. Fantastic. I worked—as a pretty hatcheck girl, as a pretty receptionist, as a pretty dancer in a three-girl chorus line in a Forest Hills nightclub—but what I did best was sit around, sit around and enjoy being congratulated for being so pretty. Fantastic! I sat around, and I slept around, ever suspicious yet ever hopeful that this lover or the next would love me even if I had an accident that scarred the face and body. Super-fantastic, because the unscarred face and body were really all I had to offer. I taught myself how to talk funny and be amusing and now and then I managed to say something that posed as thoughtfulness; I wanted desperately to be taken seriously, but that doesn't happen often to us vapids. What, truly, did I expect to get?

I know what I did get. When I was nineteen, I got first prize in the beauty contest. Kenyon Dairies was looking for The Kenyon Girl, who would epitomize robust, beautiful good health and, by way of nationwide publicity, help them sell their milk and cheese and butter. The crown came with a check for fifty thousand dollars and a year of *traveling throughout the United States and everywhere: heralded appearances at supermarket openings, smiling perpetually and holding up a lot of milk and cheese and butter in public, photographs in magazines and on billboards, clothes and sumptuous hotels, everything sublimely vapid, Cinderella's dream come true.*

And it got me W. W. Molenkamp, who owned Kenyon Dairies. Four months after the coronation, I was taken to meet him in his Princess suite in Bermuda, one of the half-dozen hotel suites he maintained year-round. Except that he was incalculably rich, all I'd heard about him was that he never went out in public, that he changed wives frequently, and that, for a busy man in his middle fifties, he spent a disproportionate amount of time in bed with young women. He stood from his desk as I was ushered in, and he bowed, but he didn't smile. He said, "It's come to my attention that you behaved in a rowdy and reprehensible manner in Houston several evenings ago."

I blinked. I'd been in Houston, for a Kenyon executives' convention at the Shamrock, to do my thing: recite my pat, gooey speech about how heavenly it was to be The Kenyon Girl, sign autographs and exchange happy inanities with the guests and their wives. One executive, reeling drunk and boisterous, led me to the center of the floor and, though there was no music, loudly demanded that I dance with him. I cooperated in the dreary gag, I explained now, because I had no way of determining just how important an executive he was, and I was afraid to say no. I denied rowdiness. It had been adolescent fun, I conceded, but I certainly didn't think—

"You are not being engaged to think," he interrupted softly. "You are being engaged to promote the image of innocence and health. Your contract doesn't require that you evaluate the importance of anyone except me. In future, you will be friendly and pleasant with everyone, but any further whorelike behavior will—"

Then I heard myself say, "You go to hell, Mr. Molenkamp," and I stalked out.

The Molenkamp-Kenyon plane that had flown me to Bermuda flew me to Miami, where I was to be photographed the following morning—a session I was sure wouldn't take place because at that moment I was certainly in the process of being fired. I entered the Fontainebleau suite. There were ten million roses and one card. The card read Congratulations. W.W.M.

I returned to the suite the next day after the pictures were shot. He was there. Smiling. He kissed me. I'd never been kissed by a millionaire. I'd never slapped a millionaire's face. I slapped that millionaire's face and I yelled, "That should go a long way to prove that I'm just not any good at whorelike behavior!" He was amused and that made me all the angrier. "Stop smiling!" I shouted. "You're the one who's rowdy and reprehensible! If I'm fired, then get it over with! If you have some idea I'm going to play matinees with you, you couldn't be wronger! I'm not being paid to think, but I'm not being paid to lay you, either!"

And thus began the romance between Moley and Judith.

There are clever ways to rationalize whoredom. The most comfortable way is to deny it. I denied it; it took me a couple of weeks, but I successfully got the hang of it. When I wasn't being The Kenyon Girl, I was being Moley's. He was invariably kind to me; owners of whores never lower themselves to such niceties. He brought me presents and remembered my birthday and fed me aspirin when I had a cold; there's a surrogate father right there, in spades. He was abysmal as a sexual lover, with the moanings about his small mannelijkheid and the periodic impotence that could be repaired, when it was, only by my whispering elaborate sickie fantasies into his ear, yet all that was rewarding and endearing, too; the rationale was that I was returning kindness to a kind man. The holidays on his long, long, fully-manned yacht took precious little getting used to; so did talking idly over dinner about a trip and then poof, deplaning at Heathrow or Orly. He had a wife somewhere. I was his mistress. The fact that he liked me made it all right.

He got it into his head that I should be in motion pictures. No, a thousand times no, I protested when I saw he was serious; Kenyon Girling was one thing; acting was something else. All that's needed is confidence, he said. Which is what I don't have a drop of, I protested. He smiled, and bought Grafton Studios.

Panic. Arguments. Threats. I was plunked in the Malibu beach house—not bad plunking of itself, but no instant cure for the who-am-I shakes, either. When Moley went out of town, I was totally unmoored. I walked on the beach, and I swam. I read, with unimpressive attention spans. Every time I tried to get drunk, I got sick instead. I found me a lover. Randy Grant-né-Vince Bugliosi was a

172

*male starlet at Universal, no actor (look who's casting stones; the
talent of the two of us couldn't have filled an ant's nostril) but
presentable and effective on screen as long as he didn't have to do
more than register concern at the approach of the Apaches. Vince
was safe as could be, as challenging as the directions on a Kool-Aid
package. The safe thing about Vince was his consistency, his unfet-
tered understanding of what women, all women, were. They were
things with openings to be filled. Okay. Vince was uncomplicated.
Okay.*

*Sam Gallagher was not okay. He was the first man, during that
Looney Tunes existence of mine, to tell me—and he did it repeatedly—that I had dimension and potential. He started to make
small noises that sounded like a marriage proposal coming on. He
got too close, and rattled me too much, and I ran, ran toward more
Moleys who would look out for me and not expect in return more
than I was able to give.*

*Strange, maybe not so strange, to remember now: One book I read
while on the run was* Season of Silence, *by Barbara Breisky and
Martha Hanaday, two young sociologists with the thesis that women
were entrapped and imprisoned by a male-dominated culture that
trained them from birth to be domestic servants and sexual serfs, that
there was only one way to escape and that was to recognize that they
were human beings before they were anything else. The title was
from something by Susan B. Anthony,* circa *1868. The full quote
was, "There shall never be another season of silence until women
have the same rights men have on this green earth."*

*The book was overheated, primarily hysterical, probably useful
for applicant spinsters with little else to do but find themselves by
themselves. It interested me but it had nothing to do with me. I was
set. I had looks and I could amuse. I wasn't going to get lost in the
woods . . .*

In Pittsburgh, Judith parked and checked into the first respectable looking hotel she came to, bought the Sunday *Press* in the lobby,
and was taken up to an agreeably impersonal room. Once alone, she
saw Tut several times, for a moment each time, and being alone
wasn't as cozy as it had promised to be in the car, but she told herself
it would be harebrained to leave because of that.

The *Press* carried a front page, wire service interview with Ray

Pallino who, with his unique blend of pugnacious authority, re-capped the Hartley charge and predicted that those who had hoped to embarrass Judith Harrison would themselves have their dirty necks wrung before the trial was done.

She also read, in the book section, that Norman Hanaday was in town, for two days, to promote his book, *How Fascism Won*. He was stopping at the Hilton.

The Hilton. I could phone him, she thought, phone and gamble that Martha isn't with him. Identify myself, maybe suggest a drink if he has the time. Jog his memory gently, remind him of how nice he was to me that night after the Columbia Heights pistol range. He'd remember. Of course he'd remember. The question is, Would he want to bother with me?

There's one direct way to find out.

She asked the Hilton operator if she might leave a message for Mr. Norman Hanaday. She was asked in turn to wait, please, and she did, and she heard a sleepy, "Yes?"

"Mr. Hanaday?"

"Yes?"

"Don't shoot me," she said. "This is Judith Harrison."

". . . Judith . . ."

"Harrison. You bought me coffee once. I never repaid you."

Awake: "Oh, yes! Hello! Where are you?"

"In Pittsburgh. At the Gateway. I obviously woke you up."

"God, I'm glad you did. What time is it?"

"About eight-thirty."

"Eight-thirty," he said. "The Gateway. What are you doing in about an hour?"

"Nothing."

"How wonderful to hear from you! I'll be there in about an hour, all right?"

"Fine," Judith answered. "It'll be nice to see you again." Then, quickly: "Oh, wait. Could you buy me a copy of *How Fascism Won*, if I promise to pay you back for it?"

"Sure," he said. "I even get a discount, I think. Hey, I could make a profit and a royalty all at one shot here. This isn't such a bad racket after all."

17

On the plane to New York Martha Hanaday felt relaxed, pleased with the way things had gone last night. Oh, she'd still been a little tense when Jan Atwell had picked her up at the airport, and even back at Jan's apartment. But she'd come out of that, and the meeting had been great, and she was in command again.

Jan Atwell's small apartment, near Scollay Square, had been a clutter of pamphlets, paintings, books, magazines and sculpture, testimonies to the grandeurs of the homosexual life. *Will she serve me something to drink and put her hand on my knee?* Martha had wondered with distaste. *I've never been alone with a lesbian before, certainly never one this openly dedicated. I've been with blacks whose every expressed thought seesawed between pronouncements of black pride and attacks on white oppression. But that's different, isn't it? No Negro ever made a sexual overture to me.*

Jan Atwell, tiny and in her thirties, wore a pantsuit and close-cropped hair, but that was the fashion; there was nothing masculine or . . . strange about her. Her implicit decency had shown itself when she'd heard Martha on the telephone *("This is Martha Hanaday. I'm at the Boston Airport. I don't know whom else to call. Would you come and get me?")* and had sped to her without a single question. In the car from the airport to here, Martha had spoken evenly, almost as if she were describing the odd, not really grave, plight of someone else, of her stupid immobility, omitting all details but wordlessly calling for kindness and getting it. "Dr. Atwell diagnoses it as a clear case of exhaustion," Jan Atwell declared benignly, when they'd reached the apartment. "You stay here with us for as long as you like. Everything's easier after a good rest. How about a drink? Brandy? Cognac if there's any left?"

"I must be such a nuisance. May I have some tea?"

"Sure. Tetley or Mary Jane?"

"Oh, either. No sugar. A little bit of lemon if you have it. Let me help. I forbid any fuss."

"Sit. Kick your shoes off."

She watched the young woman go, saw the pleasant roll of her tight buttocks. I *am* better now, she thought. But I ought to be home, not here relying on a stranger to comfort me, to mother me. I'm *me*, for Heaven's sake! *I* comfort and mother. This is . . . unseemly. And rather nice, being taken care of. Yes.

Her pleasant hostess came with the pleasant tea, and Martha, with so very much to attend to in New York, heard herself ask if it might be possible to hold last night's meeting tonight. Jan Atwell asked if she truly felt up to it and she said yes. "Let me see what I can arrange, this late in the day," the young woman said and left the room again, tight buttocks rolling again. Above the fake fireplace was a semi-abstraction of two women in naked, non-erotic embrace. What is it like to make love with another woman? Martha wondered. I've studied the root origins of homosexuality and enough abnormal psychology to qualify as an expert in the area, surely, but in an entirely intellectual capacity. What do such women, separate from acting out abnormal fantasies, give one another, receive from one another?

Warmth. Tenderness. Warmth. Whatever it is that a woman and man can't give and get from each other. Sick, certainly, because Nature's rules are immutable. Still . . . still . . .

Shocking. I don't care. I want our bodies to touch. I want to feel the warmth of our mouths, the heat of our bodies together. We'll do degrading and absurd and loving things with each other, to each other, monstrously impersonal and unheard of things. Here. Beginning and ending here. Ah yes here, don't be cold or distant or spiteful or hateful, make good, generous, voluptuous, loving love to me . . .

Jan Atwell came back, screwing a filter cigarette into a long ivory holder. "The hall's free and so are some of the key sisters," she said enthusiastically. "It won't be what last night might've been—Liz Kyle seems to be in parts unknown; guaranteed-unreliable type, anyway—but we're all set for half-past eight. Sisters will be calling other sisters, so we may have part of a slam-bang turnout, after all. Hey, your face is awfully flushed!"

176

"I'm—fine. I just assume you explained my absence last night and my availability tonight with some—ah . . ."

"Oh, that. You had a virus that you sweated out. No problem. We're all grateful to have you aboard even a day late. There ought to be a million more straights like you, brave enough to stand up publicly and be counted on to help us fight our battles. We appreciate it." There were other chairs in the room, but she sat beside Martha. "If you're sure you're okay, we could start now going over tonight's agenda."

Martha agreed. They asked each other questions, drawing each other out, and at one point in a burst of approval, the smiling young woman reached over and touched Martha's arm. Martha instinctively recoiled.

Jan Atwell's smile vanished. She sat away and said, almost icily, "I'm sorry you did that."

"Did what?" Martha asked innocently, knowing precisely what she had done.

"Some lesbians are promiscuous, Sister Martha. Some straights are, too. Some Poles are dumb and some blacks are shiftless and some Irish are drunks."

Continued innocence was pointless. "I know what you're saying," Martha nodded. "Please forgive me."

"Mmm. I hope you know. Because the supporters we don't need are the shiny liberals who suspect, deep in their hearts, that we're sexual freaks. We're not running some perpetual campaign to convert straights. What we're living for and striving to do is teach the world that we're normal human beings with the same right to life, liberty, and the pursuit of happiness as anyone else. I'm very serious about this. The sisters you'll meet tonight are very hip, very sensitive to who's with us really and who isn't."

Martha looked at her earnestly, nodded again, and they shared smiles, and the civility resumed. As they talked, Martha silently pleaded, *Help me. Someone help me. I'm drowning.*

The Sisters of Sappho hall had been a quarter filled. Martha was introduced lavishly as the noted author and columnist, indisputably the most widely admired contemporary champion of freedom for all women. "Unlike some so-called, self-styled libertarians," the introduction built, "Sister Martha has never been selectively pro-freedom, has never said, 'I'm for freedom for all women except lesbians.' She is a tower of conviction and strength, and it's with joy and humble pride that we ask you to greet her this evening."

The applause was thunderous, and Martha, vigorously and unreservedly accepted, responded with immediate, total authority. At the lectern, a moment after she began to speak, she knew it was going to go right, exquisitely right. The feeling of elation was gigantic. The nightmares hadn't happened; she was Martha Hanaday again. Her reason for being here was clear, her memory of the Elizabeth Kyle details unclouded. She spoke lucidly, needing no notes, spoke indeed with conviction and strength. *I'm where I belong,* she thought, happier than she had been in ever so long. *People are looking up to me, listening to me, respecting me and all I have to tell them. I'd forgotten who I was, who I am. I'll never falter again. I can feel it. Norman will come to his senses. Stephanie Wall will be so proud of me.*

Electricity charged the meeting, through her speech and throughout the question and discussion periods which she also controlled. Yes, she would keep the promise she made this night to devote as many of her syndicated columns as might be required to the Elizabeth Kyle case. Yes, she would be perfectly willing and ready to march with her sisters in any struggle that demanded fair play, understood they were hungry for mass-media forums she could provide, and was prepared to provide them. She wasn't sure of when or exactly how the open discussion got around to Judith Harrison, whom one of the audience maintained was no acknowledged supporter of SOS but who nonetheless was being manhandled—"the word is meant literally"—in Hartley simply because she had been born female. Would Sister Martha defend her, as well? "Of course, if I were asked to," Martha assured. "Either all women have the right to own themselves and their decisions or none of them has."

The evening was wonderful. They were made secure and confident because of her. The elation stayed.

Back in Jan Atwell's apartment—Jan's and her roommate's, a slim, almond-eyed girl named Mac—Martha sat with them, and drank wine with them, a few drops more than she usually allowed herself, and listened to them praise her as a superbly unifying, rallying force. They offered to open the couch for themselves and give her their bed; she thanked them and said she would take the couch. Jan, in a taffeta, daintily feminine robe, came to her after she was settled under a blanket. "All A-Okay?" Jan asked. "What can I get you?"

You.

No. I don't mean that at all. There's enough good feeling in me about myself now to last the rest of my life.

"Not a thing," she replied. "I couldn't be more comfortable. I'll be asleep in two and a half seconds."

"Thanks again, Sister Martha. For everything."

"Good night."

And she had fallen into a sweet, dreamless sleep with ease.

Now, on the plane to New York, her sense of well-being continued, well-being and intermittently even peace. The depression she had expected would rain down on her, once she was sufficiently clear to review the parade of emotional onslaughts over these past days, did not come. Sobriety and sadness at how unmoored she had temporarily let herself become, but not helpless and wasteful depression; she would work that unmooring into perspective, learn from it, be better for it.

There were disagreeable tie-ups at Kennedy about her suitcase that had flown ahead of her, but it was reclaimed, and the airbus driver who took her and a handful of other passengers to Manhattan was a cheery man who sang Verdi, robustly off-key, and she and the other passengers laughed. The Columbia Heights apartment was still and spotless when she entered it, and she called to Bernice, the cleaning lady who worked full days here on Saturdays and should surely not yet have left. Bernice wasn't in the apartment, nor was Martha's secretary, Nancy, who normally was here at this hour on Saturdays. There was mail in her office, and the newspapers, and Nancy had left messages. One message was about a barrage of Saturday calls from Nicole Rooney, of Sisters of Sappho New York headquarters; here is the number and please return calls. None was from Norman.

The office phone jangled as she was assembling some priority order of whom to call first, Dr. Wall's widower or Norman. Nicole

Rooney declared, "Sister Martha! *Fi*nally! I've been ringing you every hour on the hour, it seems, since Jan phoned me yesterday morning about that gung-ho meeting on Friday night. Where've you *been?*"

"I just got in. Yesterday morning? You mean this morning. The meeting was last night."

" 'The meeting was—' Oh-oh, I can see you and I're two birds of a feather, we never can keep track of time, can we?" She chuckled. "Well, the fire you lighted in Boston was Friday, for your information, and we think it's just marvelous that you're going to lead the march to Hartley. We're busting with plans and suggestions and whatever to discuss with you."

Martha sat. "Say all that again, would you? Slowly?"

The Sisters of Sappho, as many as possible from around the country, would descend on Hartley on Monday, a week from tomorrow, the day Judith Harrison's trial was to begin. With television and the press sure to be there, the spotlight of publicity would be priceless. Martha had agreed not only to participate in the march but to lead it. A statement to that effect had been issued to the press. "One of the reasons I was trying to reach you," said Nicole Rooney, "was to read you the statement before I gave it to the papers, but we really couldn't keep waiting, not with an exciting story like this one. I know you'll be satisfied."

Martha guardedly made her repeat that today was Sunday.

"Unless I'm losing my mind," the voice said cheerfully, "today is definitely, definitely Sunday."

18

Judith liked Norman Hanaday, liked him enormously.

They ate a leisurely dinner in her hotel's dining room. Neither of them minded that there was no legal sale of alcohol on Sundays in Pittsburgh. She explained what had taken her to Regal City, resisted parading a list of her still-tangled feelings—he hardly needed to listen to all that, she was sure—yet careful not to feed him the impression that she was without feeling. He was obviously weary, but they talked for a long while—the waitress glared at them from time to time—about peddling books on the air, about Hartley, about things and people that had happened to each of them since their first meeting in Columbia Heights, about Martha (though warily), and he said, "I'm awfully glad you called to repay me for that cup of coffee. I feel absolutely relaxed and absolutely happy."

"So do I," Judith said, smiling.

"How did we get to be old, close friends so fast? I'm the original birth-to-death New Englander, stodgy and stiff as a board with people until I've known them for twenty years."

"Give me all the credit," she kidded. "You had nothing to do with it. Unstodging is my specialty."

The waitress came, pointed to the check she had brought nearly an hour before and suggested, free of subtlety, that it was time to go awready. Norman nodded and reached for the check, but Judith got it first. He protested. She signed her name and room number, scribbled "Tip—20%" rather than puzzle over arithmetic, and the waitress went away with it and Judith said, "It's frustrating to be a liberated woman. Should we let you pay because we're worried about emasculating you, or do we work at equality? I called you. See what troublemakers we women can be sometimes?"

He laughed. "I've noticed. Where were you hiding when I was going to college? I was working as a janitor to help pay the tuition and expenses—thirty cents an hour—and the dates I bought dinner for were getting fat allowances from home."

"I wasn't hiding. I was all those girls you dated. Then. Shall we leave?"

He read his wristwatch in the lobby. "Midnight? Twelve o'clock? No wonder that waitress was glaring us into the floor! You must be tired."

"Not really. What about you?"

"Not in the least. Want to run up and down the block a few times?"

"To quote a Columbia professor I used to know, 'Not in the least.' " Evenly, then, not seductively: "We could talk some more up in the room if you're really not tired. It's not Villa d'Este, but there's a free ice cube machine outside the door."

"Are you *sure* you're not worn out?"

She grinned. "We do sound like a couple on a Golden Age date, don't we?"

This is mischievous fire I'm playing with, she thought as they were lifted in the elevator. I want his arms around me. I want us to sleep together, side by side, close to each other. Not sex. I'm not interested in sex, not really. How do you ask a tall order like that of a normal man: Let us be close in bed, under warm covers, but don't touch me here or here or here?

You don't. You can't.

I don't want to sleep alone.

And I don't want to use this good, very dear man. It wouldn't be a casual one night stand for either of us. Damn me, anyway. And damn him, too, for sending me all those signals that spell rapport. Here comes the next chapter of *Perils of Pauline*, maybe.

Near the ice cube machine on her floor was a soft drink machine. "Let's live it up tonight," he said, pointing to it, and Judith laughed her assent and unlocked the door, aware of damp palms. They sat in low chairs separated by a round table, sipping dreadful cherry soda pop, and the light banter gradually faded and he said, "I'd like very much to see you again."

Uh-oh. Play this right.

"I don't hear an answer," he prompted after a moment.

"I'm trying to form one," she said. "We're both busy travelers.

Tonight was coincidental luck; we both happened to be free. I have some chock-full schedules ahead of me, starting with Hartley, and I do travel like a night thief, and . . ."

"Truth, now. Are those devious ways of telling me there's a special man you're interested in?"

Okay, the truth, she decided. "No, those are devious ways of reminding you of Martha without saying her name."

He watched her. "I see. We've been skirting Martha pretty skillfully, haven't we?"

"Yes. I'm juggling more than enough sticky situations as it is, Norman. We might do something foolish, like get involved with each other, and that would invite some awfully messy problems for all of us."

He nodded understanding, and said after a small pause, "You're probably right."

And probably nuts, she thought, and warned herself, *Don't follow it up. Let it lie.* The return to safer subjects mercifully came, and finally—it was after one and the next room's squawky television set had been turned off—he spoke of how late the hour was and rose to leave. They stood inches apart, and it could have ended cleanly then, a good-luck forehead kiss, an antiseptic handshake. Judith looked at him, deliberately and seriously, and said, deliberately and seriously, "I'm glad I called to offer to repay that cup of coffee, too . . ."

It began.

It began without words, began with feigned and real astonishment that it was beginning, began with a cautious array of kisses that tested how far they were prepared to go. It began with passion, equally and for moments ungovernably, began with Judith's determination that it must not last past the night. It began with the nervous laughter at the dress zipper that stuck, with the welcoming bed, with the jolt of mutual wonderment and happiness as their bodies touched. It began with his asking if she wanted the light off and her answering, "Not unless you do," began with the bedlight on, began without embarrassment or awkwardness, began without shame.

"Not sex. I'm not interested in sex, not really" . . . When did I think up that gem? Long ago, in the elevator. *O God it's so good to make love*

with a man I truly like, truly like. Yes. Ah yes, how lovely passion is when it's real passion, how much lovelier it is when lovers have names, Norman. Norman. Norman. Norman . . .

"Norman," she said aloud. "Thank you. Thank you for staying, thank—" His mouth covered hers, and Judith clutched at him, her eyes gleaming, arms loving, body glistening, and received him, clutching all the more with her arms around him, and helped, felt velvet stroke after velvet stroke after velvet stroke and squeezed him, squeezed him deeper and still deeper, relaxed as a pace started, loved his chest falling rhythmically on her breasts, loved the chugging little sounds from his throat, loved, loved.

Love. Love. "Soon," he grunted. *Yes, darling, yes, fill me, yes, God this whole room is tilting, Tut's dead, fill me, dearest Norman, forgive me Tut, it's happening all through me, yes darling now we're making it together. Oh. Ohhhh yes oh yes oh yes yes.* "Darling! Darling!"

"What were we saying?" he asked later, gently, teasingly.

"We were saying thank you for staying, we were saying you're a wonderful man, we were saying we ought to keep holding each other and nap a while. I'm almost positive that's what we were saying."

"Then why've you stayed with Martha all these years?" Judith asked, a little before morning.

Norman shrugged. "For the most hostile of reasons, I guess: Pity. For all her seeming toughness, Martha is terribly fragile. Yes, I know the psychiatric textbook footnotes by heart: a man who stays and stays with a disturbed wife has some inner disturbances of his own. Yeah. Maybe. But the trouble with those footnotes is that they're so conveniently simplistic. 'Fault'—that's a clumsy, meaningless word when you talk about the failure of a marriage. A marriage doesn't go to hell because one partner is all bad and one partner is all good. The point is, I've had it. I'm done, *fini, kaput, finite,* and however you say *finished* in Swahili. The botched-up kids, the role-playing of wronged woman and guilty man, the fights masquerading as discussions, the hemmed-in this, the held-in that—enough and enough. Would you be grievously offended if I told you I favor this breast over this one?"

"You bet'cha."

Judith woke at eight. Norman was dressed, and sitting on the edge of the bed, smiling, his hand on her bare arm. "Nuthouse duty calls," he said. "A radio interview in an hour. I'll come right back."

"No. I'd love to stay the millennium, but no, Norman—there's much too much work waiting for me in New York. But now we know how to reach each other, and we will. *I'll* see to that. I plan to be a bloody bloodhound."

"You were right last night: this could get serious between us."

"Mmm. First, though, I have to read your book. Will you still feel that way if I send you a bad report on it?"

"You wouldn't dare." They embraced and kissed. " 'Do not go gentle into that good night,' Judith, dear. Take very good care of yourself." And he was gone.

How serious? Judith thought on the way to the Pittsburgh airport. He was convinced he was through with Martha. Judith was not so convinced. He was a man of substantial character and often acute perception. And he was also a guilty man, she suspected, loyalties perhaps not so defined as he thought. And what about me, she wondered, me, the queen of hit-and-run? I like him more than I've liked any man in an appallingly long time. I'm ready for a . . . damn, why is something as cold-sounding as 'relationship' the only accurate word?

Or am I ready? If all the barriers were down, if Norman were indeed bird-free, would *I* measure up for more than weeks or months? I could hurt him hard by pulling my copyrighted stunt of cutting out when love takes on shape and glue.

Gloomy attitude, considering that I'm happy. I *am* happy, *am* contented, and how about *that* for new fresh air? I do like that man. I do want to see him again, and then again.

At the air terminal, the sense of contentment dissolved abruptly. Waiting for a plane, she read in the Monday morning newspaper that Sisters of Sappho was preparing a massive demonstration in Hartley. With Martha Hanaday as leader.

Rage came, and then worry, and both merged with questions upon more questions during the flight to New York. Am I furious because she's out to steal my spotlight? Judith asked herself. No, I don't think so, I hope that's not why I'm fuming; anyone has a right to protest anything legitimate anywhere. I'm worried about harm, about backfiring. I remember my innings with Sisters of Sappho all too bruisingly—that overly noisy, self-defeating, indiscriminately destructive gang, as representative of all lesbians' civil rights and civil liberties as the Black Panthers are of all blacks, as the JDL is of world Jewry. They asked me to join them in blasting the Boston schools for dropping that lesbian teacher, Elizabeth Kyle, and I said, "I'll give my opinion whenever I'm asked, on changing sexual mores or repressive sexual taboos or anything else that hampers human freedom. But I won't—can't—become identified with a special problem or group without distorting the larger picture of women's rights throughout the society." They attacked me, of course. That was their right. I didn't add my personal observations and impressions, which would have gone, "You seem to be the lesbians' worst enemy. Your chief interest appears to be to throw as many monkey wrenches as possible into the machinery of progress so you can go on bleating 'See how the straight world crushes us.' I'm all for speaking out against injustices, but never in the company of closet destructivists."

Was that, is that, blatantly old-fashioned bigotry simply dressed up in fancy clothes?

No. I'm convinced it wasn't, and isn't. I agreed then and I agree now that every woman has the right to make her own decisions about her sex life. But there are practical considerations to the fight I have to fight. They can obscure the basic issues with shrill demands for their own special situations; they can make Hartley into a circus of absurdity; they can turn the people I'm trying to reach away from the basic issues.

Damn it. Damn it . . .

When the questions of intent and ramification brought only more questions that couldn't be answered at 26,000 feet, she forced herself to move on to other things. Here, on the back cover of *How Fascism Won*, was Norman—an unflattering and untrue photograph, missing the goodness in his good face. Judith had reluctantly agreed once to take a speedreading course, the better to locate key words and phrases in the tons of too-often windy written material she needed to tackle, and opened Norman's book and decided after several pages to start again, decided it would be a disservice, almost an act of taking him lightly, if she were to zip through it. What she read, when her concentration wasn't blurred by bright images in her head of Tut and Martha Hanaday and Peter, was extremely skillful, an always-reasoned yet indignant moral outcry, all the more personally effective for her, for she viewed Norman as a quiet, eminently reasoning man not given to exclamation points. She read on and—

Suddenly she glanced up, hearing herself.

Peter. I was thinking of Peter for a moment. Now isn't that strange! Or was it?

When concentration became hopeless, she closed the book, and remembered . . .

Two jokes.

One: Joe E. Lewis was called a rummy and he answered, "I resent that. I don't deny it, but I resent it."

The other: A man says, "You say you'd sleep with me for a thousand dollars. Would you sleep with me for two dollars?" The girl huffily says, "What do you think I am?" and the man says, "We've already established that. What we're establishing now is price."

Which pretty well says all there is to say about me, from the time of Moley till several years after Moley. I moved from new lover's yacht to jet to island to country to continent with all the grace of an aristocratic hooker. The working hours were long but the pay was dandy, and I was terribly good at my earn-while-you-learn job. It consisted of making nice to my keepers, one at a time, each of whom lasted an average of three to six months, of my looking presentable on his arm at openings and in splendid cafés, of entertaining his friends and clients with vivacity and don't-touch seductiveness, of lavishly applauding his feats as a lover.

Not every arrangement was a success. One keeper wanted me to make lie-down nice to his friends and clients ("What do you think I am?"). Another wanted to prove his affection for me by beating me up. On the whole, though, I had no complaints and plenty of fringe benefits. I saw a lot of the world. I met many people, shiny and decidedly non-Regal City people, most of them beautiful, many of them interesting, some of them useful to themselves and to others. There was even a pension plan provided in the job; one farseeing keeper set up a trust fund which I could call on in my old age—say, at about twenty-six. If I resented what some people were surely calling

187

me, I didn't deny it, a plus side to my character; maybe a kurveh *is what I am, you sanctimonious gawkers, but his wife and family don't treat him well and I do. So there.*

So where? There isn't much of a market for my line of work once the crow's feet sprout and the silicone injections don't take, so where did I suppose I was eventually heading? To marriage, the obvious end in itself, I kept saying; marry rich, and the sanctimonious gawkers will stop gawking and you'll hold on to all this, besides. A natural enough cake-and-eat-it-too ambition. Only I couldn't do it; I had either cold feet or the beginning of a functioning brain cell, mix 'em or match 'em, but I couldn't go through with anything as whorey as marrying without love. Doodness dwacious, not this *idealistic mooncalf! I nearly did. I met a friend of a friend of a client of a friend of a keeper, while I was between keepers and he was between weddings, and I spent a week at his villa outside St. Tropez and he popped the question and I said yes. And ran. Ran back to the perpetual ballroom, shaking a bit.*

Whoops, there she goes again—the hard luck kid whimpering I didn't know how miserable I was while I was cozying up with the Duck Flambé Belle Terrasse. *Of course I wasn't miserable. Not happy, but not often miserable, either.*

What did get curiouser and curiouser, though, as I pressed onward through that perpetual ballroom, was that no one pointed out my worst sin: letting what could be a first-rate mind stay blank and resourceless. I wasn't quite a dimwit—I read more than menus, a radical act in my sorority—but there was a continually uneasy pact between that mind and me: if I didn't bug it, it wouldn't bug me. The true name of the game was running for running's sake, to live life in pleasurable absentia, to avoid pain and reality at all costs. Above all, never to whine. People, men-people, could get easily irritated with whiners, and men-people were the ones who paid for the ballroom.

When did I take those first timid steps toward an inventory of myself? At twenty-four, very, very gradually and always with welcomed interruptions. I was still running and laughing it up, yet there were spasms of time when laughing it up made my jaws get tired, when I could look at that black thing circling about me and finally call it by its right name: depression. I was living, sort of, in

*London that summer, in a spacious Mayfair flat with Tony Barrow,
theatrical producer, veddy Etonian and veddy much devoted to his
saintly wife and supah kiddies who sped to greet him when he got
home to Brighton on weekends. At gatherings, Tony introduced me
as his protégée, not entirely a euphemism because he pulled a
complex of strings and all of a ludicrous sudden I was Judith
Harrison the television personality. "Television personality" is a
euphemism. Every time BBC did a chitchat panel show I was
summoned, bringing along the purty face and the low-cut dress and
the amusing, brainless chatter. It was scarcely a career, and I was
always sure I was falling on that purty face, but the critics liked the
smashing, featherheaded Ameddican, so I wasn't about to argue. At
a party one night in the Mayfair flat, an American named Morrie
Forrest said he produced shows for television in the States, said he'd
caught me on the telly here a few times, thought he could give me a
helping hand if and when I looked him up in New York. Thank you,
I said, retrieving my leg from his helping hand.*

*Parties followed parties, waking in the morning to depression and
rootlessness became a normal way to wake, more parties followed
more parties. The last party in London was that autumn, when one
of the guests hushed the crowded room by calling me a parasite and a
home wrecker and a whore. She was Tony Barrow's wife, and I left
the hall, head held duchess-high, and I fled to the flat and cracked
wide open. I flew to New York, a great place to hide.*

*Morrie Forrest was a television producer, after all. His specialty
was superschlocky game shows, he was a giant in the field, and we
agreed to make me a television personality. On* Dancing Dollars *I
was the cute li'l chickie in the leotards who breathlessly squealed to
the winning contestants, "Congratulations! You picked Curtain
Number Four, and this kayak will be delivered to your home!" On*
Fun For Wives, *Morrie's lasting monument, I was the bubbly
panelist who told the lady before she got the refrigerator, "You're
obviously a wonderful wife and mother and homemaker, Mrs.
Hiram Klutz. Keep up the good work!"*

*At twenty-five, still riding the up escalator and looking across and
seeing myself on the down escalator, I had my own afternoon show.
For what it's worth, I never slept with Morrie Forrest—which might*

be worth something, at that. The show's Monday-through-Friday format was simple: Have two guests on together each day, exchange mediocrities in the guise of bright and amusing conversation, come out against absolutely nothing including double pneumonia. Guests were easy to get; aside from the actors and authors eager to plug their latest numbers, I evidently had accumulated a lot of friends since the Moley era, some of them famous enough to help the ratings almost from the outset. Judith's World *went from local to network in surprisingly short order, because Mrs. Hiram Klutz out there in videoland obviously liked what she saw and heard; she saw attractive people and she heard nothing thoughtful. In the show's second month on network, Morrie singled out one newspaper follow-up review to read me: " 'The clear success of* Judith's World *is attributable to several factors. Miss Harrison's beauty is genuinely interesting, her animation seems real, her voice is pleasant, her laugh is delicious, she has few affectations, she dresses well, and she listens to her guests. Her most spectacular achievement, however, lies in her genius (there can be no other word) for appearing smart and unfailingly talking dumb. Is that what it's all about? Are women as proudly insipid as Miss Harrison seems to say each weekday? If so, she is marvelous at it, even inspirational." Morrie loved the review, called it a money review.*

With a well-earned reputation like that, there was no logical reason for a serious scholar like Dr. Peter Clements to waste his time coming on the show. Even I knew who Peter Clements was—an anthropologist and historian, an intellectual with a sense of humor, not above communicating his observations on the proper study of mankind to all the Mrs. Hiram Klutzes he could reach, with affection, without condescension. Morrie was against booking him: "These double-domes are okay on the late-night talk shows when nobody's listening. But this is daytime. We gotta push the bath oil."

"Let's try it," I said, still stung by that review I resented and couldn't deny. "Have some safe Ziegfeld girl on with him for insurance."

He was deep in his forties, a beanpole with a barber-college haircut, a rugged-plains homely face and a thoroughly amiable smile. The Ziegfeld girl was a bluehaired matron who had appeared on Broadway with John Barrymore and who was on camera this day to discuss great moments in needlepoint. Peter Clements came with a just-published book of his on cooking recipes from around the world. He was articulate and funny, spoke of his hobby of collecting offbeat recipes wherever he traveled—"not a dangerous hobby until I get into the kitchen"—sneaked in some thoughtful remarks painlessly, and was a total joy. We shared a beer afterwards and he told me he was a fan of mine. I was surprised. "You've watched this drippy show?"

He nodded. "For the past two solid weeks, every afternoon, courtesy of a long-healing appendectomy. You do what you do quite well."

"Which means?"

"Which means, might we have dinner together and talk some more?"

The next surprise was that a romp in the hay wasn't all he was interested in. I was being as virtuous as a nun that season in my own paid-for apartment—until the second time I invited him to the apartment. He lived in the country, on the Connecticut-Rhode Island border, disliked New York City, came to it for a few days and nights at a stretch to conduct whatever business called, and then hurried back. Until the fourth time we met, and then he found reasons to stay in the city longer.

It's Imbecile Teen Magazine stuff to say that Peter was my first lover. Peter was my first lover. Inside this baby-fat brain was a perfectly good one striving to get out, he said, and it's ridiculous to say that until Peter I'd never thought about much of anything, and nope, until Peter I'd never thought about much of anything. While he was pulling and tugging at that brain, the good one, he was telling me I ought to know the situation between him and his wife. No, I said. It has to be talked about some day, he said. Some day, I said; not now.

Imbecile Teen Magazine, next issue: When the thunderbolt did hit, when I discovered that every moment of my life was centered around the love of Peter Clements, he was gone. No phone call, no message, no break-off sherry at the Plaza. Gone. His admitting that he'd been funning these months with a free-lunch Galatea might've been survivable. His abrupt tent-folding was not. I went into a tailspin that hurt desperately.

191

And eventually came out of it. With bitterness and with effort, maybe not whole, but Judith's world had changed and, little by little, so did Judith's World. *My laugh-it-up crowd wasn't very funny any more, nor was I; the running palled; the prospect of one more party in one more perpetual ballroom was deadly. The show gradually began to reflect the mood. I insisted that along with the upside-down-cake guests, the stop-press scoop on what Paris is wearing, we look for people who do more than chew gum. Morrie said no. I said Yes or find yourself another purty bowl of sawdust.*

The ratings got better. I got better. I didn't change to cotton stockings, I didn't forego the light, frivolous touches when they were indicated, but I did learn how to ask interesting questions of interesting people—people involved in government, in family planning, in a social concept no one had yet thought to call women's liberation—and what we all learned was that Mrs. Hiram Klutz had a perfectly good brain striving to get out, too.

Peter and I saw each other, oh, a year and a half ago, in Washington. Arthur Keaton, a brave and outspoken senator who'd been working for years to have anti-abortion laws removed throughout the United States, had invited me to testify before his committee. The Senator and his wife and some friends and I had dinner at Gusti's later. Peter and a pincushiony young blonde came in. He lighted up, started to walk toward me, and stopped, probably because I did a colossal job of haughtily averting my eyes. It was just as well. What upset me most of all, I think, was my instant analysis of the quality of that pincushiony blonde. She appeared to be a cheapie, not unlike Guess Who . . .

Judith's plane landed. The first thing she learned in her apartment that Monday was that all hell had broken loose.

19

In this corner, wearing purple trunks, Sam Gallagher.

On Sunday, in my hospital room, with an elephant's weight still on my chest, I was visited by a ferrety little man named Fred Delmont, who claimed he was a private investigator engaged by Pallino and Pallino, Judith Harrison's attorneys, in town to gather all the information he could to submit to Raymond Pallino prior to the trial. How had he found me? I asked. Finding was how he earned his living, he answered, adding that there had been no sleight of hand; he'd heard about my beating on last night's radio news.

For all I knew, he was Oliver Starn's lord high executioner, despite the license he showed me, but I told him everything I'd told Langford, the Hartley cop. Thanks, he said, closing his notebook. The information would be phoned to Ray Pallino, who was hoping to stop off in Hartley for part of the following day, on his way from Mississippi to New York. He, Delmont, said he would check in with me from time to time during the week.

By Sunday night, Burt's office had checked around and found where Judith was. I was relieved. If she had to go to a dying father, the comparative physical safety of a dinky town in the wilderness was the best place to do it.

On Monday, feeling not much better, I read that a population of lesbians would descend on Hartley at a time to coincide with the start of Judith's trial, with Hot Lips Hanaday as group captain, to demand freedom for all women. The Starns couldn't possibly ask for more than that, I thought. Judith needed their help, I figured, like a moose needs a hatrack.

And on Monday, Raymond Pallino zoomed in to see me. Our paths had crossed once before, when I had covered a murder case he was defending, and I'd watched him in spectacular action. I admired him then and I admired him now, for an unquestionably superb mind, for a first-rate sense of theatrics, for his genuine investments in social matters that mattered, and for a personal dynamism I guess I envied. Knew I envied. There were certain reservations along with the admiration, though. Nothing really pinpointable so much as a suspicion of . . . well, a heavy capacity for ruthlessness. A rip-roaring readiness to come out shooting, even if he hadn't completely identified the target. I was mighty happy he was on our side. Still . . .

Still, and anyway, here he was, impatient and tough and in charge, a street brawler Presence in the tailor-made pinstripe suit, not a nervous guy but not still for a moment. "Lousy break, you getting roughed up," he said quickly, as if a few words of sympathy were expected of him, however perfunctory; he thanked me for having talked to Delmont, and repeated—accurately and without notes —the essentials of that talk with Delmont.

"That's what I call a memory," I said, marveling.

"Anything left out?" he asked. "The more you fill me in on now, the faster we get moving."

I didn't tell him where Judith had slept on Thursday night, but I filled in everything else that hadn't seemed all that germane when Delmont had done the questioning.

No, wait, there was one other thing I omitted besides Judith on Thursday night: Harriet Starn's abortion. I told him in detail about my hour with Noah Walters and about going to Starn's estate just to poke around, but I left out Harriet Starn; I wasn't altogether sure why, except for a feeling that if she did belong in this case—maybe she did, maybe not—Pallino should learn about her from someone other than me. I admired him, and I didn't entirely trust him.

Pallino wasn't a smiler, but Noah Walters' name made him brighten. "That's nice, hearing that Walters is still alive and kicking," he said. "I'd forgotten he was from this neck of the woods. He must be three hundred and thirty years old. God, that man was a giant! I've had two idols in my life, and he was one of them."

"Who was the other one? You?"

I said it lightly, even affectionately, and he took it okay. He grinned and nodded. "Any other way to win a game?"

Before he left, jubilantly swearing to rattle Hartley's teeth, I asked him if he planned to see Walters.

"I plan to see everyone."

"I suppose you know about Hanaday and her friends coming to town," I said.

"Yep."

"You seem pleased about it."

"Tickled."

"Why? What possible advantage is there in diversionary—"

"Gallagher, my beat-up friend," he said, "let's make a pact, all right? You say out of the lawyer business and I'll stay out of the reporter dodge. I'm going to welcome anyone who can throw the glare of publicity on what we're up to—anyone, including The Flash Artists Society of North America. Be of good cheer. I gotta run now to make my plane."

Fred Delmont popped into the room late Monday afternoon. He'd learned why Lyman Bester happened to be in a hospital bed one floor away from mine. Honey Bester, a lady of considerable enterprise if not sense, had evidently informed the Godzilla Company that I'd offered Lyman two grand to sing, and how much more were they willing to offer for him not to sing? They didn't take kindly to the proposition; poor Lyman was in awful shape.

Delmont stayed long enough to tell me, with head-shaking respect, about his client, Raymond Pallino.

"I picked him up at the airport," he recounted in awed tones. "His main reason for coming here for just a couple of hours was to meet the D.A. and feel him out a little. So what does he do? He gets off the plane and says he'd been so busy finishing up things down there in Mississippi that he forgot to have somebody call and tell Albright he was coming. I called up for him, there in the airport, I told Albright's secretary that he'd be there in half an hour. She says wait and she comes back on the line and says Albright can squeeze him in at about four o'clock. Here it is ten in the morning. I say to hold on and I tell Pallino. He grabs the phone out of my hand and he says to the girl, 'This is Pallino. Tell Mr. Albright to expect me in thirty minutes.' Like that. And he hangs up.

"I'll be damned. I drive him. I go up with him. He's not loud, he doesn't act sore, he doesn't come on like he's pushing weight around. He says it again: 'I'm Pallino.' The girl looks like she's gonna have kittens. She buzzes. Albright comes out. You've seen Albright, right?

A Mack truck, right? What's Pallino—five-eight, five-nine? Well, he stands there, and they shake hands, and he's like a head taller. They go inside and shut the door."

Delmont shook his head again. "You got to take your hat off to a guy like that. I've done investigations for him, when he's called me, for going on three years. I think if a car lost control and was coming straight at him a hundred miles an hour, he'd keep walking and make the car go around him."

I thought of Humpty Dumpty and said, "Let's hope."

Judith phoned me that night. Pallino had just returned to New York, where she was.

"How dreadful, Sam darling!" she exclaimed. "How stinking dreadful! How bad *is* it?"

"Not bad at all," I said, sounding cool, even remote. "They gave me some dry toast and prune juice here—the first gourmet meal I've had since I hit this town."

"You could've been killed!"

"Maybe, but the valiant only die once." Listen to sweet-natured Sam, to the tinge of petulance, the unveiled sarcasm. I was glad she was safe, glad to hear her voice, yet I was stamping my foot a bit at the hurt of having been run out on.

"You sound—angry with me . . ."

"Angry? I haven't had time to be angry. I've been spending every minute savoring the kindly way you said good-bye on Friday morning."

"Oh dear . . ."

I realized I was behaving like a jerk. Her weekend must've been a hard one, and I thought Enough, already. "Strike all that, Judith. I heard about your trip home and I'm sorry."

"*I'm* so terribly sorry, Sam darling. For what happened to you. I feel responsible."

"Yes, come to think of it, I did recognize you—you were the one that slammed into my kidneys. Come on, cut it out. What happened happened and I'll live. I'm fine. My doctor was just here and he guarantees I'll play the violin again—which is terrific, considering that I never played the violin before."

"That old joke, you nut . . ."

"Yeah. When will you be out here?"

"Not till the latter part of the week, it appears now. There was —Pennsylvania, for those few days, and now I'm lined up for a clutch of interviews and conferences right till the last minute. There's so much to do."

"Judith," I said suddenly, hesitantly.

"Yes, Sam?"

Yes indeed, Sam. "Listen, come to see me the minute you get here, okay?"

The pause was a half-second too long. "Of course I'll see you. Who'd keep me away?"

That girl who flees in the night, I wanted to say. "The *minute* you get here, I mean. There's something about this case I think I have to tell you. It might be important or it might not—but either way I don't want it going out over a switchboard phone."

"That sounds very cloak and daggerish. Did you tell Ray whatever it is?"

"No."

"Why not?"

"Reasons. Trust me."

"I see," she said, a slight chill in her voice. But it warmed again as quickly and she said, "All right, I'll be there first thing, Agent X-Nine. And darling . . ."

"Yeah?"

"Get well soon."

" 'Darling.' You've called me 'darling' three times in two minutes. What would you call me if you loved me?"

"I do love you, you numbskull. I love you, and I'm aghast at what they did to you, and I'm grateful you're alive."

I slept pretty well that Monday night, aches and uncertainties and all. Alma, my ex-wife, the girl who'd married me charging extreme cruelty, had once yelped, during one of her periodic reviews of my faults, that I wasn't really interested in sustaining a relationship with a woman. Alma knew me mighty well, but she was far off the mark there.

The thing is, it's hard to sustain a relationship with a woman you can't catch.

Right, darling?

20

Judith went to work as soon as she returned to New York on Monday. The press wanted interviews. Television and radio talk shows were waiting, either to tape interviews or, in several cases, to bump their guests and interview her live. She consulted first with Tony Pallino, who repeated Ray's instructions: "You're not to proclaim innocence or guilt. You say nothing about what you were or weren't doing with Luther Cobb. That's your lawyer's job. Your job is to keep hammering that no cop and no court has the right to dictate moral behavior to consenting adults."

There were two shows and two press meetings on Monday, with the promise of a continually busy Tuesday and Wednesday. There also was the correspondence to study, the letters and wires and phone messages that had flooded in since the day of the initial reports out of Hartley. Judith was gratified that the preponderance was supportive, though not entirely gratified. "I'd feel a little more comfortable if there was more handclapping from the smaller towns," she mentioned to Tony. "Big city reactions aren't always the most trusty barometers of what the whole country feels about anything."

Ray, home from Hartley, phoned her at nearly eleven on Monday night. Just checking in, he said quickly, and asked if she was okay after Regal City, and sketchily detailed his gut reactions to Hartley and his meeting with Clifford Albright, Hartley's County Prosecutor. "This is gonna be more fun than I figured on, kid," he declared. "Most D.A.'s unleash the moral indignation speeches only when they get to court, but Huckleberry Albright seems to be living his part, with the huffing and puffing right up front. *Mar*velous!" He laughed.

"Does he know his business?"

"Oh, sure," Ray conceded. "I doubt if he'd last an afternoon anywhere but where he is, but he and Hartley were made for each other. He's gonna come in wearing God on one shoulder, the flag on the other, and motherhood on his chest. And that'll go great with the natives. I have a sneaky admiration for cornballism when it's pure, and Albright's the driven snow."

"What will you be wearing?"

"No overalls, I assure you."

"At any time?" she asked, momentarily apprehensive. "Isn't there a When-In-Rome theory in law?"

"Uh-oh."

"Uh-oh what?"

"This is the second time today a layman's tried to educate me on how to practice my trade. I saw your friend Sam Gallagher in the hospital today. He's a nice boy, but he started reading Blackstone to me."

"Hospital? Sam?"

Ray hastily explained as much as he knew. Judith, alarmed, insisted on more details, less haste. "Easy, easy," he said. "The kid's maybe not ready for a decathlon match but he's all right. Look, I have to get off now. It's gonna be a rough week, and I'm juggling a dozen other balls in the air besides Hartley, and I haven't said hello to my wife yet and she's waiting in the other room to shake hands. Give Gallagher a ring. Cheer him up. You can tell him you and I'll be flying there to Sin City on Saturday."

"Saturday? Two days before the trial? Why so late?"

"Because teacher says so. You stay here and keep the pots boiling as long and as loud as possible, and then we go charging out there at curtain time. See you later, loov."

"Ray—"

Click.

The long-distance operator said there was one hospital listed in Hartley, and Judith placed a person-to-person call. Waiting, concerned for Sam, she found herself concerned about Ray as well, not at all clearly. Her faith in Ray Pallino had always been no-questions-asked unfaltering. Yet now, still unclearly . . .

"Hello," said Sam.

They talked, and she felt guilty for his hurt, and she wanted to turn to him and hold him to make the pain go away. And she heard his unspoken "I want you," and she felt like running the other way.

She came away from the call to Sam with horror at what he must have been put through by Hartley, horror at what it was capable of, and with a growing feeling of unease, the kind without a name. There would be more endless days ahead and so she prepared for sleep, although there was no sleepiness in her. In bed, she again heard Ray's answer: *Because teacher says so.* That's what the unease is about, she thought. Some of it, anyway. *Because teacher says so.*

What does Sam have to tell me about the case that he wouldn't tell Ray? Why, suddenly—suddenly, really?—am I worried about Ray? Am I just now hearing what he's answered from the beginning—*Because teacher says so*? I don't think I want that answer from you any more, Ray, not if we confirm my ugly little suspicion that what *Because teacher says so* actually means is *Women ought to be smart enough to know they're not smart enough . . .*

I hope I'm completely misreading you, dear Ray. I hope that was exhaustion speaking. I hope. I do hope.

She worked to switch her mind off for the night, without success. Tut returned, Tut in his grave, Tut swinging her around and going *"Whoo-oop, whooo-oop, whoooooo-oop!"* She stared at pounds of letters and telegrams on her night table, supposed this was as good a time as any to make a stab at them, and instead picked up Norman Hanaday's book. Oh my, she sighed, regarding his back-cover photograph again, warming to him once more, wishing once more, for his sake, for this very nice man's sake, that she hadn't encouraged their meeting again.

I'll read a few chapters, she thought.

She finished the book at five o'clock. Madness, she thought, blinking at the table clock. And slept till eight, when her alarm rang, and wakened feeling fine.

Tuesday's schedule began at ten that morning and ended at midnight, but she found a moment to phone Norman's publisher and ask how she might reach him. The proper thing to do would be to call him and tell him how much she liked his book. And him.

On Wednesday afternoon, she sat in Ray Pallino's office.

"We're swimming," he said. "Everything's under control. What more do you have to know?"

"Everything."

His desk was piled high with papers, and he was clearly impatient. "I'm not gonna put you on the stand. What do you need to bone up on? All you have to do in that courtroom is listen along with everybody else. Look, kid, we're both busy bees. The minute I walk up to that judge, the Judith Harrison case becomes the only case in the world, but until then I'm up to my eyeballs in other matters. I'll talk your ears off on the plane on Saturday if that's what'll make you happy, but for now—"

"I didn't come here to be made happy!" Judith snapped. "I'm not exactly dense. I listen very intelligently. If you tell me about preparations and movement, things I have a right to know, it needn't take all day."

"Look—"

"You look, Ray. That 'because teacher says so' stuff simply isn't enough to reassure me. You're the best there is and I certainly don't intend to read Blackstone to you, but this is my case, too, and I damned well don't intend to be handed a scorecard along with everyone else."

He grinned. "Cheeky type, aren't you?"

Judith nodded. "And pushy."

Ray nodded. "All right. I've applied for special permission to appear on behalf of the defense. That means I take over, without one of those Lester Farr with a *t* local lawyers of record on my rear end. The permission'll come through. I'll blow smoke rings through Albright's witnesses, Bester and the Cobbs, but I want a witness of my own—Andrea Lane—and I'm issuing a subpoena to her to testify. I'll get those two cops who busted you up on the stand if I decide that's profitable, those cops and the whole goddamn Hartley constabulary and Albright himself and Farr with a *t* and Donald Duck and Martin Bormann and the entire Fifth Fleet if that's what it takes to find out who was behind your getting busted."

"But will they allow that?"

"Will who allow what?"

"Aren't you restricted to the fornication charge? I thought—"

Ray Pallino waved a disparaging hand. "That, in gaudy neon letters, is what 'because teacher says so' means, dummy. What'm I going there for, to say 'It's up to the prosecution to prove beyond the shadow of a doubt that my client did indeed commit the crime of nookie with someone other than her spouse?' You were framed, for Christ's sake, you topheavy Jewess! That's what I'm gonna prove! Don't give me that 'restricted to the charge' salami. You want an attorney who plays Marquis of Queensberry, who preens at being referred to as an officer of the court, you'll find eight tons of 'em in the Yellow Pages."

He scissored fingers through his hair as he paced. "More information about preparation and movement, kid? You got it. I had a rundown done on the judge who'll preside. Name's Maurice Jamison. Maurice Jamison not only got elected to his high post on the bench by the right honorable Oliver Starn, but he parts his hair in the middle and at the age of sixty he still wears his high school signet ring. All right, all right, your honor, that's irrelevant and immaterial. But what's relevant as hell is that he's Starn's handpicked boy, and I expect to play a merry tune or two on that harmonica. Matter of fact, they all seem to be Starn spear carriers, directly or indirectly—Jamison, Albright, the lot of 'em.

"Yet again more information, sexy? Darned glad you inquired. That state's law against fornication has been on the books since the state was born, and you know what? The last time it was argued in court was in 1922, so a little birdie whispers to me there's an Ethiopian in the petrol tank, right? Right. In answer to your next and final question, before you ask it: Yes, I'm absolutely positive that Oliver Starn did everything but physically flash a badge and arrest you, and no, I don't have a tincture of evidence I could take to court. Not yet. But help's on the way, Miz Scahlett, so don't you fret none."

He kissed her head. "Don't noodge me *overmuch*, kid," he said with—for Ray—extreme gentleness. "You're right: I *am* the best there is. And you're the best there is, and I love you, and now you scram out of here and go to your five o'clock interview and do what you do best, which is making wonderful layman sense to other laymen. *Capish?*"

By the time Judith and Norman Hanaday spoke together by telephone, late Wednesday night, her suitcase was packed to leave for Hartley on Thursday. The directive to be passive, girly-passive, had churned in her, annoyed, grated. She had phoned Sam to say she was coming. Sam promised to contact his *Rowland's* contact and see that she had Airport Motor Inn accommodations, no slipup this time.

Hearing Norman's voice, she discovered herself feeling several almost embarrassing tingles. She praised the book, and him for having written it, and said she was on her way to Hartley in the morning, and they talked around their affection for each other, and she regretted, after the call was done, that she had not had the courage to say the truth: *This isn't love I feel, yet it's miles beyond fondness. It's sexual, sure, but that's hardly the all of it. I wish you were here with me now, Norman. Or I there with you.*

On Thursday, alone, she flew to Hartley. Ray would be furious. So be it, she thought. Maybe this is the last place I belong, on my own, right now.

She was soon to find out.

21

On Tuesday Hanaday's publisher's office had phoned to tell him to be in Chicago the following day, to tape *The Mel Kruger Show*. "I thought Kruger's producer'd turned me down," Hanaday had said.

"That was last week," Andy Masters said. "The book's gathering steam, Norm. You going on the Kruger show's a hell of a good break. Oh, and by the way," he added, "you might be heading on out to the Coast from there. We'll let you know."

Hanaday had placed a call to his son Richard, a sophomore at Northwestern, luckily got him in, said he was coming to Chicago tomorrow and hoped they could get together. The boy disappointed him by not even pretending to sound pleased. "Uh, how long will you be in town, Dad? This week's a crusher for me, with exams and all . . ."

"I'll be there for a few days, at the Ambassador East. I'm sure you can find ten minutes out of your busy schedule to see me."

"Gee, I hope so."

"So do I," Hanaday said sternly.

"Hey, incidentally—isn't that simply delicious, Mother teaming up with SOS? That should give the Establishment something to scream about."

"Mm. We'll talk about it."

Nothing about the short telephone call had been satisfying, Hanaday thought from time to time on Tuesday and on Wednesday, but he reminded himself that they had never been especially comfortable with each other. No, that wasn't so; they had been close in the early years, as he and his daughter Audrey had been close in the early years. Until Martha got her by-the-book paws on them, undercut and overruled his judgment and advice and authority at every crucial turn, almost had *Mother knows best* embroidered on them.

Oh, what sniveling rot! he cursed. Of course kids don't go sour because one parent screws them up. Where was I during the souring process? Around. Not off at the wars, not constantly down at the office, not looking the other way. Around, watching. Half believing that maybe Martha, an often most persuasive woman, did know best.

There was no message from Richard when Hanaday reached his Chicago hotel on Wednesday, but there was one from Judith: would he be free to call her at any time after ten tonight, New York time? Absolutely, he thought excitedly, happily, and in his room took a call from Marilyn Rose, R. A. Storm's Chicago representative. They were in luck, she said; other shows besides Kruger's wanted interviews with him while he was in town, and so did the press. She confessed that some of the spoken interest in him had to do with his wife being in the news, that he should be prepared to—

"That's out," he interrupted, surprised by the briskness in his voice. "My wife is perfectly capable of speaking for herself. I'll have no comment to make about Mrs. Hanaday."

"Well . . ."

"Get back to whomever with that message and then get back to me, would you, please? I'll understand if they want to forget the interviews, but it's something I'm going to stay adamant about."

From the first moment he had learned about Martha's tangling herself up with those Sisters of Sappho people, of her plan to travel with them to Hartley, he had known he should talk with her, to determine if she was really serious, to ask her just what the hell she supposed she might accomplish by tying in with them. And repeatedly he had replaced the receiver before dialing the last digit.

He lifted the receiver now and dialed the Columbia Heights apartment. Martha answered, and he plunged into his questions without preliminary.

"Certainly I intend to go through with it," Martha said. "Is that honestly why you called me out of a blue sky, Norman? After hanging up on me when I called you at a time of very deep depression? Why are you suddenly so concerned about my welfare?"

"Because I think you've been given some awfully bad advice, Martha. You don't need sideshow capers like this. I don't want you to get hurt."

"I wonder why I have this strong feeling that this is a grossly dishonest phone call. It's possible that Judith Harrison and *her* sideshow friends are the ones you don't want to get hurt. Isn't that what you're truly saying?"

He sighed. "There you go again, automatically assuming you

know what I'm *truly* saying. Very well, Martha, have it your way. I expect to see Richard while I'm here. I'll tell him I talked with you."

"Richard?"

"Richard."

"But you said you were calling from Chicago."

"That's right. Richard's in Chicago, remember?"

Silence. A strange, thick silence.

"Martha?" Silence. "Martha?"

"I'm here. Yes, by all means, visit with Richard and tell him I love him. Don't tell him how much you hate me, how much you've always hated me."

Silence again, and he realized she was no longer on the line. He replaced the receiver, thinking *What the hell . . .* ? He dialed Richard's number. The boy's roommate, sounding even more effeminate than Richard, explained that Dickie had left word that he would ring as soon as he had a free moment.

Hanaday met Marilyn Rose in the hotel lobby. She was a breezy lady with yellow hair, and she said, "My car's outside. Mel Kruger's no big distance from here." She had called the other shows with his ultimatum, she explained on the way. All but two had canceled out. "Those two are worth doing, though," she said, not at all convincingly.

Mel Kruger didn't ask about Martha, but one of the other guests did. She was a television comedienne named Dixie Richmond, and she considered Martha's early book, *Season of Silence,* a classic and *Private Parts* even more so, called her a woman of great integrity and depth, and said, "One of the classiest things about Judith Harrison is that she gives so much credit to Martha Hanaday for having led the way." The present-tense praise for Martha continued, and Hanaday heard himself join in. He swung a lie successfully—the agreement between Martha and him that he wouldn't discuss Hartley in public—and talked about his book at every appropriate opening, and discovered he was touched that someone had been kind enough to say positive things, obviously genuinely felt, about Martha, about his wife.

Marilyn Rose drove him to the next taping, delivered him back to the hotel, and said breezily, although he had offered not a hint of invitation, "I'd love to stay a while, but my old man gets restless when

I'm out too late. You know how it is." Unasked, she showed him her marriage band and said, "See you in the morning, honey." He grinned as he watched her go, and asked at the desk for messages. No messages. He phoned Judith from his room. She wasn't in, but she'd left word with her answering service that she would be back no later than eleven o'clock, Chicago time, and would call him if that was all right. "Yes," he said.

Waiting, he phoned down for a Scotch and soda, undressed to his shorts, and watched himself on *The Mel Kruger Show*. He disliked his voice, and the sparse hair, and the seemingly sullen slouch, but he was satisfied that he was an infinitely improved performer, far better than he had been at the start of the tour, back there at the time of the Peloponnesian War. He hadn't thought to tell Richard or the roommate about the Kruger show, and he resented Richard once again, resented the kid's flat-out rejection of him. *"Isn't that simply delicious, Mother teaming up with SOS?"* It figured. It figured, and Hanaday resented his own jealousy.

Resented Martha. Resented his sleepwalking cooperation with her in training the children to venerate her while vaguely remembering his name. The deed had been done subtly, not by conscious design, but done nonetheless, and he had been a participant. He recalled how odd Martha had seemed on the phone today, and he was concerned again about her welfare, and none of it served to lessen his resentment.

He signed the waiter's check, and walked about the room with the Scotch, and listened to Dixie Richmond praise Martha, and asked himself if any of the twenty-two years with Martha had been good.

Yes. Of course.

He was twenty-seven, in his third year of teaching at Satterley College for Women in northern Vermont, and fairly content with the way things were going. His salary was barely above the poverty level, but he was allowed to teach without on-high interference, and each semester there were at least a few bright, inquisitive students to keep him on his toes and make him feel he wasn't lecturing the walls. He lived off-campus, in a furnished apartment big enough to contain the hundreds of books he had accumulated, and a desk on which he was writing a history text that was flawless one night and hopelessly inept the next, and a bed on which he occasionally shared

207

an hour with Regina Dodd, who taught medieval history. The male members of Satterley's faculty were hired and retained if they were (a) adequate teachers and (b) eunuchs, the latter requirement probably more important than the former, for the maintenance of the students' virtue was almost guaranteed in the brochure. Hanaday understood and always scrupulously averted his eyes from the student body's frequently appealing bodies.

He didn't meet Martha—she was Martha Frerichs then—until she took his modern history course, but he knew who she was. Everyone on the small campus did: she was twenty-one and a senior, a sociology major and a Mensa member, a typhoon of vivacity and scholarship and popularity, the cheerful girl who writes the petitions outlawing war and hunger and makes you feel proud rather than foolish as you sign them. She was tiny, more striking than pretty—her almost blindingly white teeth were a trace too large for the rest of her face, a perfectly nice face—yet there was an energy and immediacy about her that refused to be ignored.

By far the best reason to steer clear of her away from the classroom was that her uncle was the fattest of cats, the trustee who contributed generous sums of money every year in memory of his Satterley alumna mother.

The first most personally imposing thing about Martha Frerichs was that she took the modern history course as an elective. The second was that she was incontestably the most attentive and imaginative student he'd ever had, coming to class not only completely prepared but armed with questions and ideas and arguments that tested him and sometimes proved that she knew more about aspects of the subject than he. The third was that she flattered him a lot. The fourth was that she changed in his mind—just when, just how, he couldn't be certain—from a rather sexless young lady to quite the opposite.

They huddled together that starless night in his arthritic, asthmatic Dodge, shivering with cold and with the realization that finally, after months of gazes meeting and darting away, of gazes meeting and holding, of touching accidentally, of touching purposely, finally It was about to happen.

She (as he brought the packet out of his pocket): "Why that?"

He: "Why not that?"

208

She: "It's so—artificial. Let's not worry. This is the time of month when I'm safe."

It was not a time of the month when she was safe. A doctor confirmed her pregnancy, and she was white with shame and self-recrimination, and Hanaday, without the remotest notion of how to go about finding an abortionist, solemnly agreed with her that it was his obligation to find one. He did, and borrowed the five hundred dollar advance fee from the bank—an equally oppressive task—to pay for it. As he drove her to the operation, she flew unexpectedly into hysterics, wailing that she couldn't possibly participate in a murder. Hanaday, his own nerve ends screeching, barked, "This is one hell of a fine time to come to a decision like that!" She was apologetic but resolute. He pointed up every imaginable consequence of bearing an unwanted child, and she nodded and stayed resolute, and eventually he could do nothing but turn the car around.

She would not blame him if he ditched her and never spoke to her again, she said coldly. As coldly she said she loved him, would never love anyone but him. The thought of marrying her, of marrying anyone under these conditions, was dismal. The thought of deserting her was sweet and abruptly unconscionable. Over the next very long week he brought her reasons upon more reasons why she must not have the child. No murder, she said coldly.

They were married by a justice of the peace. They spent their wedding night in a drafty motel room, just outside Burlington. The wallpaper was a prison-green. The toilet bowl made apologetic, insistent, froglike grumping noises through the night. "I made you do all this," she wept.

Partly, he thought. What was memorable about the wedding night was her passion, unrestrained and exquisite. She was so loving that for a time he was almost glad it had happened.

When Satterley's dean learned about the marriage—its fact, not its reason—Hanaday fully expected the sky to fall. Because graduation was so close, and because Martha was to be valedictorian—and doubtless because the dean had grave questions about how Martha's uncle would react to the news, now at annual contribution time—the understanding was that Hanaday would quietly stay until the end of the semester and then chart his own future course, plans not to include Satterley.

With the help of the right strings-pulling friends, Hanaday was offered a junior teaching berth in Columbia's history department in New York, and he grabbed it. He and Martha rented an apartment near the university. He began teaching in September, and Martha, very pregnant, began postgraduate studies in Columbia's sociology department. In February, when Audrey was born, Martha was hard at work on a book collaboration with Barbara Breisky, a social worker not much older than she, the book that was to become Season of Silence.

Inexhaustibly, Martha seemed to have time for everything, the book, the race for her M.A., the baby, her friends, Hanaday's friends, the marriage. The good marriage, mostly cheerful and loving and workable. They were blessed with Mrs. Rogers, Audrey's baby nurse who had contracted to come for a month and who decided to stay on, at a salary they could handle, as nurse and housekeeper and cook. Her dependability released Martha from the humdrum household chores, and Martha used her new freedom to spread her wings all the wider, and Hanaday watched her galaxy of activities with measured pride. She became increasingly preoccupied with those activities, less so with his, but so gradually that it didn't matter. He loved her. He respected her interests and her drive. He enjoyed her. He read Season of Silence *at every invited step of the way, praised it when he thought it right, made specific recommendations for changes and restructuring when he thought they were needed, and she listened and invariably agreed, and dedicated the book to him. The dedication was embarrassingly flowery, and he was ecstatic.*

The book was published on Audrey's second birthday. It was favorably reviewed and, despite the charts and graphs and voluminous statistics, was a popular success as well. The byline read By Barbara Breisky and Martha Hanaday, *but Martha soon became identified as its sole author because Miss Breisky was inordinately shy in public and preferred the shadows while Martha pursued every opportunity available to publicize it. In those 1950s when few voices were seriously questioning the holy decree that females were born to serve their mates, Martha was out loudly disagreeing, wherever and whenever a platform could be found, out persuasively arguing that female independence did not have to be incompatible with marriage and family.*

Her modest celebrity burgeoned, and she was asked to try her hand at a newspaper column dealing not with women's total independence—then too radical a germ to spread—but with, well, women. "What about women over fifty?" Hanaday suggested. "They're a group no one seems to pay much attention to in these advice-column things, and there must be a lot of them."

Martha wrote some sample columns titled Women over Fifty *while she was pregnant with Richard. The syndication started with four outlets and, when Richard was nine years old and Audrey was thirteen, was up to forty outlets.* Women over Fifty *evolved in these years to, simply,* Martha Hanaday, *still basically a question-and-answer advice column but one that had shifted to encompass all ages of women.* Martha Hanaday *was successful because Martha's advice and observations were sound, never lofty yet rarely simplistic. The marriage stayed essentially sound, too. Their arguments—not arguments; disagreements—centered mainly around his belief that she wasn't attending to her family enough, her belief that the quality of attention counted far more than quantity. Look at the children, she would say. Could you hope for more emotionally healthy children? There's the key. Obviously.*

Money was earned—from the column and other writings, from lectures, from royalties, from her own radio show—but little money was saved. Audrey had developed a series of nervous tics, was stealing erasers and jewelry from her friends and denying thievery when thievery was proved, was sending up little frightening flares that she was on the verge of becoming sexually precocious. Martha consulted a psychoanalyst who recommended immediate and intensive treatment. Martha subsidized the treatment, commenced therapy herself, and mentioned one night just before she rushed to New Haven to deliver a lecture on mental health that she was considering putting Richard, a brilliant child making poor school grades, into treatment. "Ridiculous!" Hanaday protested. "There have to be less complicated and certainly less expensive ways to help those kids if they do have problems. Let them know they have two parents, for starters." Martha, sweetly: "Norman, dear, I haven't said one word about your sharing the expense. My decision is my responsibility. Obviously."

He continued to protest, to forbid, to reason, to threaten. Martha won.

She was in California, on tour with her new book Private Parts *on the Friday night Hanaday telephoned her excitedly to say his full professorship had just been confirmed. She was happy for him and asked if Audrey had got to her analyst's appointment on time. Colleagues and friends who had heard the great news called him to congratulate him, and one, Jack Horrigan, invited him to a makeshift victory party on Saturday night at the Horrigan flat on Central Park West. He was hesitant because Martha wasn't in town to come with him, but Pat, Jack's wife, got on the line and insisted, and so he went. He met Anne Carpenter that night, a pretty divorcée he saw home. She said awesome things like, "I could go for you in an earth-splintering way, but let's play this by ear, all right?" He stayed the night, an incomparably happy night. They sang snippets from* Mikado *and* Pinafore *as she fried ham and eggs in the morning, and they made love again, and he promised to phone her, and didn't. It was impossible that she, that any woman, would be content with an affair without any obligations from either side, the only kind he could afford.*

About a year later, desperate for companionship, he found Anne Carpenter's number and phoned her. She remembered him, and hung up.

Some of the campaigns that Martha led were trivial, some were important, and all were entered into with zeal: the fight to force government contractors and subcontractors to end job discrimination against women; the fight to abolish "Help wanted—Male" ads in the classified sections; the fight to prohibit airlines from firing stewardesses who married or who passed the age of thirty. She fought, believed deeply in each fight, and Hanaday respected each fight, helped her to see she should trim sails here or go for broke there, supported her. While other feminists were merely bitching about their low status as women, she was out helping to change it. Not alone, to be sure. But those who joined and followed and fought along with her did so primarily because of that special fierce dedication that was Martha's.

She remained the wife and mother she had been—basically neglectful though never totally removed from the family's occasional crises—but as a feminist her emphases, her very personality began to change, from reasonableness to stridency. Her pro-women speeches became anti-men. Her public pronouncements—once so carefully and thoughtfully organized, so laced with compassion and even humor—now came out sounding shrill, often downright ludicrous.

Her equality-in-marriage statement, for example: "Wives must be paid salaries as dishwashers, nursemaids, and bedwarmers." She spoke it during a widely viewed television show, and the interviewer swooped. "Let's pursue that reasoning to some conclusion," he said. "Who pays when a wife and husband have a night on the town? The evening out—the baby-sitter, the restaurant, the theater, the car's parking lot? Do they go Dutch, like two roommates?"

"I thought I was invited here for a serious discussion."

"You were."

"It's a stupid question, a frivolous question."

"Why is it?"

"Frivolous and classically male chauvinist. A wife is an employee. Sometimes she's taken to dinner by her husband, her employer. It's scarcely the employee's responsibility to ease her employer's exploitative conscience further by forfeiting a penny of her hard-earned salary."

"But if they're both—"

"I've said all I intend to say on the subject."

Hanaday, afterwards, at home: "The salary thing isn't what I'm talking about. You must honestly believe in it or you wouldn't have brought it up. What you did wrong was not following it through."

Martha: "That man is a dolt. All he's there for is to sell corn flakes."

Hanaday: "Then you should've just jollied along or not gone on in the first place. You always told me you saw yourself first and foremost as a teacher. That wasn't teaching tonight, Martha. Snapping the way you did, opening the door to be laughed at—if he does represent what you call the chauvinists, you couldn't have reinforced his attitudes more if you'd—"

Martha: "I won't have you shout at me!"

Hanaday: "Who on earth is shouting?"

Martha: "You are! You have no cause to feel threatened, anyway, certainly not with your income. I'm going to bed. My migraine is splitting me in two. I'll sleep in my office tonight."

Hanaday: "Martha, come back here."

Office door opened, closed, locked.

She had breakfast ready for him that next morning—rare for Martha—and he was surprised to see her so cheerful. She apologized for those brutal words about his income. "I was on edge, but that's no excuse for saying such a castrating thing; that nonsense about which spouse earns more than the other is so transparently the sick vagina-penis competition that I'm ashamed it popped into my head for even an instant." She was dressed to leave, too busy to continue any more discussion. He called her back again. She was gone. He returned home that evening to find not Martha but an extravagantly handsome billfold with his initials engraved in gold, and a note inside: Darling N., Happy unbirthday. This small gift is my inadequate way of telling you what I tell you each day of my life, though you may not hear—that I deeply love you and always shall. Pax vobiscum? M.

Over the next year, her newspaper outlets, one by one and eventually as many as a half-dozen at a time, chose not to publish her column any longer, citing editor and reader and advertiser complaints that it had become too parochial or too controversial, that its brightly common-sense approach to human behavior now seemed too often erratic, garbled, frequently plain fanatic. Hanaday read Martha Hanaday and had to agree. He told her so, as supportively and constructively as he could. Martha would have none of it. "They want me to go back to being a cookie cutter. They want me safe," she raged. "They want me to take them by the hand and show them what to do for colic and what cheese dip to serve when the husband's boss and his wife come for cocktails. Well, the hoopskirt age is over. Hasn't anyone out there heard that? If they're afraid of my putting a mirror in front of them and making them look at themselves, making them see they're fifty-one percent of the population and still groveling in the dirt; if that threatens them so much that they run from the truth, then that's just too bad. I've come too far and I know too much about human behavior to be insulted by swine. Martha Hanaday speaks and writes and lives as Martha Hanaday, not as some marionette."

He began to take sober inventory, several months before he uttered the hard word "divorce" to Martha. Despite—perhaps partially because of—the parade of psychiatrists, analysts and therapists, all of them earnest and full of knowledge and costly (costly to Martha,

214

*true, but costly, nonetheless), despite his sometimes confused efforts
to be an effective husband and father, there was no family. Audrey,
still unfreed of those facial tics, had had two abortions before she was
seventeen. She was twenty-two now and married—of all square,
mid-Victorian things, married!—to a certified stumblebum who
spent his nights memorizing Herman Hesse and his days ripping off
other people's credit cards because that was the way to get back at The
Establishment. They were gypsying, the last time Hanaday had
heard, somewhere in the vicinity of San Diego. Richard, eighteen,
was in college, determined to have a productive adulthood in fine
arts but in his way a gypsy, too. Hanaday had detected the boy's
invisible nervous tics early, had striven to be a strong, guiding
father, succeeded, failed, succeeded, failed, always with Martha
appearing in the corridor suddenly from nowhere cooing* Come to
Mommy, dear baby, your father means well but he doesn't
understand how sensitive you are the way Dr. Kristall and I
do, does he?

*And there was Martha. Twenty-two good, numbing, maddening,
fuzzy years with Martha.*

The rumors, the withering gossip overheard: Nutsy as a fruit-
cake. Getting there, anyway, the way she acts in public these
days. The teacher nuns in Rhode Island invite her to come
talk to them about how to train their girl students to grow up
to be useful citizens and independent women at the same
time. So what's she into, five minutes into the speech?
"Train them to be professors, not teachers; doctors, not
nurses; priests if necessary but never nuns. Teach them
anything but subservience." Oh, did those sisters applaud at
the end like their hands were all frostbitten!

And more: Did you hear what that batty Hanaday broad
told the Hunter graduating class? "If you decide to marry,
draw up a contract, and specify payment for services rendered. Housekeeping—$25. Hostessing business party
—$25. Sex—$100." That's what you call career guidance,
all right.

*He requested an appointment with Martha's analyst, Stephanie
Wall.*

"Is my wife disturbed, Dr. Wall?"

"It's important for you to learn what you think, Professor Hanaday."

"Doctor, this is my forty dollars for this hour, and—"

"Fifty. Go on."

"My question seems to me a fair one. If Martha is seriously ill emotionally, I ought to know that and know how to be of help. If she's no more ill than the rest of us, I should know that, too."

" 'No more ill than the rest of us.' Interesting."

"What?"

"Nothing. Professor Hanaday, if I may be frank, Martha has been in treatment with me for eight years. I find it interesting that you've waited till now to ask for a consultation."

"Are we back to my motives?"

"It's more important what you think."

"I think I'm not getting an answer to my question: after eight years, what is your diagnosis? and prognosis? I went along thinking Martha was fundamentally in command of herself and control of herself. I'm asking you if she is or isn't. If she's sick, how sick, and what can I do?"

Dr. Wall accepted a seven-minute telephone call, at his expense, and returned to the room and said, "Be kind. Be understanding."

"Is that all you have to say? 'Be kind. Be understanding.' Is that it?"

"Your anger is interesting, Professor. After eight years—"

"After eight years, no analyst should be leeching off the same patient; that's what I find interesting. 'Be kind. Be understanding,' " he snorted, and got up to leave.

"You still have more of your hour left," she said, indicating her clock. "If you have anything to say about your marital relationship, it would be interesting to hear it."

"Nothing more."

"Oh, by the way. Shall I bill you at your residence or your school?"

"Bill me? For what?"

"For our session."

"You're laboring under a misapprehension, Doctor. I'm sending you a bill—for being thoroughly asinine on my time."

He sped home, where Martha arrived long past their promised dinner together. He told her about his meeting, told her he con-

216

*sidered Wall an outright charlatan, told her he loved her and would
look out for her and take care of her.*

*The camel's back was broken and the last laugh occurred a week
later, when he learned that Martha had forwarded to Stephanie
Wall, M.D., a separate check in the amount of fifty dollars.*

Judith returned Hanaday's Chicago call at half-past eleven. She
had learned he was in Chicago from his publisher's office.

"I finished your book," she exclaimed. "It's excellent!"

He was delighted, and said so. What was most delightful, he
thought, was that her enthusiasm sounded real; *she* sounded real,
tuned-in, connected with him. They talked for a very long while and
he asked, "When do you head for Fort Apache?"

"Tomorrow."

"Shipshape?"

"Not stupendously steady at the helm this second, Admiral, but
yes, aye-aye, I guess I'm looking forward to it."

"Are you looking forward to Martha, too? I ask you that just to
prove that I read the newspapers."

Pause. "No, I can't say I'm wiggling my toes at that development. I
don't think it'll be good for anyone. But it might turn out to be more
of a nuisance than a calamity."

"I'll want to be in touch. Where will you be staying?"

"The Airport Inn. The Airport *Motor* Inn."

"I wish I could be there."

"Oh God, that's what I wish, Norman! How wonderful it would be
to see you and be with you!"

Norman Hanaday realized, the moment he replaced the receiver,
that Chicago wasn't where he belonged. Chicago, or the West Coast,
or home.

He went through the motions of work on Thursday and Friday.
Richard didn't call, nor did he call Richard.

On Friday evening, he found Andy Masters' New York home
number and phoned him to cancel the tour.

"Why, when the momentum's picking up?"

"There's something I have to do," Hanaday answered, and then
called the airport to reserve a seat on Saturday's first flight to
Hartley.

217

22

The fact of physical violence had always repelled Judith as the ultimate obscenity. She saw Sam in his hospital bed now, and started to say something flip, not to minimize her outrage and concern but to avoid appearing sloppy-emotional. She tried flip jokes. They formed in her throat and stuck there. She kissed him, and filled up.

"It's okay," Sam said, patting her. "It's okay."

"For the world's handsomest man, you look awful."

"Ho ho, you think I look awful now? You should've seen me when they hauled me in here, or at least when I woke up. I looked like I'd been attended to by a first-week embalming student—with a hangover."

"What hurts most?"

"The boredom of talking about what hurts most. It was fun for a while, but it became a drag. Where's Pallino? Did you come to town together?"

"No," Judith said, and explained her restlessness in New York, though careful not to suggest a hint of criticism of Ray or even doubt. Sam asked her quite direct questions about him, her estimate of him as someone who could be trusted to play in the crunch with a grain of civilized conduct. "Why do you ask that?" she asked warily.

"Just observation and hunch," he answered. "A first-rate lawyer, sure, I know all that, but the impression I got when he was here was that Pallino's chief client is Pallino."

"Not when he's working," she said, and praised Ray, and Sam nodded as though unconvinced, and told her finally what he had not told Ray, why he had waited for her to come. "Wow," she said softly when he was done.

" 'Wow' is exactly the right word," Sam agreed. "It's a ticklish business, Judith. Get to Harriet Starn and you maybe get to the bottom of everything. But how do you get to her? And even if you do, what keys to the kingdom would she be willing to fork over? In any case, velvet gloves are absolutely required for someone that frail, and my hunch says that Pallino doesn't know from velvet gloves."

For nearly an hour, Sam told her everything he had told Ray, and more, things she knew and did not know, about Lyman Bester and why he was in this hospital, observations she listened to and respected. Before she left, she kissed him again and smiled and said, "I'll be back, Pulitzer darling."

"You watch your step, lady."

"Don't I always?"

"What a droll rejoinder," he snorted in mock contempt, and called her back and lightly kissed her lips.

She went to Lyman Bester's room. The motel clerk and a chubby woman were watching a small television screen. He saw her and instinctively grabbed the woman's wrist. The woman looked around and gasped, "You—!"

"Mr. Bester, we have some things to discuss," Judith said.

"Get out of here," he said huskily.

"It won't take long."

The woman stood up from the edge of the bed. "You heard my husband," she said, "Go away from us. You've caused enough trouble already."

"I'm afraid there's going to be a lot more unless we talk."

"I said get out," Bester croaked. "I'm a sick man. You want the cops on you again?"

His wife almost literally pushed her out of the semi-private room. And as Judith stood in the corridor, wondering at her next move, the chubby woman emerged, an overpainted, hard-looking woman with worry spraying about her. She circled her forefinger in the direction of the alcove across the hall, and they walked there together. "What're you bothering my Lyman for?" she demanded, shakily lighting a cigarette. "Nobody wants to talk to you."

"Sit down, Mrs. Bester."

"I don't take orders from tramps."

Firmly: "Sit down, Mrs. Bester."

Mrs. Bester sat.

"I know about your call to Sam Gallagher, and about your other call," Judith said, sitting with her. "And you and I know your husband was beaten up as insurance that he says no more to anyone than the District Attorney wants him to say."

"You know a whole lot for somebody who doesn't know nothing. Well, you got it all wrong."

"I don't really expect you to tell me now what you were ready to tell Mr. Gallagher, but I suggest you think over what I have to say, Mrs. Bester, you and your husband. If he testifies that he saw Luther Cobb and me together, he'll be telling the truth. But he'll be asked about his beating, he'll be asked about a lot of things by my attorney, a very tough attorney, and he's definitely going to put your husband through the mill. I'm sure you've heard of perjury. Perjury can send your husband to prison. We wouldn't hesitate for a minute to help him get there."

The woman blanched. "Nobody goes to jail for telling the truth." She rose, but she was obviously affected. "You leave us be."

"One second, Mrs. Bester," Judith said, rising, too. "I'm staying at the Airport Motor Inn. If you cooperate with the *whole* truth, your husband's in no trouble. If he's ordered in court to tell everything he knows, and he lies—"

"You leave us be!" the woman repeated, and hurried away.

Judith drove her rented car to the Airport Inn. Maybe I blew it, she thought. A lawyer who pleads his own case has a fool for a client. A client who speaks for her lawyer, especially a client with a pretty touch-and-go knowledge of the law, probably deserves to be hit with the custard pie. We'll see. I'm here now. Unarmed and winging it, but here.

In her motel room, she considered ways to reach Harriet Starn.

There weren't any easy ones, Sam had said, and more, had cautioned her not to try on her own. The goons who had trailed him to the Starn house, or relief goons, would surely be in the vicinity if she were crazy enough to go there, he'd warned. And, goons being goons, and her face being immediately recognizable, she dared not risk that face, or neck, or similar valuables.

She wrote a letter to Harriet Starn, a smoking-out and implicitly threatening letter, she knew without pride. She was sure that Miss Starn knew about the upcoming trial from one source or another, perhaps knew much about it and its details, she began. She wrote that there were forces in Hartley intent on punishing her for her stand on abortion, wrote that she had good cause to believe that Miss Starn would deplore such a railroading, requested that they have a meeting as soon as possible. She wrote the motel's phone number and the number of her room.

The short letter took a great deal of time to compose. Judith used a blank envelope rather than any of the desk drawer envelopes bearing the motel's name, and addressed it—Rachel Drive, Sam had said—not to Harriet but to Oliver Starn. Sam had mentioned that Harriet handled her father's social mail that was delivered to the house, and that a letter with her own name on the envelope stood an excellent chance of being intercepted by the guardians before she got it. Judith sealed the letter, fully aware that Harriet Starn might not even receive it, much less respond to it. She wrote one more letter, to Mr. and Mrs. Cobb, urging them to call her at the Airport Inn, stressing that a call would be in their best interests.

A post office was nearby. She bought a special delivery stamp and posted the Harriet Starn letter. On her way to the car, she heard, "Miss Harrison?" A broadly grinning mailman said he was sure glad to see Judith Harrison in the flesh, and wait'll he tells the wife who never used to miss her on the boob tube. He pumped her hand, and asked her for an autograph for his wife, sign it to Myrtle. "To Myrtle," she wrote on a paper he found in what seemed to be his fiftieth pocket, and she smiled and thanked him, and he thanked her, and she slid into the car thinking, *He* wouldn't vote to convict me to five to twenty years. She drove to Cliveden Avenue, where the phone directory had told her Luther Cobb lived. The shades were drawn and no one answered her knock. A black lady was on the front porch next door. Judith asked if she had any idea of when Mr. or Mrs. Cobb would be home. The lady shook her head, with an impassive gaze that said *White folks don't come around here except to sell toothaches.* Judith placed the letter to the Cobbs in their empty mailbox.

Back in her room, she phoned Andrea Lane. And left her name and number with the maid who said that Mrs. Lane wasn't expected in till late evening. "Please ask her to ring me, no matter how late," Judith said.

She had dinner in her room and didn't leave it, fearful of missing messages, but she called Sam, who guardedly approved of her letter.

"Come on over and we'll neck," he said. "Leave word that if Harriet calls you just got tired of hanging around."

There was one call, at ten. A woman's voice bleated, "We know where you're at, you atheist! You'll get what's coming to you in the courthouse next week. 'They that not believeth in Me shall perish.' You'll burn in the fiery flames of Hell for all time to be, you smutty atheist!"

Part of the eleven o'clock television news dealt with the case and Monday's trial. The facts were right. The treatment was smirky.

The telephone was mute, discouraging but not surprising, Judith thought. Starn's daughter wouldn't've received the special delivery yet. *I don't honestly expect the Cobbs or the Besters to contact me.*

Andrea Lane is disappointing, though. What possible danger would she *be in if she spoke with me?*

Judith's phone wakened her early on Friday morning, a dismally rainy morning. A leafy, extremely nervous voice whispered quickly, "Please—we won't exchange names. Your letter came. Can you be in the vestry of the First Baptist Church on Winick Street in one hour?"

"Yes."

Harriet Starn, a frightened little girl in a grown woman's body, wearing an elderly librarian's dress and Mary Todd Lincoln's coiffure, was a reasonably young and reasonably attractive woman masquerading as a cartoon frump. Anguish and sharp fear were palpable in her every helpless birdlike move, her every helpless, imploring glance, and Judith thought, *I don't really have the stomach for this, you poor, whipped soul.*

"What are you trying to do to my father and me?" She tried to pretend forcefulness, but did it badly. "Is it blackmail? I couldn't possibly take any money out of my account to give you without a hundred questions being asked. Please don't do anything to hurt me. I'm not well. I never have been."

"Miss Starn," Judith said feelingly, wishing she could hug her, cradle her. "I'm deeply sorry if my letter seemed threatening, but I felt it was urgent that we talk."

"What is it you want of me? I can't bear threats, I can't bear ugliness. I'm ill and my father's getting old. Why can't you leave us alone? We've never harmed you."

"I think your father's working to harm much of what I believe in,

Miss Starn. I think he's responsible not only for my arrest but for involving and corrupting a lot of people in order to get at me."

"My father doesn't corrupt anyone. You're a monster and a menace. We all know that. Whatever happens to you, you've brought on yourself."

Careful, be very careful, Judith prayed. Slowly, calmly, she said, "He *is* behind all this, isn't he?"

"I don't know anything!"

"You must. You seem to know I'm a monster and a menace."

"He says you are, and my father knows what he's talking about. He's devoted his life to defending the American way of life against people who would destroy it."

"Is it the American way to lie, to have innocent people hounded for crimes that don't exist? Because that's what someone is doing to me, and I think your father is leading it. Is that what you believe in?"

"No. You're lying. I have nothing against you. I shouldn't have come here."

"But you did."

"I was afraid you'd come to my house. I was afraid you'd make trouble for us. Please, what is it you *want?*"

"I want you to listen to me, to what really happened. And then decide whether you think I should go to jail or not."

"What good would that do? What *I* think doesn't matter."

"But it does, really. Because I need help in reaching your father. You *must* listen."

"You're threatening me. Why don't you come out and admit it?"

Judith sighed. "No, I'm appealing to you, not looking for vengeance. *Will* you listen, *please?*"

They sat on a hard bench and Judith began to talk, groping for a way to tell the truth without seeming to attack Oliver Starn, yet determined to make this pathetic woman understand the menace he represented—to Judith in the trumped-up criminal charge, and to all women who dared to challenge him.

She watched for reactions. Harriet Starn listened in large-eyed silence, obviously agitated, signs of comprehension surfacing quickly and then as quickly vanishing, and when Judith reached the part about the airport mix-up she seemed as if she would interrupt, but then subsided.

Finally Judith said, "And that's what happened in that motel room—nothing. But someone went to a lot of trouble to orchestrate that comedy of errors, and that someone didn't do it as a joke. Unless I can find out who arranged it, and can get him to admit it, I could go to prison. I need your help."

Harriet Starn was visibly trembling as she stood. "Even if everything you say is so, I can tell you my father isn't the kind of man who would do such awful things—have people beaten and all that. And why should I believe you, anyway? The whole world knows what kind of woman you are. And now you're here trying to blackmail me because of a . . . mistake . . . that happened ever so long ago. If my father is evil, what are you?"

"Harriet, I think you know that everything I've said is the truth. I'd hoped you'd understand how ruthless your father can be, and that you'd try to keep him from ruining another life. But blackmail?" She shook her head. "No. I couldn't do that, even to save myself."

She sat for a while after the woman had gone, gazing at the small stained-glass window that had been patched with cardboard. *So much for secret weapons,* she thought, wondering if she would ever see that sad little figure again.

23

The service for Dr. Stephanie Wall at the Corley, Locke, and Edwin Memorial Chapel on Madison Avenue was non-denominational and—shocking to Martha—poorly attended. A colleague of Stephanie's, Dr. Otto Feuerbach, spoke the eulogy in a maddeningly emotionless monotone. His Viennese accent was so thick that Martha understood barely a third of what he said. Even more shocking was the fact that the *Times'* obituary had been so brief, so flat. What had happened to public gratitude, to appreciation of wisdom and contribution? How was it possible for the *Times* to squander so much space on the passing of an ancient character actor and only a short, dismissing paragraph to someone as valuable as Stephanie Wall?

Filing out, Martha saw a man in tears. She went to him, touched him. "You loved her, too, didn't you?" she asked tenderly.

He nodded as he blew his nose. "My life is finished now," he said.

"Would you like to talk about it?"

He shook his head sadly. "Have to get back to work."

Between Monday and Saturday, Martha and Nicole Rooney were in touch continually. Nicole phoned on Wednesday with good news and what she considered troubling news: "As it stands now, there'll be from two to three hundred sisters in Hartley. Isn't that a terrific response?" The problem, she said, was where to put up all those coming and those staying on. There were hotels and motels and guesthouses in and near Hartley, though not enough. Her office had checked the big city roughly a dozen miles from Hartley and found that for a city its size there were surprisingly few hotels. "We'll work it out, though," she said happily. "Some of the ruggeder sisters can sleep in station wagons if necessary. Anyway, you and I are booked into a place called the Airport Motor Inn that's supposed to be close to everything. We've reserved their banquet hall for the press conference on Sunday."

Coolly, Martha said, "Nicole, I do hope it's being emphasized to these people that the march has got to have a precise time limit. I've explained this to you, more than once. One day of it, properly organized, will have a lot more impact than if it's straggled out to three days or even two. I realize you're talking primarily about sleeping accommodations the night before the march. But longer than that—"

"Oh, I agree, Sister Martha. On the other hand, we can't very easily have those sisters traveling a thousand miles there to march and then force them to turn around and go right back home, can we?"

"I rather think we can," Martha said decisively. "I was asked to be in charge. If I am, then my decisions will have to be respected. If I'm not, we both had best come to some understanding now."

There's your perfect opening, she thought, your chance to hem and haw or start some polite argument so that I can gracefully resign. Please . . .

Nicole Rooney didn't take the bait. Martha, she insisted, would definitely be in charge from beginning to end.

Norman called on Wednesday. Martha's immediate impulse was to forgive him. He asked her about Hartley and she wanted to say Don't let me go there, Norman. I got into it before I had the foggiest idea of what I was doing. All I knew was that someone was reaching out to me, someone was taking me seriously. I'm so frightened, Norman. They're using me. Everyone's using me. With Stephanie gone, and you gone, I'm alone and I'm terrified. I'm in such pain. There are times, more and more now, when I can't distinguish between reality and fantasy. I can't keep up with everything happening at once. You always leaned on me, you always saw me as so strong. I'm drowning, Norman. It's so painful and I'm drowning, help me, help me.

But Norman was using her, too. He was cold on the telephone, distant, indifferent to her pain, scolding her, talking to her as if he were wiping out the fact that they had had a wonderful life together, obstinately facing away from the truth that their life could be wonderful again if he would only let his defensive guard down ever so slightly. But his affect gave her no space, no room to welcome him back, and so she hurt him as he was hurting her.

"Yes, by all means, visit with Richard and tell him I love him," she said. "Don't tell him how much you hate me, how much you've always hated me," she said, and softly lowered the receiver to its cradle.

Richard, she thought. My own baby Richard. For a moment I couldn't even place him, couldn't see him. I love that child. How very strange.

As the weekend neared, Martha realized she was swallowing as many as a dozen Valiums a day, realized too that she had to keep reminding herself that Dr. Wall was dead, that she would not only never see her again but could never hear that comforting, steadying voice on the telephone again. There were no other Stephanies, none to whom she could go and say, Nearly a week ago I mislaid an entire Saturday. It took me an entire Saturday to fly from Boston to New York. Tell me where I was that day and that night. Help me. Help me.

Her daughter Audrey called on Thursday, collect, from California. "I need three hundred dollars," she said.

"Three— Sweetheart, I sent you money last week."

"It was more than a week. This is important, Martha. Roger has a chance to connect with this band, but he has to get a bunch of things out of hock first because—oh, it's a long, dreary story. Can you wire the money like the second I hang up? And this time without the church sermons? We're in a hurry."

Carefully: "No."

"What do you mean, no?"

"No, sweetheart. For one thing, I don't have that kind of money to throw around any more. For another—"

"I heard you the first time. I can go take a royal crap for myself."

"Audrey!"

"You don't have money to throw around? Who're you turning down, the Salvation Army? I said it was important, didn't I?"

"I'm sure you think so, but there's simply no way I can go on and on and on supplying you with large amounts of money, even if I could afford it. It implies that I approve the life style you've chosen for yourself. There has to come a time when I say no, lovingly and firmly, and this is the time, darling. If it were truly an emergency, Heaven forbid, naturally there would be no question . . ."

"Oh, baby, but that's hot marbles," said Audrey, who had never heard *no* before. "Plenty of money to deliver over to the shrinks, but your own daughter can go get lost. How many thousands did you shell out to my four shrinks without batting a muscle, even when they were fucking me up so bad I wanted to jump off a roof? Okay. *Okay!* You don't dig my life style? That's real hard shit, man. You never had the time of day for me, so you parked me with the shrinkos. I didn't need them, I needed *you!* You sonofabitch, you wouldn't even let me have a father!"

"Aud—"

"Every time you saw he was coming through to Richard and me you cut off his nuts, and he gave up, and I gave up, and now what do you have to show for all your fucking around, big-dick mommy? A son who's a raging queen and a daughter you won't even lay a little money on when it's important. Okay, big dick, *okay*. I hope you die, you frigid, meddling, selfish shitheel. We'll all be better off without you. I hope you die today."

And the telephone slammed down.

On Friday night, as she was preparing for the Saturday flight to Hartley, Martha had a person-to-person call from a Rob Lincoln in Massachusetts.

"What do you mean you don't know me?" he snapped.

"Should I?"

"Oh, I get it. Someone's there."

"How do we know each other?"

"Is this a gag?"

"I don't understand," she said.

"I don't, either. I'm the one paying for this long distance call, so let's climb off this cutey-poo merry-go-round, shall we? I'm going to be in my pad all next week, after all—she's not coming—so it's all right for you to come on out."

"I really don't follow any of this. Your name and your voice are familiar, but who are you?"

"Stuff it. Stuff it up high."

Moments later, she remembered. She had spent that last Saturday and Saturday night with him in Brockton. Him. Rob Lincoln.

More moments later, suffocating, it was all pieced together.

A year ago—more? less?—the New York radio station had de- cided not to renew her option, but there still were guests eager to get on The Martha Hanaday Show. *One was Rob Lincoln, in style that season as a New England sculptor who sculpted women not in worshipful hymns but with genuine love for them as equal and superior human beings. He arrived barely minutes before air time, astonishingly youthful and ruddy cheeked and good-looking, corn-colored hair flowing, brimming with energy, boundlessly alive and vibrant. "I'm twenty-two, but I trust that won't be held against me," he said at the microphone. He was boyish yet immensely articulate, acutely sensitive to the aspirations and problems of women striving for independence, respectful to Martha though not obsequious.*

When the show was finished, she thanked him and offered to drop him off somewhere if he was headed crosstown and if he could wait the ten minutes till she wrote up the day's log. He agreed, halfway between surliness and impertinence. Waiting for the elevator together, on the twenty-seventh floor, he asked, one eyebrow cocked, "Are you as deep-down glacial as you appear to appear?"

Inappropriate, of course, but a joke; artists were supposed to say inappropriate things at inappropriate times. " 'Glacial' doesn't do it," she said cheerfully. "Try again. Try 'friendly.' "

" 'Friendly.' "

"Give the young man a cigar."

The corners of his full lips turned down, and he shook his head. " 'Friendly' doesn't do it. Deep down, with the right fuse, I suspect you'd be straight firecracker."

"What grand talk, so early in the afternoon," she said, still cheerfully, not quite so cheerfully.

The elevator was vacant when they stepped in. He pressed Lobby-Express, *wrapped his arms around her, and said, "I estimate we have between sixty and ninety seconds, uninterrupted."*

Startled, she fought.

In the lobby he said, "I'm heading back to Brockton, Mass. If you're ever in the neighborhood, I'm in the book." And sauntered off.

Without a recollection of how she had got there, she was at the Brockton bus terminal. "Throw the bell four fast rings, so I'll know it's you," he said when she phoned. "Oh, and we're fresh out of wine. Bring a bottle of Campari. Bring a couple."

He lived in a loft studio and greeted her in dungarees, a lanky and beautiful boy, naked above the waist, barefoot, dried clay on his

*beautiful fingers. A moment before they made love, she asked, "Why
do I interest you, when there are so many young girls around?"*

*"Because you're the youngest of them all," he said. "And because
you're here. An answer?"*

"I . . . Yes."

*Miracle. Miracle. Miracle. There was nothing strange or wrong
about any of it, this beautiful child beautiful man beautiful person
was enhancing her, dominating her and supplicating himself, festooning her with need and with strength, mostly need which was most
beautiful of all. All of it perfection, miles off the ground, from the
unsick sick games at the beginning (the emphasis on genitalia, the
lovemaking at the mirror, the released, remarkably free language) to
the incredibly sweet peace afterwards. His young friends threaded
into the loft through the day and evening, artists, intellectuals,
young, all of them young, all of them beautiful. He thought it would
be a colossal idea for her to welcome each of them in the wide bed and
she agreed. "Hold me till I make it," one said.*

"Yes, baby, yes," she said.

She had taken fifteen Valiums this day. She took sixteen. The
sixteenth didn't help, either.

24

On Friday afternoon, talking long-distance with Ray Pallino, Judith could almost see his glare. She explained her restless reasons for having come to Hartley ahead of him, omitting any reference to Harriet Starn, and eventually brought him out of his crankiness. "Done is done," he conceded. "As long as you're there already, shaking your can for all the farmers to go gee-whiz at, we might as well keep you busy. Wait for a call from Dorothy. Oh, and one more thang, wampus star: see that you don't put that can anywhere near harm's way. Fred Delmont's out there sherlocking for me. From the vibes he sends me, some of those gee-whiz farmers don't love you any more than they loved Gallagher. You getting your teeth bloodied by avenging angels would be a big publicity plus, but I suspect having your jaw reset would be a little expensive."

"That's the sweetest thing you've ever said to me, Ray dear."

Dorothy, Ray's secretary, did call. The major city near Hartley had four television stations, three network affiliates and one independent. The independent station, invisibly but definitely controlled by Oliver Starn, had said no to a Judith Harrison appearance on an interview show. The ABC outlet had said yes to a taping. "Can you be there at ten tonight for a ten-fifteen interview?" Dorothy asked, and Judith agreed and copied the address. The secretary had also arranged for her to be transferred today from this Airport Motor Inn room to its single suite for a press conference the following day, Saturday.

In Sam's hospital room, Judith brought him up-to-date, emphasizing her growing certainty that Harriet Starn wasn't merely a penned-in innocent totally sealed off from the Oliver Starn facts of life. "The tip-off was the special, the *dif*ferent way she looked when I got into the business of the changed reservation and the call I had in Chicago changing my flight time," Judith said. "It was as if I wasn't telling her anything new."

"You figure she made those calls for Pop?" asked Sam.

"Or she knows who did. I reached some decency in her, Sam. I *think* I did. The question is, what do I realistically expect her to do with it? Turn her father in? Confess that she participated in a railroading? That's not very likely. I'm convinced there's a clean sense of honor in her, but there're equal helpings of confusion and terror, too. So what did I accomplish? And why am I burdening you with all this?"

"I'm one of the interested parties, remember? I have the contusions to prove it. And the love."

Uh-oh, she thought uncomfortably. *You're not playing fair when you say "love" so seriously, when you pronounce it that meaningfully. You're supposed to be friendly old Sam, all breeziness and safety. Don't go complicating things. Let go my hand, Sam. Most of all, don't give me that searching look. It's out of character for you, and I have enough to contend with as it is. Please, Sam . . .*

"Love," he repeated. "Me Sam, you Judith. I've been carving it on the wall all day: 'Sam loves Judith.' For real. You hear me, don't you?"

"I hear Sam, who deserves a woman who can love him back on all cylinders, not some part-timer with the fidgets," she said gently, as gently freeing her hand, as gently smiling.

"Positive?" he asked. "As it is, the hospital's threatening to bill me an arm and a leg for those carving damages. Loving me back is the least you could do."

Then Sam smiled, too. The smile returned them to breeziness, and she was relieved, and they explored avenues of Monday's trial together, and Sam mentioned his feelings for her again only when she rose to go. "That love stuff," he said. "I meant it. I'll keep meaning it."

A nurse came into the room with his dinner tray, saving Judith from a surely expected reply. She promised to be back and blew him a kiss and left.

From Sam's floor she went to Lyman Bester's, expecting nothing. She got nothing; the door was closed and the patients' nameplates on the door read *T. Gonzales* and *R. Benedict.* In the parking lot, she saw a heavyset man in front of her car door, clipping his fingernails. He saw her, his fleshy face impassive. He didn't move as she approached, even as she stood a few feet away from him, and she guessed she ought to be faintly frightened. "Would you mind standing somewhere else?"

"You Judith Harrison?"

"No, I'm John Dillinger. Who are you?"

He showed her a wallet badge. "Langford. Hartley Police," he drawled. "Mind telling me what you were doing inside there?"

"Certainly I mind! Suppose you tell me why you're trailing me. Better yet, kindly show me something other than that badge that says you have the right to block my path."

"That's the wrong attitude when somebody's trying to help you. Nobody's blocking you. You're free to come and go's you please, long's you're on bail."

"How grateful I am to hear that. Make your point if you have one."

"I just want to make sure for your sake you're not looking for more trouble than you're in already. That reporter fella with the big mouth, for instance; he's not gonna help you any."

"Who might, then?"

"Me. With some sound advice. Don't go poking around, stirring things up. Behave yourself. Hartley may not be New York City, but we're not some one-horse burg, either. You can be asking for more headaches than you need if you keep nosing where you don't belong."

"That's a pretty clumsy-sounding threat, Mr. Hartley-Police-Department."

"Whoa—you said threat, not me. Advising you to respect the law's no threat."

"All right, then thank you for the civics lesson. I'll repeat your advice to my attorney as soon as he gets here. I'll quote you, Mr. Hartley-Police-Department-Langford, and I'm sure he'll be in touch with you to learn more about the law. Now step away from my car. At once."

She drove back to the motel, unaccountably exhausted. There were no messages but her suite was ready, she was told at the desk, and her belongings had been moved from the single room. They had indeed, she found soon after entering the pleasant new quarters. Her plaid raincoat was hanging neatly in a closet, one pocket inside out. Her locked attaché case hadn't been tampered with, evidently, but the bellhop or chambermaid who had packed her clothing had obviously gone through everything. Looking for what? Dope? Atom bomb secrets? Annoyed and disturbed, she made doubly certain the suite's doors were bolted, unsettled by the image of the Langfords watching her breathe, and she was glad Ray was coming, wished he were here now.

She dressed for the ABC television taping, studied the door that led outside, and changed her mind and phoned the ABC contact. Apologizing, she said she couldn't make tonight's taping and asked if the interview might be done the next day instead. Sorry, no, she was told. She stayed indoors this night, as she had the night before, though for a different reason. I'm uneasy, she thought, and then amended it. No, not uneasy. Plain scared.

Living scared, even for a night, is a hideous way to live, she reproached herself, and supposed she understood the Andrea Lanes a little better.

She could not sleep, and she almost welcomed the nameless telephone callers. They began at midnight—the first ring was at the very stroke of midnight, the corny dramatics of which she imagined she might recall one day as amusing. In the first call she was a nigger-lover who belonged not in a jail but under it. In the second call a chummy drunk offered to come over with a pint and they'd set around a while and then turn on the heat. In the third call she was a nigger-lover *and* a pushy Jew heathen who walked arm in arm with Satan. She decided to call it quits during the fourth call: a man's resonant and refined voice said he was deeply sorry to have read somewhere of her father's death and then, abruptly shifting gears, cackled that she could soon expect to be joining the filthy Christ-killer in his grave.

She gazed at the receiver that was wet with sweat and considered calling the police. And remembered she was in Hartley, very much in Hartley. She rang the switchboard operator, instead, and said she would accept no more calls till eight o'clock wakeup call. Feeling nothing, she switched on the smudge-colored television set and watched *Her Jungle Love*. The sounds and the substance of the fourth call came back to her and for a time she chose to reflect on them and the caller clinically. The man was sick. There could be no other interpretation. Lonely and unloved and maybe too aware of his own too-brief mortality, but sick. I have no more right, she thought, to hate helpless, sick people than I have the—

Suddenly, without announcement, she needed to spring to the bathroom, where she vomited, and shook, and vomited some more. *I do hate you, you vicious, contemptible bastard!* she raged. *I marvel at all the evil you're able to collect in your diseased brain and empty heart, your need to vomit it out at another human being. I marvel and I hate you. I hate you, you miserable coward, hate you, I hate you and you won't defeat me, you won't make me cry* . . .

She walked to compose herself, more imprisoned than she had been in the Hartley jail. A perky, winking girl on the television screen was selling Betti-Jo Bras, "for the man in my life and the life in my man." Another wink. *Her Jungle Love* returned. Dorothy Lamour and a chimp were having a sprightly conversation and feeding each other bananas. Judith was still in the armchair, and the set was still on, when the eight o'clock wakeup call wakened her. On her way to the shower, she glanced at her watch. It read not eight but ten. Angrily she phoned the switchboard and demanded an explanation. "This is what it says here on my wakeup sheet, Miss," the operator defended. " 'Penthouse: Ten A.M.' Listen, don't bawl me out. You want to come down and see for yourself where it says ten o'clock?"

The phone was ringing as she came out of the shower.

"You're *here?*" she exclaimed to Norman. "In the motel?"

He had arrived well-past midnight, he said. Preposterously complicated plane connections. No cars for rent at the airport, and an interminable wait for a taxi. He hadn't had the heart to ring her, once he'd checked in and verified she was here, assuming she'd be sound asleep. ("How awful!" she cried. "I was watching seventy-year-old movies for most of the night!") And then this morning, he went on, he'd been advised she was taking no calls till ten.

"But what are you doing here? I'm happy you are, so terribly happy, Norman, but what happened to your tour?"

"You did. I wanted to come to see you, that's all. For a cautious old history professor, I'd call that pretty impetuous."

Excitement glowing, she said, "I'd call it wonderful. Can you come up right now? In a few minutes, I mean, after I put on some clothes?"

"Yes."

"Press *P* in the elevator. I'm not sure if that stands for Penthouse or Purgatory, but it'll get you here. In a very few minutes, I hope," she said, and dressed quickly, profoundly happy now. There could be problems, she thought. Ray was coming. There was a press conference. If he and I move a millimeter together in public, she thought, the hemisphere is guaranteed to swoop down and chortle *You're you and he's Martha Hanaday's husband!* Oh, nuts to looking for problems before they exist! You're here, darling Norman. How toe-wiggling glad I am, good-omen Norman, how serenely glad!

The telephone sounded again an instant before she opened the sitting room door to admit him. It continued to ring and he asked, "Shouldn't someone answer that?"

"They'll go away," she whispered. "Where were we? Oh, yes: we were kissing."

Norman cooperatively returned to his own room when Ray Pallino arrived at the Airport Motor Inn an hour before Judith's scheduled press conference. In the suite, she told Ray about the detective named Langford and about the anonymous calls. "Mosquitoes. Just don't let them under your skin," he said. She told him about Norman Hanaday. "A mistake," he said. "Why it's a mistake I'm not altogether sure yet, but it's a mistake. Just take care the wrong kids on the block don't see the two of you together till the trial's over."

There was a discreet tap at the door as they talked, and waiters rolled in tables of liquor and sandwiches for the press, on Ray's advance instructions. They left and Judith told him—carefully —about Harriet Starn. He was furious. "Your boyfriend Gallagher knew all this when I went to see him and held it back till now? What're the two of you hatching, a trial to run independent of mine? Why don't I simply bow out and you and the Irishman take over?"

"Don't be childish."

"*Child*ish? The Irishman doesn't zero me in because he figures I can't be trusted, that I'll run to plaster Starn's groovy little secret on all the billboards. Okay, maybe I can buy that. But *you*, dammit!

What were *you* standing around all these valuable days for, waiting for me to show you my scrapbooks, my law degree? Well, *answer* me! What the hell were you afraid of?"

"That you might be only too willing to destroy her. She's an extremely fragile—"

"Destroy her? She seemed willing enough to destroy *you!* Starn's ready to destroy you and spit out the seeds! Christ sake, dumbo, grow up! This is the big, wide world; marauders like Starn not only never play fair, they have nothing but contempt for the ones who do." Ray paced, the inevitable fingers scissoring through the hair. "Starn's in Greece. We put him on the giant silver bird and get him back here."

"How?"

"With a cablegram. A nice, snotty cable that doesn't say the daughter's name but lets him know he'd better hustle on back to hearth and home before this trial's many days old."

Judith listened and agreed and said, "With the complete understanding between you and me, Ray, that that's all. Smoking him out, fine. Holding that club over him, using it to bluff him once he gets here, *if* he gets here, fine, but that club is absolutely never to come down. Agreed? Because otherwise I'm here and now making it clear that you're to leave the whole thing entirely alone."

Ray frowned at her, but nodded. "Use your *kopf,* kiddo. There's a lot more to gain by keeping it as a weapon than by letting the kitty-cat out of the bag." The phone rang. The reporters were gathering in the lobby. "Send 'em up," Ray directed, and dropped the receiver on its cradle and said, "I have work to do, unless you want me to hang around."

"I'm all set."

"Don't pull punches," he said, rising. "Let those babies know there's a war on." He saw her copy of *How Fascism Won,* picked it up. "This the new beau?" he asked. Judith, rising too, nodded. "Looks like an old beau. An old *some*thing," he said. "Well, they claim that geriatrics is one of the still-unexplored, worthwhile fields of study."

Edgily she said, "There's a point, Ray, at which your reputation for wit begins to get on my nerves."

"Have I reached it yet?"

"Not entirely."

"I'll try harder."

He had mentioned that he would be looking in on Sam Gallagher today. She asked him to say nothing about Norman. Ray shook his head, as if in wonderment, but promised.

The wire services and major papers were represented, but the press conference went less well than Judith had hoped. "There was this reporter from the Starn newspaper chain," she told Norman at dinner in the motel suite. "A tightlipped little man named Quigley in a narrow brown bow tie. He was pure Cheshire cat for the first fifteen minutes or so, and then he got suddenly hell-for-leather determined to associate me with the Sisters of Sappho. What's my relationship? What are my sympathies? Is it true I sent them a telegram begging for their support? If not, did I ask them not to show up and embarrass me? He knew exactly what kind of corner he was painting me into. In the Starn-Quigley type of journalism, 'Yes-but' answers are the certain way to put your foot in your mouth. If I approve of the Sappho demonstration then I approve of the Sapphos; if I disapprove then I'm denying lesbians the rights all women should have, to live and responsibly express themselves as they choose. It was damned if yes and damned if no, and smug Mr. Quigley was as clever with the needle as he could be."

"How did you handle it?"

Judith sighed. "Badly, I'm sure. I did the worst possible thing: I rambled. My God, I even made something dangerously close to a speech—which ain't the sharpest way to keep the press awake. The more I tried to explain the case as I saw it, the more I seemed to be saying 'I wish those obstreperous lesbians would go work their own side of the street while the queen here is on stage.' The more honor I bestowed on Martha as the mother of us all, the more it came out like a funeral oration." She speared an onion ring. "I must be aging fast. Press conferences used to be a breeze."

She detected a next-county look in his eyes at Martha's name. "You're concerned about Martha, aren't you, Norman?" she asked softly.

He nodded. "Nothing's ever simple, it seems. I'm convinced I'm telling you and me the truth when I say I honestly don't want to see her again, and at the same time I hope she doesn't make a fool of herself when she gets here. If those people she's tied herself in with are as nutty and irresponsible as I gather they are . . ."

Ray phoned. Judith took the call in the bedroom.

"Well, the Irishman isn't altogether useless, after all," he said. "I pay that Delmont gumshoe a fortune and it takes Gallagher to come up with the Harriet Starn thing. Most of all, it takes Gallagher to find out for me where to locate Oliver Starn. I stop in to see him at the hospital and he picks up the phone like a pasha and calls the almighty *Rowland's*. Zip-zip-zip, they check and they call right back. Starn's staying at Grande Bretagne in Athens. Don't tell anybody, but I'm getting to like that fresh kid." He read for her what he had cabled Athens: " 'Matters have arisen in Harrison trial affecting welfare of you and your family. Urgently suggest you return immediately and confer with undersigned before case goes to jury.' " And added, "Here's fifty that says he'll be home before he's finished reading it."

And teased, "Oh, by the way, speaking of fifty— How's Gramps? Still there?"

She hung up.

And sat and considered the good man in the next room. She had mentioned Ray's suggestion that for a time they not be seen together. He had understood and agreed. He would attend the trial, from the rear of the courtroom, and would be available for sturdy-oak purposes. "I wanted to come to see you, that's all," he'd said.

No, that's not all, dearest Norman, she thought.

But so be it. What matters is that you're here and we're together and I'm warm near you. For now, that's all that matters.

25

"No," Martha said on Sunday's flight to Hartley.

"They're merely suggestions," Nicole Rooney said.

"I'm totally opposed, and I won't go along with any of it," Martha said sternly. Seven other New York members of Sisters of Sappho were on the plane. Two of them were in the seats in front of Martha and Nicole, listening. "Signs and posters reading 'Free All Women' are precisely right because they're what the protest is about," she continued. "Signs that call for equal rights for lesbians are perfectly appropriate. But some of these other slogans . . . no."

"We thought that capturing attention fast—"

"Frankly, I'm rather surprised at you," said Martha. "Didn't we agree on the necessity for dignity? Equality for women is a serious matter or it isn't. This 'Gay Girls Is Where It's At,' for instance. In the context of a protest march I'd personally find it as offensive as I would a blacks' protest referring to dice and gin."

"The word 'gay' is misunderstood."

"It may well be. But a poster's no place to make it understood, and certainly not in a conservative stronghold like Hartley. Our position there is to plead a serious cause seriously. This 'Gay Girls Is Where It's At' sort of drivel immediately associates the movement with cheap thrills and self-gratification."

"We don't exactly see it that way, Sister Martha."

"I'm afraid you'll have to start if I'm to be of any help to you."

The remainder of the flight was civilized, endurably chilly.

A banner at the air terminal announced HARTLEY—THE "HART" OF AMERICA. They were met and effusively welcomed by two women—one young, one nearly elderly—who said that the station wagon could squeeze five passengers; the others could get to the nearby Airport Motor Inn by cab. Martha responded to the cordial greetings and was herself cordial during the short ride in the station wagon. The queasiness began to set in only when they reached the Inn's lobby and she was reminded that she and Nicole would be sharing the same room. Nicole had mentioned something earlier in the week about the possibility of their doubling up—the Motor Inn had over a hundred rooms but space wasn't limitless —and sharing a room had sounded logical.

Doubts came now as she waited to be registered. Aware of pass-ersby looking at her, consciously aware for perhaps the first time since she'd agreed to lead the project that there might be those who would view her as a lesbian simply because she was identifying herself with the cause, she quietly removed herself from Nicole Rooney's knot of women at the front desk. At the newsstand, she bought a local newspaper, the *Statesman-Patriot*, and pretended to immerse herself in it. There was a picture of Judith Harrison on the left lower half of the front page. There was a picture of herself—a grainy, ghastly picture—on the right lower half. She had time only to gather a quick impression of how the newspaper was treating the dual arrivals. The impression was that it was not only negative but mocking and hostile. Prominently placed was the directive "See Editorial 'Descending Locusts' on Page 3."

"What took so long down there," Nicole said in the elevator, "was that the clerk was confused. Seems there's another Hanaday regis-tered here."

"Odd. It's not that common a name," Martha said, and thought of Norman and decided it was impossible that he was the other Hana-day. There was no reason for him to have come here. He'd made that emphatically clear on the telephone.

The large, airy room had twin beds separated by a night table. Martha was relieved, yet scolded herself: *I've got to get over this nonsen-sical notion that all lesbians are perpetually in carnal heat. Why would she try to seduce me, anyway? She mentioned at our very first meeting at the Russian Tea Room that the sadness of having ended a long-time love affair had that week been remedied by the beginning of a new and far better one. I remember thinking it odd that a stranger would talk that way to me, another stranger. Maybe she was just being ebullient. Maybe it was a message of some kind . . .*

They agreed to unpack only the essentials because SOS's key regional directors would be coming soon, but they read the

Statesman-Patriot together, the twin stories about SOS and Judith Harrison's upcoming trial, and they read the editorial. It was a beastly piece, loaded to appeal to the lowest mentalities, decrying the presence in moral, family-and-church-oriented Hartley of one "Northern woman proudly known to be a fornicator" and "a female band of sexual nuts and lunatics and perverts."

Incredibly, Nicole wasn't upset by the editorial. Unbuttoning her blouse, preparing to shower, she teased, "Still hooked on dignity, Sister Martha? Still think we can afford to speak softly when we're up against gangsterism like this? 'Perverts.' I've heard the word so often it doesn't even faze me any more. All it does is make me ready to battle those mothers all the harder." Martha regarded her. She was somewhere between forty-five and fifty, a big woman, nearly flat-chested despite her size, almost neuter in build. She grinned and said, "I'll be out in two shakes." Alone, Martha re-read the newspaper's paragraph about herself. It called her "a former spokesman for the so-called women's liberation movement."

Former.

It stung, even coming from an obviously hateful and demented sheet such as this. I'm here and now, she thought angrily. She waited for the sound of the shower and cried aloud, "I'm here and now, do you hear me, you ignorant, sadistic gravediggers? I'm here and I'm now!"

There were enough chairs and enough space on the beds' edges to accommodate the eleven women who came to the room. About a third of them struck Martha as perceptibly mannish in dress and manner. One in particular, a muscled, mean-looking thing introduced as Guv, folded her arms and fastened hostile eyes on Martha almost from the moment she arrived. The nearly elderly lady who'd been at the airport pursed her thin lips, not seductively, surely, but as if to follow the discussion better, and seemed completely out of place here. The others gave every evidence of femininity; in dress and manner, there was no hint that any of them was—different.

Ignoring Guv's disconcerting stare, Martha spoke her opening remarks with authority and ease. She would be meeting with the press at six o'clock this evening in the Oak Room downstairs, she said, and she would stress that the demonstration of several hundred Sisters of Sappho in front of the courthouse early tomorrow morning would be purely for the purpose of insisting on respect and equality for all women, heterosexual as well as homosexual. And she said:

"You've seen, or you should see, the editorial attacking you in today's local paper. It's mindless and scurrilous, but I have no question that it will be read as gospel by a lot of people, some of whom are always only too ready to sling mud. I'm not suggesting that we be scared off by it or tuck our tails between our legs (*uh-oh, wrong choice of words; unerasable*), but I do think we should respect it as a barometer of inbred antipathies toward anyone who marches to a different drummer. The editorial was full of such inflammatory language as 'female perverts' and 'godless sinners playing Halloween in men's attire'—"

Hoots and catcalls.

Martha tapped the wall. "Let's not waste time booing the enemy here. The reason I consider this a valuable editorial and worth drawing to your attention is to assure you, if assurance is needed, that we're all in something other than friendly territory. We're here to try to persuade everyone who'll be looking in on this community that lesbians, that all women, are demanding social justice and dignity, and we'll do it with the voice of solidarity. But I must emphasize that the slightest show of—well, vulgarity on anyone's part can be nothing but counterproductive. I must . . ."

She felt she was losing them, some of them. Guv, yawning, squinted at Nicole and said, "See why I was burning up the phone wires all the way from Tallahassee, Nic? If this march is to have any impact at all, it calls for one of us to wear the chief's feathers. The Birchers don't look to the Kunstlers to lead them. The Jews don't call up Eichmann to dance them over to Hadassah. And now I have it verified that I brought a bunch of sisters all this distance to line up behind Uncle Tom."

Another, less querulous: "Guv's right on. No disrespect to you," she said to Martha, "but maybe you're just too straight to dig the torture the straights put us through every day of our lives."

"Damn right I'm right on," Guv declared. "We're not out here to kiss duffs—"

Another, to laughter: "Not on the street, anyway."

243

Guv: "—and beg the straights to *tole*rate us. We're fighting for our goddamn *life*, our goddamn self-re*spect* as human *be*ings! What's this *dig*nity crappo? I don't feel dignified. I feel *me*, and whoever else I feel like feeling if that's how the wind blows. And no cracks from you other cracks about blowing, you gutter-minded dykes."

Fully half of them were suddenly vocal at once, some laughing, some chuckling, some darting embarrassed or appraising glances at Martha and calling for a vote on how the Monday march should proceed, most maintaining that Guv was telling it right. *But I agreed to come here on the express understanding*—Martha was saying, and they were ignoring her, pointedly ignoring her; suddenly no one was still, the rowdies had taken over, they were in movement and jabbering childishly among themselves and crowding her out; talking as she tried to talk, and then something was building in this volatile room . . . Something, something bubbling upward and directed against her, some *see-how-independent-and-naughty-we-are?* conspiracy that had to have been firmly planned against her in advance. An almost mass nose-thumbing at Martha Hanaday, a ballet of derision; a smirking couple on the bed were groping each other and kissing, the act not loving but gratuitously lewd; the approving, encouraging language from the watchers was boisterous, smutty. She watched, awed, watched the wild irresponsibility of these grown children, all these hostile, degenerate children, heard no one support her demand for order, heard Guv close to her rumbling, "Now you get the picture, man. We're *us*, we don't need dignity sermons, we've shuffled long enough and it got us zilch, we go the way *we* go, and that's what we expect you to lay on the press boys: The straights don't have to buy our style—we don't need to recruit *no*body—but they're gonna have to learn fast and once and for all that we're for real, the shuffling's done, we're here to stay. Say it as fancy and high-ass as you like, but that's the message, dig?"

Once more, Martha, appalled, strove to insist that they settle down and listen, looked for someone, anyone, to give her a sign of acceptance, kindness, respect. She watched the flaring restlessness, the nervous chatter and laughter, the finger-snapping caricatures of women; she heard playful, feverish conversations about sex organs, saw another couple grappling and others cheering them on, and everywhere there was laughter, cheap, adolescent, degrading, self-degrading, everything unreal. Unreal . . . the nearly elderly lady, silent and pleasant-faced, sat perched and observant, either stone deaf or under the delusion that she was at a ladies' afternoon bridge club luncheon. Unreal . . . Martha turned to Nicole Rooney and entreated, "Can't you stop all this?" Nicole shrugged, her smile whimsical, a smile that plainly approved the unreality.

And Martha's own reality crystallized. You arranged this, she accused Nicole wordlessly. You used my good name to focus attention on your barbarism. You and your Boston friends, none of you had the vaguest intention of having me do anything except provide you with initial publicity. Disgusting, pathological, all of you . . . you're not from Lesbos, you're all from the bottom of the barrel, how dare you fool me, how dare you, how—

"—dare you!" she shrieked.

The voices, the frenetic activity, stopped.

She was on her feet. "Trickery! I've had enough trickery! What gave any of you the idea you could use Martha Hanaday and then toss her away at your psychotic convenience? I'm Martha *Han*aday! My knowledge and my wisdom are admired by mature people you couldn't even begin to look up to! The only people who don't follow my advice are people like you, sick souls writhing your pathetic little lives away in fantasy! I don't need you, you sad, disgusting little freaks and perverts, Martha Hanaday doesn't need you, never, not ever!"

Her head reeling, her eyes half-blinded in tears and fright, she charged to her purse and suitcase on the luggage rack, and voices started again, soft voices and loud voices, and she struggled with alarmingly numb fingers to close the suitcase, and someone was yawping for her to apologize for the names she'd called them, and someone was laughing and someone else was saying let the has-been go, and she snapped her coat from the closet, and at the door one of the very feminine looking ones grinned cruelly at her and said, "Kitchen get too hot for you, baby? We can read it on you a mile away: you put gays down, but that's not where your bottom drawer's at. You're lookin' to cook with us, right? Right, stuff?"

She wanted to slap the slimy impudence out of this pervert, this abomination, and sensed that she would be struck back. The sounds behind her had not stilled. She pushed the abomination, who was laughing, and opened the door and fled, not to the elevator but the stairway.

She ran.

She missed her step on the second flight of stairs and tumbled the last half-dozen steps to the ground. For a time she lay sprawled on the hard floor, in weeping and in anguish, and rubbed her leg, and peered at her opened suitcase, its halves parted wide like spreading thighs, clothing strewn about the floor. Other belongings were up in that foul room, dresses and her briefcase, and she sat up finally and whimpered and hugged her knees against her chin as she had done as a little girl in the treehouse her father had built for her, no longer weeping but waiting, forcing an even breathing and patiently waiting for reality to return, for reality to reassure her that the oppressive dream would soon be done, for everyone to come to her and apologize.

"Ma'am?"

She was being shaken, gently.

"Ma'am? You all right?"

She opened her eyes to see a black woman in a chambermaid's dress near her. "You must've taken a real spill. Do you think you can move? Should I go get the doctor?"

"No. I—guess I passed out for a moment. Thank you."

"Lucky I came by. Not many folks use these stairs." The chambermaid helped her up, cautioning her to take it slow and easy. Martha thanked her again and saw her putting the clothes into the suitcase and asked her not to bother. "Never you mind about bother. I tripped going down some steps last Good Friday and I was laid up for two weeks." She closed the suitcase. "Sure you're all right now? Let me help you to the ladies' room, right through here."

The hairbrush and lipstick helped. She noticed a run in her stocking. She removed both stockings and threw them in the trash can. Her wristwatch read a quarter-past six. That couldn't be—the meeting upstairs had started precisely at three. The lobby was uncrowded. The lobby clock read six-twenty. The bell captain gave her directions to the Oak Room, and she asked him to mind her coat and suitcase for a time. There were two dark walnut doors to the Oak Room, both closed. She chose the rear door, and paused for a moment before she pulled it open. She heard mingled, muffled sounds, punctuated by sounds of laughter.

246

The press meeting was in progress as Martha stole into the large, crowded room—in progress and clearly in disarray. Most of the SOS people who had been upstairs were present in the front, from Nicole Rooney to the monstrous Guv, yet no one appeared to be in charge. The mood was that of a happy free-for-all; they were all gathered here, it seemed, the Sapphos and the journalists alike, not for an orderly congress of questions and answers but, incredibly, for some kind of sport, for mutual needling and heckling.

Martha watched from the back wall. Four of the women were talking at once, apparently about four different issues, amusing their audience with obscene allusions and foul language. Guv wasn't seated but shambling about, in caged-lion style, now grinning, now winking, now bellowing "Right on! Right on! Right on!" over the good-natured din as though enjoying the chaos. One featherbobbed girl in a prim Peter Pan collar was shouting that gay gals were the only honest women, and as she shouted an even younger girl —surely no more than seventeen; where on earth had she come from?—was complaining loudly that gays everywhere had to put up not only with all the nowhere, outmoded rules and regulations on motherhood, marriage between straights, jobs, "the whole crashing-bore bit," but they were also discriminated against and looked down on like dirt every minute of every day by "you friggin'—no, make that *non*-friggin'—envious straights." It was outrage uttered as a laugh line, and some of the reporters cooperated by laughing, throwing vulgarities back at the women, insults returned, insults wrapped in humor.

It was all a game, a hate-spewing game, the Guvs courting contempt with their own contemptuous frivolities, the press evidently having decided that they'd been invited to a freak show so they might as well roll with the ribald jokes as long as the free liquor poured. Martha, in horror, knew she must publicly disassociate herself from these maniacs instantly, explain their vile betrayal of her good faith and trust, clear herself.

She stepped forward. She suddenly heard her name called out, over the noise. They saw her, everyone saw her, and she could not move. She saw all their eyes, glimpsed someone who looked like Norman, saw the reporters directing themselves to her, saw the Guvs glaring at her with naked scorn. "Well, look who's here, straight from Straight City: Ole Black Josie with the strummin' banjo

247

and the pushbutton loyalties!" Guv crowed, and there were hisses and roaring boos from the women, and then they were hurling abusive language at her, shockingly abusive. Martha stood frozen. *Why are they doing this? What did I do to make them want to hurt me so? Why does everyone want to hurt me?* They were denouncing her, calling her a has-been, a coward, a traitor to the women's movement . . .

Norman? Is that Norman over there? Why is everything blurring, why is everyone so brutal to me?

And then Norman was at her shoulder, leading her away from the violence.

The public rooms were much too public, and her own room, the room that wasn't hers any longer, was out of the question, so she agreed to go with him to his. Strange, she thought as he closed the door, this is my husband, my very gentle husband, and I don't feel safe alone with him. Maybe it's because he hasn't smiled at me.

He had gone to the Oak Room, he said, because he had learned she was going to speak there; had gone in curiosity and in the hope she would be all right. The reporters had asked about her absence at the outset, before the meeting had given way to pandemonium. He had gathered—and hoped the press had gathered, from the invective of those women at the mention of her name—that she had returned to her senses. He had stayed on in curiosity that grew to fascination, relief that she was free of them.

"It's good that you came for me," Martha said. "We can go back home now."

"No," he said. "We can't."

He spoke of his wish that nothing bad happen to her and of his resolute decision to go through with the divorce. ("Divorce? What are you talking about?" "The divorce I talked about in the apartment that morning." "You're talking in riddles. You never said a word to me about anything like that. I don't understand why you're taking sadistic advantage of my upset, Norman, you of all people, but I simply won't have it. We'll check out of this loathsome place and fly home tonight." "You're not hearing me, Martha.") Presently, because he quietly insisted, she heard. She listened to a preposterous monologue about their marriage as an ongoing mistake, unconscionable rubbish, every bit of it.

She listened for an indulgently long while, inwardly sighing at the picture of this proper, aging man who was saying, in his own clumsy way and without a drop of insight, that he needed freedom in order that he might escape the aging process. The solution was time, of course. They would go home together, and perhaps vacation at the Cape when the weather permitted, and she would hear him out during leisurely strolls on the beach and help him come to insight and everything would be right between them again.

The telephone rang beside her and she automatically picked it up. "Hello."

". . . Is this Professor Hanaday's room?" she heard. Familiar voice.

"Yes." She looked at Norman, saw him tighten.

"May I speak with him, please?"

"Who's calling, please?"

"Judith Harrison. Is that—Martha?"

Familiar voice. Yes.

"Yes, Miss Harrison, I'm Mrs. Hanaday. One moment." She offered the receiver to Norman. "Miss Harrison would like to speak with you."

Everything clicked into place for Martha Hanaday as she sat motionless, observing his obvious discomfort as he answered. The call was predictably short, mostly monosyllabic, clearly an embarrassment for him. Then he was done and Martha, pleased with her sense of emotional strength and well-being, devised a supportive smile, absolutely determined to avoid clichés at all costs. There would be no hysteria, not even displays of disapproval.

But one question was justified, she believed. "How long has it been going on? Since that night you spent hours and hours finding a taxi for her?"

Judith Harrison was not the origin or the cause of his wanting a divorce, he said. It was important that she know that.

Civilized smile widening, she said, "My naïveté surprises me even more than your dishonesties, Norman. I always had the idea I was fairly perceptive, but then I always had the idea, too, that for all your inadequacies you were basically an honorable man. Most surprising on both counts, don't you agree?" She stood, still smiling. "I wonder if I might use your telephone?"

"Hell, Martha, this formality—"

"Room four-one-seven," she said into the mouthpiece, catching a glimpse of herself in the table mirror, seeing cool efficiency and control, appreciating the image. Nicole Rooney answered and Martha said cheerfully, "Oh, good, you're in. This is Martha Hanaday. There are some belongings of mine in your room. A bellboy will be there in the next few minutes with a container of some kind to collect them. Do have them ready." She then phoned the bell captain with instructions, replaced the receiver, and said to her husband, "I wish you and Judith all the goodness and happiness and understanding you deserved and never once got from me during all our years together, Norman. You have my promise that I'll see the divorce is as easy and uncomplicated as humanly possible."

"Where are you going now?"

"Upward, my dear, upward. What is positively *man*datory is that you carry on without any guilt about a decision you've made wisely, and without the slightest worry about me. I land on my feet, always. When I travel I travel upward, always."

I suppose I ought to be falling apart, and yet I feel perfectly fine, even content, Martha thought on the descent to the lobby, *as though a whole series of pressures and burdens have been lifted off me.* She didn't bother to check out; the room had been paid for in advance. The bell captain had her suitcase and coat. A bellhop brought her the things from Room 417. She gave twenty-five cents to each man and thanked them both, puzzled by their abrupt switch from courtesy to surliness.

Calmly, rationally, she considered her next step. There were no more direct flights to New York this evening, but easy connecting flights were available. The prospect of home was extremely inviting. Yes, she thought; I'll go home. It's probably a ferocious amount of traveling to do in one day, but I'm not in the least tired. Home is home base, where I do my best thinking. Distance enhances perspective. I can chart my course with equanimity there, with Stephanie Wall's help and my own clarity. Yes. I want to be in my own home.

"More coffee, ma'am?"

She looked up. She wasn't in the motel lobby. This was a highway diner and the clock above the cash register read nine o'clock and she was alone in a booth with the Sunday edition of the *Statesman-Patriot* before her. She blinked, tracing how she had got here, unable to.

She nodded for more coffee. Curious. Unimportant. The name in the newspaper was Clifford C. Albright. There was a telephone booth in the diner, and she found Clifford C. Albright's home number in the directory and dialed it. A lady's voice answered and said her husband was in but accepting only urgent calls for the next several days.

Martha gave her name. "Tell him it's vital to the Harrison trial that he and I talk together at once," she said.

26

Sam Gallagher, tall, dark and handsome?

I was able to get out of the hospital bed on my own by Saturday, long enough to receive Ray Pallino, catch a bit of hell from him, and agree to be on deck for the trial. By Sunday I was even hobbling up and down the corridor on a crutch, but the young doctor who'd more or less guaranteed I would be out of there in roughly a week after I checked in brought me a revision. Some of my plumbing wasn't healing as tidily as anticipated, and I was urged to stay put for another five or six days. No way, I said; I had a date in court I wasn't going to miss. We wrangled, and worked out a compromise: I could attend the trial as long as I came back into the hospital every afternoon and stayed the night. Okay, I agreed, seeing the sense of it. The elephant hadn't stepped off my chest, altogether. Staying close to the young doctor—Croft, his name was—seemed smart, because he'd come to learn the intricacies of my plumbing. Besides, the prospect of exchanging those marvelous hospital meals of Jell-o and lettuce for that Airport Motor Inn swill—I swear I'd seen a family of African pygmies dipping their arrows in it—was manifestly unappealing.

I had a nice phone call on Sunday, from Noah Walters. He'd been ailing a bit since our get-together—nothing worth writing home about, he assured—and he'd just heard about me. I assured him that my ailing wasn't worth writing home about, either, and I answered all his questions as well as I could. My impression was that he hadn't too much use for the Raymond Pallino school of earthquake lawyering, though he didn't make it any big deal. Sure, he'd be glad to help in any way if he were asked to, but he certainly wasn't going to stick his nose in unless and until. "You look behind you next time," he said, and there was affection and sweetness in that gruff old voice. "This world needs all the good young fellows like you it can get." Awfully nice thing to say, wasn't it?

Monday morning came.

Judith called for me at nine o'clock. Pallino was already in court. She drove, smiling but tense. I kept the conversation light. She stayed tense, and said, "All I hope is that we can slip inside without spotlights on us."

That wasn't to be, we learned when we parked her car near the courthouse; the only way to get in was up the front steps. The area was absolutely swamped with people. Rubberneckers and reporters and camera crews and more rubberneckers and the Sisters of Sappho.

Oi, those Sisters of Sappho. I forget who it was who later on estimated that they numbered about a hundred and fifty, but I'm convinced there were a million and fifty. Everywhere, like carpenter ants, with signs and shrill voices. There were lots of foot patrolmen—too many to represent Hartley's finest; most of them had probably been borrowed from neighboring towns for the occasion—and there were wooden barricades and even cops on horses. But keeping the peace seemed an almost hopeless job. The noise and the crush were terrific. Someone hollered that Judith Harrison was here, and every eye flashed our way, and the taunts began.

Judith held herself straight. The cops weren't straining themselves to clear a path for us. A matron with naturally blue hair called Judith a Jezebel and spat, with impeccable aim. One gallus-snapping whiz-banger yawped, "Hey, there, Miss Whore-isson, how's about we go equal? You grease the tractor and I'll warsh the clothes. You bring in the bacon and I'll leave you play with my tits. Hee-hee-hee-hee." I told her my slowpoking was holding her back, told her to zip up the steps and inside alone. She shook her head. We moved slowly out of necessity. No one blocked us, but getting through that heavy crowd was almost a career.

We inched. The only good thing about those Sisters of Sappho was that their hijinks served to divert the attention of some of the jaspers away from Judith. That was the only good thing about them. Their signs contained such sensitive pleas for understanding as *Lesbian Power* and *What's So Great About Straight?* and *Gay's the Way* and *Love Is Sweeping the Country—Don't Brush Off Lesbians* and *Gay Girls Is Where It's At* and *Shake It Take It Make It!!!* and my favorite, the poignant *Would You Want Your Daughter To Marry A Man?* The television cameras kept grinding, although it was a sure bet the audio boys would be working overtime to bleep the gutter language these deranged broads were belting out. They weren't there to help Judith, or all women's rights, and they sure as hell weren't there to help lesbians' rights, unless there's something positive in milking scorn. One true believer, a leather-lungs bull dyke type who came on like she got her Saturday night jollies by beating up stevedores, was preaching above all the other shattering noises that every straight who'd ever lived secretly longed to be gay.

Inching forward a little more successfully now, we saw some police breaking up what seemed to be a fight. It wasn't a fight. Two of the lovelies were having at it on the courthouse steps, dressed but roiling against each other like overheated coyotes. The cops yanked them apart and the more decorous of the lovelies loudly cooed, "Frig off, pig!"

If Martha Hanaday, whom I would have recognized from photographs, was anywhere among that cavalcade of stars, I didn't see her.

At last we were mounting those courthouse steps—no cinch for me and my crutch, certainly no cinch for Judith, who was visibly trembling. The crewcut carrying the *Lesbian Power* sign rushed at Judith, threw sinewy arms around her, bellowed, "Let's all hear you say you're one of us, Sister Judith!" and planted an unsisterly kiss as close as she could to Judith's mouth. Quickly coming out of shock, Judith shoved her, but not before a photographer snapped the historic event from three feet away. The crewcut fell, which presumably didn't help matters. Judith hustled in, alone.

I found her, about twenty minutes to ten. She had been crying, and I held her, and she broke down again with a queen-sizer of a cry. Finally the nose was blown, the smile returned, and she said, "Last one into the courtroom's a rotten egg." We went in together. The bandages across my chest were too tight, and I felt crummy. The only reason I mention that is to enlist sympathy.

Ten o'clock, Monday morning. A very crowded courtroom.

The press wasn't welcomed with open arms to attend the show entitled *The State* v. *Judith Harrison*. Albright, the prosecutor, glowered at me, but I was at the defense table as a member of Pallino's staff. So there, Albright.

A moment before the judge was ushered in, I pinched Judith

under the table for good luck. She pinched me back. She wasn't trembling any more.

The trial began. As soon as the court reporter was ready to go, Ray Pallino moved for a change of venue. "The basis for your motion?" Judge Jamison asked.

"It's brought to my attention that the news media's preliminary coverage of this case through the rest of the country is balanced and objective, whereas the press treatment in and around Hartley is blatantly loaded and prejudicial and guarantees that my client will be unable to get a fair trial."

Jamison, a mite testy for so early in the game—though I must say that from the outset Pallino was wearing an almost visible sandwich board announcing that he wasn't looking for sweethearts—advised, "Let counsel be assured that the bench only presides over fair trials. Is that understood?"

"It's noted."

"Further, reception would be similar in any other part of the state. Motion denied."

"Exception."

"Exception noted."

Pallino's next motion—for dismissal—was based on the equal protection under law concept. "We read a panel list of ninety-six prospective jurors, eight of whom are females," he said. "The fact that the state excludes women as jurors, except as volunteers, is in itself automatically prejudicial in a case directly involving sexism. I move that there be a more proportionate representation of women."

"Denied."

"Exception."

"Noted."

The potential jurors were shepherded in, and questioned. Clifford Albright took speedy advantage of his peremptory challenges by excusing the sprinkling of blacks and most of the women, but he had a solicitous, sunny disposition toward those who came through as shuffling cretins. Pallino was solicitous to no one. He asked Mrs. Stuart Biggs, potted-palm housewife and grandmother, "Do you feel you could be impartial and judge this case on its merits?"

"Oh yes indeed!" said Mrs. Biggs.

"How much have you read or heard about the charges against the defendant?"

"Oh, very little, which is why I can be impartial. I don't get to do much reading except my Bible, of course, and once in a while the *Reader's Digest*, what with my home and tenants to take care of and my church work, but I'm very good at being impartial."

He excused her—probably sensing what I sensed: she was so impartial that she was champing to hang Judith by the thumbs—and then asked Alvin Kirk, house painter, "Been reading much about this case?"

"Only what's been in the local paper, sir."

"The *Statesman-Patriot*?"

"That's right."

"Formed a few opinions?"

"Oh no, sir."

"Do you think what consenting adults do in private is any business of this court, of any court?"

Albright: "That's not pertinent."

The judge agreed.

Pallino let it go. "Tell me, Mr. Kirk," he said, "are you married?"

"Yes sir."

"Fine wife, I'm sure."

"None better."

"Married how long?"

"Let's see . . . twenty-nine years. No, sorry, twenty-seven."

"Congratulations. Now in those twenty-seven years, you and Mrs. Kirk have exchanged a cross word or two, haven't you?"

"Do we fight, do you mean?"

"Have disagreements. The happiest married couples have disagreements from time to time. Raise their voices, say unpleasant things they may think better of an hour later or the next day."

"Well"—a wooden grin—"yes sir, you could say that. Never anything serious mostly, but we've had a couple of battle royals now and then. Nothing serious."

"You've criticized your wife?"

"Sure."

"And you're saying she's criticized you?"

An impatient Albright said, "Your Honor, the court's valuable time is being wasted with this nonsense. Might we get on—"

Whipping around, Pallino snapped at Albright, "*My* time is valuable, too! See that you remember that!"

"Counsel is advised to learn decorum quickly," the judge cautioned.

Ignoring him, Pallino asked Kirk, "Your wife has criticized you?"

"Now and again, but—"

"Then I submit to you, Mr. Kirk, that your good wife is in danger of arrest and prosecution. There is a law in this state that a wife may never speak ill to or of her husband, never criticize or question him harshly. She must be sweet-tempered and respectful at all times, on pain of seizure by authorities."

"Your Honor . . ." Albright groaned.

His Honor: "What is your point, counselor?"

Still ignoring him, doing it grandly, Pallino asked, "Are you aware of that law, Mr. Kirk?"

"No sir."

"It was passed in the year 1817. It's never been revoked, so it remains an enforceable law. Just out of curiosity, Mr. Kirk, would you have any idea of how many more jails this state would have to build if that law were strictly enforced?"

On his feet, Albright stormed, "Is Your Honor really going to allow this asinine conduct?"

"Oh, never mind," Pallino said, as though bored. "This juror is acceptable to defense. As a matter of fact, in order that we not waste the court's and the prosecution's valuable time, I accept without challenge every juror the prosecution takes a liking to."

"Playful kid," I whispered to Judith.

She nodded, not smiling.

Clifford Albright's opening statement to the jury was of corntassel excellence. Consentual behavior was not at issue. A law had been violated. All laws were made by the people's legislative representatives for the purpose of protecting the people—"You and you and you"—from all and any of the antisocial evils enumerated in the Ten Commandments. Granum County's citizens were upstanding folks who subscribed to the Christian ethic of the sanctity of home and family and religious adherence, and had decided in their wisdom to view morality not as some outmoded shoebutton to be laughed at and ignored, but as a living, breathing, abiding force in everyday life.

"Everyone, under our system of jurisprudence, is equal in the eyes of the law," Albright intoned, fingering his tie clasp four inches below the knot. "We are confronted in this trial, however, with a defendant who for many years has pictured herself as considerably more equal than the rest of us. How immorally she comports herself in communities outside Hartley is not our legal affair. But when she comes to our community, yours and mine and our children's, and entices a stranger to perform lewd and lascivious and filthy acts with her, as the court will prove, our paramount concern must direct itself not only to our own sensibilities but to those of our beloved young ones. The concept that sexual mores and the law have nothing to do with each other presumably works well in pagan societies. Ours, though, happens to be dedicated to decency and—if my learned colleague will forgive an unsophisticated, old-fashioned term—moral righteousness. Without a strong code of morality we are telling our children and our children's children, 'It's perfectly all right to indulge your senses in any paganism if it feels good. Anything goes. It's only those old fogeys who believe in God and goodness who say the piper must be paid.'

"I reject that. I know you will."

Raymond Pallino swaggered to the jury box. Insolent as hell.

"If what Judith Harrison was doing in the Polo Motel in the early evening of June seventh of this year is what this trial is all about," he said, "I assume the prosecution will make that clearer than it was made in his opening remarks. If Judith Harrison's sexual history is what this trial is all about—her private past plus her professional life—I'm hopeful the prosecution will eventually clear that up for us, too. For you and you and you and me.

"The people's charge against Judith Harrison—the stated one—is that she committed the crime of fornication. It's long been my information as an outsider, and I naturally welcome correction, that fornication is an act performed by more than one person at a given time. Since there is no accusation that Judith Harrison forcibly raped Luther Cobb—although I can't imagine how that accusation was overlooked—I have the feeling that Mr. Cobb wasn't in that motel room, with all his clothes off, to invite her to church services. Yet there is Mr. Cobb, seated over there on the side of the prosecution's angels. No charge against him.

"Would you like to know why not? Because men don't fornicate; women do. That's what the prosecution just told you.

258

"If rationality were in vogue around these parts, then what my client and Mr. Cobb did or did not do in private would be a matter purely between them—them and conceivably Mrs. Cobb as well, who is also sitting over there on the side of the angels. Let's concede for the time being that Mr. Albright is correct, that the only issue relative here is whether or not a specific act of illegal sexual intercourse was done on a specific date. If that's so, then a crime is a crime, no matter who commits it, and quite obviously the fact that the defendant's name is Judith Harrison or Jane Doe or Mazie Shultz is entirely immaterial. But very well—I'm completely willing to go along with the prosecution playing it both ways. Let's let him have his cake and eat it.

"Stripping everything down, what the prosecution is asking you to do is to convict and send to the penitentiary someone you're not supposed to like or approve of.

"I'll tell you what I'm up to. It won't be to attempt to persuade you that Judith Harrison models chastity belts, *if* that's the tack the prosecution chooses to take in order to scandalize you.

"I'm going to scandalize you, too, but with something even better than sex. I'm going to prove that Judith Harrison was framed. By some upstanding citizens in your community. I'm going to prove that other upstanding citizens in your community knew of the frame as it was being planned, participated in it, and some of them are in this courtroom this minute."

To Albright he said, "Your turn."

The first witness, Brian Whitlock, was one of the two cops who'd arrested Judith at Andrea Lane's. He simply recounted the event of the arrest itself, and Pallino, conferring quickly with Judith who nodded, seemed otherwise disinterested, as though he would have only a perfunctory question if any, until Whitlock mentioned that, on the way to the station house, the defendant had behaved in a rowdy manner.

In his examination, Pallino said, "Define 'rowdy manner.'"

"The defendant employed loud, raucous, and coarse language."

"I see. Were you offended?"

"I'm answering your question."

"So you are. Give us a sample of her coarse language."

"I'd rather not. There are ladies present here."

259

"There's also justice present here, or so I've been told. It's possible you and I are both wrong. Now then, Officer—"

A gavel bang and an angry judge. "You're straining the bench's patience, counselor."

"Now then, Officer," Pallino said, "let's hear some of that language."

"Well, when she refused to come along quietly, I touched her arm, like guiding her, and she slapped me and she yelled out, 'Take your hands off of me, you pig sonofabitch.'"

"What type of language did you expect her to use when she was being busted like a common criminal—'Mercy sakes, nice man'?"

"Objection," from Albright.

"Sustained," from Jamison.

"Do you happen to know, Officer," said Pallino, "that when Miss Harrison isn't in trouble with the law in Hartley, she's a spokesperson for what's sometimes called women's liberation?"

"I know that. As far as I'm concerned—"

"As far as you're concerned is of absolutely no interest to me. What does interest me, especially since we're talking about language, is whether you're aware that certain words are positively never used by feminists. At the very top of the list is 'sonofabitch.' 'Bastard,' maybe. 'Sonofabitch,' positively never."

"That I don't know about. All I know is what she said."

"Your memory is to be commended. But I wonder if it's a faultless memory. Are you sure it was her arm you touched? Might it have been her hip?"

"No!"

"Didn't she in fact slap your face because while in the process of arresting her you rested your hand on her hip?"

"No! Whoever made up a lie like that, she's got to be sick!"

"I move to strike out everything after 'No.' I've no further questions."

The next witness called was Luther Cobb, and Judith squeezed my hand hard. He moved toward the stand only slightly faster than if he were heading for the green door that led to the hot seat, but before he got there Pallino called out, "Just a moment, Officer Whitlock. Consider yourself still under oath. Where's your partner? There were two of you arresting officers."

"He's home with the flu."

"What's his name again?"

"Herman Stacey."

"I ask the court to direct that Officer Stacey be made available for questioning if we so wish. Or to supply a doctor's report testifying that his health precludes an appearance, in which case we'll move to visit him at his bedside."

Luther Cobb avoided looking at Judith. For that matter, his thimble-sized wife, at the table no more than a dozen feet away, wasn't looking at her, either, or at anyone, including Cobb, almost as if staring into space would help curtain unpleasantness.

Cobb was sworn in. My legal expertise leaves a lot to be desired, but I know when the hell has been coached out of a witness in advance, and Luther Cobb had had the hell coached out of him, right down to answering questions before they were completely asked. He had driven her to the Polo, and carried her suitcase into the motel room. And stayed, at her invitation, because the room was cozier than waiting for her in the car with the rain coming down and because he could watch television while she showered and changed clothes in the bathroom. He heard the shower. She came into the room, wet, with a towel in front of her, and smiled, and dropped the towel, and suggested they do some sport. He tried to get away partly because he was a married man but mainly because he remembered his daddy in Georgia telling him about black men getting lynched for having any truck with white ladies. He was scared but he was human, too. She wasn't only a mighty fine-looking lady, she teased him and coaxed him and teased him some more until he forgot all his daddy had told him and it seemed like all of a sudden he was as bare naked as she was. And his missus had been following him and caught them, and there was all that hollering. He sure didn't want his missus to go calling the policemen on her, but she went and did.

Had they actually had intercourse?

Not to the end. His wife came banging at the door just after they were getting started.

"My God," Judith whispered to me. "That poor man and those lies . . ."

The courtroom gasps and titters weren't bothersome enough for the judge to call for order. Albright, done, offered Cobb to Pallino, but the judge had other ideas. "The hour being late, we will resume at ten o'clock tomorrow morning. Court adjourned," he said.

I learned about this Norman Hanaday fellow after Monday's session concluded. From Judith, and in straight-shoulder fashion; I'll give her that. No, I didn't shower my blessings upon her. I got sore. I even threw half a tantrum. What the hell did she mean, she thought she was in love? I heard her out, and I said no, I wasn't one of those stiff-upper-lip noblemen who waxes philosophical when socked between the eyes. I heard how I sounded. It wasn't my finest hour, but I *was* sore and I let her know it. Dumb, of course. If you fall for someone else you fall for someone else; she hadn't worn the corsage I'd bought her for the senior dance since back in Malibu, but that was entirely beside the point. No, she didn't have to drive me to the hospital; I could get there myself, I said. Oh, boy. Why didn't I stamp my foot while I was at it and quiver my lower lip?

I returned to Hartley Hospital, home away from home, by taxi, stopping on the way to buy a quantity of Scotch. In my room and in my jammies, I poured one for myself and one for young Dr. Croft, who protested that he never drank during working hours. I prescribed a dose for his health, and he applauded my medical know-how. He was slightly high when he left, three generous belts later. "Best of luck in brain surgery," I said. And decided the boozing was a bore, and began to talk my recollections of Monday's trial into the tape recorder Burt Oehlrich's office had brought me, and quit when Judith kept getting in the way.

The evening television news coverage on Starn's station was predictable. Here were the marching lesbians with their shocking signs and savage manners. Here was the lesbian kissing Judith Harrison, the camera instantly cutting away so we wouldn't have to bother watching Judith react and angrily push the lesbian. Here was the commentator in the trench coat not slanting any news, Heaven forfend, but leaving you and me with the impression, natural enough, that The Northern Woman endorsed and was personally responsible for bringing all those Sappho folks to Hartley. I poured me another sorrowful blast and accepted a call from my boss, Howard Bracken, who had been calling me every other day from his rolling lawn hamburger grill in Weston, Connecticut. I told him about the day and he told me to get well, to not worry about the hospital cost. The beauty part about Howard was that he could be depended on to answer there was no cause to worry about the hospital cost despite the fact that the question had not been raised.

I was temporarily lifted from the glooms that evening by the large manila envelope that arrived. In it was the Hartley Police Department's photograph of Officer Herman Stacey, Brian Whitlock's partner, the cop home with the flu. Ray Pallino's attached note asked if the face was familiar. I called Pallino at once. He was in his room at the Motor Inn and I exclaimed, "You bet the face is familiar! This is one of the gents who clobbered me, the one I caught in the eye! Where'd you get the picture?"

"By way of outright theft. You're sure that you're sure he's the one?"

"No mistake. That flu he's home with localized itself in his left eye."

"Bravo, Irishman. On the evening of the day you were roughed, a Dr. Clyde Murdoch treated Stacey for an eye laceration. We'll see what fun we can squeeze out of that."

I mentioned my Sunday call from Noah Walters, and added that I was a little surprised that Pallino hadn't bothered to contact him as he'd promised. He corrected me in a hurry: "For your information, Walters was one of the first calls I made. His wife told me he hasn't been well at all, and she'd be grateful if I wouldn't disturb him unless it was necessary. So it isn't necessary, so don't accuse me of ignoring my other idol. See you later, Irishman."

Judith phoned at nine. "Can we make up?"

"I don't feel like it," I said. But a couple of minutes into the basically one-way conversation—she talking, I pouting—Sam the sucker began to melt. She told me a bit more than I cared to know about meeting and then remeeting this guy Hanaday, and she used the word "happy" a few times too often, so what could I do? I stayed manfully surly, and suggested she come to her occasionally admired senses before too long, but of course I didn't throw her out into the June snow. Not Judith.

Helene, the night nurse with the lovely personality that measured thirty-six inches in the thoracic area, came in to give me my back rub. I placed my mighty viselike grip on her thigh and she squealed, "Fresh!"

"That's me," I said. "If memory serves."

I was still awake at midnight, studying the ceiling and saying, *I love you Judith damn you I love you Judith damn you I love you* . . .

27

Soon after Judith finished the call to Sam on Monday night, the misgivings she had tidily tucked out of sight chose to reappear.

It would be easier for everyone—everyone meaning me—if you completed whatever remains to be completed with Martha away from Hartley, she wished she could summon the courage to say to Norman. *Martha knows about us, thanks to my wow of a blunder in phoning your room while she was there. Okay, that was pretty rough. Still, I believe you should be done with her if you're as convinced as you insist you are.*

Yet I'm less convinced than I was yesterday that your staying here is the way to do it. No matter how much Martha contributed consciously or unconsciously to the break, she's off somewhere now, surely blanketed in the wounds of rejection while you're here in the blankets with her successor.

You say you've had enough, you say you're through. Mmm. You checked this morning and she and her belongings are out of this motel. Simple? Not so Hollywood-happy-ending simple as it seemed long, long ago, yesterday.

Something else isn't so simple: this pose of mine of pure altruism. In truth, in ungracious truth, I don't really care all that much about the bruising of Martha Hanaday's sensibilities. I want the warmth of you without the responsibility of you—and, however indirect, of Martha. I'm nervous about Sex Maniac Destroys Happy Home *headlines. That doesn't make me a* Profiles in Courage *nominee, I know.*

I value you, Norman. I think I love you, or think I'm in love with you, which probably isn't the same thing but lovely, nonetheless. But do I go around framing Judith Hanaday *in my mind, picturing it on match covers and cocktail napkins? Am I really ready for that?*

Okay, maybe that's what's at the core of these all-of-a-sudden mental pacings of mine. Maybe I'm starting to recognize for real that you wouldn't or couldn't tolerate anything less from me than full commitment. Maybe what I'm afraid of is that you'll see I'm a darn sight less put-together than you seem to think I am, that serious emotional involvement and I have a way of parting company as soon as the signs start pointing to a brighter and closer tomorrow and tomorrow and tomorrow.

See what staying close can let you in for, dear, good Norman?

No, you don't see, because I'm too chicken to spell it out for you, as of course I ought to. Chicken, and evergreen-hopeful that the old dog can learn new tricks despite the shoddy track record. Damn. Damn.

Those tomorrows scare the bejaysus out of me, Norman. But I love having your arms around me.

28

Gallagher again, endearing vagabond and lovable rogue.

If you're so smart, you tell me how I should've acted, with Judith at the wheel, on that Tuesday morning drive to the courthouse. The Dutch Uncle approach might have delivered the shock of understanding: *Psychiatry isn't my bag, but just consider that losing your Dad and meeting up with this senior citizen named Hanaday at roughly the same time could be more than mere coincidence. After all, when you're ninety-five, he'll be a hundred and fifteen.* Or Pagliacci might have made a sparkling aria: *That sound you hear is my heart breaking, cara mia, but have you heard the one about the Polish tattoo artist?*

Neither tack was appropriate or entirely where my feelings were. Psychiatry wasn't my bag—who was I to explain her psyche to her, especially if I was all wrong?—but neither was I into the joke bag. I told her that what I'd said about loving her had been on the level, told her I disenjoyed speaking of love only to turn the corner and learn I was being crowded out.

That brief drive was not one of my finer moments, but, looking back, it couldn't have been movie popcorn for Judith, either. She listened. There wasn't any condescension in her earnest nods. She was sorry, she said, not for falling for the other guy but for not taking my seriousness seriously enough early on. Or that was the gist of it. The substance of what she said without saying it was, *You're a way station I'll always love, but in my fashion. I never meant for you to get fancy ideas about us. That's what I'm sorry about—that you did.*

"Right," I said. "Did I ever tell you about the nearsighted snake who tried to rape a rope?"

Nine-forty, Tuesday morning. The Sisters of Sappho were on or around the courthouse steps, fewer of them than on Monday, but the remainders were just that, remainders—dregs, grubs, greasy hair, greasy fingernails and kneecaps shouting up a storm at the TV cameras and the floral-shirted locals with the Instamatics, loudly basking in the laughter and jeers. The posters' letters seemed larger and more offensive than they had the day before. Certainly the language was more appalling, designed to remove any possible vestige of sympathy or even pity among the locals. A couple danced, cheek to cheek, groin to groin, psychosis to psychosis. Others badgered bug-eyed onlookers to sign petitions demanding instantaneous agreement by both the Republican and Democratic parties that the next United States President be gay. The crush and confusion continued, with lots of cops still on deck. There were no cops on horseback, though, which should have suggested that the peril to the peace had diminished since Monday. The foot patrolmen stood as Parthenon friezes, even when the Sisters spotted Judith, went *Yah yah yahhhh,* and advanced as one to gather her unto them for the watchful audience as their friend, blood foe, and fundamental savior. Judith and I managed to get through and past them, without a chair and whip, without help from the fuzz.

Why no fuzz help? A fair question. Why none of the Sisters arrested or run out of town? Another fair question. A fair answer: Why interfere with anyone who makes the women's movement look bad?

We got inside. Judith appeared none the worse for wear, though I did notice little ripples of agitation around the edges. Not many ripples, and most appealing edges.

Tuesday, ten A.M. Luther Cobb on the stand.

"Mr. Cobb," said Pallino, "when someone deliberately lies under oath, he's committing perjury. He's willfully making false statements, and that can earn him a jail sentence. Do you know that?"

"Yes suh."

"The worst that can happen to a heathen who places his hand on the Book of God and swears to be truthful and then knowingly lies is a prison term. A believing man, a religious man who does the same is liable to a punishment longer and certainly greater than a term behind bars. I'm talking about the Afterlife. Are you a believer in the Afterlife, Mr. Cobb?"

"'deed."

"You're a lay deacon at the Black Abyssinian Church in Hartley, is that correct?"

"Yes suh."

"Then you're familiar with the Commandments?"

"Yes suh."

"Do you believe they were divinely handed down?"

"Oh yes, suh."

"But maybe there are a few you take more seriously than the others, or a few less than the others?"

"They all the same, they's all impawtant."

"How about the Eighth Commandment? Would you recite it for me, please?"

" 'Thou shalt not bear false witness against thy neighbuh.' "

"Excellent. Now would you recite the Sixth Commandment?"

" 'Thou shalt not commit 'dultery.' "

"Right. The Lord just threw that one in for laughs, though, wouldn't you agree?"

Albright objected to the levity. Jamison sustained.

"You told this court yesterday," Pallino said, "your version of what took place in the Polo Motel on the early evening of June seventh. You said you broke the Sixth Commandment. God gave Moses a set of laws for you to live by, and you honor them all, but you broke law number six. Am I correct?"

"Yes suh. But like I say, the lady was teasin' and coaxin'—"

"Come on now, Mr. Cobb. Each Commandment is clear and precise. Does that law number six read 'Thou shalt not commit adultery except when a lady teases and coaxes?' "

"No suh."

"Do any of the Commandments allow for any bending of the rules? Is giving in to temptation occasionally okay?"

"No suh."

"But you're saying temptation made you violate law number six."

"Yes suh. I didn't say I done right."

"What kind of temptation can you conceive of that would make you break law number eight?"

". . . None. No temptation."

"Speak up. The court can't hear you."

Cobb cleared his throat and repeated his answer.

"Why should we take your word for that?" Pallino asked. "If you have reason to ignore the Sixth Commandment, why not ignore the First or Tenth or all of them if you're teased and coaxed? Why not simply pick and choose the convenient ones to follow and pretend the inconvenient ones don't exist? Obviously all the Commandments aren't of equal importance if you can violate the ones you want to."

Albright complained that the witness was being badgered. Before the judge could rule, Pallino said, "Do you feel badgered, Mr. Cobb? I'm asking questions of a church deacon, questions that have to do with religious and ethical conduct. Do you feel badgered because I'm trying to pry the truth out of you? Is it possible you've been advised that truth is anything you and your attorney can get a jury to swallow?"

Jamison ordered that stricken and warned Pallino that his abusive and argumentative behavior was inviting a contempt citation. Pallino pitched him an up-yours frown, and walked a couple of steps in silence and then resumed.

"Something puzzles me, Mr. Cobb. When two people in a motel room are engaged in an act as private as sexual intercourse, isn't it customary to see that the door is locked?"

"I guess so."

"You guess so. I happen to know so, and I happen to think everyone on this jury knows so. Now there was the defendant in the motel room, teasing, coaxing, fornicating. Let's pretend for a moment that the defendant never thinks to lock doors at such a time because she's so crazy with passion when she's about to fornicate that a second out to insure privacy would be an interruption. Let's say that her reputation is so questionable, anyway, that she figures she doesn't have much to lose if she's caught in the act. But wouldn't *you* have an awful lot to lose—you, a married man *and* a deacon?"

"It all happen so fast—"

"—that she had you completely in her power before you had a chance to remember that the Sixth Commandment means what it says."

The judge sustained Albright's objection and said, "The bench will not permit you to put words in the witness's mouth, counselor.

I'm further going to insist that as of this moment you start to practice law and to keep uppermost in your mind that gratuitous insolence will not be tolerated. You may proceed."

"Mr. Cobb," said Pallino, "who is Oliver Starn?"

I saw Jamison sit up. Albright sat up, too.

"Olivah—?"

"Starn. Who is he?"

"He owns the newspapuh."

"And Hartley as well, right?"

"Your Honor," Albright said, "why is someone with absolutely no relation to this case being brought—"

"Ask *me* that question!" Pallino spat at Albright. "The court has no way of knowing yet—I don't think so, at least—what the answer is."

Came the gavel. "Court is indulging you in enormous latitude, counselor, as I've indicated more than once. What's the relevancy of this line?"

"I'll establish relevancy shortly."

"See that you do."

"I'll try my hardest," Pallino said sarcastically. Then, to Cobb: "Inasmuch as Oliver Starn and his associates and employees are directly or indirectly involved in much of the life of Hartley—the city council, the school board, any number of things—would it be fair to say that as a workingman in this community, perhaps in your part-time job as a driver, you've worked for Mr. Starn or someone connected with him?"

"Not that I knows of. I don't ask folks their business."

"Very well. Now, with the recollection of your hand on the Holy Bible, Mr. Cobb," Pallino said carefully, "with the recollection of your having sworn to tell nothing but the truth so help you God, I now place this question to you: At the time you were paid or threatened to participate in the framing of Judith Harrison—"

"Your Honor!" from Albright.

"—wasn't the shadow of Oliver Starn hovering somewhere?"

"Your Honor!"

Came the gavel again. Jamison ordered both attorneys to chambers.

"Wonder how smart his shenanigans are, really," I said to Judith.

"Isn't the whole idea of a trial to woo a judge and jury with candy and flowers?"

Judith said she figured he was probably forcing the court into errors in case of appeal.

"I thought the other idea was to win the case here."

"Ray knows what he's doing."

"You hope."

Judith didn't answer.

They returned, and court resumed. Pallino wasn't chastened but grinning, even when Jamison had the record show that defense counsel, for having injured the dignity of the court, now had himself a citation for contempt.

Cobb, brought back, held to his story. He was excused, with provision that he be available for recall.

Rosetta Cobb was called next, and she answered Albright's spoon-fed questions in a voice softer and shakier than her husband's. Yes, they were childless, she said. She worked as a cook for a local caterer and when things were slow there she hired out as a domestic. Luther was a hard-working, good man, also with more than one trade: he was a cabinetmaker but he took extra jobs, as handyman and private driver, to send what money he could to his folks in the South. She and Luther were far from well-off, but out of necessity each of them owned an automobile in order to get to and from work. Decent as Luther was, she had begun to notice little signs, starting about six months back, that he was seeing other women. She had followed him on June seventh, and she detailed what she had seen in Room 5 of the Polo Motel. She had been hurt and angry, though angrier more at that white lady for leading her good, weak husband into temptation. In that anger she had sworn out the complaint. She would do it again.

Pallino's turn. For nearly an hour he made her go over and over and over every nit-picking detail of her following Cobb and Judith Harrison in her car, emphasizing his mock astonishment that she could have followed in a car her husband surely would recognize unless she were following from a mile behind, mock astonishment at her apparently split-second timing in breaking into Room 5. She twisted her marriage band a lot and looked intensely miserable.

271

Pallino: "Describe, Mrs. Cobb, these 'little signs' you had that your husband wasn't completely faithful to you."

"Well, he come home an hour later'n he s'posed to one night—he's always on the dot or he calls up—and he says he was drivin' these folks, and I smelled this perfume. He swore up an' down I was wrong, what I accused, and I b'lieved him later but I didn't b'lieve him then."

"Describe other 'little signs' you had."

"That was all. There wasn't nothin' more till he got hisself in the hands o' that white hussy."

I expected Pallino to move to have that stricken. He didn't. He calmly recapped all her testimony, highlighting inconsistencies and, again, mock astonishment at her collection of coincidences. He excused her, with the warning that he planned to call her back. I watched the jury's faces. I couldn't read a thing on any one of them.

Tuesday lunch in the diner across the way from the courthouse —Judith, Pallino, and me. He was still grinning as he filled us in on what he called the session of chambers music. "Baby finally hit a raw nerve," he crowed over his single bourbon and water. "The duck came down and the magic word was 'Starn.' Jamison spanked me good. Not a whisper about Starn, natch. Asked me if I was deliberately trying to show contempt for the court. I said 'No, I'm trying to conceal it.' No sense of humor, these corrupt hacks. He was harrumphing like Sydney Greenstreet. In all his harrumpty-ump years on the bench, he'd never had a lawyer pee on him so openly, and if I didn't snap it up and start performing like a court officer instead of a clowny one-man band, I was gonna be able to paper my walls with citations."

Judith wasn't amused. Wasn't he maybe overdoing the hijinks a bit?

"We win either way," he said. "If the thumbs go down here, we'll keep this pot boiling big and loud all the distance to appeal. I'm gonna make thirty-six kinds of a chimp out of Jamison. Citations? They'll not only be killed, but I'll be loaded down with medals for public service."

I had two-cents worth, and I put them in. "What happens next?"

Pallino touched his index fingers to the bridge of his nose. "Wait your turn, along with the rest of the great unwashed, Irishman," he said. "As it saith in the Old and New Testaments combined, 'Pallino uses his beano.' "

That didn't seem to amuse Judith, either.

Tuesday afternoon. Lyman Bester, limping a bit.

He'd had an accident, he admitted to Albright, and Albright thanked him for leaving his convalescent bed to testify. His testimony for Albright consisted of the racket coming from the Polo's Room 5, his going there to investigate, Mrs. Cobb hollering, Judith and Cobb naked. For a guy with no cause to be relaxed, I must say he was coming through as a neatly confident witness.

Pallino's turn. He asked permission to excuse Bester for a short time and have Mrs. Bester, who was in the courtroom and under defense's subpoena, called to the stand. "When it's time to present the defendant's case," Albright snorted, "counsel may call all the witnesses he cares to."

Pallino nodded. "Do you work days or nights at the Polo Motel, Mr. Bester?"

"It varies. Usually four to midnight."

"How long have you been there?"

"Couple years."

"Would you call it an interesting line of work? I've always been fascinated by hotels—the constant change of people, different kinds of people moving in and out."

"We wouldn't mind if it was constant 365 days a year. Every business has their seasons. Yes, it's interesting sometimes."

"When someone comes in to register, would you say it's part of your job to size him or her up? To make a quick, personal judgment as to whether he or she might turn out to be a troublemaker, I mean. Whether he or she strikes you as someone who'll skip off without paying the bill."

"Well, yes, you get that. What you do is get their license number when they register. And you run their credit card through the machine if they have one. And you try to be courteous."

"That's your main consideration, am I right—to make sure you're paid for services?"

"Isn't that what any business is about?"

"Yes, indeed. Now who wouldn't you let in, even if he or she is prepared to pay in advance?"

"If you're asking do we let colored people in, the law says we're not allowed to turn anybody away because of race or that."

"That wasn't what I had in mind, but thank you."

"No drunks if we can help it, especially if they act like they're gonna be disorderly or destroy property."

"What happens when a couple registers? Do you have some radar equipment in your head that tells you they're checking in for the express purpose of having sex illegally?"

A Bester pause. "You read Mister and Missus on the register, you assume they're mister and missus."

"Yes, but let's be hypothetical. Let's say you know, or you have a sensational suspicion, that they're not married to each other. They pay in advance and they're sober as a, uh, judge, but they're not married."

"Then I tell 'em sorry, we're full up."

"Even if you're not? Isn't being paid for services what business is all about?"

"We run a decent place."

"Really, Mr. Bester, are you honestly telling me you refuse space to a paying couple who'll be quiet as churchmice and won't leave cigarette burns in the carpet?"

"That's right. It's the law in this state. I forget the exact wording, but an innkeeper isn't allowed to let 'em in if he's got reason to believe a couple's unmarried and they're there for deviltry."

"Do you agree with that law?"

"Obeying it is my job."

"No, no, I asked if you agree with it."

"Well, sure I do! There's always reasons for laws."

"I commend your good citizenship. Would I be correct in gathering that you learned this grand respect for the law while you were serving time in this state's penitentiary three years ago for hiking and forging checks?"

Witness was not on trial, Albright roared. Jamison agreed.

"You're absolutely right and I'm deeply apologetic," Pallino purred, a colossal put-on. "Now then, Mr. Bester, let's talk about your accident."

Albright: Irrelevant, immaterial, and—

Pallino: I'll establish relevancy.

Judge: Proceed, on condition that you indeed do.

"How did the accident occur?"

"I was hanging curtains for my wife in the apartment. I fell down."

At our desk, Pallino retrieved a paper, told the judge it was Hartley Hospital's admittance report on Lyman Bester, listing bodily wounds sustained as a consequence of a severe physical beating. The bailiff gave it to Jamison, who glanced at it and denied its entry into the testimony on the grounds that it was irrelevant to the issue at bar. "Exception," Pallino said, and asked Bester, "Isn't it an exhilarating feeling to have a friend in court, Mr. Bester!"

A second citation for contempt.

"Who beat you up, Mr. Bester?"

"I was hanging curtains for my wife and I fell down."

"And I submit that what you're hanging now is yourself with that clearly phony story. Weren't you in fact clapped around—by 'unknown assailants,' we'll say for the time being—because for the sum of two thousand dollars in cash you offered to spill the beans to a reporter about a Hartley conspiracy against Judith Harrison? And didn't those unknown assailants get to you before the reporter could?"

"No!"

"Under oath, aren't you first and foremost a greedy man who had the brainstorm of working both sides of the street, of hoping to persuade other persons that it was worth *three* thousand dollars in cash not to spill those beans to the reporter named Sam Gallagher?"

"No!"

"I call you a liar, Mr. Bester. I submit that you know a great deal more of the real truth than you think you're going to tell before this trial is done, and I here and now invite you to avoid a perjury charge I otherwise have every intention of seeing you served with! Now suppose we shock the jury by letting the fresh air of truth into this courtroom for a change. Who beat you up, and why?"

"Nobody beat me up! I told you I fell off a ladder while I was painting the apartment."

"Really? I could have sworn you said you were hanging curtains. Shall we have the clerk read back your testimony?"

"I was doing both, painting and hanging curtains. We were renovating the place."

"I can see why you'd be a valuable employee, Mr. Bester. Anyone who can paint and hang curtains at the same time ought to be worth his weight in dollars. Maybe three thousand of them, right?"

Albright objected that the witness was being badgered, the court sustained, and Pallino mimed great shock.

"I certainly wouldn't want to badger poor Mr. Bester," he said. "He looks as if he couldn't take much more." He turned back to Bester, smiling. "Well now, sir, you may have a faulty memory when it comes to things like how you got beaten up, but may I assume your eyesight is fine?"

"I can see okay, yes."

"And when you went up to the door of Room 5, you saw Miss Harrison and Mr. Cobb naked, fornicating, while Mrs. Cobb shouted at them—is that correct?"

"They were naked, standing there. I didn't exactly see them —doing what you said—but they *were* buck-naked, and Mrs. Cobb was sure yelling."

"You didn't *exactly* see them doing what I said. Tell me: in your long experience, do couples who get buck-naked for sex usually leave the door standing open? Or do they generally lock it?"

"I don't know. It—"

"What's that? You don't *know*?"

"I mean Mrs. Cobb probably left it open when she busted in on them. I didn't see them doing anything, but Cobb said they were, didn't he?"

"I believe he did say that, somewhere in his evasions and lies. Do you suppose he got three thousand dollars for saying that, or was he just afraid he'd fall off a ladder while painting—excuse me, hanging curtains?"

Objection. Sustained. Stern warning about further contempt. Pallino waved it all away and dismissed the witness, again reserving the right of recall at a later time.

Bester limped down from the stand, looking like a wounded rabbit with no hole to hide in.

Albright produced a single character witness for the State. Martha Hanaday.

A surprise witness, and how. What I got from the expressions on Judith's and Pallino's faces was that they wouldn't have been any more surprised to see the Light Brigade materialize, led by Garbo, Lazarus, and Judge Crater, all nude.

I'd had this image of the latter-day Martha Hanaday as a dumpy battle-axe with a collection of nervous tics. Nope. She was well-groomed, well-poised and, as she got going, quite effective. Albright asked her credentials and she gave them, in a cream-enriched, self-assured voice. There was neither grandstanding nor excessive modesty; she listed her achievements in the arena of women's rights, and she brought herself across as someone with head set on straight. She had come to Hartley for two purposes. The first was to ally herself with what she had been expected to believe was the central aim of an organization of women who happened to be lesbians—to demand, through peaceful demonstration, freedom and independence for all women. She'd been betrayed, she added; she had disassociated herself from the Sisters the instant she'd realized their intent was to disrupt for disruption's sake alone.

And her second reason? Fear. Fear that this trial of this defendant might be erroneously viewed by some observers as the crucifixion of a noble soul with noble convictions. Whether the defendant was guilty or innocent of the State's charge against her was of no importance to Martha Hanaday. What was of importance, paramount importance, was that someone come forward to set the record straight as to this defendant's total lack of ethical or moral scruples in her self-appointed role as leader of the women's movement.

Pallino sat tight, but Judith seemed stunned, or awed, or maybe both. I watched the jury as Albright began his questioning.

"Tell the court just when and how you first met the defendant," he said, pointing to Judith.

She didn't look our way, but stared straight ahead. "We first met approximately two and a half years ago, at a meeting in my apartment in New York. I had heard of her—a pretty playgirl with a television show, mainly—and I was surprised at her interest in women's rights, but when she asked to attend one of our meetings I welcomed her. Colleagues warned me that she wasn't to be trusted, and it turned out they were right."

"In what way did she reveal that her motives were self-serving and devious?" Albright asked. I waited for Pallino to object, and even the judge looked toward him expectantly. He made no move.

"Well, first there was the caliber of her questions," she went on.

"We were there to plan new campaigns, but her questions were—at first, anyway—challenging and hostile. She derided our goals and seemed scornful of our methods, and her attitude was most upsetting and disruptive. But more than that—it became clear that she'd come looking for a fashionable cause to champion, not because she believed in it but because it could give her a new image. Perhaps her popularity was slipping, or maybe she wanted to overcome her sexpot reputation. Or, more likely, she saw ways to make money from the movement—a new product to peddle, as it were. In any case, we were disgusted by her brash and brassy ways. Before the evening was over, I had to ask her to leave."

"How did the other ladies in your group react to Miss Harrison's—uh—performance?" Albright asked.

"They were most upset. They tried to make her understand that the rights of women was a cause of great seriousness and importance to us, but she was insulting and abusive. She seemed obsessed with her own importance and determined to put us in our places, to make us feel we were naïve amateurs. It was all most distasteful, and all the women were relieved when she left, and when we could get back to the serious business we'd gathered for."

"And when did you next meet Miss Harrison?"

"We never actually met again, until this—episode. She tried to contact me many times, but by now I was painfully aware of her self-serving motives. I did talk with her once, though, a few weeks after that unpleasant evening in my home. She'd been calling on the phone, and finally I accepted a call. She told me she was still determined to become a name in the women's movement—a 'superstar,' I believe the term is—and that she had the popularity and the connections to make it work. If I really believed that getting the message across to the public was the most important thing, I would want to make use of those connections—and of her, uh, sex appeal, I believe she said. I asked how we could do that, and she said she would make public appearances—on television and on the lecture circuit—in behalf of the cause, if *I* would take care of the arrangements and write the speeches for her."

"She asked you to write her speeches?" Albright asked, his tones dramatic with disbelief. I looked at Judith, who was shaking her head sadly.

"Well, she said we would collaborate on them, but it was evident that what she wanted was the public exposure, not the hard work of writing and attending to details. She would get the money and the 'image' of a girl crusader, she said, and I would get the satisfaction of seeing battles won. I said it sounded dishonorable, but it was clear that she didn't even know what I meant by honor."

"Yes," Albright said quickly, glancing at Pallino. "And was anything else said about her intentions?"

"No. Yes, actually one other thing does stick in my mind from that conversation. I asked her how she could be so sure of television appearances on the top shows. She laughed and said something like, 'Those bookings are handled by men, aren't they? There are ways.' "

The lady was going good. Those Midwest dowagers were practically wriggling out of their corsets behind us in the courtroom.

"Naturally I was revolted. I hung up and assumed that would be the end of it. I was wrong, though. I underrated the gullibility of Americans who will buy anything if the package is pretty enough, or if the person selling wears short enough skirts. I also underrated Miss Harrison's capacity for cashing in on the hard work of others."

"And what connection have you had with her since then?" Albright prompted.

"None, directly. I went on with my work and she went on with her own campaigns, flitting from issue to issue and from bed to bed."

Everyone, including the judge, looked at Pallino, who was playing with a pencil. Then His Honor, seeing that no objection was forthcoming and no doubt thinking of the court record, arranged his face into a grim look and said, "I must caution the witness to refrain from indulging in personalities." He sat back, the picture of judicial fairness.

"I'm sorry," Martha Hanaday said. "I have always tried to avoid publicly criticizing anyone identified with the women's rights movement, even those who are obviously opportunists. But I really believe this woman is dangerous, because the public could easily confuse her personal immorality and radical views with the goals and beliefs of the movement as a whole."

"What radical views do you refer to?" Albright said.

"The left-wing political bias, for one thing," she said. "For example, during this country's involvement in Vietnam, she attended a

279

rally conducted by known communists and supporters of our enemies, and she joined in labeling our acts as atrocities and she cheered as Viet Cong flags were waved."

Gasps from the courtroom.

"And at a time when the vast majority of our Negro citizens were striving to develop a unity of black pride and identity, she was uttering statements in favor of interracial sex and interracial marriage. I could go on and on with her mindless destructiveness."

Clearly she didn't need to. Watching that jury, I had the feeling they were ready to hang this pushy Red Jew atheist who wanted our sons killed and our daughters defiled by the coloreds.

Her windup was controlled and dignified, the voice of sanity in a naughty world:

"I would like to emphasize that I take no pleasure in making what could appear to be personal attacks on another human being. But I have followed the career of this woman—with her skill for publicizing herself, it would be impossible to ignore her—and I would be less than honest if I said she was merely an embarrassment to the movement. She has been, and certainly is now, a thoroughly negative and destructive influence. We who are committed to the dignity and freedom of women protest any suggestion that may be made during this trial that she represents anything other than her own megalomania and severe character disorder."

Pallino, who hadn't raised a single objection during her love song, strolled up to her for his cross-examination.

He shrugged elaborately. "What's your point, Mrs. Hanaday?"
"Pardon me?"

"What's really behind all that vicious malice?"

"I think I explained myself adequately. If I know the correct definition of the word 'malice'—a desire to inflict suffering or injury on another for personal reasons—then the word is totally inaccurate. I do indeed disapprove of the defendant, but purely for the reason I gave: it would be a mockery of all women struggling for dignity if someone as shallow as Judith Harrison were held up as a Joan of Arc."

"You just plain wish she'd get out of your ballpark, right?"

A condescending smile. "Mr. Pallino, I recognize that you have an interest in trying to characterize me as consumed by threats of rivalry, but I'm afraid you'll have no luck there. I've never needed nor wanted my own ballpark, as you call it. I've never lusted for personal power. That's been a male concept since the beginning of time, and I've never felt the urge to mimic it. I'll leave the personality cults to the personally ambitious."

"Yet you're a personality. And deservedly so, and I say that with sincerity. I've read and admired your books, *Season of Silence* and *Private Parts.* I confess I don't get to your newspaper column often, but you've been a hard fighter and a constructive force over the years, and I'd like you to know that I have high regard for your valuable contributions to feminism."

Warily she said, "Thank you."

"Which might well be the last compliment you'll hear in this courtroom, Mrs. Hanaday. No one can minimize your fine work *in the past,* but isn't it true that you're an ex-queen bee, and isn't it true that you're a lonely, embittered soul making a last-ditch effort to regain the position you've lost to the younger women—women like Judith Harrison—through an outrageous assortment of innuendoes and downright lies?"

"Objection, your honor!" Albright was on his feet.

"Sustained. And I must warn counsel against this abusive language."

"And speaking of abusive language, Mrs. Hanaday, did you ever, personally, actually hear Judith Harrison cheer for Viet Cong flags?"

"No, I wasn't at that rally, but her views were known."

"I'm sorry you weren't invited to the rally, Mrs. Hanaday, but since you weren't there how can you testify as to what was said, or by whom?"

"I think I read it, probably in the papers."

"You *think* you read it, *probably.* In what paper, Mrs. Hanaday?"

"I don't recall. I would appreciate your not standing so close to me."

"You don't recall. Do you recall just when you heard Miss Harrison advocate interracial sex? Or was that in the same newspaper you've now forgotten?"

"I repeat, her views were well known. I don't remember where I read about her statements on sex with Negroes, but I'm sure she said it."

"You can't recall where or when you read it or heard it, and you were never actually present at any of the meetings where Miss Harrison gave her views, yet you're certain of exactly what she said. Is that what you're telling us?"

"Everybody knows what she stands for."

" 'Everybody knows.' 'It was plain that . . .' 'It became clear . . .' Mrs. Hanaday, I'm going to give you a free, five-second course in law, one you should've been given before you got on that stand and took that solemn oath. If you say that you hate me—even under oath—then that is opinion, and it won't break my bones. But if you say, under oath, that I stole your watch or shot your dog, then you'd better come prepared with something at least remotely resembling truth. With *facts*, Mrs. Hanaday, not assumptions or half-remembered things from forgotten newspapers or outright slurs, but *facts*. Now, would you care to retract anything you've said so far?"

"No!" She looked at Jamison. "Would Your Honor please have this man stand farther away from me and not shout at me?"

"Counsel will—" Jamison began, but Pallino had already retreated.

"Speaking of 'severe character disorder'—I believe that was the phrase you used to describe Miss Harrison, along with 'megalomania' and a few others. Tell me, who made the professional diagnosis of 'severe character disorder?' Besides you, I mean."

"It was common knowledge."

"I see. More 'common knowledge.' When will we get some *un*common knowledge from you Mrs. Hanaday? When will we hear one single *fact*? When will we hear opinion labeled as opinion, and spite as spite? When will you substantiate these serious charges you've made? Because if you can't, then I submit that all you've brought to this witness stand is personal spite and sick imagination!"

She looked in Albright's direction, as if to say *Make this man go away*. She was silent for a moment, her face troubled, empty of confidence now, eyes pleading. There was something suddenly, pervasively pathetic about her, she was a slight woman suddenly smaller, and she said, so very quietly that the court reporter asked her to repeat it, "You haven't the right to abuse me like that. I'm Martha Hanaday . . ."

"Yes, I know you're Martha Hanaday," Pallino blazed. "This jury

282

knows you're Martha Hanaday. This jury also knows the sky isn't falling unless there's some evidence that the sky *is* falling. I repeat: Will you now retract *any* of the remarks we've heard from you so far?"

Softly: "No. You're standing too close to me. Please . . ."

"Are you under psychiatric treatment, Mrs. Hanaday?"

Still softly: "That's not your affair."

Judith's whispered "Uh-oh" agreed, seemed to agree that the question, the abrupt opening of that can of corn, was a cheap shot. Pallino said, "Whether you're a responsible witness is very much the affair of this court." I think I saw what he was playing with: *You show me my yids and godless Reds, I'll show you your shrinks.* "Are you under psychiatric care?"

". . . No. Are you?"

"No, but I know how to define paranoia. Paranoia is a projection of personal conflicts, isn't it?"

"It's referred—ah—to as systematized delusion. But—"

"Yes. Attributed to the supposed hostility of others. Now, if Judith Harrison is evil for having stolen your crown, isn't it reasonable to presume she's capable of stealing anything else of yours, your purse or even your husband?"

Judith muttered, "God damn you, Ray. God damn you."

"Is your husband's name Norman Hanaday and is he now in this courtroom?"

Martha Hanaday clapped her hands to her ears. "Don't shout at me! I can't bear shouting!"

"I'm going to demand a straight answer to this question: Weren't you galvanized into testifying against Judith Harrison because in your systematized delusion you imagine there's a romantic involvement between her and your husband?"

Then the damnedest thing. She had been quiet till that moment, sometimes almost inaudible. Albright was adding to the room's general feel of restrained uproar by loudly protesting witness-badgering, and Jamison was gavel-banging, and what the damnedest thing was was that she leapt from her seat, face spookily contorted in pain and fury, she weaved for just a moment as though she were about to either drop or run, the damnedest thing of all was the loony cry that sprang not from her throat alone but her entire quivering body. "Don't come *near* me!" she screamed. "How *dare* you, how dare you attack me when all I've ever, when my only mission in life has been to lift humanity, raise it to the zenith? How dare *anyone* treat me like dirt when *she's*"—a finger at the stunned Judith—"the dirt, she's the whore, the whore, the whore, the whore, the whore, the whore, why won't anyone listen to me? I imagine nothing! I'm Martha Hanaday and everything I say is so, everything I've always said is so! How dare anyone try to discredit me? What are you saying, that he left me for her because I'm a frigid woman? My children adore me, that's my monument, I envy no one no matter how they, whatever happened to warmth? Audrey? Stephanie? Audrey?"

As if we all weren't in the midst of something grotesque enough, a cop came out of the judge's chambers and whispered into Jamison's ear as this woman was babbling. I'd heard, or thought I'd heard, a telephone, and supposed the cop was bringing a phone message. I saw the judge nod. I also saw a man come down the courtroom's middle aisle and stand near Judith, who still seemed stunned. He identified himself as Norman Hanaday and asked if he might approach the bench. Jamison said yes. We couldn't hear any of it—we could only watch his wife sit again, very slowly—but I gathered he was asking if he could take her the hell out of there. Jamison okayed the request and spoke to the court reporter, announced there would be a short recess and left. Martha Hanaday's gaze was quizzical, as though she were trying to place her husband, as he gently helped her from the chair.

He led her, slowly, the way one leads a very old person, or someone who's fallen hard. They walked from the witness stand, and Martha stared ahead, her eyes vacant and her face serene. As they reached our table, Norman Hanaday stopped before Pallino. If looks could kill, Ray Pallino's family would have to start shopping for basic black.

Hanaday stared, coldly, for a moment, then said, in a quiet, soft voice, "You are a contemptible son-of-a-bitch." He took Martha's arm again, and they walked on. He had not once even glanced at Judith.

And how was Judith reacting? She wasn't jumping over the tennis net to shake Pallino's hand, but she didn't smite him with a terrible swift sword, maybe because she didn't want to gratify the audience that had switched its attention from the Hanadays to her.

She didn't talk, even after Pallino and Albright were called to the judge's chambers. She doodled circles on a scratch pad. "Come on out to the corridor with me and watch me smoke a cigarette," I said. "I blow smoke rings that come out square."

She shook her head.

In the corridor, Al Chase of AP gave me a match. We rapped until I spotted the Cobbs, standing by themselves, about thirty feet away. Something in the way Luther Cobb looked at me suggested he had something to say but that I'd have to do the approaching. I excused myself from Al and hobbled to them. Mr. Cobb started to talk, stopped, started, fumbled, and eventually got some words together. They'd seen me sitting with Judith; was I her friend? Yes. Would I tell her they had something to tell her? Yes, wait right here.

I hobbled back toward the courtroom, as fast as my good leg would take me. And now I'll butt out for the time being, because I wasn't in on what happened in Jamison's chambers. But you wait right there, too. You haven't heard the last of me.

29

In chambers, Maurice Jamison asked both attorneys if they didn't agree there were good reasons to bring the trial to a halt this very day; it promised to be long and costly, in dollars and man-hours, and he was coming to the conclusion that dragging it on would furnish more heat but probably little more light than had been shed these two days so far. He had not sought to preside over the case, he said, sounding conciliatory, even chummy; he had been assigned it, considered it an essentially much-ado-about-nothing case, and he had an offer to make that ought to satisfy both sides. He would have the record show that the inordinate publicity attending the trial was disrupting the community and that he now believed the publicity was serving to prejudice the defendant's ability to be tried altogether fairly. If she would take a disturbing-the-peace plea, they could button the whole thing up fast and everyone could go home. Buttoning up the whole thing also meant dropping the contempt citations, he added.

Albright was surprised, or feigned surprise, claimed he was sure he was winning his case, but that his sole function as prosecutor was to see that justice was served, and yes he had plenty of more pressing chores waiting on his desk, and yes he would abide by the judge's decision.

Raymond Pallino laughed. Jamison asked what was so funny. "You," he said. "You're a riot. Your boss is screwing the Constitution seven ways to Sunday, and now that the heat's getting hotter the nice thing for me to do is take my client home by the slapped wrist and let's all forgive and forget. Yes sir, that's what you yokels would call a real thigh slapper."

"Let's watch that 'boss' business . . ."

"No, you watch it. I gather Starn's back in Hartley. Well, you get this word to him pronto, Jamison. You tell him he's not the only one who's up to his fascist ass in trouble. Yesterday and today I just moved some furniture around. Tomorrow I really start wrecking this joint. I'll pull Starn's D.A. here off the rubber stamp long enough to find out in open court how come he's never bothered with a fornication case in all his years on the job till this one. I'll put everyone on that stand, and I mean everyone, Jamison, and I don't care how many hides get nailed to the wall alongside Starn's. Instead of cozying up to me, I advise you to advise your boss there are other laws besides the law against getting laid. There are laws against false arrest, character defamation, suborning perjury, criminal con-spiracy—and the niftiest one of all has to do with public officials who knowingly participate in a criminal conspiracy."

Amid blood-drained bluster from Albright and warnings from Jamison, Raymond Pallino said, "Don't give *me* that petty-thief righteous indignation. You have orders from on high to all of a sudden unscramble eggs? Well, tell the boss you did your beautiful best but it didn't pan out."

To Albright, Pallino said, "By the way, old boy, I did something unforgivable this morning when I talked to the press. I told them that in view of Hartley's recent wave of violence—Bester and that reporter, Gallagher—I had asked you to ask the Chief of Police to provide police protection for Miss Harrison and me. I told them that you immediately agreed to arrange it and I appreciated your coop-eration. What I did that was unforgivable was that I spelled your name with two l's instead of one. I apologize; I have two l's in my last name and I go berserk when they give me only one in print. Anyway, they know and they're printing that if anything untoward happens to anyone before the end of this trial, it won't be because you personally didn't guarantee full and total protection. You're a saint, fella."

And to Jamison: "Unless you have some moral pronouncements to intone from the bench, let's wrap up this cockamamie court for the day. We both have work to do. I have a lot of phone calls to make and telegrams to send and citizens to see. You're probably anxious to call your boss and let him know I'm staying at the Airport Motor Inn. The Airport Motor Inn is on Hubley Boulevard. Hubley begins with an 'h,' just like 'heck' and 'happiness' and 'Harriet.' "

Gallagher was in the courtroom when Pallino returned, but Judith

287

wasn't. There was the formality of the red-faced Jamison resuming court in order to adjourn it till the following morning, and then Pallino swiftly stuffed papers into his case and said, "When Judith gets back, Irishman, tell her to sit still in the motel till she hears from me."

"Don't you want to know where she is?"

"Probably social-working the Hanadays, right? No, I don't have time; too much to do. Just tell her there ought to be a whole flock of thunderbolts before this day's out."

Hurrying into the corridor, Judith caught a glimpse of the Cobbs in the elevator just before its door closed after them. People were watching her, but she moved quickly down the two flights of stairs to the lobby, her mind's eye filled with Norman automatically rushing to his primary responsibility, with the obscene crumbling and devastation of Martha Hanaday, with a crowding in of muddy pictures and loss and ominously uneasy doubts.

The Cobbs emerged from the elevator, obviously terrified, obviously having thought better of their request to Sam, and saw Judith and attempted to escape. She blocked them. "Hasn't this gone far enough?" she entreated. "I know you're both frightened. I don't know why, but why you lied will have to be explained some time, can't you see that? *Please* talk to me!"

Luther Cobb searched the faces and the walls about him. He looked at Judith blankly, and shook his head, and he and his wife scurried away. She followed them until Rosetta Cobb insisted that she leave them alone. They fled through the lobby's revolving door.

Back in the courtroom, Sam gave her Ray's message. "Will you come with me, Sam?" she asked.

"Sure. To the motel?"

"No. I think I'm done with folding my arms on the sidelines."

She drove to Cliveden Avenue. Maybe the Cobbs wouldn't talk to her in their house, she said, maybe especially not in their house, but she had to make another stab at getting to them. With no particular diplomacy, Sam suggested that her complete faith in Ray Pallino was possibly wobbling a bit: "Pulling Hanaday's name out of the air during the cross-examination, for instance—that couldn't have bathed you in rapture."

Judith was quiet for a time, and then said, "Let's not get into Ray. It isn't as if I didn't know his blowtorch style ahead of time."

"You have a few misgivings, though."

"I have more than a few," she conceded, "but I'm in no mood for your famous Iago act, Pulitzer. If and when I decide he's stepping entirely out of line, he'll know about it."

Most of the misgivings are about myself, she thought. Of course I knew the kind of lawyer and person Ray is. He plays to win, always. It was—is—up to me to either give him carte blanche or to warn him that there's a point at which the any-means-to-an-end tactics can't be justified, won't be tolerated, by me. Yes, I'm worried. I'm worried about Ray's fleet of steamrollers revving up in his garage.

And I'm worried that Norman won't leave Martha. And I'm worried that he will . . .

30

Gallagher. I told you I'd be back.

The Cobbs finally let us into their home. They had a nervous, voiceless debate about it, but they let us in. Judith and I had agreed in advance that if they displayed any qualms upon seeing my splendid County Galway countenance, I would dematerialize in a flash. No sweat; I was allowed in with her.

Their parlor was rather dark because of the drawn green window shade, but it was an immaculate room. The furniture was made by hand, presumably Luther Cobb's hand, and the feeling was one of sturdiness, of solidity. The wall pictures and calendar art were limited to a single subject and a small cast of characters: The Lord's Prayer, Jesus and the Disciples, Christ on the Cross—a Caucasian cast, but that was their business. When the talking got started, Mr. Cobb did the bulk of it, with Mrs. Cobb providing the punctuations. Together, they came on like a pair weary and out of breath from running too long and too much, resigned now to quit the race. Judith asked questions only when she had to, simply and supportively; otherwise, she kept still, nodding when *that* punctuation was indicated. It worked. Pallino would've pummeled them with his questions, and after nothing there would have been nothing.

They had lied. They had been ordered to lie. They had lied even though they'd placed their hands on the Bible, and they'd known then and knew even better now that that lawyer in the court was exactly right: eternal damnation awaits the false witness . . .

It had started barely two months before. Lonnie Perkins, Rosetta Cobb's youngest brother, came up from Georgia to stay for a time. He was seventeen, handsome, bright, strong as a bull, not certain about much but plain certain he wasn't going to live and die a sharecropper like Daddy and Daddy's Daddy. He joked a lot, snapped his fingers a lot. Cabinetmaking, Cobb's skill, didn't interest him, nor

290

did Cobb's recommendation that he get as much schooling as he could. "Got to walk before you run," Cobb said, and took him along on snow-plowing jobs and, when the season changed so suddenly, on gardening jobs; taught him gardening, impatient that the kid paid more attention to the homes than the grounds, more to getting ahead than to preparations for getting ahead. There wasn't anything mean or bad about him. He liked cars. He liked girls. He was going to burn up the world. Rosetta Cobb adored him, and a wary Luther Cobb wished him well.

The kid made all the mistakes a mindless seventeen-year-old American kid makes, but his biggest mistake was that he made them as a mindless seventeen-year-old American black kid, and in a community that went ashen on reading about nigger lynchings but that liked its negras visible only on cue. He raised harmless hell by night and did underpaid but rudimentary gardening and lawn mowing by day. Twice a week he tended the grounds of the Lanes on Three Oaks Drive. Mrs. Lane—Mrs. Andrea Lane—took a liking to him, served him soda pop after work, was nice to him, asked him about the terrible conditions his people had to endure under those fascist bullies in the South, praised Roy Wilkins and the NAACP, spoke of her labors on behalf of racial integration and equality, fed him more soda pop, introduced him to her seventeen-year-old daughter Deirdre, beamed as he and Deirdre rapped about this and that. He phoned Deirdre that night, asked if they could take a walk after he did the lawn on Wednesday. She said yes. Rosetta Cobb got a call on Tuesday. Mrs. Lane was awfully sorry but young Lonnie wasn't quite working out. No need for him to come back.

He promised Rosetta and Luther he would go with them to church on that Wednesday evening. He didn't show, and they found out why. There had been a parked Volks on Main Street, with the key in the ignition, a gleaming new Volks begging to be tried out. He'd tried it out, meaning to love it up for a couple of blocks, and return it safe and sound. He loved it for a half-hour's worth of blocks, brought it to where he'd found it. The arrest was as fast as his impulse had been stupid. What he remembered first about the police station was that the folks who were processing him into a cell were neither friendly nor unfriendly; except for booking him, he didn't *exist. He kept speaking Luther Cobb's name. A cop led him to a cell and asked him if it was true that boogs had big dicks. He cursed the cop, which was yet another mistake. The cop pitched him to the floor of the cell, and yanked the kid's pants off and punched him in the groin, nowhere but in the groin, repeatedly until the kid passed out.*

The charge was more than car theft. The arresting officer, Herman Stacey, had found three marijuana cigarettes in Lonnie Perkins' possession. The kid swore they'd had to be planted in his jacket pocket because he'd never seen a marijuana cigarette in his life. Luther Cobb paid the bond. Lonnie Perkins continued to insist that the marijuana thing was all wrong, all wrong.

The offer came from Mr. Bancroft, the fine gentleman Luther often drove to and from the airport, the well-dressed gentleman who always smelled so fine: "That boy's in a peck of trouble, Luther. He could spend the best part of his life behind bars, what with all those serious charges against him. I can help, I can see to it that he's freed right off and your Rosetta won't have to wring her hands any more; I can see that he gets himself a clean bill of health, but you and Rosetta will have to help a bit. You do as I say, and swear to the Lord Jesus you'll never say a word about this to anybody, and I'll see that the boy's never bothered again. Let's hear you, Luther. I'd hate it if you got a bad name over at the bank, what with how industrious you've been all these years."

The Harrison lady, coming to Hartley, was a bad lady. A Jezebel, Luther. Anti-Christ, Luther. Killed your Lord, hates your people, flaunts herself like the trash she is despite her big words. You do exactly as we say and the boy will be home free and Mr. Courtney at the bank will do right by you. Hasn't your Rosetta been upset enough?

They went through with it. It took persuasion, and drilling, and Testament quotes about looking out for those who would look out for you, and more drilling, and they prayed and threw up somewhat, but they did it.

I spoke. "Would Mr. Bancroft be Marcus Bancroft?"

Cobb believed so. I knew that fine gentleman, Marcus Bancroft, Vice-President and Executive Editor of the entire Starn newspaper chain, I said, from the time of my *Rowland's* research on Starn. The jigsaw was fitting nicely now, though there were some missing pieces. Luther Cobb supplied them. Bancroft had guaranteed that their involvement would end the moment Mrs. Cobb called the police. Their names would never be brought into it; the law and the newspapers would take over from there, and the charges against Lonnie would be automatically dropped. When the Cobbs squawked that it wasn't turning out that way, they were told they had no choice but to see it through. Once they left the witness stand, Lonnie would go free—and stay free, as long as they stayed hushed up. Their fingering wouldn't hurt Bancroft, who would naturally and successfully deny everything, but Lonnie's record was being kept in a special file and he could be re-arrested at any time and face a long penitentiary sentence.

Our obvious question—why didn't they seek out legal advice the moment all this began?—yielded blank stares that answered plenty: folks taught from the cradle to step aside for The Man fare best when they do as they're told. Peace comes after you've crossed the Rivuh Jordan.

Judith looked shocked. Luther Cobb's eyes had tears as he begged her forgiveness and swore he and Rosetta wished all of it could be righted. But it couldn't, not by them, they had to stay in Hartley, this was where their home was and their work was. No. They were sorry, they were petrified, they had to have her know their sin, but they weren't strong people, they couldn't survive the trouble that was sure to come if they dared to speak the truth in public. Wouldn't she understand?

She was trying to, she said, still shaken, and asked them if they honestly thought they could live with their guilt. She stressed Bancroft's name, emphasized that he wasn't above the law, emphasized that he and his crowd would go on stomping and cheapening other human beings unless they were exposed once and for all. She would help the Cobbs, she promised, she would help Lonnie, but she and the law could do next to nothing as long as frightened people stayed frightened.

No. Sorry, sorry, sorry. No.

There was a message, when we got back to the Airport Motor Inn, for Judith to call Pallino at once. The message contained a phone number, and she placed the call from the lobby booth. Waiting, I

293

bought Tuesday's *Statesman-Patriot.* Considering that the paper had been treating *Humankind* v. *Judith Harrison* these past many days as the news story of the century, it was a bit jarring to have to search for mention of it. I found it on the second page, a brief and bloodless account of Monday's doings, so sharply low-keyed after more than a week's orgy of exclamation points that there couldn't have been any doubt that someone upstairs had clapped a lid on.

Judith was flushed as she came out of the booth. "I'm about to meet your hero Noah Walters," she said. "Ray's at his house, and I'm to speed over there. And alone, Sam."

"Why alone?"

"Because Oliver Starn says so."

Shazam. "Feed me that name again. Slowly."

She nodded, and hurriedly gave me the patchy details. I understood why I was disinvited—I didn't like it, but I understood. I gimped with her back to her car, told her the simplest way to get to the Walters' house, ordered her to stay loose—sappy advice—and watched her drive off.

I drank Scotch in the motel's lounge, less than euphoric. A reporter who's restrained from covering the flood is always less than euphoric, though, as I say, I understood. Starn had phoned Walters, less than an hour before, asking for a meet with Judith as soon as possible, at Walters' home and with Walters there. There was no love lost between those two old gladiators, yet Noah Walters was a logical conduit; Starn evidently had a proposition, and what better referee and potential impasse-breaker than his ancient adversary, unworshiped but totally honest and fair? My showing up, with or without my press card, apparently wasn't what Genghis Starn had in mind. So I sat there in that saloon that was all knotty pine and tally-ho fox hunt pictures and drank my Scotch, damn it.

I'll see you later.

31

Although Judith knew of Noah Walters, from Sam's adoring descriptions and from her own knowledge of him as one of the last of the great, good warriors, she was not prepared to fall in love with him. She did, almost instantaneously. He welcomed her with a courtly string of compliments into a house perhaps twice as old as he was, and Judith, who had never said aloud that she was honored to meet someone, said so now. Goodness billowed from this man, goodness and integrity rescued from pomposity by a genuine sense of humor.

In his rambling living room, he said, "Mr. Pallino's on the telephone in my study, Mrs. Walters is off babysitting with one of the grandchildren. Please sit." She did. Some wine? Something to eat? No, thank you. "My notion of a first-rate time would be to settle back and ask you a long bunch of questions about yourself," he said, "but it appears that'll have to wait a bit. Company's coming. Mr. Pallino tells me you know why you're here."

"Not entirely."

"That makes three of us," he chuckled. "It's been a lot of years since Ollie Starn's bothered to contact me for anything. He asked me to try to round you up to come here for a private talk—just you and him, with me sort of sitting by as timekeeper, I guess. He claimed it would have to be a meeting without Mr. Pallino. I claimed I was pretty sure you'd want your attorney present. The Ollie I've known and loved since Creation would've kicked up an awful fuss at that in the old days, but all he did was bark a little and let it go. This is a man who needs something very badly—a truce of some kind—and very fast."

"Will he admit anything?"

"Oh, in his fashion. My hunch is that he wanted you discredited but he didn't mean for it to go this far—not out of consideration for you, but because it's hard to stop a forest fire even if you're in charge of all the forest rangers. His problem is that he was in Europe when the fire got out of control. I think he probably had word sent down to that Albright puppet of his, something on the order of 'Give her a black eye and ship her out of town.' I think Albright got carried away and decided to run off with the show, either because he misunderstood that it was to be short and sweet or because he figured he could keep Ollie happy and be governor at the same time."

"Governor?"

Noah Walters nodded. "Cliff Albright has some mighty fancy political ambitions. How do you get to be governor of a state? The easiest way is to get your picture in the papers by prosecuting sinners. Anyway, we'll see what we'll see. In the meantime, Miss Harrison, I'd like to offer you a small piece of unsolicited advice."

"Of course."

"About Mr. Pallino. I'm not talking behind his back now—I made my observations clear to him before you came. He views this case in terms of issues bigger than the simple defense of his client. So do I, and I'm sure so do you. But he belongs to a school that says cases are to be won—preferably with honor, but above all won. In other words, don't hand me a bomb and order me not to throw it . . ."

Carefully, Judith asked, "Would that bomb be Harriet Starn?"

Again he nodded. "All I'm advising you is what I advised him: He's your counselor, and he has the right and the duty to talk law when Ollie comes, but you should carry the ball as much as possible. Hear Ollie out. I'm not suggesting you curtsey, God knows, but I know Ollie Starn and I'm convinced if he's hit with a ton of bricks too soon, if Mr. Pallino tries to outshout him too early—and I gather that's what he has planned . . ."

Ray entered the room, ears perked. Mr. Walters seemed first to sense his presence and then looked at him through those immense eyeglasses. "I was just saying to Miss Harrison—" he began.

"Yes, I heard," Ray said crisply and asked Judith where the hell she'd been.

She told them about the Cobbs.

"Marcus Bancroft," Ray repeated. "Starn's boy . . ." as the doorbell sounded.

Alone with Judith for a moment, Ray shook his head. "The old codger's gone and gotten himself senile," he grumbled, almost to himself. "Muscle is okay but only if it's polite. Don't let's be beastly to the beasts. Christ!"

Striving for calm, aware that the ball was indeed hers to carry, tense yet suddenly sure of herself, she quickly warned him not to start throwing punches before he heard Starn out.

Glaring at her, he snapped, "You're not talking to a thumb-sucker, lady! Don't teach me how to swat flies!"

"Then don't try to swat this one with a sledge hammer!" she snapped back.

And stopped, just before Noah Walters appeared with Oliver Starn.

He was, Judith thought, Warren Harding without the cornflower, a striking man with tough, tight skin and full red lips and bristly eyebrows and glacial eyes, eyes that darted about continuously, rarely fixed. Noah Walters began to make introductions, but Starn would have none of it. "That won't be necessary," he said in a metallic, surprisingly thin voice. "Everyone here knows me, and I know everyone here. May we get to my reason for coming?" He was invited to sit, and preferred to stand. "First of all, I'm acquainted with Mr. Pallino's reputation for loud theatrics and bombast. If voices and tempers are kept down, I believe we'll be able to come to an understanding. May we agree on that?"

"Yes," Judith said, to Ray as well as to Starn.

"Thank you. I have personally been accused of creating an atmosphere that caused this young lady's arrest and trial. I deeply resent such unfounded allegations, and under normal circumstances I would take the normal legal steps to see them refuted. But there's a time factor involved here. The longer this thing continues, the more it will hurt those personally close to me. I have no intention of allowing that to happen."

A glance at Judith. "Your invasion of my innocent daughter's needed privacy was unspeakable. You and your attorney's threat to use her as some type of bargaining wheel is far more reprehensible than any crime you could imagine me capable of. But I'm not an ignorant man. I realize that you have no more respect for my concepts of morality than I have for yours. I realize you planned to use that courtroom as a forum to promote your beliefs to the world, and now here comes someone who's asking you to remove yourself from that forum and quietly go away. I'm—I am asking that."

Ray, relatively subdued for Ray, said, "Miss Harrison happens to be charged in a court of law with a criminal act."

Starn nodded, with restless impatience. "That can be rectified easily." As though ignoring Ray, he said to Judith, "I'm not a lawyer, but it's conceivable that once this matter is dissolved your attorney *and* Noah could suggest that you were subjected to damaging publicity and held up to public ridicule and vilification. I think you're intelligent enough to concede that that's patent nonsense. Those who regard you as a disgraceful and immoral woman may not change their minds, but publicity is what you seem to thrive on and you've enjoyed a tremendous amount of it since the moment you stepped foot in Hartley. Now. All court costs and whatever other expenditures were or are incurred will not be your obligation. My papers and my stations can't very well assume any public connection to your adventure, but we will state that though we have always disagreed with your philosophies, we believe as responsible journalists and broadcasters that you were treated unfairly and unwisely by well-meaning people whose fervor exceeded their judgment. In addition, you will be given money, in cash, to do with as you choose—to spend on yourself, to share with your attorney, to further your—ah—interests. I would think fifty thousand dollars is not ungenerous."

Judith, softly: "No, it isn't."

"In return, you will give your word, not to me but to Noah, that everything spoken in this room will never leave this room. You and your attorney will never attempt to perform any contact with my daughter or say her name to anyone, ever." A pause. "All agreed?"

Ray Pallino said, "You're a slimy bastard, Starn. To the teeth."

Starn merely blinked. Uncomfortably, Noah Walters said, "We can all do without the abusive lang—"

"You're cute as a button, Starn," Pallino said. "We've got you and your half-pint fascists by the balls and you know it. Fifty grand and a few words from your local announcer about civil liberties, and you're off the hook? No sale, baby, not in today's inflationary market. What we're charging you is going to cost you a hell of a lot more than money."

Now, thought Judith.

"That's enough," she said quietly, firmly, and faced Oliver Starn and said, "I'm prepared to accept your offers," and silenced the protesting Ray with a commanding frown. "With something from you in place of cash. I want you to see that Rosetta and Luther Cobb are completely exonerated."

Starn's eyebrows met. "Exonerated? Of what? Neither of them has been— Oh, I see—that young buck brother of hers, that indictment. Certainly. I'm sure it can be erased."

"That's not what I mean," Judith said, and told him of her meeting with the Cobbs, and of Marcus Bancroft.

Bancroft's name distinctly struck a nerve. "Forgive me," he said, "but I'm talking about a sizable sum of money and what amounts to a public apology to you, and you're talking about some colored people."

"Yes."

"This isn't clear to me at all. I consider myself a reasonable man. I came here in good faith. I came here to apologize for any inconvenience you might have been caused and to make it up to you." His tone of reasonableness changed as he spoke, and then suddenly he blurted, "Don't you wave Marcus Bancroft at me! This is a life and death situation I'm talking about!"

Anger and agony crowded his face. "*Life* and *death!* I'm not a beggar. Do you want to hear a father beg? I flew home to find my daughter in a highly agitated state, more than I've ever seen her. You're concerned about a couple of worthless darkies? Let's see if your bleeding-heart humanity extends to people of your own color if not your religion. This is my *daughter* I'm talking about!"

"Nobody's deaf here, Ollie," said Noah Walters, and Ray seemed to be enjoying the spectacle, and Judith was still.

"My daughter's taking sedatives, Miss; would you like to crow over that? She was still asleep at noon today. The colored maid tried to wake her up and couldn't. She finally came around, thanks to God, not to you. She was so agitated by this whole sickening affair that in her confusion she accidentally took more of those infernal sedatives than any doctor would've permitted. Is *that* what you want on your conscience, Miss, do you want her to *die?* Because that's what will happen if you don't leave us in peace!"

Judith stood.

Slowly and deliberately, she said, "You're right in one regard, Mr. Starn: neither of us respects the other. I'll mourn if Harriet does eventually do away with herself. I'll mourn the final waste of someone who started the wasting process a long time ago, maybe on the day she learned she had no right to her own mind and body."

"I'll listen to no speeches."

"It must be painful to go through life as a craven coward, Mr. Starn. You generate evil and corruption, and when you're found out the responsibility for your evil must go on someone else's shoulders. If Harriet kills herself, it's my fault. If—"

"Don't keep saying that! What kind of sadist are you? It was an accidental—"

"If your railroading me gets derailed, it's the fault of your lieutenants. But they're your lieutenants, aren't they, Mr. Starn? You created them, you taught them all they know. You'll listen to no speeches? Very well, then listen to a threat, a quite simple one. It has nothing to do with Harriet. I've directed Mr. Pallino that under no circumstances will our side drag her into this." Ray shot her a You're-blowing-it gaze, but she continued. "Mr. and Mrs. Cobb are to be allowed to speak the truth, in open court, without any repercussions afterwards."

"Marc Bancroft is a family man. He could go to the penitentiary . . ."

"No one goes to the penitentiary without first being convicted of a crime. I want the file on Lonnie Perkins brought from whatever secret dungeon it's in up into the sunlight. Your alternative is to watch this trial grow, this trial and the trials I assure you will follow. There are courtrooms outside of Hartley, Mr. Starn, and judges and district attorneys and jurors and citizens who don't quiver at the sound of your name. As you say, you're not an ignorant man. Harriet will be protected, but do you imagine for a moment all your dirty-linen closets will stay locked?"

Oliver Starn looked helplessly at Noah Walters, who said, "Buy it, Ollie."

Oliver Starn nodded.

"I'm getting out of here, too," Ray said, moments after Starn left. "The poignant idealism around these parts is giving me a nagging backache." In the direct center of the room, he whirled and blistered at Judith, "Are you satisfied? Against my better—no, my best judgment, I shut up for you. Is this what all the work was leading up to—ninety-nine percent capitulation to that schmuck?"

Mr. Walters said, "Your frustration is understan—"

"Don't tell *me* about frustration, you placating old relic! Go back and read your scrapbooks. Try to remember when you were young enough to fight with your fists, not with powderpuffs and quaint little homilies."

"Stop this!" Judith demanded.

"Stop what? We could've massacred him and his lice for good. You *bet* there's frustration. Well, the hell with it. I'll leave and you two pantywaist liberals can rock in your rocking chairs and praise Pyrrhic victories and drink a toast to all those dirty necks you saved. Great. *Salut.* Drink up. But keep the windows and doors bolted, nice bleeding hearts, because the Starns of the world are running loose and it won't be long before they come after you with their machine guns."

Then he was gone, and Judith missed him.

32

Seamus Terence Gallagher, known affectionately as Sam, banjo-eyed favorite of millions.

A funny thing happened on the way to Judith's going her way and my going mine. We didn't get married. Weren't you thinking all along we would?

I'll tell you about us in a minute.

Neither Judith nor Pallino was responsible for the ceiling that fell on Oliver Starn. Nor was Marcus Bancroft, who dutifully testified that he'd taken it upon himself to choreograph the Cobbs' ballet because, on his own initiative and informing only his conscience, he believed that the Judith Harrisons were subversive dangers and deserved to be themselves subverted. The penalty for suborning perjury comes higher than a parking ticket, so a good question is why did Bancroft totally include Starn out throughout his testimony? Good answer: he had been Starn's Sancho Panza for a passel of years, and Starn had enough on him to guarantee him fifty years in the electric chair. So Bancroft confesses to independent zealousness, is promised that the Governor in Starn's pocket will quietly grant clemency when the fur stops flying, serves a disagreeable but comparatively short stretch, and goes home to his loving and looked-out-for family. End of waves.

Only it wasn't quite that neat. While he was singing about himself, Harriet Starn was rushed to Hartley Hospital—there wasn't time to get to a private one outside town—and had thirty-three billion sleeping pills pumped out of her. Starn assured her he would let her go to St. Croix, an island she liked, to recuperate from her accident, the moment the doctor said she was up to it. She insisted on talking only with Judith, insisted that otherwise her next suicide try would be a success. I went to her bedside with Judith, and I scribbled it all down as she talked, talked about her Andrea Lane telephone impersonation on her father's instructions, talked about the diary she kept of who was involved in what corruptions under her father's baton, and in what drawer in her bedroom the diary could be found. I hustled to Pallino, and two federal marshals served the papers that got the diary that named the names that killed the cat that ate the rat that stole the cheese that set off the chain of indictments.

Federal indictments, that started in low gear and then poured like confetti. Talk about the domino theory; all those black blocks with the white dots went boom-boom-boom, from Lyman Bester who pointed to the Herman Stacey strong-arm cops who pointed to the police chief who pointed to the D.A. who—well, it's warming to know how quickly loyal henchmen will unhench and find God when they're faced with the possibility of all expenses paid inside a federal pen. By the time the government had nailed down a solid criminal conspiracy case implicating Starn, that door opened onto others. The God-finders became horse-trading informers, and before long Oliver Starn realized that those other unlocking charges against him—making very funny with tax returns, bribery, coercion by threat, and a couple of cases of outright fraud were just openers —would have kept him awfully busy. He sat down one night and wrote a rambling note about patriotism and leftist conspiracies and parental love and the decline of old-fashioned American virtues. His last deceit was probably his crowning best: the obits in his newspapers and on his television and radio stations claimed that the hunting rifle had gone off accidentally while he was cleaning it. The funeral was closed to the public and to Harriet.

The last I heard, Ray Pallino was in the Southwest, serving as advocate, without fee, for a family of Sioux Indians who'd been suckered off their land. The communiqués he delivered to the media focused on the issues involved, only passingly on the Sioux family themselves as people. Okay, I'm straining when I suggest that Pallino and Starn were more alike than either of them would have admitted or even recognized, the similarity being that neither had much patience or feeling for human values. But which one of them would I call to if I were in trouble? Guess.

Sisters of Sappho, part of the Hartley scenery, suffered a numbing scandal when one of their number said something pro-homosexual without a wink, a leer, and an implicit plea to be mocked. No accounting for tastes, if you'll excuse a little schoolboy humor.

Norman Hanaday took Martha home, not to rebuild a marriage—in the sense that most of us think of marriage, anyway —but to care for her, and they're living together still. I know this because Judith told me she and Hanaday bumped into each other a few weeks ago and drank some coffee together. I gather it was an awkward meeting, friendly but awkward. I gather, too, that Judith digs why she went into that mooncalf affair with him. It was a kind of flight from reality for both of them, a comforting affair that was perfectly safe because of his practical unavailability. They had coffee and exchanged good wishes. I'm going to assume that was that.

I'm going to assume it because now I come back to full circle. Judith and I are, as the gossip columns used to put it so eloquently, an item. We do oddball things like sit for hours and talk with each other. We go to the movies and fool around in the dark. Right now we're in her East Eighties living room. She's over there, reading the latest Supreme Court decision, written by Justice Paula Demling. I'm over here, occasionally working well on the sequel to my Saigon book. Toscanini is conducting *Eroica*.

The possibility that this might turn out to be a permanent deal enters. my mind, of course, but it doesn't linger for long at a time. You don't tame or contain someone like Judith, not in this year, not in this day, not in this third quarter of this Twentieth Century. But this is nice. This is very nice. You take care.